ANNE HOLT

A MEMORY FOR MURDER

Translated from the Norwegian

by Anne Bruce

CORVUS

First published in Great Britain in 2021 by Corvus,
an imprint of Atlantic Books Ltd.

Copyright © Anne Holt, 2021

English translation copyright © Anne Bruce, 2021

Originally published in Norwegian as *Mandela-effekten*. Published by

This translation has been published with the financial support of NORLA.

N NORLA
NORWEGIAN LITERATURE ABROAD

10 9 8 7 6 5 4 3 2 1

A CIP catalogue record for this book is available from the British Library.

Paperback ISBN: 978 1 78649 857 1
E-book ISBN: 978 1 78649 858 8

Printed in Great Britain.

Corvus
An imprint of Atlantic Books Ltd
Ormond House
26–27 Boswell Street
London
WC1N 3JZ

www.corvus-books.co.uk

To Jan Guillou, my friend, with thanks.

Creation

Although she kept slurring her words and grinning, she was lovely. Elegant and charming, the way younger girls hardly ever were. A bit mumsy, really, but pretty brazen with it. Attractive. A full mouth with lips that looked real. Reddish-blonde hair that definitely wasn't. Well and truly plastered. She was standing there spewing into a rubbish bin by the fountains at Spikersuppa when he spotted her. He had lingered, watching her for a while, until she straightened her back, looked across at him and suddenly waved him over. He obeyed just as a rat scampered past her feet, the poor creature's mouth stuffed with kebab or something. She was too far-gone to notice the beast. He felt sorry for her. He often felt sorry for people.

For himself too.

Things had progressed the way he wanted and she let him go home with her.

'How old are you really?' he asked for the third time.

'Tick-tock, tick-tock.'

Maybe the woman was actually crying. Mostly she'd laughed, even though he'd had to hold on tight to stop her falling into the gap between platform and carriage at the National Theatre subway station. Her laughter was infectious, even in her drunken state. All the same, she didn't seem particularly happy.

'Tick-tock.'

Her apartment was drop-dead gorgeous. Not that he would exactly want to live in fucking Manglerud, at least not in a gigantic high-rise block. The place wasn't especially spacious either, but the bird had seriously good taste, the sort you find in the pages of interior magazines: fairly dark colours, just enough books on the shelves and a far-too-discreet flatscreen TV, sort of thing. And those groups of empty vases and candles, arranged on wooden trays in an effort to look absolutely casual. Here and there, dotted all around, but not too many. The apartment was the perfect place to crash for the night, something he was totally dependent on at present. Any acquaintance or stranger, as long as it was clean enough and they were nice people, and he was saved until the next day.

'Far too old,' she complained. 'The clock is ticking.'

He had brewed a huge pot of coffee and also poured a lot of water down the woman's throat. He knew how she was feeling. It wasn't often he drank enough to be totally sloshed, but when it happened, it was best to sleep it off. Hell on earth when you finally woke up, of course, but all the same.

'Maybe you should sleep,' he suggested as he got up from the settee.

'No,' she insisted, trying to pull him towards her. 'You're so sweet. So nice. I'm sure you'll make a wonderful dad. Can't we make a baby together?'

He laughed.

'How many times do I have to tell you? I'm gay. G-A-Y. I don't feel any desire for women ... no offence ...'

Taking a step back, he turned up his hands and showed his palms.

'... and the last thing I want is children. I'm only twenty-one.'

'It would be so easy,' she said, struggling to sit more comfortably. 'I've got all we need, and it's the right time of the month, and ...'

Her consonants must have been left at the bottom of a glass somewhere. Her hand dangled over the edge of the settee when she tried to stand up and she fell back again. No longer looking so good.

He guessed forty years old.

'Thirty-eight,' she said with a hiccup. 'I'm thirty-eight, and it's getting late.'

A snigger.

'That rhymed! Come on, let's make a baby.'

She shut her eyes. A few more minutes and she'd be fast asleep. He seized the chance to look around again. He spotted an iPad beside the pathetic flatscreen. She must have bought it in the US – it was only a month since Apple had launched the coolest gadget of the times. Bloody expensive. Bloody beautiful.

Sometimes he stole things.

Never much. Mostly food and drink. An odd time money, but only small amounts, and only in moments of desperate need. The tablet, with its bright red leather cover, looked really tempting.

'A baby,' she said in an unexpectedly firm tone of voice.

This time she managed to stand up. The grin was gone. She shook her head ever so slightly. Drained the half-full cup of lukewarm coffee. Put it down and stretched her back with her hands above her head, as if she had just woken up. He had hoped she would doze off on the settee, so he could lie down in the enticing bed that was most likely behind the nearby door. Now it would probably be the other way round. Fair enough. Beggars can't be choosers, and the settee was absolutely fine.

She padded across the floor towards the open-plan kitchen, surprisingly steady on her feet now. Rattling in a drawer. Several drawers. He was staring at the iPad. He knew she also had an iPhone. In her handbag, the one hanging from a hook in the hallway, containing both her wallet and loads of makeup. It had toppled over between her feet on the subway and he'd had to help her gather everything up again.

'Here,' the woman said, raising an enormous syringe above her head.

Something for a horse. Or an elephant. It didn't have a proper point, he could see that. No metal at all, in fact. Blunt and strange. It looked a bit like a toy hypodermic, the kind kept inside the dinky doctors' medical bags that had a red cross on the front.

'Do you have any food?' he asked.

'Yes, of course. Afterwards. First this.'

He wasn't stupid. At junior high, he'd been top of the class. Smart and cocky, he'd heard his teachers say. Then his mother had died and there was no more school for him. Life went its merry way, in a sense. He stumbled along after it as best he could. Mostly living from hand to mouth. Sometimes like a prince. Most often not. He hadn't had a fixed abode since his father had at long last lost patience with him and thrown him out the door.

When he was seventeen.

For four years he had lived off Social Security and the generosity of others. All the same, he wasn't stupid, and when the woman waved the big plastic syringe yet again, he understood what she wanted.

'Are you healthy?' she asked.

'Yes. But I can't be bothered—'

'No HIV infection?'

'Course not,' he answered, annoyed now. 'I'm careful.'

'Hereditary illnesses?'

Her consonants were back in place.

'No,' he replied. 'At any rate, we're not making a baby with that gadget there.'

She was right in front of him now. Her breath stank of vomit and coffee and red wine. Her tongue was a strange shade of pale blue. Her eyes even bluer.

'Ten thousand kroner,' she said flatly.

'What?'

He took a pace back.

'You'll get ten thousand kroner. All you have to do is wank into a cup. In the bathroom or something. Give the cup to me and you'll get ten thousand kroner. You look as if you need it.'

He hadn't had ten thousand kroner in cash since his confirmation.

'Thirty,' he said in a flash. 'I want thirty thousand.'

'No,' she said, crossing the room to the small unit where the iPad and flatscreen were.

From a little drawer she produced a wad of pale-brown notes, held together with something that looked like a hairband.

'Ten thousand kroner,' she insisted. 'I don't even know your name, so you're taking no risks. No demands. Not for financial support or turning up at family birthdays. You give me what I want, you get the money in return and ...'

She hiccupped and had to take a step to one side to retain her balance.

'Christ,' he said, 'this is crazy. You can't just make a kid like this. Kids shouldn't ...'

He ran his hand through his longish hair.

'Why don't you just go to Denmark or something? Or have a chat with a friend? Or find yourself a guy, for Christ's sake, you're—'

She was waving the banknotes.

'You're lovely,' she said. 'You're Norwegian and blond and young. You're kind. You helped me home. I've no idea how smart you are, but I'm sharp enough for two.'

He could strike her down. Take the money and run. She wasn't just as out-of-it as she'd been when he'd found her a couple of hours ago, but it would be easy to overpower her. And she didn't have a clue who he was.

'Ten thousand kroner for a few seconds' work,' she said.

She was spot-on about that. It wouldn't take long at all.

'Plus the iPad,' he said, pointing.

'No. Ten thousand. Take it or leave it.'

'But why me? Haven't you got—'

'You know nothing about me. I know nothing about you. Let's keep it like that. Now I need an answer.'

He answered.

Ten minutes later, he stood alone in the hallway of the small apartment with an entire fortune in his pocket. The woman had taken the cup and syringe into her bedroom and asked him to leave. Without offering him any food as she had promised. It didn't matter, now he could buy something. Her handbag still hung on the hook at the front door and he opened it carefully and drew out her wallet. She liked cash, this woman. Behind a photo of an Alsatian dog, there was a bundle of 200-kroner notes. Her credit card was firmly fixed inside the tight slot in the leather, but with a bit of jiggling, he managed to pull it out far enough to read her name.

If she had no idea who he was, at least he would know who he might be having a child with. On the other hand, getting pregnant at that age, after a more or less random attempt at artificial insemination while under the influence, would probably wind up being pretty difficult. After a moment's hesitation, he pushed the card back into place without touching the cash. Then he dashed out to get some grub and somewhere else to sleep. Once he was some distance away from the apartment block, he made up his mind to pretend the whole absurd episode had never happened at all.

Curiously enough, though, he never forgot her name.

The Assassination

When the shot hit Selma Falck, she was in fact only astonished.

It wasn't especially painful. Just a jolt to her shoulder, at the very top of her left arm. She instinctively grabbed the entry wound, and noticed with increasing bafflement that blood was already seeping through her velvet jacket, staining it dark crimson.

A hell of a hullabaloo kicked off.

Tables toppled and people screamed. Cups, glasses and chairs flew in all directions. The customers in the crowded pavement restaurant threw themselves to the ground or sprang up to flee the scene. A pram parked at the far edge of the jumble of small tables tipped over and the mother's shrieks cut through all the noise.

Only Selma Falck sat completely still. As the blood spread under her right hand, she grew gradually dizzier. Later she would insist that many seconds had passed, perhaps as much as a couple of minutes, before she realized Linda was dead.

The shot had struck Selma's old friend from the national handball team in the head.

A sharp report had ripped through the autumn air. Not two, Selma firmly insisted. She remained seated, nausea denying her

7

the ability to stand, while she struggled to shut out the cacophony of weeping and wailing and harsh warnings.

One single shot. Definitely not two. Linda had been sitting on her left. Vanja Vegge, Selma's oldest friend, sat opposite them both. A stressed-out waiter had just thrown down a glass of water on the rickety little table. It was perched so far over, teetering on the edge, that it risked tipping over once the waiter turned his back to squeeze past the jam-packed tables. Linda Bruseth's reflexes might not have been as good as they had been thirty years earlier, but she had avoided the accident at the final split second. Her hand was still clutching the glass and her head had dropped forward. It might even look as if she had dozed off in a drunken stupor. But all that had been on the table a few seconds earlier was the water, two cans of Pepsi Max and a cappuccino.

A fine-calibre firearm was what crossed Selma's mind. The bullet had hit Linda at the back, on the side of her skull, where it had deposited mass and weight as it rotated inside her brain, changed angle and continued its journey through another, larger hole in Linda's cranium before striking Selma's arm. Dots danced in front of her eyes, black and green, but she managed to lift her injured arm sufficiently to see there was no exit wound.

'The same bullet,' she muttered. 'And now it's inside me.'

'We have to leave!' Vanja Vegge screamed hysterically from beneath the table.

'She saved me,' Selma said.

'What? We have to go, Selma! There could be more shots!'

'Linda saved me,' Selma repeated. 'But I don't think she knew that.'

Then she got to her feet, swaying slightly. Taking a stronger grip of her left upper arm, she walked with surprisingly steady steps towards the wailing ambulance that was miraculously already approaching.

'Anine must never learn of this,' she mumbled all the way, over and over again. 'My daughter simply mustn't get to hear of this.'

As if that could possibly be avoided.

The Interview

Private investigator Selma Falck and Police Inspector Fredrik Smedstuen sat side by side in a cleaners' cupboard at Ullevål Hospital. It was remarkably large. On the other hand, it smelled far from fresh. Damp patches formed rough patterns on the windowless exterior wall and putrid floor cloths were piled up in a corner.

'Placing you in a four-person ward,' the police officer mumbled, shaking his head. 'In the richest country in the world. That's how things have turned out.'

'It's fine,' Selma snapped. 'Anyway, I'll soon be discharged. Just a flesh wound. And they did at least lend us this cupboard, didn't they? For this little ... chat of ours.'

She raised her eyes and let them run over the space. One wall was covered in enamelled metal shelves, crammed with so many poisonous cleaning agents that they could have killed off the entire hospital if they fell into the wrong hands. Iron hooks that looked as if they had been made by an old-fashioned blacksmith were screwed all along the opposite wall. They were all different sizes and brushes and mops hung from each of them, attached by plaited string, all so filthy that Selma optimistically assumed the cupboard was no longer in use. It was just a superfluous space in a gigantic hospital complex that would soon be razed to the ground. At any rate, the hospital was to be relocated, sparking such voluble protests from a virtually united medical profession that she thought they must be right. Here and now, though, she changed her mind. Twenty-four hours in a ward far higher than it was wide, with three gabbling wardmates and a sickly smell of urine from the shared bathroom, had made her long for the far newer National Hospital where a year ago she had spent six weeks and eventually come to enjoy it.

She was sitting in a wheelchair without really knowing why. The nurse had insisted. Smedstuen's bulky thighs spilled over the sides of a flimsy tubular chair and he kept wriggling. On the shelf beside them, he had placed an iPhone in sound recording mode between a bottle of lye and a four-litre drum of undiluted ammonia.

'As I said,' he continued, 'this is just a preliminary, absolutely informal interview. The case is top priority. We're all over it. A Member of Parliament killed in broad daylight. Reminds me of Sweden, in fact. I thought you'd be keen to add your pennyworth. You know ...'

Selma made no response. Something about this guy affected her. It was clear he had respect for her – he had opened the conversation by expressing his admiration and regard for Selma's earlier feats. She had greeted him with her usual friendliness and cordiality when he had arrived unannounced at her bedside. It was automatic: she fell into the role of her other self in dealings with everyone except a small handful of people. Affable and amusing. A bit of a flirt and always agreeable. It worked every time. But not with this man. There was something reserved about him, something aloof – as if he really couldn't care less. As if even in a case like this, a fatal shot fired at a crowd of people in an open street, fundamentally bored him.

Maybe he just felt uncomfortable. He was big, heavy and unkempt. His pilot's jacket was a touch too small. His hair was slightly greasy. He had tried to conceal the smell of cigarettes on his breath with Fisherman's Friend lozenges. As for Selma, she had managed to take a shower before he called in, her arm taped up with plasters. Vanja had dropped by with clean clothes from her apartment, Armani jeans and a midnight-blue oversized *Acne* shirt. Sighing deeply, the policeman shrugged as he shifted the mobile several millimetres closer to her.

'A single shot,' he declared. 'You're certain of that.'

'Yes.'

'Eye witnesses heard more than that. Some say two, others three. Still others think it might have been an automatic weapon. A number of shots in a series.'

'Witnesses tell lies. We humans are chronically unreliable. We make up pictures in our heads that are far from correct. Have you heard of —'

He interrupted her with an impatient toss of the head.

'Yes, of course. But what makes you so sure?'

'My ears. I heard one shot. Only one. And that's what the forensic investigations will show you. One bullet. It hit the back of Linda's head, changed direction inside her brain, flew out again and then hit me in the arm. Where it lodged.'

The policeman smacked and licked his lips.

'What's left of the bullet has been sent for examination,' he said, nodding towards her shoulder. 'We got it straight from the operating theatre. It's so deformed we'll be lucky if it's at all possible to work out what type it is.'

'But we're talking about a high-velocity small-calibre gun, are we not?'

'In all likelihood. Which demands a good marksman. A heavy-calibre weapon would have blown the head off your friend. Where did you learn this? About firearms and calibres and suchlike, I mean?'

Selma did not find it necessary to answer. The policeman, obviously feeling increasingly uncomfortable, was tugging at his shirt collar, even though it was open. Scratching his three-day-old stubble. He seemed really completely uninterested in both the case and Selma Falck herself.

'We'll see what the technicians find out,' he muttered. 'Strictly speaking, we can't know whether it was you or the other woman, condolences by the way, who ...'

He touched his breast pocket, as if searching for a notebook.

'Linda Bruseth,' Selma helped him out.

'Yes, Linda, that was it. We don't know whether it was you or her who was the target of that bullet. Or anyone else. That woman Varda, for example.'

'Vanja. Vanja Vegge doesn't have an enemy in the world. She's a friendly psychologist that everybody loves. The only provocative thing about Vanja is her colourful, fluttering clothes. Hardly something to get killed for.'

Smedstuen mumbled something that might mean even the police felt Vanja Vegge was an unlikely target for an assassin.

'It doesn't have to have been anyone at all,' he went on. 'It could have been an act of terrorism. A shot in the dark, intended to scare people.'

Selma laughed, jarring the stitches where she knew a drain had been inserted. She grew suddenly serious and settled her arm more comfortably in the sling. Tried to relax her hand, as she had been told to do.

'An act of terrorism,' she repeated. If the policeman wouldn't buy her affability, he would certainly catch her irony instead. 'Exactly. It was a typical act of terrorism, of course. Settling down to fire off a single shot at a pavement restaurant. Where there were probably about thirty people seated. And where only I, by chance the only famous person in that whole crowd of people, was hit. Before the terrorist packed up his gear and sneaked off in all the confusion. Yes, of course.'

'Not only you. Linda ...'

'Bruseth,' Selma finished for him when he hesitated again.

'Yes. She too was hit. Two birds with one stone, so to speak.'

'Obviously because she suddenly leaned forward. She was trying to save a glass of water that was about to topple over.'

'We've heard that, yes,' he said, nodding apathetically. 'That other friend of yours ...'

Once again he patted his chest.

'Vanja Vegge,' Selma reminded him.

'Precisely. I talked to her yesterday. She says the same as you. One shot, and a sudden movement from Linda. Almost simultaneously.'

'As I said, it—'

'All the same, she could have been the target.'

This time, Selma contented herself with a smile. 'Linda was the most anonymous backbencher in Parliament,' she said.

'Yes, but—'

'From Indre Vestfold, as kind as the day is long and ...'

Selma was about to blurt out that the old handball goalkeeper was a bit simple, but caught herself in time.

'... with such a sunny disposition. You could wrap her round your little finger with no trouble at all. If anyone really wanted to murder her, I could come up with better methods for you on the spot. Much better than a sniper lying hidden in Grünerløkka firing a shot into a café, I mean.'

'That also applies to you.'

'Me? What do you mean?'

'That there are simpler ways of killing you.'

Selma leaned forward in the wheelchair. 'About this time last year, I was walking around naked on the Hardangervidda,' she said softly. 'For five days. In a snowstorm. With serious injuries. With no proper food and drink for three whole days and nights. I'm not so easy to kill.'

The policeman reached his hand out to the mobile, but changed his mind.

'It's too early to say what actually happened,' he sighed. 'We want to conduct a reconstruction as soon as you're able for it.'

'Any time at all. If I'm not discharged today, I'll sign myself out. This wheelchair stuff is just nonsense. I can walk.'

Selma was fed up. Despite the size of the cupboard, all of a sudden it seemed more confined. She wanted to get away. Her arm was sore, but not so bad that that she couldn't just as well take some Paralgin Forte and rest on the settee at home for a couple of days.

'Would you like police protection?'

'What?'

'You're obviously convinced the shot was meant for you. We're not so sure. But if you believe that someone is willing to shoot you in broad daylight, then maybe you need—'

'No, thanks.'

Selma was lost in thought. The idea that struck her immediately after she was shot had slipped her mind by the time she had been driven to the hospital and operated on without delay. It had not been able to find its way back through the morphine fog until now.

'Shit,' she whispered.

'What?'

'Nothing,' she brushed it off.

The episode at Grünerløkka had been splashed all over the headlines for more than twenty-four hours. Nevertheless, Anine, Selma's daughter, had not been in touch.

'Shit,' she formed the word once again with her lips without making a sound.

The policeman pulled a bag of Fisherman's Friends out of his jacket pocket, dug out a lozenge and used his stubby fingers to drop it in his mouth.

'So you don't want protection, then. OK. We'll come back to that. Who knew you were to meet your friends at that particular café?'

'What?'

'You heard me. Had you told anyone you intended to meet up at that particular pavement restaurant at that particular time?'

Selma shook her head slightly. 'No, I don't think so. Well, of course we had said it to each other, naturally.'

He did not even smile. 'Are you sure?'

'I think so. Or ...' She gave it some thought. 'The arrangement was made on Monday,' she said after a few seconds. 'Via text message. I live alone, and I can ...'

Yet another pause before she shook her head.

'No, I haven't spoken to anyone else about that appointment. No one apart from the two women I was to meet.'

'Have you written it down anywhere?'

'No. It's nowhere other than on my list of texts.'

'No automatic diary on your mobile?'

'No. Of course I appreciate why you're asking, but I think I can swear to it that I didn't tell anyone at all.'

'Who do you think the others could have mentioned it to?'

'I've no idea!'

He was sucking noisily on the lozenge. 'Who could have known the three of you were meeting?'

Selma really had to pull herself together to avoid expressing her disapproval. He kept smacking his lips and the strong smell of peppermint was almost unbearable in a space already reeking of damp and cleaning products.

'Linda's husband, maybe. Ingolf. He doesn't live in Oslo, but as far as I know they had a good relationship.'

It suddenly struck Selma that she ought to phone him and express her condolences. It had not occurred to her before now and she lost her concentration for a moment.

'I see,' the policeman said, rotating his hand to get her going again.

'Usually Linda went home to Vestfold at weekends,' Selma continued. 'And she spoke to Ingolf every day by phone. As far as I'm aware. There could also have been someone at the Parliament who knew. Maybe they have a system where they have to report their activities and whereabouts. In case of voting and suchlike, I mean. I don't really have a clue. You'd have to check.'

'Isn't your husband also a Member of Parliament?'

'Ex-husband. Yes. But I don't know what routines they have. As I said, you'd have to find out for yourself.'

'I'll do that. Vanja, then, what about her?'

'You can ask her yourself.'

'Yes, but now I'm asking you.'

Selma sighed. 'Vanja is married to Kristina. They have a symbiotic relationship. They lost their only boy a couple of years ago and since then it's been almost impossible to get one to come to anything without the other. Kristina should actually also have been with us at the café, but she had a sore throat. Anyway, I've got a pretty sore arm, so I hope we'll soon be finished with this.'

Now he had begun to jot down some notes. 'Uh-huh,' he said inconsequentially. 'Uh-huh.'

All at once he looked up and straight into her eyes. 'Do you have any enemies?'

Selma's eyes narrowed. She hesitated. 'I think you're right,' she said instead of answering him. 'It was probably Linda who was the target.'

'Why do you say that? Three minutes ago you scoffed at the idea, and I—'

'Despite all that, she was a Member of Parliament. An important person. And we've agreed that the sniper was an expert. So it was hardly a bad shot.'

'We'll come back to all that,' the police officer said in annoyance. 'Please answer my question.'

'Which one?'

'Does anyone wish you harm? Enemies of any kind?'

Selma tried to look bored. It was extraordinarily difficult. More than anything she felt compelled to phone her daughter Anine and make it crystal clear that Linda Bruseth had been the one who was the assassin's target. Selma had just been terribly unlucky. What were the odds, in fact – it would never happen again.

'Two or three years ago I would have said no,' she told him in the end. 'I mean, my ex-husband and children have not been exactly over the moon about me for a while, but they don't really wish me any harm. I assume. Apart from that, I have only friends. No enemies. I believe, at least. But right now?'

She made a face. He stared at her, straight into her eyes. There was a glint beneath the bushy eyebrows that merged above the bridge of his nose into a bristling V. His gaze was suddenly razor sharp, as if up till now he had tried to trick her by seeming different from the way he was. Selma cocked her head.

'I would certainly claim to have enemies now, yes.'

He did not blink. Selma felt an increasing aversion. It was as if he was holding something back. As if he had arranged in advance with the nurse in charge to borrow this horrible broom cupboard as an interview room. And to force her into a totally unnecessary wheelchair to make her weaker than she actually was.

'In addition to an extensive secret paramilitary organization,' she began, 'with resources and weapons and—'

'*Operation Rugged/Storm-scarred* was destroyed last year. Thanks to you.'

'Destroyed?'

It was difficult not to laugh again. 'You think it's possible to destroy such an outfit?'

'Well, yes, after all, there was such an infernal racket, and a whole string of court cases, political scandals, lots of—'

'You asked me if I have enemies,' she broke in. 'I'm trying to answer. *Rugged/Storm-scarred* was an operation. The actual organization was nameless, in fact. Ill-defined. Impossible to grasp. I'm convinced there are still people out there who wish me six foot under. On top of that there are loads of folk in the Norwegian cross-country community who would be delighted if I suffered real misfortune ...'

She had started to count carefully on the fingers protruding from the chalk-white sling.

'But they'd scarcely lie on the roof of a building to shoot you,' Fredrik Smedstuen said. 'If they had, they'd have to be biathletes.'

He smiled for the first time. His teeth had a greyish tinge.

'We also have an angry diamond thief,' Selma said, impassive, pointing at the ring finger of her left hand. 'But he's behind bars. Late last winter, when I could at last move about after last year's little ... trip to the mountains, I exposed a disloyal employee in *Telenor*. He's still on the run, but the last reported sighting was in Bali. Probably won't dare to come home again for a while. And then we have—'

'You don't need to go though all your cases. I get the picture.'

'In addition to all of these, you have the people I've turned down.'

'Turned down? You mean—'

'No, not men. Not like that. Clients. I get five or six applications a week. At least. I accept one case every other month or so. Some of the ones forced to leave with unsettled business can get quite agitated.'

She shrugged her uninjured shoulder and added: 'Which I can well understand.'

'What are you working on now?'

'Now? Right now I'm sitting in a broom cupboard with you, wondering whether we'll soon be finished. My arm is aching and it stinks in here.'

Heaving a sigh, the policeman got to his feet with some difficulty.

'Stay in Oslo, then. In principle, by the way, you have the right to a victim's advocate to represent you.'

Selma shook her head. 'No, thanks. I'm sure I'll manage. I'm fairly sure now it wasn't me the man was after.'

She felt how much easier it was to tell a lie rather than speak the truth.

'Or woman,' she added quickly. 'To be fair, we don't know the sex.'

'Call me when you feel up to a proper interview. At Police Headquarters. And a reconstruction, as I said. I guess that will be pretty soon.'

He opened the door to the busy sound of footsteps and talking and the occasional shout. The perpetual odour of sixties-style dinners lay thick in the corridor. Since her operation, it had made her feel queasy. However, compared to the putrid floor cloths the smell of industrial meatballs was heavenly.

Fredrik Smedstuen stood with his big hand on the door handle. 'You didn't answer,' he said.

'Answer what?'

'What sort of case you're working on at the moment?'

Selma hesitated. A slip-up. A good lie sprang to her lips, smooth as silk. Never too detailed, but not so brief either that it offered the opportunity for further questions. It came of its own accord, without delay, precise and utterly effortless.

'Nothing,' she said abruptly, compensating with a smile so broad and dazzling she could swear it brought a blush to the Police Inspector's cheeks.

The Smiley Face

Her shoulder and upper arm were throbbing like mad when Selma Falck finally stood in front of the entrance to her own apartment in Sagene. Five well-wrapped bouquets of flowers were propped against the wall between her and her neighbour. She instantly assumed they were intended for her, since the media had given detailed reports of the shooting episode at Grünerløkka on all platforms. To top it all, *DGTV* had started broadcasting from the crime scene only twenty-two minutes after it all happened. The sensation caused by a Member of Parliament being killed in what appeared to be a straightforward assassination was immense enough in itself. The immediate rife speculation that Selma Falck was the intended target made the story even more riveting.

As always, Selma was in the spotlight. She had left behind sixteen floral arrangements at the hospital. The auxiliaries had run out of vases after the last one arrived this morning.

Using her right hand, she rummaged in her bag for her keys. She noticed her fingers were tingling and realized the slight trembling in her right arm had something to do with the injury in the left one. She caught herself wishing Lupus were still alive. The half-wild dog that had saved her life a year ago had passed away a couple of weeks after their rescue. Warmth, food and care after what had turned out to have been six months alone on the mountain plateau was too much for the old animal.

Lupus had looked after her. Now she would have to look after herself.

After fumbling to insert the key in the lock, she rotated it. First one, then the security lock. She opened the door a crack.

Someone had been here. Again.

There were many ways to check whether an uninvited person had visited a place. An alarm system was obviously the simplest. When she had moved into this new building in Sagene almost two years ago, it had all been already installed. Not exactly state of the art, but OK, and Selma had not seen the point of cameras in the small apartment. The system was new and good enough. All the same, three weeks ago she had come home and felt a disquieting awareness that someone had been there. Inside her home. Inside her modern, secure apartment, where there were only two ways in. One through the front door, the other via the balcony, the only one of its kind on the smooth exterior wall, suspended more than eight metres above the ground. Neither of the two doors showed the least sign of a break-in. The idea that someone might have climbed up the front wall in a densely populated area without drawing any attention was difficult to imagine. Impossible, actually. The person in question would have had to enter through the front door. Which meant he or she had a key. You could of course enter the building by waiting for a careless resident who left the door slightly open, but Selma's own apartment was something else again. The person in question would have to possess a key and somehow switch the alarm off and then back on again.

No one else had a key to her apartment as far as she knew. No one knew the code for the alarm. To the best of her knowledge.

In what felt like a lifetime ago, during the period before she almost lost her life on the Hardangervidda, she had been involved with a young man. A far too young man for a middle-aged woman like her. In a moment of thoughtlessness, she had given him a set of keys. He had handed them back when she had brutally broken up with him, not because she wanted to, but because it was necessary.

He had simply left them on the hallway shelf one day and disappeared. Since then she had not seen him. He had never been given the alarm code. When she had finally been discharged from hospital at the end of October, she had tried to contact him. Without success. Whether it had been wounded vanity or a slightly broken heart that took hold of her she was never completely certain.

When she had been suffused with this disquieting feeling about uninvited guests three weeks earlier, she had not entirely understood why. It was only a feeling. It struck her as soon as she stepped foot in the apartment, even though nothing had been disturbed. At least as far as she could see. It was all like a paranormal shift, a vague stirring of a foreign substance. Not a smell, nothing visible. A sort of presence was how it seemed and she had felt her pulse rate soar when she walked on into her bedroom.

No sign of a break-in there either. Eventually she had dismissed the notion. She had changed in the last year. Become a touch more anxious. A bit jittery, even though she never showed it to anyone. She had begun to consider death. Anything else would have been strange: Selma Falck had literally been minutes from the hereafter when she had finally been found by a mountain rescue patrol last autumn.

Maybe it was just her age.

So she had written it all off as sheer fantasy, until she was about to turn in for the night. The bed was not made. The single quilt was curled up against the pillow, and when she lifted it, she caught sight of the packet of chewing gum.

A packet of KIP.

Three small, rectangular pieces of gum, red, green and yellow, tightly wrapped in cellophane.

She had shaken the pillow after she got up. It was plumped up and in the right place, with no sign of a hollow made by her head. In the middle, in a tiny depression someone must have used two fingers to make, lay the packet. The best treat Selma Falck had known when she was little.

She had loved KIP. The taste, fruity and far too short-lived, but also the consistency, was worth all the pennies she managed to rake in for want of regular pocket money. The tabs were crisp, almost floury, at the first chew, before it melded into a perfect, rubbery balance between hard and soft. After only a few minutes they were usually exhausting to chew and had lost their flavour into the bargain, but those first few seconds of a KIP held such good memories that she felt a faint cramp in her jaw at the mere sight of a packet.

The small tabs had not been in production for forty years or so. Selma had never clapped eyes on a packet since then.

But now one lay here on her pillow.

Several seconds of total bewilderment were succeeded by an unfamiliar dread.

It had washed through her so intensely that she had not even dared to pick up the packet. For a long time she simply stood and stared. In the end she took the second quilt and pillow from the other side of the double bed and lay down on the settee. Without being able to catch a wink of sleep.

There were only two people on the face of this earth who could know that Selma Falck, as a young girl, would have gone through fire and water for a packet of KIP. Vanja Vegge, her oldest friend, and Selma's little brother Herman.

It was out of the question that Vanja had broken into Selma's apartment without leaving a trace. She did not have keys and did not know the code. Herman had died years ago.

Following a sleepless night, she had dismissed the thought of calling the police. With her background, they would probably take the incident seriously, despite the strangeness of the threat, but on second thoughts it occurred to Selma that it had not really been a threat at all, strictly speaking. It revolved around a packet of chewing gum that had been discontinued long ago. It might all be a bizarre joke. No harm had been done, apart from the annoyance of being scared. Selma had spent weeks and months giving statements in the cases proceeding from the exposure of the *Rugged/Storm-scarred* operation. The desire to pay any further visits to police headquarters at Grønlandsleiret 44 as soon as this was far from compelling. When daylight forced its way through the gap in the living room curtains around half past five in the morning, she was no longer afraid.

Nevertheless, she had embarked on the potato flour trap. A fine layer of powder on the pale oak flooring just inside the threshold before she went out, closed the door and locked up.

For three weeks she had continued with this. With no fresh signs of uninvited guests. In the past forty-eight hours there had been other things to think about, and the piles of floral bouquets had almost made her forget to take care as she moved inside. Fortunately she had thought of it before she opened the door.

Someone had stepped on the potato flour. Selma had to crouch down to see the partial footprint, a barely visible tip of a shoe. When she pulled her glasses down her nose and studied the print more closely, she was so startled that she fell back. Her throat constricted and she had to breathe through her open mouth. Her head was spinning when she finally dared to kneel down and examine it for a second time.

Her eyes had not deceived her.

The toe tip had formed a zigzag pattern in the potato flour. That was terrifying in itself. What was worse, however, was the smiley face beside it, maybe five centimetres in diameter and drawn with something slimmer than a finger.

Selma stopped breathing altogether when she spotted that the emoji was winking boldly at her.

The Memorial Service

The Labour Party's parliamentary group had chosen to tone down the memorial service as much as possible.

Linda Bruseth was a name people outside her home region had scarcely heard. Her road to the Vestfold bench in the parliament building had started in small ways. In a tiny inland village she had been repeatedly re-elected as chair of the school's PTA thanks to her parentage of a bunch of five boys. That lasted for more than fifteen years in total, and when the last child waved goodbye to the farm to venture into the big city, her existence became unbearably bleak. She found something else to fill her days. After her triumphant efforts in a popular movement to stop the compulsory acquisition of three properties in connection with a planned wind farm up on the moors, she ended up on the Labour Party's list for the local council elections. In the secure surroundings of her local area, she did a magnificent job. She knew everyone and was well liked by her opponents as well as her party comrades. Tall and heavy but nonetheless athletic, as she had always been. A great lass, people said of Linda Bruseth – a bridge builder of the old-fashioned kind.

Always a smile, always something to give, for everyone.

During the huge surge of refugees in the autumn of 2015, Linda resolutely took charge. An old meeting house and a recently closed-down hospital were transformed within a fortnight into reception centres. The village opened its arms and welcomed Syrians and Afghanis with warmth and enthusiasm. At the same time they created twenty badly needed job opportunities in the village. It all became so efficient, inclusive and successful that Linda Bruseth, prime mover of the project, was invited as a guest on to NRK's flagship TV programme, *Kvelden før Kvelden*: the day before Christmas Eve 2015, in a miasma of crisp roast pork ribs, between Christmas carols and lavishly decorated trees, Linda and two handsome little boys from Syria sat smiling.

Heart-warming, people commented on social media.

At long last, an empathic Labour Party politician, wrote others.

She would persuade me back into the party, at any rate, observed quite a few.

Linda Bruseth was that rare thing, a results-oriented politician. Throughout 2016, she grew increasingly popular across the region and early the next year she was nominated to a secure place on the Vestfold Labour Party's list of candidates for the parliamentary elections later that same year.

Only to plummet into oblivion once elected.

She was allocated a place on the Justice Committee, but had no clue about legal matters. She was used to sound common sense and resolute action in a familiar environment, not screeds of documents in the big city. She was so uncomfortable in her new role that she made sure to be moved as quickly as possible and her next stop was the Rural Affairs Committee. However, she did not feel at ease there either. For the first time in her life, she admitted to a diagnosis. Dyslexia. For more than fifty years she had managed remarkably well despite her secret difficulties with reading and writing, but now they had really begun to bother her. In the end, only a few months into a four-year period everyone now knew would be both her first and last stint, she was tucked away into the Family and Culture Committee.

There, things went slightly better.

Children were a topic of which the mother of five had a good grasp. Sports also. But culture was not her strongest suit, and she still had problems with reading.

In the statistics of talkative representatives, she was at the very bottom.

And now she was dead. Shot in a café because she got in the way of a bullet meant for the far-more-high-profile Selma Falck.

The Party had chosen the lobby for the brief memorial service. A space in the middle of the parliament building meant, perhaps appropriately, for comings and goings. Admittedly, it also served other purposes, both formal and informal, and not least was a hunting ground for the press pack every time a political storm was brewing, when politicians would really prefer to hide away.

Faint individual voices had been raised in preference for the Labour Party's group meeting room. They felt that would be a touch more caring. Smaller and more intimate. Some claimed it would give stronger emphasis to Linda Bruseth's connection to the Party. Such objections were dismissed without further discussion.

This was something that simply had to be done. The Party's most anonymous representative would receive her small mark of respect, without laying the groundwork for anything more than a minimum of comment on an unfortunate member. Although it was true that the press were far kinder to dead politicians than they were to the living, there was every reason to spare the family from seeing the insults already appearing on social networks.

Lars Winther, news journalist on the *Aftenavisen* newspaper, stood in one of the large arched corridors beside the doors to the assembly hall. He had come alone, without a photographer. Some photographic service or other would probably offer something. He was in a bad mood because he had not been allowed to visit Selma Falck. Since the time a year ago when she had presented him with the journalistic scoop of the century, the two of them had become even better friends. Such good friends that his editor would not permit him to have any professional contact with her whatsoever.

Instead he was now listening to the leader of the Parliamentary

Party rattling off a eulogy in front of the sparse assembly. The politician had delved deep into the member's past to find suitable and relatively truthful words of praise. Beside him there was a small table with a burning candle and a book of condolences in which no one had written. When he had finished, he scribbled down a few words of farewell and handed the microphone to the oldest of the members from Linda Bruseth's home region. He launched into a speech of which the introductory words at least contained considerably more warmth than the previous speaker's. And of course he had also known the deceased politician for more than twenty years. Kind was a word that was repeated in every second sentence.

Lars Winther felt a nudge in his back and wheeled round in irritation.

'Hello,' muttered a colleague from *NTB*. 'This is not where it's happening, you know. You can see that for yourself. There should have been a lot more of a commotion about an MP being murdered. This stuff here is just embarrassing beating around the bush. It was Selma Falck who was supposed to die. Not Linda Bruseth.'

When the speaker in the distance stopped abruptly, a vague sense of confusion spread through the gathering. Lars took a step out into the lobby and craned his head forward. At the opposite end, the President of the Parliament, who should really have been present at the memorial service, was walking towards them with determined footsteps. Behind her were four men and one woman Lars did not recognize. Their stride, the look on their faces and the fact they were almost marching in step, however, meant he immediately understood who they were.

'Well, the police at least have their doubts,' he said under his breath to his cocksure colleague. 'As far as they're concerned, this is not so cut and dried. They're on their way to search Linda Bruseth's office.'

The Graveyard Walker

It was late and darkness had settled over Oslo several hours ago. A drizzly rain was falling from the leaden low-lying clouds. The path was slick with wet leaves. Even though the days could still be warm, the first frosty night was probably not far off. The man approached the graveyard from the west and had crossed the motorway through an underpass. His left knee ached less than usual. He tried to walk steadily, without a limp. If he overtaxed the right leg, it would become painful too.

Not a soul to be seen.

He walked slowly between the graves. Here and there, people had placed battery-operated lights that created a gloomy, sinister atmosphere. As usual, he had a grave candle in his pocket, along with matches and a packet of cigarettes. Stopping for a second, he fished out a smoke and stood in the shelter of an oak tree with his hands curled round the match he had torn off.

They should have stopped, the two of them. Both he and Grethe. All through the nineties, fewer people around them smoked. Even when his wife was diagnosed with lung cancer with metastasis in 2002, they had both continued. Grethe just could not put the cigarettes away and by then there was hardly any point in him doing so either. Anyway, he was absent most of the time.

When she died the following year, he switched to smoking in secret. In addition he stopped drinking. Not that alcohol had ever been a problem for him, but when he buried his wife, he entirely lost the pleasure in taking a glass or two. Instead the tiniest drink pushed him down into a darkness he found increasingly difficult to crawl back out of. So he stopped, just as he had cut out almost everything else in the painful numbness of having become a widower.

Apart from smoking, and then only when no one else saw him.

And his work. He continued until the age of fifty-five, when he had received a gilt-edged opportunity to retire. Since then there had been plenty to occupy him, as he possessed a sought-after expertise. The social side was not so successful. Grethe had been the gregarious one and she had seen to everything on the home front. House and family and social company. The boy and the garden and finances and everything associated with family life.

His existence had taken a slightly too sudden turn for the worse when she succumbed and died. Only by the skin of his teeth had he managed to get through it without giving up the ghost. Even now, so many years later, he never felt really happy. Life had become sepia-coloured, but there was still momentary comfort to be found in the very first drag of a newly-lit Marlboro. The glowing tip gave off a cheerful light as he took a mega-drag and walked on.

The marble stone was small, low and roughly hewn, just as Grethe had wanted it. In a thick envelope on the bedside table, adjacent to the bed where she had drawn her last breath, instructions had been left. The contents were straightforward and mostly practical, dealing with the title deeds to the house and spare keys for the cabin. Insurance documents and family jewels and the agreement with their neighbour about dividing the road that nothing would come of. Nevertheless, between the lines, he also read into this the odd glimmer of deep love, of harmony and twenty-one good, secure years.

Grethe lay at the very far end, the farthest and lowest point in a burial ground surrounded by heavy traffic and light industry. The stone leaned a little to the south-west, where the fjord lay, as if it longed to go home to Italy from whence it had come.

Her name was on a bronze plaque. The letters were relief engraved on a narrower panel screwed on to the larger one. There was something un-Norwegian about it – the usual practice was to engrave the name and dates on the actual stone. But this too was something his wife had decided before she died. Maybe she had seen it somewhere abroad.

He hunkered down though the pain in his knee brought tears to his eyes. Thirty squats a day were still routine for him despite no discernible improvement coming of it. The day he skipped his morning gymnastics, however, everything would be knackered. He would never manage to get down into that position again. It was unthinkable to let oneself deteriorate like that. Of all the little things that still made everyday life move on from one date to the next, the satisfaction he derived from keeping himself trim was among the most important.

His fingers ran over the ice-cold lettering. The bronze plaque, which until a few weeks ago had been dark green, almost black in some places, was recently polished to a golden shine. Beneath Grethe's name, a space had been cleared for another. He had been present when the stonemason had re-attached the plaque.

The patch of ground beneath the colossal elm tree had become a grave for two.

The name at the bottom had not yet been fitted. The guy from the undertakers had seemed taken aback when the widower had turned down the idea of screwing on the second plate. Servile and silent, he had nevertheless accepted the instruction and handed over the small panel with the name and dates of birth and death. It was at his home now, where it would remain, wrapped in tissue paper in Grethe's old bedside table drawer, until it was all over. Until everything had been accomplished and it was possible to breathe again.

This was the only thing he wanted in life now – to be able to take a deep breath down into his lungs and let it leak out again slowly. Time after time. Feeling the life-giving oxygen circulate to the many muscles of the body, making him feel alive. He did not know what was going to happen. It didn't matter. In truth, he had made unforgivable mistakes in his life, but far greater wrongs had been inflicted on him and his little flock.

He had lost far too much.

If only Grethe had been allowed to live, the world would be different.

He mumbled a few words and slowly rose to his feet. Lighting the grave candle he had brought, he set it down on the wet, dead grass. Perhaps he was saying a prayer. He was not entirely sure. It was probably Grethe rather than God he was addressing. In the end his thoughts petered out.

Once again he fished out a smoke and sauntered back the way he had come.

SUNDAY 8 SEPTEMBER

The Helper

'How can a smiley face wink? Did it move?'

Einar Falsen wiped his yellow-stained hands on his trousers and sat down on his ancient settee. A cat slinked cosily on to his lap and began to lick the cheese puff grease from his owner's fingers.

'Of course not,' Selma Falck said, with a touch of irritation in her voice, as she slapped a document folder down on the coffee table with a thud and took a seat on a rickety armchair. 'One eye is drawn like that. Closed, I mean. As if the face was winking.'

She demonstrated while she struggled to find a more comfortable position for her sore arm.

'Take off that awful wig,' Einar told her. 'And what's that?'

Selma ripped off the false hair and stuffed it into her bag. All her years of going in disguise to and from Oslo's illegal gambling dens had left her with a sizeable selection of wigs, glasses and headgear. The need to avoid recognition was at least as great now. She had long ago learned to vary her gait. And she had forced her recently operated arm into a sleeve before she had made her way out via the basement garage instead of using the usual exit. After that she had walked the mere quarter of an hour down to Einar Falsen's small apartment. Even though she really hoped Linda

Bruseth had been the assassin's target, she could not be sure and so she took her precautions.

'These,' Selma said, placing her palm on the bundle in front of her, 'are all the cases I've had dealings with since I quit as a lawyer and started out as a private investigator.'

She pushed them several centimetres towards him.

'What am I supposed to do with them?' Einar asked. The former policeman stared sceptically at the pile of papers.

'You're going to go through every single one very carefully,' Selma said.

'Why?'

'Because ...' Annoyed, she stood up, crumpled the foul-smelling empty cheese puff packet and headed into the kitchen to dispose of it. 'Did you not take in any of what I told you on the phone?' she asked loudly.

'You should be pleased I even took the call when you phoned. I nearly jumped out of my skin. You're not to use it in anything but extreme emergency, I've told you. Lots of times.'

'This *is* an emergency. I was shot at.'

'Let the police take care of that case. They'll get to the bottom of it.'

Selma returned and sat down. She let her gaze linger on the man on the opposite side of the three-legged, crooked coffee table. He was having a good spell. He did not exclusively eat cheese puffs, even though his consumption of them was still excessive. As far as she could understand, he was careful to take his prescribed antipsychotics. Following a couple of decades as a rough sleeper, it had done him good to move indoors. Even into an apartment like this, draughty and damp, for which he compensated by having numerous panel heaters on full blast at all times of the day and night.

'It's as hot as a sauna in here,' she sighed, tugging at the neckline of her sweater.

'Just right,' Einar replied with a smile, moving the cat to his shoulder. 'Pussycat thinks so too.'

He had definitely improved in the past year and was so much healthier that he almost always called her Selma rather than Mariska after an American actress everyone thought she looked like.

For far too many years, Selma had been compelled to have him admitted to hospital with forty degrees of fever and gurgling lungs at least once during the dark days of the year. Last winter he had, however, scraped through without a single instance of serious illness. With his improved physical condition, his mental state also stabilized. He still suffered from delusions about everything from lethal electro-hypersensitivity to the idea that the country was subject to a totalitarian, total-surveillance, secret regime. Controlled by the CIA, of course. The entire *Rugged/Storm-scarred* case had not exactly helped. Even now he could sometimes succumb to deep anxiety and delirium about conspiracy theories. But these periods were increasingly rare and never lasted as long as before. These past few weeks, he had behaved almost normally. He kept the apartment fairly clean and showered a couple of times a week at any rate. Einar Falsen seemed satisfied with his life for the first time in twenty years.

Things were not going so well for Selma.

She was exhausted. It was no longer so easy to keep up appearances. The previous year's near-death experience had taken more out of her than she liked to admit. For as long as she could remember, probably since childhood, she had been split between her real self and her outward image. That was how she had chosen to live her life. Much of the perpetual restlessness within her had been transformed into positive energy. She got things done. The uneasiness left over had made her a gambling addict, something that had almost completely destroyed her a couple of years earlier.

But not entirely. Selma Falck always got back on her feet.

Her fame from the time when she had been one of the best handball players in the world had over the years changed into celebrity for constantly evolving reasons. First as a high-profile lawyer. She often accepted or rejected clients based on the kind of attention the case was going to bring her. Politically, she sat on the fence and had a unique ability to land full-square in the middle of what was generally acceptable when she was occasionally challenged about her political views.

Selma provoked no one.

There was scarcely a reality contest she had not taken part in. She had won several of them. Social media also seemed made for Selma Falck. Through selfies and snapshots she had walled herself in behind success, impressive enough without becoming an object of much jealousy. Her exercise tips had previously been followed by almost 300,000 subscribers on YouTube, a number that climbed even higher after she had generously allowed the world to participate in last year's impressive rehabilitation of a damaged body of well over fifty.

Selma Falck was seldom completely herself.

Living like this had gone well. Selma could not get the hang of anything else. Her mouth widened into a smile when she encountered other people. Her memory was enviable and allowed her to face most people with empathic questions about their lives and wellbeing and grandchildren.

A year ago she would have exploited the situation she now found herself in. She would have let herself be interviewed from her hospital bedside if the doctors had granted permission, as she had chosen to do last year as soon as she was well enough. The photographers would have been allowed their pictures, now as then. Her Instagram account would have been continually filled with photos from the hospital, accompanied by hashtags such as *#shotbyasniper* and *#detectivelife*.

Instead she had turned away all attempts at contact.

'Is something wrong?' Einar asked, sounding surprised, as he put the cat down on the floor.

'Yes. Someone tried to kill me. And I've no idea who it was. That's bound to affect your mood, you know.'

'As I said, you should let the police deal with that. Anyway, it could have been your pal the guy was after. She was the one who died.'

Selma did not reply. Slowly, she leaned back in the chair until she was sitting like a defiant teenager with her legs stretched straight out.

'Yes, of course. I wish that's how it was. I want that to be how it was. But I still don't believe it.'

She gestured towards the folder and straightened up.

'Go through these, please. On top are the cases I did actually take on. You can skim through them. Since I've solved them all, those clients love me. Further down the pile you'll find a concise overview of the people who've contacted me in the past two years and I've been unwilling or unable to help them.'

'What am I looking for?'

'To see whether there's someone who has more reason to be after me than the others. I haven't managed to find any myself. But there could be a pattern I've missed. Are you feeling in top form?'

'I'm in top form, yes! Haven't felt better in ages. I take Pussycat out for a walk at night to meet as few people as possible. The Chinese guy at the kiosk—'

'He's from Vietnam.'

'Same thing. He delivers cheese puffs to my door now. Every Tuesday and Friday. And the *Meny* supermarket up here ...'

He waved lethargically at the window in approximately the right direction.

'... they're open until half past ten at night. Just before closing time there's hardly any folk in there. And I only need to shop every fortnight. Things are absolutely tip top.'

Selma hesitated. Einar Falsen could not have access to the Internet whenever he wanted. Last year she had bought a laptop, wrapping it up well in lies claiming it was free from radiation and taught him how to use it. Things had gone really badly. He had found confirmation of his most confused delusions all over the place out there on the Internet, and had suffered such a setback that it had almost been the end of him.

In his good spells, on the other hand, she could let him use the machine. That had happened twice and had been extremely successful. As early as his first encounter with the vast World Wide Web, he had demonstrated a talent for searching and compiling information. If he were disciplined enough to avoid getting embroiled in places he could not cope with, he also gained great pleasure from the innocent games Selma had bought for him.

'You can have the laptop,' she said, producing it from her shoulder bag.

Einar's face lit up. 'Can I download a new HOG?'

'HOG?'

'Hidden objects game. Really great fun.'

'OK. One. Only one.'

The laptop was still protected with something Einar believed to be a magnetic field-eliminating cover of spray-painted plastic. Selma fired up the machine.

'Let me see,' Einar said enthusiastically, waving her over to him on the settee. 'I'll choose a game myself.'

To be on the safe side, he picked up his helmet from the floor, an old ice-hockey helmet Selma had covered in aluminium foil held in place by silver gaffer tape. He fumbled with the chinstrap and settled more comfortably on the settee.

'No games until you've worked for at least three hours,' Selma warned him as she uploaded *Big Fish* and let the man scroll through the numerous offers. 'And you can only play for one hour.'

'Two,' Einar said firmly. 'And you must first tell me what I have to find out.'

Selma began to download the game he had pointed at.

'I want to know as much as possible about all these people,' she said, nodding towards the stack of papers. 'There's a lot there already. Rationalize it all. Then find out everything. Marriage, interests. Friends. See if any of them have anything in common. Work, holiday home, travels. Social media is normally the best source, but—'

'I've got it now.'

'Then I'm off. Does your printer work? Have you paper for the printouts? Have you got enough ink?'

'Yes. Yes. Yes. Off you go.'

He did not even look up from the screen. The bundle of case folders lay untouched.

'You must tell me one thing before you leave,' he said.

The sounds from the machine betrayed that he had already launched the game.

'Work first,' Selma said sternly.

Now he glanced up. 'When the police are already investigating the incident at Løkka as a possible murder attempt on you, why won't you tell them about the stall-ker who magically enters your apartment and leaves behind little greetings, without setting off the alarm and without breaking in?'

He mispronounced the word 'stalker'.

'Staw-ker,' Selma corrected him as she moved away. 'It's pronounced staw-ker.'

'Pack it in. Answer me instead.'

'Because,' she said, turning slowly to face him again.

Silence ensued.

'Because what?' Einar insisted.

'Because Anine won't like me being shot at in broad daylight. Admittedly, I'm convinced I was the intended target, but I really hope the police get bogged down in Linda's life. Then I can talk Anine round and be allowed to have Skjalg. At home, at the very least. On the other hand, if she finds out I'm being followed all the way into my own apartment, you can bet your life she won't let me see the boy until all this is over and wrapped up. And that could take time.'

'Skjalg,' Einar repeated with a toothless grin. 'To think that Selma Falck has fallen head over heels in love at last.'

Selma left him without another word. The restlessness that always drove her on and kept her in perpetual motion, welcome and life giving, was different now.

What she actually felt was fear.

The Assignment

Lars Winther was at work despite it being his day off. With a house full of children, weekends had developed into a war zone at home. His wife was also a journalist and also worn out, and in common with Lars would far rather spend Sundays relaxing by working. Now he was the one who had won the battle, through a strategic retreat even before the youngest kid had woken up.

For the first few hours he had quite simply caught up with sleep. He felt like a new person when he crept out from under the blanket on the settee in the largest conference room. He stretched, drank a bottle of water and straightened his clothes. For the sake of appearances he would have to go home in an hour or two but he had plenty to do in the meantime. Visiting Selma was top priority. If he wasn't allowed to work on the shooting episode in Grünerløkka, no power on earth could prevent him from paying a call on a sick friend. The media had reported that Selma Falck had been discharged and Lars assumed she was still in enough pain to keep her at home.

As he strode out through the door and into the open-plan editorial offices, he heard the editor shout his name.

'Bloody hell,' he whispered, but all the same padded into her office at the other end of the huge space.

She was new. When the old editor had retired three months earlier, most people had expected an internal promotion. They were wrong. In came a thirty-eight-year-old woman from *Stavanger Aftenblad*. She was one of the youngest in the entire newspaper, but in short order had established an authority that Lars Winther found pretty fascinating. She was always in the office. Monday to Friday as well as weekends and holidays. The employees had begun to whisper in corners that she had still not found herself anywhere to live.

'At last you're awake,' she snapped as she motioned for him to take a seat. 'Have you deserted the family idyll? A bit of a chore being home at weekends?'

Lars muttered an indistinct affirmation.

'Here,' she said brusquely when he finally sat down.

She pushed a voluminous green plastic folder towards him. When he opened it, he saw that a memory stick was taped on the inside and the remaining contents were a bundle of printouts he estimated at around one hundred sheets.

'What's this?' he asked sceptically.

'I'm not entirely sure.'

'What do you expect me to do with it?' He closed the folder and pushed it back across the pristine desk.

'It's a story Jonathan Herse was working on,' she said.

'Jonathan?'

Lars's eyes narrowed. His colleague had died three weeks earlier in a tragic road accident at the Bislett roundabout. The young journalist was riding a bike without a helmet and cycling far too fast when he crashed. Most evidence suggested that the taxi driver he collided with was the innocent party. The accident had occurred late one Friday night and there were few witnesses. Most of them were also so drunk at the time of the accident that their statements were all over the place. The most crucial fact in the case was that Jonathan's blood alcohol count was 0.17 per cent and the vehicle driver was sober.

'Why do you want me to look at it?'

Lars Winther gazed at the folder with what most of all resembled distaste. Taking over stories that had already been started was worse than writing obituaries, which he had sometimes been forced to do as a summer temp on local papers in his teenage years. Journalism depended a great deal on method and he had his own. As had most reporters. It was always tricky to find a clear thread in stories others had embarked upon and the end result was often that you had to start all over again from scratch.

'What's it about?' he asked. 'It's always hellish to—'

He was interrupted by a cleaner coming in. Wearing a dark chador, she only wanted to empty the bin.

'Child welfare,' the editor said without paying her any attention.

Lars smacked his forehead and groaned demonstratively. The cleaner set down an empty wastepaper basket, took the rubbish away in a bag and made herself scarce.

'Christ, no!' Lars almost shouted. 'A fucking hornet's nest! People who run into that department go stark raving mad. They're conspiracy theorists, dimwits and net trolls. It's out of the question that—'

The editor raised her right hand so abruptly that he held back.

'I've spent a lot of time working my way into … the environment here,' she said sharply. 'And it's my firm understanding that you really want to transfer to the politics section.'

Lars stared at her without nodding.

'And that you almost expected it,' she went on, 'after the success of exposing the *Rugged/Storm-scarred* operation. The point is …'

Steepling her hands, she rested her arms on the desk. Her eyes were bluer than any he had ever seen and her blonde hair appeared genuine. If it hadn't been for her tight, almost lipless mouth, she would have been attractive.

'You got that story free of charge,' she declared. 'Handed to you on a silver platter by Selma Falck. In this …'

A well-manicured, pink-varnished nail tapped the plastic folder.

'Inside here, as far as I know, there is the start of something. But it's an interesting start. I haven't seen any of it myself, but Jonathan was both enthusiastic and slightly …'

She was sampling her way to the right word.

'… worried, almost.'

'Please,' he gave a faint moan. 'Child welfare, for heaven's sake! Be good enough to let me pass on it!'

'No,' she said with a smile.

This time he did not shove the folder back.

'Jonathan was far from clear and fairly secretive with it,' she said. 'I regret not pushing him harder when he asked for three weeks off from everything else. But I'm guessing this is not about individual cases, nasty bureaucrats and whinging parents. This here—'

Yet again she leaned forward and caught his eye.

'This case is about something far more serious,' she said. 'If I understood Jonathan correctly.'

Lars gave another loud sigh as he grabbed the folder without opening it. The editor gave a faint nod towards the door and he got to his feet.

'If you crack this, the road to politics will be far shorter!' Her voice sounded almost cheerful behind his back.

'Child welfare,' he snarled almost inaudibly and let the door slam behind him with a bang that was a bit too emphatic.

He changed into his jogging gear for the run to Sagene. When Selma answered neither her phone nor the three text messages he fired off with only a minute in between, he ran the whole way home instead.

Child welfare. The worst hornet's nest of them all, as Lars Winther knew, and he made up his mind not to give a shit about the editor's instructions.

At least for the moment.

The Stalker

Poker-Turk, Selma's old client and jack-of-all-trades, turned up at once. As he always did when she phoned.

On the way home from Einar's, Selma had felt her fear rise with each step as she approached Sagene and the small apartment that had been her secure bunker until now. A bedroom where she had spent better nights than she ever had in the villa on Ormøya island with her husband and children a lifetime ago. A living room she had finally arranged exactly the way she wanted it. Practical and snug, no more nor less. The balcony was her favourite spot, undisturbed and alone on the high and otherwise smooth façade. From there she could look out over extensive parts of the city and next to no one could see her.

The apartment was a sanctuary.

Or – it had been.

Now she barely dared to step inside it. Only minutes after she had come home, or after she had restlessly, with racing pulse, paced back and forth across the living room floor with regular anxious detours out on to the balcony, she realized that something would have to be done. The uninvited guest must either have been an employee of the security company that had set up her alarm system, or in some other way have access to both the key and the code. Maybe a hacker. There were many of them.

Far too many.

Poker-Turk appeared three quarters of an hour after she had called him. Pleasant as always. In a cloud of expensive aftershave, he had turned the place upside-down. First she had asked him to dismantle the old alarm apparatus. He had cocked his head, given this some thought, and then declared that this course of action would be stupid. Since it had not been installed with the inclusion of cameras, fortunately, she could just use it as she normally did. Switch it on when she went out and off again when she came back. Or else just forget about it. He did not get his wife to use their own set-up unless they were away for a longer period.

'Perfectly normal, you know.'

Poker-Turk's equipment resembled something from *Mission: Impossible*.

He hid tiny components, all wireless, in picture frames, between the slats on the venetian blinds and under the cornices. After an hour's work he asked for her mobile phone. Three minutes later, everything could be controlled by an app. With the use of four well-concealed cameras, she could see almost every nook and cranny in the apartment. He handed her the phone with a serious expression.

'Do you want me to take control of it too? For the sake of your own security? I can download—'

'No, thanks. I'll manage it by myself.'

'But you want to change the lock? Even though it will be discovered if he tries to come in again?'

'Or her. And yes. I want a new lock. Two locks, in fact. Like now. Changing the lock is not so unusual, after all. He or she might think it's just sheer chance. It'll prevent him from entering, but not necessarily tell him I know he's been here.'

'The smiley face is surely a sign that he wants you to know?'

'Yes. That's the most frightening thing about it all, to be honest. However, he can't be sure I've spotted it. But ...'

She shivered, quite literally, a shudder that ran through her body and made Poker-Turk place his hand on her arm. The uninjured one. Almost imperceptibly, she drew away.

'I don't want him in here,' she said firmly.

Poker-Turk nodded. It did not take him long to do as she asked. The work seemed solid enough, even though it had caused some obvious scratches on the door.

'Jack of all trades, master of none.'

He smiled, packed up his tools and was on the point of leaving when she asked him how much she owed.

'You owe me nothing,' was the reply.

As always.

'You saved me from being jailed for four years, Selma. And you sorted my tax return. Also, you've lost plenty around my gambling tables, which by the way you haven't visited for a long time.'

With a loud guffaw, he gave her a quick fist bump and departed.

Selma was left on her own again, somewhat calmer now.

But not calm enough. There was only one medicine for what was gnawing beneath her breastbone, those painful twinges at the top of her stomach that just kept growing worse. She flipped open her laptop and logged on to one of her usual domains.

The sight of the online poker logo reduced her pulse rate. The stern king of hearts looked right through her, while the queen of spades gazed coyly at a jack in a coat of mail. Selma's fingers were already tapping in the code. She was breathing more easily. Her distress was about to be converted into excitement as a glorious sense of wellbeing displaced the anxiety in a matter of seconds.

Halfway into the combination of letters and numbers, she suddenly stopped. The photo of Skjalg as a newborn, enlarged to an absolutely ridiculous size and hung on the living room wall beside the bedroom door was serving its intended purpose. Selma slammed the laptop shut and pushed it aside.

Four and a half months had gone by since she had last gambled.

When Selma's daughter Anine had unexpectedly turned up at the hospital following last year's ordeal on the Hardangervidda, Selma learned she was to be a grandmother. The little child must have come into being only a week or two before her son-in-law died at his own wedding.

Little Skjalg was born in April.

He was a godsend. His eyes were dark and his mouth broad with full lips. The cupid's bow was so distinctive that it might even resemble the scar from a successful harelip operation. The staff in the maternity ward were over the moon that an infant boy could be such a spitting image of his grandmother. Anine lay there in bed, blonde and blue-eyed, and Selma, after her third visit in less than twelve hours, had finally twigged that she ought to leave her daughter in peace until she went home. Before she left, however, she had let two doctors and three nurses take selfies of the brand new grandmother cradling her grandchild in her arms.

Anine got annoyed, of course, but on the other hand, she did that often. The most important thing now was that she needed her.

Life as a single mother was far from ideal. The boy's paternal grandfather and grandmother were divorced and family ties were weakened because of that. Skjalg's uncle had not even seen his nephew. Even though the boy was called after his dead daddy, his surviving relatives had shown negligible interest in the baby. In contrast, Selma was absolutely dotty, as they said when she came swanning in with a new car seat and a whole suitcase filled with baby clothes to drive the tiny little family home after two and a half days spent at Ullevål Hospital.

Anine accepted Selma's enthusiasm. So far and only because she needed it. Her compliance, however, came with one clear condition.

No gambling.

She should not take the tiniest risk of losing the apartment at Sagene, which had become a place where Skjalg felt safe. Selma Falck had already gambled away more than her shirt in the past.

Selma had promised. She had sworn a solemn oath that this period in her life was over. The agreement was easy to enter into. Sticking to it was sometimes unbearably hard.

But she had managed it.

Little Skjalg was a miracle. Selma saw herself mirrored in him in a way she never had with her own children. She saw herself in his little face. In his hair, which had stayed completely dark as he grew older. Unusually enough, his first two tiny teeth appeared when he was only four months old. Even more unusually, they popped through on his upper jaw, not the lower, exactly as Selma had seen on the few photos there were of her at that age. One of them, taken in the early spring of 1967, on a beach in a location that must be somewhere in California, depicted a serious youngster. Propped up with towels behind her and tucked in around her backside, squinting in the strong sunlight, she showed two grains of rice below her top lip. Her parents had called her Chip'n'Dale until she was four, when all pet names had faded and died away completely.

Anine would not find out if Selma indulged in some gambling. Just one hour. She could set a limit for losses. Small change.

Nothing serious: she could put a time lock on the computer, a device she had installed in a period when it had all become a bit much. Not that it had helped any, she had to admit, because of course there was also a code to override it.

On the other hand, Anine was a living lie detector, and she quizzed her mother about gambling every time they met. Selma's ability to fib and tell white lies as well as flagrant ones when it suited her had brought her far in this world. Anine, unlike all the others, had stopped being deceived as early as around the age of eight. It must have been about that time their relationship had splintered, Selma thought as she pushed the laptop further across the table.

She would have to think of something.

Lars had been trying to get hold of her. Repeatedly. They could find something to do but she wasn't particularly keen to talk to him.

On her way into the bedroom for the third time, her gaze fell on the pile of copies of the folder she had given Einar. Grabbing it glumly, she headed for the settee and collapsed on to the cushions. She winced when pain shot through her shoulder, simply because she had begun to forget her injury in between each careless movement.

On top lay the list of cases she had actually accepted. She laid them aside. Absent-mindedly, she began to leaf through the ones she had turned down. Now she was glad she always made a brief note of every application she received, no matter how banal it might be. Settling the sheaf of papers on her knees, she stretched her feet out on the coffee table.

The letters would not play along with her. She could see them, but could not concentrate on stringing them together into words, far less form sentences. Her anxiety, this counter-productive, unfamiliar dread that would not release its grip, made her heart beat far too fast. It felt as if she could feel her blood pressure rise. There was a dull pounding in her head, her ears were ringing and she began to gasp for breath. A flashback from the days she had spent in a stone shelter through a winter storm, naked and surrounded by the stench of urine, excrement and cold tomato soup, suddenly made her screw up her eyes and get to her feet.

The papers fell to the floor.

The cyberstalkers, she thought, on the verge of a panic attack.

That must be where the answer lay. She already had these persecutors, people who could not leave her in peace. Ones she had mentally flicked away for a long time, but who had begun to bother her increasingly in the past year. Not because they were necessarily more annoying but because she no longer had the energy to dismiss them.

Selma Falck wasn't strong enough to be herself and sometimes that was unbearable.

She dashed to the kitchen, found the paper bag she had to use a bit too often these days, and used the thumb and forefinger of her right hand to shape the opening into a mouth-sized hole.

Three deep breaths later, she felt better. The dizziness subsided and she took the bag from her lips. Inhaled while counting to five in silence. Held her breath for four seconds. Exhaled for three. And opened her eyes.

No one could come in now. No one had keys for the new locks.

If only Lupus had been here.

She poured a big glass of water from the tap and drank it slowly. Her pulse rate slowed noticeably. All the same, the anxiety did not disappear completely. On a whim, she went into the bathroom. Locked the door with the key, the one she had never used before. She sat down in the shower recess and drew her knees up to her chest.

The phone display lit up when she touched it.

Fredrikke Augustsson was the name she was looking for.

Selma was well aware of how difficult it was to be active on social media without attracting followers like Fredrikke Augustsson. This particular variant was hung up on law and order. On jurisprudence, no less, or at least a misconception of the subject. Ages ago, perhaps as far back as 2014, Selma had stood up for a high-profile lawyer colleague in a way she had felt was pretty amusing. Just snappy enough, the way you should be on Twitter. Her colleague had done nothing but point out that Fredrikke Augustsson gave paid legal advice without being qualified as a lawyer, something that was in fact illegal. Simple. The hot-tempered amateur piled even more hate speech on the guy when he advised the Solicitors Regulation Authority of what the woman was up to. They gave her a sharp rebuke and since then things had gone from bad to worse.

Selma should have known better than to get involved. After a few weeks of cantankerous attacks from the furious woman, who lived of all places in an enormous villa in Holmenkollen, Selma had concluded that Twitter was not the arena for her. Until that point she had enjoyed it. Many trendsetting legal minds used the micro-blog service as an arena for discussion and the professional advantages of links and references were numerous. Nevertheless it had all grown tiresome after a while, and Fredrikke Augustsson's enraged persecution forced her to deactivate her account.

All the same, Selma was genuinely curious.

In order to avoid entirely missing out on the gossip, legal chat and everything else going on, she reactivated her account from time to time. Preferably at night. It could be both entertaining and useful to know who said what to whom and why. Unfortunately, Fredrikke Augustsson also persisted with her campaign. She ranted angrily and threw out a continuous stream of insults aimed especially at two sometimes-synchronous groups: lawyers and more or less organized sceptics. Anti-conspiracy theorists. Fact-hunters. The problem was that they responded to her. The more she attacked them, the harder they fought back. Sometimes they went well beyond the pale in their obvious enjoyment of riling the woman. It was like watching a gang of boys circling round a captured lemming.

But it was really quite amusing to follow it all.

Fredrikke Augustsson was a wannabe lawyer who had left no trace behind her on the Internet apart from a whole host of angry troll accounts on social media. She probably spent most of her time in the vicinity of a keyboard. Her profile actually told Selma nothing except that she fitted right into her own neighbourhood according to all the prejudices on display. A slim woman with fair hair, dressed in clothes with an Austrian style. Loden and wool and thin quilted jackets. A member of the country set, aged around fifty.

She could not possibly pose a danger to anyone other than herself.

'Batty,' Selma whispered, and then Janna Underbar crossed her mind.

This could not possibly be her real name, but she had certainly been the most annoying cyberstalker of them all. When the Internet was in its infancy, Janna Underbar had set up a website that looked as if it belonged to Selma. Selma could not fathom where she had got hold of the pictures the Swedish woman seemed to possess. Sometimes the odd childhood photograph had turned up on the adoring home page with the domain name *selmafalck.com*. It had all felt slightly uncomfortable but pretty harmless all the same. Only when the lady in question had popped up beside her on a flight between Oslo and Stockholm had Selma become worried. How her persecutor had secured that particular seat was impossible to understand. It could scarcely have been by chance.

The passenger by her side had been sweating and shaking with excitement and pulled out a pile of photos for signing before the landing wheels had even been hauled up.

At first Selma had thought Janna Underbar merely unhealthily besotted from a distance. However, after the woman had spent a small fortune shuttling from her home in Uddevalla to various places in Norway to meet Selma, the police were brought in. The woman was usually drunk, always extremely forward and lost her temper each time Selma shunned her with escalating brusqueness.

In the end she had been banned from any contact according to paragraph 57 of the Penal Code. Six months later, Janne Underbar was murdered by her lesbian live-in partner after a drunken quarrel. Selma was hugely relieved when she received a formal letter from the Swedish police about the death. When she later discovered the conviction carried the minimum sentence, six years imprisonment, it was clear there had been numerous extenuating circumstances. Selma could vividly imagine.

She hadn't given Janna Underbar a thought for years.

Janna Underbar was dead. She could be forgotten.

But that wasn't the case with Creedmore.

He had sent her letters for almost a year. When she had finally come home after her hospital stay in the autumn of 2018, there were already four envelopes from him in her post. Lars Winther had emptied the mailbox in Selma's absence, and tried to sort out the essentials from things that could be tossed in the bin. The letters from Creedmore had landed in the first bundle. The envelopes were ordinary ones that could be bought in any branch of *Clas Ohlson* or *Staples*, the paper similar. The man, and Selma was fairly certain it was a man, had written the letters by hand. The first of these contained flattery and little hints that they ought to meet. Selma had skimmed them – they weren't long – and then stuffed them into the waste paper. When they continued to arrive, she began to keep them. They were still not threatening but simply began to be repellent in their persistence. When she discovered, on further investigation, that the signature, Creedmore, was a type of ammunition, it all became unpleasant. A couple of times the thought had entered her head that she should alert the police. She had many friends there and could do so off the record. Just seek some professional advice.

It never went further than the thought. After all, he did not seem dangerous.

The underfloor heating was roasting her backside. Staggering to her feet, Selma almost fell over and had to use her injured arm to save herself. The shower door hit the tiles and shattered. Selma swore. She stood staring at the pulverized glass on the floor while she picked shards out of her hair. When she tried to brush a few fragments from her shoulder, she cut her hand.

She held her hand under the tap and let cold water splash over it.

Her pulse had soared to 120, she realized. And was still climbing. Nausea washed over her and she began to retch. Nothing came up apart from sour bile that burnt her gullet and tongue. The water turned a paler and paler shade of red. In the end it ran clear. Her hand was shaking. Without knowing if she dared, she used her fingers to fumble her way to the pulse counter on her fitness watch.

Her heart was thumping 167 beats a minute.

Something was seriously wrong. She tottered out of the bathroom. She had to get out of the apartment, away from all this. She could stay at Einar's. At a hotel. In the forest, if it came to that, or with Vanja and Kristina. Before she reached the front door, she had tapped her way to what she firmly believed was Anine's number.

'Medical emergencies,' was the response at the other end. 'How can I help you?'

MONDAY 9 SEPTEMBER

The Committee Meeting

'It is eight years, one month, two weeks and four days ago now.'
The tall, grey-clad man sat at the head of the table. The atmosphere among the six professionals around the conference table had been almost cheerful while they waited for the chairman.

'Since what?' one of them asked above the others' chatter.

'Since 22 July 2011.'

The babble was immediately silenced.

'Why do you mention that?' a young woman ventured to ask.

'Because we were promised an improvement in resilience,' Karstein Braaten answered sharply, banging his fist on the table. 'Against terrorism. Against natural catastrophes. Against cyber attacks. Against invasion and pandemics and Uncle Tom Cobley and all. Every single fucking politician in this country spent weeks, months and years promising better resilience for the nation and its people. And then this happens ...'

Grabbing his mobile phone, he let his fingers run over the display. 'Then this happens,' he repeated, holding the phone up to the others.

'The Social Security scandal?'

'Yes, the Social Security scandal.'

None of the others seemed to grasp what he meant. One

of Norway's largest public services, NAV, the Social Security agency, had responsibility for the organization and financing of job creation programmes, social benefits and social welfare. They administered one third of the entire state budget and were themselves the backbone of the welfare state most Norwegians were so proud of. Recently it had come to light that the agency had been the cause of a large number of miscarriages of justice for benefit fraud, as well as depriving several thousand people of support payments to which they were actually entitled. The scandal had arisen because of a misinterpretation of EEA regulations. Over many years. Perhaps decades. Not only had NAV apparently closed their eyes to warnings of malpractice for a long period of time, but also their mistaken application of law had been based on instructions from Norway's Parliament as well as the prosecution service and the judiciary. The most serious legal scandal in modern Norwegian history was an established fact.

'I don't quite understand where you're going with this,' said the youngest person in the room, a man who could hardly be more than thirty, but who already had a PhD in Macroeconomics from the London School of Economics and a Masters in Statistics from the Massachusetts Institute of Technology.

The man in grey put down his phone and held his face in both hands for several seconds. He had scarcely slept for five nights and momentarily felt both nauseous and faint.

'My mother died last Saturday,' he said unexpectedly, grasping the edge of the table as he forced out a smile.

Condolences were muttered around the table. He gave no thanks.

'It happened fairly suddenly. Even though she was nearly ninety, and from that point of view death can't exactly come as a bombshell. That may be why I'm being slightly more ...'

He looked towards the young, over-educated loudmouth.

'... blunt. Apologies.'

He stooped to one side and picked up a stack of reports everyone around the table recognized, resilience plans for every imaginable, and some unthinkable, catastrophic situations. Karstein Braaten cleared his throat, holding his clenched hand in front of his mouth, and his voice sounded calmer when he continued:

'In certain situations, the government will have the authority to make enormous inroads into the rights of the Norwegian people. In their freedom of movement. Their finances. In prioritization within the health service. They will be able to deploy the Home Guard and the Police Force. Acts we normally regard as part and parcel of everyday life, practically safeguarded by our human rights, could be forbidden overnight.'

The room had fallen silent. Some looked down. Others, such as the young woman at the very foot of the table, stared straight at him with eyes that grew narrower by the minute. Karstein Braaten had no idea whether she was expressing comprehension or confusion. For far too many years, he had worked on security. The safety of the populace. Ensuring the country was prepared for situations for which the irresponsible never spared a thought. The young woman, smart as such women always were, educated and well informed, nevertheless did not have a clue. She would not have for many years to come, not until she had lived as long as he had behind closed office doors and among documents that warned about the world and the realities only the smallest minority were willing to see.

'And people are going to comply, obediently,' he went on eventually with a brief nod. 'All prognoses suggest that, in a crisis situation, Norwegians will do as they're told. There will be a lot of yelling and a bit of screeching, but when it comes down to brass tacks, we do what our government asks of us. Why?'

His eyes circled around the table but no one felt called upon to answer.

'Trust?' one person finally dared to suggest.

'Exactly. Trust. We live in a society based on trust. For the moment. We rely on one another. Mostly. In the authorities and state institutions. We have one of the most well ordered governments in the world. It rests on a foundation of trust. Even that dreadful, unendurable summer Friday in 2011 did not really alter that. This people ...'

He looked lingeringly out through the window.

'This nation retained its trust in an apparatus that totally failed when everything went wrong. The mere sight of that defective rubber boat, crowded with police officers who ...'

He gripped the glass of water that someone had filled before he arrived. Draining it, he forced out something he hoped would resemble a smile.

'A lot of water has gone under the bridge since that time,' he said in a steadier voice. 'I think there would be a demand for more heads to roll if the terrorist attack happened today. In retrospect, while we waited for more freedom, more democracy, more love ...'

His voice was on the verge of breaking with contempt for the well-worn platitudes in the aftermath of 22 July.

'... we have in fact ended up with the opposite. Increased polarization. More intense hatred. Sharper verbal exchanges. More disdain for the police. More blatant racism.'

'Perhaps we should make a start on today's agenda?' suggested the young woman as she fiddled with the papers in front of her on the table.

She was obviously both unused to and uncomfortable with the board chairman's emotional outburst.

Karstein Braaten did not respond. He glanced again at his phone and let his thumb swipe from article to article.

'People have been unjustly imprisoned,' he murmured. 'They've been punished without legal grounds. What a nightmare for a constitutional democracy! Serious miscarriages of justice as a consequence of a gang of ignorant lawyers not bothering to do anything other than what they're told. Which was that it was illegal to travel abroad and be paid benefits at the same time. With severe punishment as a result. Leaving Norway, for many people, became losing their livelihood. Most of them complied and through that were deprived of absolutely fundamental human rights. Such as visiting a dying sister in Germany. Such as salvaging what little property you own in Sweden from water damage. No one saw the absurdity of that. This ...'

He banged the phone so hard on the table that the glass cracked. Dumbfounded, he sat staring at the display. No one spoke.

'Confucius,' he said in the end, putting down the mobile. 'As early as half a millennium before our own era, he stipulated that a ruler needs three things: weapons, food and trust.'

He counted on his fingers.

'The first of these he should give up when things get tough is the weapons. Then the food. Because trust, the idea that your subjects trust in you, is the only thing you really can't do without.'

'We're not exactly living in a dictatorship these days, though.'

The young scholar adjusted his glasses and continued: 'Just as important as trust is a good dose of distrust. It's difficult to call ourselves a democracy if people don't retain some healthy scepticism.'

Karstein Braaten nodded.

'That's correct. In a land such as ours, there's a fine balance between trust and distrust, between subordination and protest, which enables us to face crises. Opposing voices have to be present. As they are being raised now. That's what makes us into a democracy. It's the opposing voices, the criticism ... the distrust, if you will, that makes us stronger and takes us forward. Belief in the system must nevertheless be absolutely fundamental. How all this will specifically affect this fine balance ...'

He seesawed his hands as if they were scales and stole a glance at his damaged phone.

'... is in the lap of the gods.'

'It will surely get sorted out,' said the eldest woman in the room, smiling from ear to ear. 'Anyway, this scandal has only impacted people who are generally a bit ...'

She moved her head from side to side in an unmistakeable gesture, before rounding off: 'Shall we just get started, then?'

There was fluttering of papers and a sense of deep relief. Only Karstein Braaten went on sitting without moving a muscle before he rose from the table and left the meeting without uttering another word.

Nothing like it had ever happened before.

The Psychiatrist

Helle Viksfjord had specialized in psychiatry for all of seven months. What had been her greatest strength until now, having progressed so far on her educational path at such an impressively young age, had recently become an Achilles heel.

She was thirty-one but her stocky body shape, round face and unruly, loose curls took years off her age. It also seemed to rob her of gravity. Her patients usually reacted to her with surprise or stupefaction, followed by scepticism, which they never quite managed to overcome before she had to send them on within the system. Only children met her with open minds and she did not see much of them in this new job of hers.

Selma Falck was the first person who seemed to take the young doctor's youth in her stride. The tall woman smiled at her when she entered the consulting room and held out her hand without hesitation. Her movements were gracious and athletic at the same time – a calm gaze around the small room, a smooth, flowing motion as she sat down and crossed one leg over the other.

Then another smile. Her gaze was direct, a questioning look, seemingly, almost teasing.

'Well, then,' Helle Viksfjord said, turning to the computer screen for a moment before it struck her that this was hardly the right thing to do. She swivelled her chair back again. 'How are you feeling?'

'Fine, really. I do still have some pain in my arm ...' Selma Falck touched her left shoulder. 'But I've got a pretty high pain threshold. So it's OK. Thanks for asking!'

'Now I was thinking more of ...'

The psychiatrist gave a quick smile. It was virtually impossible not to seek refuge in DIPS, the patient record program open on the monitor.

'It seems you had a fairly distressing attack yesterday,' she said, taking a deep breath. 'And as you now know, there's nothing physically wrong with you.'

The woman opposite smiled broadly.

'Well, I have a total of half a kilo of titanium all through my body,' she said. 'And a relatively recent gunshot wound. So saying there's nothing physically wrong with me is something of an understatement.'

Her words could be understood as a reprimand, but the smile and frank gaze took the edge off the implicit criticism.

'You were found unconscious.'

'Just a bad turn. I'm exhausted after a few nights of next to no sleep.'

The patient pushed her injured shoulder forward a few centimetres, followed by a grimace of pain so fleeting that Helle Viksfjord was unsure if her eyes had deceived her.

'All the same, we don't like it when people of your physical condition and age suddenly pass out,' she said. 'And certainly not when they're so frightened before they faint that they phone for help. You're going to be examined from top to toe.'

Now she could no longer restrain herself and began to point at the computer monitor with a pen.

'Your heart is fine, despite what you've said about ... the episode. Your blood tests also indicate nothing to be worried about. On the contrary. Your liver function is excellent. The CT scan of your head shows nothing wrong there either. Overall ...'

Putting down her pen, she folded her hands in the hope that this would make her appear more relaxed.

'From a physical point of view, you must be one of the fittest patients I've ever seen.'

She regretted this immediately. Selma Falck's smile said what she did not need to put into words – that Helle Viksfjord's experience with patients was not exactly impressive.

'Thanks! I keep myself in shape. As you know.'

The doctor tried to restrain her blushes. She had followed Selma Falck on Instagram and YouTube for a long time now.

'Yes, of course,' she replied, swallowing audibly. 'You've probably checked whether ...'

All of a sudden she straightened up in her seat. She was so much shorter than her patient that she had to look up slightly to make eye contact, even when seated.

'But, to be honest,' she began again. 'All this ...'

She stole another glance at the monitor.

'... looks very like a fairly severe panic attack. What do you think yourself?'

Selma nodded. She was serious now, with a tiny worried frown between her eyes.

'I think that sounds absolutely right,' she said. 'Not that I've ever experienced such an attack, but from what I've read and heard, I'm in complete agreement with you.'

'I see. So you think you may have had—'

'No, not at all. As I said, I'm convinced I just had a bad turn. I felt no anxiety except that for a second I thought I might be having a heart attack. It was quite scary, I have to admit. I'm well aware that heart attacks can happen to even the fittest of people.'

With a nod of the head, she paused for a moment before she went on: 'And that was why I phoned for help. Which I assume was the right thing to do?'

'Yes, of course. But you said after you were admitted that you had felt a sudden sharp increase in your pulse rate, problems with ...'

Selma Falck glanced at the clock above the door.

'A bad turn always has a reason,' the doctor said hurriedly. 'Naturally, it may be harmless, but I'm sure we share an interest in getting to the bottom of this?'

'Absolutely. I'm grateful for the help I've received. It almost makes me feel guilty. Twenty-four hours in hospital without there being anything wrong with me apart from feeling really tired after a gunshot injury.'

Selma Falck's face was truly fascinating. She was not actually beautiful, maybe not even good-looking, but it was as if she used every muscle in her face when she talked. It made her words more colourful and gave her sentences more depth. Her voice was fairly low-pitched and always friendly. Nonetheless, Helle Viksfjord felt uncertain. A look in her eyes, the suggestion of a smile at the corner of her mouth – the constantly changing facial expressions aroused a suspicion that Selma Falck was as often ironic as honest. Her description of the previous day's incident, as detailed in the records, seemed however to be both truthful and genuine. At the very least she must have been really scared when she told the cardiologist about it.

'You've described quite an intense feeling of anxiety?'

Selma nodded again.

'Yes, I thought I'd had a heart attack. That's frightening for most people, I'd think.'

'We know now that it wasn't a heart attack.'

Once again that nod of the head.

'Yes, and I'm really glad of that.'

'Have you had attacks like this in the past?'

'It wasn't an attack. As I said, I took a bad turn. As a result of lack of sleep. It's embarrassing to have bothered an already hard-pressed health service with such trivia. You've almost certainly got more sensible things to do. I'm absolutely fine. I've had some painkillers prescribed and expect I'll sleep better now.'

'You must feel troubled about Friday's incident, though?'

'Thursday. It was on Thursday that I was shot.'

'Yes, sorry. Thursday. It seems someone was out to kill you. Does that not scare you in the least? Especially after all you went through last year? Have you had any help at all with working through what you experienced?'

Selma Falck ran her hand through her shoulder-length hair. Even now the doctor thought she could discern a faint smile, but her eyes were serious when she looked directly at her and, after a brief pause, said:

'That was a lot of questions all at once. And yes, it scares me a little. But not so much that I can't live with it.'

Out of the blue, Selma Falck grabbed the jacket she had draped over the chair when she sat down. Her mobile came to life when she pulled it out of her pocket. The psychiatrist had not heard either the ring tone or the buzzing.

'The police,' Selma said apologetically. 'They want to see me. Was there anything else, or can we just draw a line under things now?'

She was already on her feet, carefully putting on her jacket.

'Well,' the doctor said, 'I'm not entirely comfortable with ...'

Selma was ready. She adjusted her denim jacket, the yoke of which was decorated with colourful embroidery.

'I really have to go when the police ask me to,' she said. 'But thank you so much for your concern. If I may be permitted to say so ...'

Her smile lit up the whole room, showing teeth so white they must have been bleached. As her eyes narrowed, a faint network of fine crow's feet appeared on each temple.

'Your hair is really beautiful. I've always wanted curls.'

She used her uninjured arm to lift her handbag and headed for the door. On her way out, she half-turned back.

'And by the way,' she added, more serious now. 'You seem unusually young to be a qualified psychiatrist. I'm sure it's not an easy thing to do. We're all full of prejudices, whether we want to be or not. I don't really know what I had expected. A grey-haired woman in her sixties, maybe? With glasses.'

Helle Viksfjord was at a loss for what to say in response.

'At the moment I'm the youngest in the country,' she piped up for want of anything better to say and regretted it immediately.

'Congratulations,' Selma Falck said warmly. 'Don't let anyone use your age against you. Never. Thanks for a nice chat.'

A lovely waft of fragrance was left in her wake. Helle Viksfjord stared into space for several minutes before she collected herself and finally entered some notes in the DIPS record.

They were extremely brief.

The Folder

Lars Winther could not for the life of him understand what Jonathan Herse had been working on.

It had taken him four hours to go through all the papers left behind by his dead colleague. After only half an hour he had

66

called on the editor and again begged her to let him give it a bodyswerve. It was out of the question. She had, admittedly with a smile, declared that he was not allowed to give up until he had written a report that clearly showed he had made a decent effort to get to grips with it.

He was still far from that. Mainly there were three types of documents, around half taken from specific child welfare cases. A total of six, he thought he had now established. These comprised reports from the Child Welfare Service, decisions by the Regional Social Welfare Board and statements from teachers and nursery employees as well as observations made in the homes of the families in question. Lars had to admit he scarcely knew what the Regional Social Welfare Board was, but after a Google search he was somewhat wiser. The government's court-like public administration agency decided cases in accordance with the Child Welfare Act, among other things. They could determine that children, because of their parents' substantial neglect, should be removed from their homes and placed in institutions or with foster parents. They decided on the type and frequency of visits and could also order relief measures, assistance and treatment. Their decisions could be reviewed by the actual courts and in two of the cases there were also legal judgements. In neither of these had the findings of the Regional Social Welfare Board been overturned.

Six families. Six tragic instances of incompetent parents, all deprived of their children. With very good reason, in Lars's opinion. Two of the cases mainly concerned the parents' drug misuse, while one had to do with what he felt in his heart of hearts verged on learning disabilities in all concerned. Two of them were more typical, Lars imagined – single mothers who quite simply could not cope. Who were incapable. Who gave the youngsters cola for breakfast and ice cream with chocolate sauce for dinner so that they could get five minutes' peace, who never turned up for parents' meetings and who never even sent apologies when continually summoned to the public health nurse for check-ups. Who did not send packed lunches to school and also obviously didn't inspect their children's clothing before they sent them out in blizzard conditions of minus ten degrees Celsius. The final case concerned a Somali girl of sixteen who became pregnant while living in a foster home. She already had a criminal record, had dropped out of school some time earlier and was barely able to look after herself, far less a baby. The child was given up for adoption.

Lars had felt a kind of sympathy for these adults who quite simply were unable to put their lives in order. It was too uncomfortable to think of the kids: he himself had three who were enough of a handful. Life as a parent of young children was sometimes a challenge, but both he and his wife did at least insist on the children brushing their teeth before they went to bed. One of the children in Jonathan's case file had such rotten milk teeth by the age of five that they all had to be extracted.

Sad and sorry and absolutely no basis for journalism. Not for Lars Winther, at any rate.

For the second time, he laid aside all the papers from these specific cases.

The remaining bundle could be divided into two, more or less down the middle. One half was printouts of Internet articles, mostly from the Norwegian quality media. *Aftenavisen* itself, *NRK*, *DG* and *Dagbladet* as well as a couple of regional newspapers. Some of the articles were really ancient. The oldest was from 1997, and had to be a photostat copy. They all dealt with child welfare issues, some with specific cases, whereas others were more general.

The rest were articles and documents in foreign languages, a few of them written in English. They all portrayed the Norwegian

Child Welfare Service as an out-and-out terrorist organization. Others were in a language Lars assumed to be Polish. A couple might be from Hungarian newspapers, or Czech, he didn't quite know, but a fair number of them were Russian. They were easier to identify, both because of easily recognizable words and the Cyrillic letters, but impossible all the same for him to comprehend any of it.

Lars stared despondently at the three bundles.

They told him nothing except that life was harder for some people than others. However much the conspiracy theory Internet trolls twisted and turned things, it was a fact that some people could not manage to look after their offspring. Child welfare in Norway functioned fairly well, even though some foreigners gave the fanatical critics here at home support for their view that the Child Welfare Service could be compared to the Gestapo.

Which was sheer nonsense.

There was no story in this material, at least not one Lars Winther could discern. He felt a certain relief. It would take him ten minutes to encapsulate what he had gone through. After that, he would slap the folder back down on the editor's desk and never again go anywhere near a child-welfare story unless forced to do so.

One sheet of paper had fallen to the floor and, pushing his chair back from the desk, he picked it up: a printout of an article from his own paper. *Attorney General Furious – blames European Court of Human Rights for leaks in controversial child welfare case* was the headline. Lars could only vaguely recall having seen the article not so long ago. Without reading it.

ECHR. The European Court of Human Rights. Lars had learned that a number of Norwegian child welfare cases were queued up for hearings there, something the Norwegian government had seemed to take with equanimity until now. The proceedings in this particular case had ended long ago, but the judgement was overdue. All the same, a professor of law at the University of Oslo had tweeted animatedly that the result would be especially embarrassing for Norway. He obviously had sources he certainly shouldn't have had access to.

Lars spotted the date, 4 September, in the right-hand corner of the clipping.

This article was dated only five days ago. That couldn't be right. Lars quickly began to leaf through the other articles in the pile. The most recent one was from July of this year. He picked up the folder that had held the papers. The green plastic folder was worn at the corners and one of the elastic cords was about to come adrift.

Jonathan had died in an accident on 17 August. Two and a half weeks prior to 4 September.

Until then, he had clearly spent a lot of time on this story, or non-story as Lars considered it to be. After his death, someone had gone to the bother of looking up one article and printing it out, before placing it in the folder in a space where it logically belonged.

A banal article about the Attorney General's anger.

Remarkable.

It could have been the editor herself, of course.

No. She had said she hadn't looked through the folder. That she simply attached importance to what Jonathan had told her before his sudden death.

Which could be a lie, though for the moment Lars couldn't think of any reason for her to come up with such an untruth. Then it would have been more likely for her to saddle another journalist with the story rather than giving it to Lars. One who had already done the same as him and perhaps made some inroads. Who had found an article that seemed interesting and added it to the pile.

Could be. There could in fact be countless explanations, but all the same Lars could not rid himself of the little germ of curiosity the mystery had aroused.

Without thinking it all the way through, he tore off the memory stick taped inside the folder and inserted it into the USB port on his computer. Something made him change his mind. He snatched it out again, took his own MacBook from a drawer and pushed it in there instead. Just seconds later, he was into *Finder*.

No name appeared on the screen under the list of devices. Jonathan had not even gone to the bother of giving the memory stick a name. Lars attempted to open it, and that proved possible, but it did not take him any further forward. There were two documents on the storage device, called *A.docx* and *archive.zip*. Strange descriptions. He had never saved anything without coming up with a name to tell him something about the contents, the only simple way to retrieve it later.

The anonymous files also required a password to open them. It was pointless to start guessing. Lars didn't even try. Instead, he spotted the editor on her way into her office.

'Elisabeth!' he called out as he got to his feet.

Several of his colleagues glowered at him in annoyance. He threw out his arms in a gesture of apology. The editor, having heard his shout, approached him with determination in her short steps.

'Yes?' she asked as she came closer, obviously just as irritated as the others.

'This story of Jonathan's,' Lars said, gesticulating towards the folder. 'Have you looked at it yourself?'

'No. I told you. The reason I wanted someone to take a closer look at it was that Jonathan seemed really incensed when he came to me two days before he died. Almost stressed out, and overly cryptic, which of course got on my nerves. If you can't confide in your editor, you should really find another place of work. All the same there was something that ...'

Lars had never seen her hesitate before. She appeared uncertain, almost worried, as she glanced down at the green plastic folder. A couple of steps closer and she lowered her voice: 'To be honest, it could well be that he had to hold his cards close to his chest because he was scared.'

'Scared?'

'Sort of. Not really. But he ... I didn't really know him, after all. All the same, I got the impression that this could be something ... big.'

She used both hands to tuck her blonde hair behind her ears and lifted her chin.

'Unfortunately I don't know any of you well enough yet. Enough said. Have you taken a closer look at the papers?'

'Yes. Has anyone else already done that? Before me, was what I was wondering?'

'What do you mean?' She seemed really taken aback.

'Well,' he hesitated. 'Did you already try to get someone else to take on this story?'

Now she seemed exasperated. Lars had no idea whether it was sincere.

'No, why would I have done that?' she asked. 'I collected this folder from Jonathan's desk the day after he died.'

'That means 18 August?'

'Er ... yes. Yes, it must have been. In the morning, as I recall, I was at work on the Sunday to get everything done that had to be attended to after his tragic demise.'

For someone under the age of forty, her speech was rather old-fashioned.

'Where did you put it?'

'Why do you ask?'

'Because—'

'In one of the cupboards in my office.'

'Did you lock it? The cupboard, I mean.'

Her annoyance grew increasingly obvious and she spoke more slowly and clearly than usual.

'No. I lock my office when I leave for the day, but not my cupboards. Where are you actually going with this?'

Lars smiled as broadly as he could.

'Nowhere,' he said, sitting down on his office chair. 'Forget it. You'll get a summary from me some time tomorrow. I don't really think there's anything here, but you can judge for yourself.'

She seemed to hesitate again before abruptly turning on her sensible heels and departing.

Lars watched her until she was inside her own office. Then, letting his laptop spit out the memory stick, he pushed it deep into his pocket.

Maybe he shouldn't give up on Jonathan's story after all. Not reject it out of hand, at least. It was time to talk to Selma Falck.

Police Headquarters

Selma's trek from the cold, forbidding Police Headquarters entrance to Inspector Fredrik Smedstuen's office on the second floor had taken half an hour. The curved, grey building in Grønlandsleiret reeked as usual of floor polish, creaking bureaucracy and the tense perspiration of the impatient queue waiting to renew passports in the foyer. Even in her early days as an unseasoned lawyer, Selma had grown accustomed to wending her way slowly through people who wanted to say hello, give her a hug and have a chat. The pleasure everyone showed at seeing her in the building – now officially called Grønland Police Station – had not diminished in the past year.

'Christ, you're late.'

Fredrik Smedstuen wore exactly the same clothes as at their last meeting. The pale-blue shirt could have been washed and it could well be that he had two exactly the same, but it was crumpled. The points of the collar curled up towards his still-unshaven chin.

'Sorry,' Selma said as she sat down without waiting to be invited. 'There were so many people in here who wanted to talk to me.'

She made a fuss of settling her arm comfortably in the sling, which she had pulled out of her pocket and put on just after stepping out of her taxi.

'Any news?'

'Yes.'

The Inspector nodded towards a flatscreen on the wall and picked up the remote.

'We've had some luck with CCTV cameras in the vicinity,' he said, pressing a button. 'There are three in all that either completely or partially cover the café where you were sitting. In addition we've got hold of a few clips from mobile phones belonging to members of the public.'

The screen flickered for a couple of seconds before a frozen black-and-white image appeared. It was taken from a high angle and Selma quickly calculated that it must have been located on the eastern side of Thorvald Meyers gate, on the same side as the pavement restaurant. Just north of where they had been seated. The majority of the tables were visible. Since Selma and her two friends had been sitting at the far edge of the kerb, Selma's back was cut off on the right of the picture. The policeman pressed the button again.

This image, also frozen, must have been taken with a camera on the opposite side of the street. The perspective was a bit lower. You could clearly see Selma's red velvet jacket, the one she had been sent as a gift by Jenny Skavlan, the TV presenter and actress, last year. Linda sat on her left-hand side, half in profile, while Vanja's laughing face could just be glimpsed above Selma's right shoulder.

Another image came up.

This one was taken from the south. The camera belonged to the transport company *Ruter* and had been placed there to monitor the extensive re-laying of tramlines in the street. It encompassed a far larger area than the two previous pictures. All the same, Selma swiftly caught sight of herself at the café table on the far right towards the edge of the photograph.

'Are these from film footage or stills?'

'Film,' Smedstuen answered impatiently. 'Just wait.'

Setting down the remote, he picked up a packet of *Nicorette* gum from a dish on the desk. The plastic crackled as he forced out two tabs and popped them in his mouth.

'These recordings are interesting,' he slurped, 'and fortunately they're all time-stamped.'

Once again he nodded at the screen, where Selma could also see a digital clock stopped at 16.15.32.

'And so we've managed to piece together some film,' he went on.

Looking at her, he gave a brief, appreciative nod: 'You were right. One shot was fired. Only one. There are no sound recordings from the CCTV cameras. However, these images, along with a total of four films taken with mobile phones in the area, make us reasonably certain. The mobile clips have sound and two of them were taken before and during the incident.'

Again he pressed the remote control.

A baby came into sight, smiling and sweet. The handheld camera zoomed in on the child's face as a loud bang was heard. In the ensuing chaos, the only thing you could say with certainty was that the woman who had the baby on her lap leapt through the café doors unscathed and the phone's owner followed close on her heels.

No further shots.

'Can I see the whole film, please?' Selma asked. 'I mean, the one you've stitched together?'

'Yes. That's why I asked you to come in. Coffee?' He pushed a cup towards her and lifted a thermos.

'Is it full-length, this film?' Selma asked.

'No. Three and a half minutes.'

'Then I'll pass on the coffee, thanks all the same.'

Fredrik Smedstuen poured himself some and raised the mug to his mouth as he searched for the right film. Selma turned her chair ever so slightly and stared slit-eyed at the screen.

It was as if she was there all over again. She remembered everything. The dog tied to a neighbouring table. The hassled waiter who, at the very start of the footage, managed to spill a cola and almost knock over a four- or five-year-old haring about between the tables. She recalled the story Vanja had just related that made both her and Linda laugh so heartily. After around forty-five seconds the water Vanja had ordered ten minutes earlier arrived at last. Her cappuccino cup was already empty but the waiter had neglected to remove it.

The glass of water was teetering. The waiter stood with his back to them, annoyed that the people at the next table had dragged an extra chair across, making it almost impossible for him to negotiate his way back to the kitchen. With a movement so abrupt it was only a shadow on the technically deficient film, Linda reached out for the glass. Even though the angle on the footage was not ideal, it clearly showed her head getting in the way of Selma's, based on the probable trajectory of the shot. As the bullet struck, the image froze for three seconds.

Linda was smiling when she died. She had managed to catch the glass of water. Yet another save, like the many she had achieved as the keeper of the Norwegian national team more than thirty years earlier. Her curly hair was like a cloud around her head. Selma could see herself about to pull back in her seat.

She could not remember that.

'Can you move one frame forward?' she mumbled without taking her eyes off the screen. 'And then another?'

The policeman complied.

'I'm pulling back,' Selma said, almost to herself. 'Very fast. Have I heard the shot? Is it a reflex action?'

Smedstuen did not reply. The film moved on, but the rest was of little interest. Chaos, screams and shouts, and Selma sitting with her right hand pressed on her left upper arm. A short string of clips taken with diverse mobile cameras after the shot had fired told her next to nothing.

All was quiet. Smedstuen gulped down some coffee and scratched his seemingly perpetual three-day stubble. Raising his eyes, he gave Selma a quizzical look.

'Well done,' she said and meant it sincerely.

'Thanks. It will help us during the reconstruction. The reason I wanted to have you watch this now is simply because we're still not sure about who the intended target was, you or Linda Bruseth. Or someone else, for that matter.'

The policeman had at least learned Linda's full name since last time.

'As you know,' he continued, 'it's also of the greatest importance that we examine your lives in detail. Both yours and Linda's. A motive for killing one of you would simplify all this. That's why—'

He was interrupted by someone knocking on the door.

'Come in,' he barked, draining the rest of his coffee in one gulp.

The slim man who opened up seemed imperious. His head was shaved and the mere millimetre of grey, prickly stubble over his entire scalp showed he had certainly not lost his hair. Selma stood up to shake his outstretched hand.

'Birger Jarl Nilsen,' he introduced himself amiably. 'Pleased to meet you.'

His voice contained vestiges of a singsong accent from the west of Norway, eroded by many years spent away from home. Selma guessed he hailed from the Sogn and Fjordane area.

'Birger is our ballistics expert,' Smedstuen said. 'Teaches sharp-shooting at the Police College. And he's also an expert on weapons. Or, at least, one of them.'

'I try my best,' the man said soberly. 'But I can come back later. I didn't know you were busy.'

Selma was about to stand up again when she was interrupted by the weapons expert: 'I believe Linda was the killer's target. If you're interested. And I'm sure you are.'

Selma remained seated.

'Others disagree,' Smedstuen said brusquely. 'Petter Kystvik insists the opposite.'

'Yes, I know,' Nilsen replied. 'None of us can be absolutely certain as yet. Not to badmouth Petter, he's almost as experienced as I am. But ...'

Leaning across Smedstuen's desk and grabbing a pen and a blank sheet of paper, he drew up an equation Selma thought she had seen before.

'The impact force equation,' she said softly. 'A bullet's kinetic energy. That is to say, the force with which a bullet hits a target.'

The man raised his head. The corners of his mouth stretched up into something resembling an appreciative smile.

'Spot on, where m is the mass of the projectile and v is the velocity, given in metres per second. It's a useful equation for many people. For big-game hunters, for example, because there are rules about the lowest estimated kinetic energy required for elk, deer and suchlike. But—'

'Where are you going with this?'

Fredrik Smedstuen wriggled irritably in his chair. Birger Jarl Nilsen laid aside the pen and paper and rose to his full height. A faint fragrance from recent shaving mixed with an increasingly foul smell from the smoking habit Smedstuen was obviously trying to wean himself from. Without success. It would perhaps have helped if he laundered his clothes. He spat out a huge gob of quit-smoking gum into the wastepaper basket before stuffing two more tabs into his mouth.

'I just want to get a really simple point across,' Nilsen said, unfazed. 'Which is that it doesn't matter what type of weapon or calibre is used. Or ...'

He ran his hand over his shaved head and took a deep breath.

'Of course we ought to come as close as possible. The appearance of the bullet taken from your arm ...'

His gaze fixed on Selma's upper arm.

'... can't help us. It's completely deformed and has lost around half its weight on its journey. Something we can ascertain through metallurgical analysis and other tests, and that's all to the good. Both the gun and ammunition will be important indicators in the investigation. But in deciding the really pressing question of who the killer was actually aiming for, all of this is immaterial.'

Selma listened intently. There was something about this man. Something that reminded her of Robert Mood, the President of the Norwegian Red Cross. On closer inspection, he was slim, bordering on skinny, but his straight spine and sinewy neck radiated a strength, the proximity of which disconcerted her a little.

'Why?' she asked.

'Because the killer wasn't particularly far away.'

'We've no idea where he shot from,' Smedstuen exclaimed. 'It's best you stick to what you know, and leave the rest of us to ...'

He held back when he saw the other two were paying him scant attention.

'How have you arrived at that conclusion?' Selma asked.

'I've been there. In the street where you were shot.'

He stole a quick glance at his watch, a blue-and-gold Rolex Submariner, Selma noted, and it struck her immediately: this man has been in the military. From his sharply defined face with deep furrows scored along the bridge of his nose and forehead, she guessed him to be around fifty-five. Probably older. Also, a scar under his chin that ran all the way from his right cheek to his left made his face appear even more striking. A former officer, Selma guessed. He was wearing a navy-blue sweater with a shirt underneath. Pristine and newly ironed, the points of the collar fitted snugly at the neckline. His posture, his self-assured gaze and the fact that he placed his arms behind his back now that he had put down the writing materials – it all pointed far from this grey, shabby police station in Grønland, wedged between the old prison and Norway's most beautiful mosque.

The man lacked only a beret and stiff uniform.

'The shot was fired from a maximum distance of one hundred metres. That makes the velocity of the bullet immaterial. No matter what kind of ammunition, it will reach the target so fast that it's only of marginal significance whether the sniper could have taken your friend's sudden movement into account. Experienced. It's certainly more difficult to handle than a heavier, larger ...'

'Now you really must cut that out, Birger!'

Fredrik Smedstuen heaved himself to his feet. Beside Birger Jarl Nilsen, he looked like something a young officer had dragged in from the street for an on-the-spot fine.

'Selma Falck is a victim in this case,' he said crossly. 'She's not a police lawyer. And she's certainly not part of the investigation team. I suggest you contact me later.'

For a second it looked as if Nilsen was keen to say more.

'I noticed your name,' Selma said with a smile, beating him to the punch. 'Nilsen is a fairly common surname, but there can't possibly be many people in this country called Birger Jarl. I could maybe give you a call?'

Although he did not smile as he walked to the door, once there he stopped and said quietly, with his back turned: 'I'm in the phone book. It was Linda Bruseth who was meant to die, and I'll be happy to explain why I'm so sure of that. If you're interested, that is.'

The Memory Stick

'I need help!'

They said this in chorus. Lars Winther began to laugh. He gave Selma a quick hug and stepped in when she opened the door wide. Under his arm he was carrying a huge folder that he put down on the chest of drawers in the hallway while he wrenched off his all-weather jacket and dropped his cycle helmet on the floor.

'Shoes,' Selma said, sounding disapproving as she pointed at his feet. 'Have you been on a long-distance bike ride, or what?'

'It's raining,' he said tersely as he flipped off his shoes, grabbed the folder and dashed into the living room.

Once he reached the dining table, he pulled out a chair and sat down.

'I love this apartment,' he murmured. 'When I get divorced, I'm going to get one just like this.'

'You can't afford to get divorced and nor have you the opportunity,' Selma said before fetching two bottles of Pepsi Max from the fridge. 'And I'm sure you don't want to, either.'

Muttering something inaudible, he opened the folder. 'Shall we deal with mine first?'

Selma sat down beside him without answering. She opened the bottles and by the time he, without the go-ahead, had finished running through the contents of Jonathan Herse's folder, her bottle was almost empty. Lars had not yet touched his.

'I can't wrap my head around any of it,' Selma said. 'Apart from lots of people being angry with the Child Welfare Service, both here at home and out there in the wide world. Especially in Eastern Europe. But then of course they thrash their kids, don't they?'

'Well, they probably don't exactly—'

'At any rate, they do have a completely different attitude to parenthood from us. You should just slap this back down on your editor's desk as fast as you can. I can't see any story in this, but I do see an incredible amount of trouble heading in your direction for your pains if you so much as poke your finger into this thorny subject.'

She drained the last dregs and screwed the lid back on before turning towards the open-plan kitchen and lobbing the empty bottle in an elegant curve into the sink. It didn't miss.

'Keep out of it,' she said. 'I sometimes get these kinds of people at my door. At least I used to, when I was a lawyer. They moan and whinge and feel they're victims of outrageous injustice. I play along and then send them away with a flea in their ear as soon as I get the chance. The problem with Norwegian child welfare is not that they intervene too often. It's that they don't do it often enough. What's that, by the way?'

She pointed at the memory stick on the table that Lars had dug out of his pocket.

'You can see for yourself,' Lars replied.

'What's on it?'

'I don't really know. It was taped to the folder. It contains two documents, which both require a password.'

'It's encrypted, you mean? I'm talking about the memory stick.'

'Er … Yes, no … all I can do is open the list of contents, but each document needs a password in order to read it.'

'So maybe not encrypted,' Selma said, taking out her laptop. 'We can probably sort that.'

Lars sat in silence, watching as she inserted the memory stick into the port. Her fingers moved at lightning speed as she keyed in commands that opened a program he obviously didn't recognize. Selma caught herself smiling. Only seconds later, an hourglass appeared in the centre of the screen.

'It can take a while,' she said, half-turning towards him. 'Now it's my turn.'

'What's that there?' Lars asked, pointing.

'A fairly simple program for breaking a fairly simple code.'

'How—'

'I'm a private investigator, Lars. I know lots of people on both sides of the law. Anyway, this here …'

She fixed her gaze on the hourglass.

'… is a program available for purchase online. If these documents from your colleague are enormous, such as complicated calculation programs, or if they're secured with something more advanced than they appear to be …'

She gestured demonstratively with her hands.

'… then we'll have to find another solution. But before we know any more, we can see if you can help me.'

'With what?'

Selma thought for a moment. 'What do you know about stalkers?'

Lars Winther seemed totally bewildered.

'Stalkers? You mean the kind of people who … follow you about?'

'Yes.'

He leaned back with a frown on his face.

'I thought you were going to ask me about something to do with the shooting incident.'

He gave a nod in the direction of Selma's shoulder.

'I'll do that too, but answer my question first. What do you know about stalkers?'

'I don't understand the question. What I know ...'

Finally he grabbed his bottle of Pepsi Max. 'Ian McEwan has written a good novel about the phenomenon,' he said.

'I don't read novels.'

'Maybe you should. It's called *Enduring Love*. You can borrow it from me. It's about a man who's on a picnic with a woman and—'

'I'll ask you again,' Selma broke in. 'What do you know about stalkers? You know, in real life, not in fiction.'

'Well, it can involve a number of different things. Loving someone from a distance, for example. Idolizing them, sort of thing. If the object of attention is a celebrity, maybe. Or as a matter of fact, in *Enduring Love* it's not—'

A sharp intake of breath from Selma and Lars took the hint.

'Or hatred,' he added quickly. 'Maybe that's just as common? I don't know. It depends on what you mean by the word stalker. On social media it's not unusual for people to follow you. I've experienced a few times people breaking into every thread with hobbyhorses that have no business there at all. If I'm going on about the quality of recreational football here in Norway, the cost of student accommodation or ask for suggestions about good fishing spots in Nordmarka, the same idiot will turn up, ranting about Norwegian immigration policy or something or other he's seized upon that I wrote about three years ago. And I say "he" deliberately. They're nearly always men.'

'Not without exception, though,' Selma said, thinking of Fredrikke Augustsson.

'I'm sure not. I block them when they get too out of hand, and then have to put up with all that guy's friends spamming me from then on until I get rid of them too. Tiresome. But I expect that's the price of an open society.'

The last comment was said sarcastically and accompanied by pulling a face.

'But why do you ask?'

Selma got to her feet. The now familiar physical discomfort had started grumbling in her gut and she tried to control it by stretching her back and breathing calmly. A stabbing pain in the bullet wound, which normally she no longer noticed much, began to bother her too. She let her eyes wander around the room. Pictures. Photographs. A sculpture on a neat pedestal in the corner, a thoughtful orang-utan in bronze she had bought in Thailand during a holiday with the handball girls twenty years ago.

No books.

Not a single bookshelf. Her professional literature was stacked in a cupboard and three large illustrated books she had never as much as leafed through were displayed on the coffee table.

'Someone is following me,' she said quietly.

'There's always somebody following someone else,' Lars said with a touch of impatience. 'That's just how it is. As I said, I'm always finding that—'

'Someone's been breaking in here. Without leaving a trace of the break-in. Someone who just prowls around and who knows secrets from when I was a child.'

'Eh ... what?'

At one time Selma Falck had thought she could not cry. For more than thirty years she had not shed a tear, in the sure and certain knowledge that her tear ducts were damaged after a serious sports accident.

'Are … are you crying, Selma?'

'No.' She opened her eyes wide and gazed at the ceiling. 'But I really don't want to go on living here any longer.'

'Tell me about it,' Lars said, patting the seat beside him.

Selma hesitantly sat down but pulled the chair further away from him. The hourglass on the screen whirred and turned. Without taking her eyes off it, she began to tell him.

She talked until she had nothing more to say. Of a feeling that there was a strange presence in the apartment. Of a packet of KIP on her pillow. Of potato flour traps at the front door and the exit to the balcony. She pretended not to notice Lars's little smile. She told him about a winking emoji, about Poker-Turk and her new surveillance system and about nights so anxious that she was seriously considering selling the whole apartment.

When she had finished, she finally looked him in the eye.

He was no longer smiling. Far from it. A solemn expression she had rarely seen on his boyish face made her feel even more afraid.

'You can't put up with this,' he said softly, placing his hand on hers on the table.

She withdrew it at once.

'You have to speak to the police. Maybe there's a connection between whatever this is all about and the shooting at Løkka.'

'I don't think so. And the police mustn't find out about these … break-ins.'

'Why not?'

'Because Anine will go completely crazy. It's bad enough that I was shot at. I must have access to Skjalg. I must be allowed to look after him.'

'I really get that. My boys are such a bloody nuisance at times but I don't know what I'd have done if I lost contact with them. All the same, you really should get in touch with the police.'

'It's out of the question, OK? I'm not taking this to the police.'

Lars sighed almost inaudibly. 'What do you want me to say, then?'

'I don't know. Something or other. Something about it being impossible for him to come back now that the locks have been changed. That I've just imagined it all. I don't know, Lars. Maybe I just need ... some sympathy.'

Lars put the bottle to his mouth and drank deeply. For a long time. At last he put it down, screwed the cap back on and sat with his hands clasped around the label.

'Did you take a photo of the print?' he asked.

'Yes.'

Picking up her mobile, Selma found the picture and held it out to him. It had been taken from a distance of half a metre and showed a clear footprint.

'The tip of a shoe,' Lars mumbled. 'But why is it pointing inwards?'

'What do you mean?'

'Well, the door is here,' he said, pointing. 'If the guy or girl or whoever it was came in through the front door, then surely it would be the heel we saw. Here it looks more like the person in question is on the way out of the apartment rather than on the way in.'

Selma pulled the phone back.

'You're right,' she said in an undertone. 'Maybe he didn't spot the potato flour straight away when he opened the door. And then he stepped over it all. I didn't sprinkle it very far into the room. And so he may have left the footprint later, on the way out, or ...'

She studied the picture more intently. Her heart had begun to race again. If it hadn't been for the cardiologist at Ullevål Hospital reassuring her two days earlier that everything about the beating organ was in top-notch condition, she would have flown into a panic again. Her throat felt uncomfortably congested when she continued speaking, as if the pulse there had doubled in size and was squeezing her windpipe.

'He must have left it there deliberately,' she said hoarsely. 'Of course. Why would he draw that smiley face if he didn't want me to discover it?'

'Well, not likely, though,' Lars said. 'I understand the emoji is there to frighten you, but the footprint would presumably be a lead for the police. It would be pretty idiotic to do something like that, if it really were deliberate.'

'Unless,' Selma began.

Nothing more was forthcoming.

Selma stood up. For a moment she remained staring at the screen, where the digital hourglass was still running out of sand before turning on its head every tenth second. All of a sudden she wheeled round and walked to the balcony door. She ran her fingers over the doorframe without a word.

'Unless what?' Lars repeated.

'He knows me,' Selma said sotto voce, opening the door.

Now Lars also got to his feet and crossed the room to join her. Selma glanced up at the little contact sensor attached to the door and frame, intended to alert her if the door were opened when the alarm was switched on.

'Knows you?' Lars said. 'What do you mean?'

'His visits are a blatant provocation. Most people would have gone straight to the police if they discovered that someone was coming into their apartment. He knows I won't do that.'

'But who ... who the hell would know that, Selma? Even I didn't know that until you told me a few minutes ago. Who else could in any way ...'

She stood on tiptoe, squinting at the contact points on the alarm. They were whole, smooth and seemed untouched. She tugged at the door to open it and stepped out on to the balcony. Lars followed her. She peered down into the courtyard below.

'How far down is it?' she asked. 'Approximately.'

Lars did a mental calculation.

'Nine metres? This is the third floor. If you reckon 280 centimetres for each storey, including the floors, plus a bit more ... eight or nine.'

'And there's nothing here to help you climb up,' Selma decided, inspecting the smooth concrete wall.

'A good climber would probably ...' Lars interrupted himself and craned his head back. 'Who lives above you?'

Selma leaned with her back to the railings and pointed. 'There are two apartments up there, each with a window directly above my balcony. In that one there,' she used her finger to point to the left, 'lives a young family with a small child. The other one there,' she hesitated for a second, 'that one's for sale, I think. An elderly man lived there until a few weeks ago. Or ...'

She thought of a notice on the board beside the mailboxes in the hall downstairs.

'No. That one is sold. Also to a little family. There were queues of people here during the viewing. Now I remember. Six weeks ago or so. The sale was completed after a frenetic round of bidding, as far as I understand.'

'Have you met them?'

'No. I try to keep myself at arm's length from the people who live in this block. Best that way. But we're on nodding terms, most of us. Some of them are a bit pushy to start with, but that soon passes.'

'If I desperately wanted to enter your apartment, I would do one of two things,' Lars said. 'Either break in through the front door, or drop down from one of them.'

Once again he pointed at the two windows directly above Selma's balcony. He was right. It would not be dangerous to come that way. Selma, however, had difficulty envisaging the twenty-something hipster, with his narrow shoulders and anaemic complexion, undertaking such a manoeuvre. Not to mention his very pregnant wife.

A faint ping was heard from the living room. Lars and Selma exchanged glances before rushing back to the dining table. On the laptop screen, the hourglass had now disappeared.

'Open sesame!' Selma sat down. 'What have we here?' she muttered as Lars drew his chair closer. 'A.docx is open. A fairly ordinary Word document.'

Neither of them said anything. They read at almost the same speed, and the text was not long enough to require Selma to scroll down.

'What the hell is this?' Lars asked.

'I don't have a clue,' Selma mumbled in response.

The document looked like an overview, some kind of inventory, Selma thought, although she could not figure out of what. The list was numbered, giving what looked like details of both time and place. Along with a lot of numbers and letters she could make neither head nor tail of.

She let her finger slide along under the first line.

1. 02.01.19 MCF HBP Cnr 1, doc 2+3, Sf archive.zip 01.13.14

'Could it be ... degrees of latitude or something?' Lars suggested.

'Maybe,' she replied. 'The introductory numbers look more like dates. The second of January this year. But MCF?'

Lars did not respond. His mouth was half-open, and he was breathing fast. He moved closer and closer to the screen, as if the solution to the codes could be found somewhere between the letters if only he looked at them hard enough.

'You must be right about the date,' he almost whispered. 'You see that each line, numbered 1,2,3 and so on, is followed by something that looks like successive dates. Most of them are in

January and February.' His finger ran down the screen. 'Two are in March. Then it ends. But MCF—'

'That combination of letters is repeated in all the lines. Except ...'

She grabbed a pen from the table and used it as a pointer.

'Here. Line number 7. 8 March. Then MCF is replaced by a question mark. And what ... HBP? What is that?'

The pen slid soundlessly down the lines.

'HBP is repeated on most of the lines. Except ... here ... and here. It says AL instead.'

'Initials?'

Selma shrugged ever so slightly. Her gunshot wound had almost stopped throbbing. It felt liberating to fill her mind with something completely different from how on earth it was possible for someone to move unseen and uninvited in and out of her apartment.

'That could well be,' she nodded, adjusting her glasses. 'MCF could also be a person's initials, for that matter, but ...'

Now she was drumming her fingers on the glass of the screen.

'Let's decide that the first numbers are dates. Moving on, it's generally agreed that doc means document. Doc 2+3 must in other words mean two specific, numbered documents.'

Lars mumbled something she interpreted as agreement.

'It also refers to archive.zip here,' she said. 'On every single line, in fact. A zip file is a compressed file, isn't it? So that the data doesn't take up too much space? Could this here then be some sort of list of what is found in the next document?'

'Yes, could be.' Lars hesitated. Now his nose was only fifteen centimetres from the screen. "But what on earth would be the point of that?'

Selma gave no answer.

'Couldn't we use this hacking program of yours and open the next one, so that we—'

'Cnr,' Selma broke in, loudly and almost triumphantly. 'C-n-r. Case number! A common abbreviation. Case number 1. That's what it means!'

She drew an invisible circle around the letters.

Lars sat up straight and ran both hands through his Tintin quiff. 'Case number 1,' he reiterated. 'Then we can hardly be talking about public documents.'

'Why not?'

'Have you ever received official papers with case number 1 on them? And 2, 3, 4 and 5? The last time I had anything to do with officialdom, the case number was ten thousand and something.'

His finger ran down the lines. It was true that the cases were marked with the same number as the line number. Selma licked her lips and made a face. She nibbled at her pen before resolutely laying it aside and getting to her feet.

'Let's take a step back,' she said. 'Jonathan Herse was working on something to do with child welfare, isn't that right?'

Lars looked dejectedly up from the screen and only just made the effort to nod.

'According to the documents in the folder, that is the physical papers you have there, it's difficult to see any journalistic angle. Agreed?'

Again a brief nod of the head.

'Since the memory stick was stored with the other documents, there's every reason to assume the contents have to do with the same subject.'

Now he was just staring blankly at her.

'The paper documents are in a sense the raw material,' Selma went on. 'They don't contain any secrets. The bundle is mostly comprised of newspaper articles.'

'And case papers,' Lars said. 'They're not so easy to get hold of.'

'Yes, of course. He could, for example, have got them from the clients themselves. Or from their lawyers. Skip that. My point is that he hasn't gone to the bother of hiding them away in digital format. But ...'

She tapped her fingertip on her forehead.

'I had an idea,' she said quickly. 'MCF. MCF.'

An autumnal wasp had buzzed in through the open balcony door and was wobbling lethargically around the room. Selma ignored it.

'Ministry for Children and Families! MCF! This *does* all deal with child welfare issues after all!'

Lars looked at her. His mouth opened but he could not find the words. Selma picked up the pen again and pointed at the first line.

1. 02.01.19 MCF HBP Cnr 1, doc 2+3, Sf archive.zip 01.13.14

'The number one signifies that it is quite simply the first line, and therefore also the first case. 02.01.19 is the date of something or other. MCF is the Ministry for Children and Families. HBP – heaven knows what that means. Cnr means case number. Doc 2+3 fairly obviously stands for documents two and three, and—'

She leaned in closer. 'Does it say Sf?'

'Yes.'

'No idea what that stands for. But it refers then to something found in the next documents, that is to say the zip document, and the final number—'

'01.13.14. That can't really be a date. There aren't thirteen months.'

'It could be written the American way. That is the thirteenth of January 2014.'

'Why then would the date be written the Norwegian way at the beginning of the line, though,' Lars began, 'and then suddenly a different date appears written in a foreign style at the end of it?'

Selma had no answer for that.

The wasp had taken a trip into the kitchen. Now it was on its way back, flying around so dizzy and befuddled that it hit the monitor with an audible thump. Lars tried to swat it away as it moved in for an emergency landing on the keyboard. Selma sat like a pillar of salt.

'Every ministry creates documents covered by the Freedom of Information Act,' she finally said. 'You have the right to see them. But of course they do also have a number of cases that are exceptions to the law. Since Jonathan Herse has gone to the bother of concealing these so effectively, I expect what must be in the zip file isn't exactly something you can delve into the records and demand a copy of.'

'Secret documents, you mean?'

'Sort of. If not exactly secret, then at least withheld from the public eye. And if they have to do with child welfare, which all logic suggests they have, then this could be fairly—'

'Run your hacking program on the archive.zip! If it—'

'That's too simple. The hacking program, I mean.'

'Are there other similar programs? More advanced ones, in particular?'

'Bound to be. But perhaps not legal. I can find out. Ask someone.'

'Damn and blast. This document here tells us very little about anything at all if we can't cross-refer it to the other one.'

'Shh.' Selma had thought of something again.

The wasp had settled on the W key. Lars stared at it for a while before flicking it away so brutally that it fell dead on the floor.

'So zip is a method of compressing files. There's no point in compressing ordinary written documents. At the very least there must be countless numbers of them because normally they take up very little space.'

'Film footage uses up space,' Lars suggested. 'And vast calculation programs.'

'Mm,' Selma said distractedly as she once again let the pen slide along the first line of the document. 'The likelihood that your dear colleague has stored calculation programs in the midst of all these child welfare documents is relatively small. Sound files, on the other hand ...'

Her pen eagerly tapped the screen.

'Sf! That could stand for sound file! Could they be sound recordings, no more nor less? Then the last number could be a time indication! The reference to the case might well be at one hour, thirteen minutes and fourteen seconds into the recording?'

'A sound file? Why would Jonathan be interested in sound recordings from the Ministry for Children and Families? What would they contain? And ... how could he have got hold of something like that?'

'We don't know that yet,' Selma said, closing the document before releasing the memory stick and handing it to Lars.

He held it doubtfully in his hand. 'How will we manage to open it?'

'I don't know that either. But I do know people. Don't lose it, for heaven's sake. If Jonathan Herse really has obtained sound files from the MCF, recordings he thought were so crucial that he's gone to all this bother ...'

She made a sweeping motion with her hand over the laptop and the plastic folder. All of a sudden she froze, abruptly sat down and opened the machine again. A few seconds later she was looking at the Ministry's home page.

Lars said not a word as she keyed her way into the Children's section. 'Bingo!' Selma said under her breath. 'Look at this!'

Lars let his eye run over the public home page but failed to notice anything sensational. 'What am I looking for?'

'The Director General. Look at his name!'

'Horatio Bull-Pedersen,' Lars read out in astonishment. 'Weird name. I've probably heard it before. On *CSI: Miami*, for instance, Horatio Caine, but never for a Norwegian.'

'Horatio Bull-Pedersen,' Selma said with a sharp intake of breath. 'HBP. The initials on the document overview. Do you still not get it? H-B-P! Could all of this revolve around sound recordings of him?'

'A whole heap of them?' Lars asked, equally dumbfounded. 'I don't get any of this. Why should ...'

Selma continued searching on the webpage without listening to him. To her great disappointment, only the directors general were named with accompanying photographs. She quickly moved on into the home pages.

'Bingo,' she whispered again. 'Senior Adviser Alvhilde Leonardsen. Horatio Bull-Pedersen's immediate subordinate. "AL" from the codes.'

She put the name straight into the Google search field and asked for 'images'.

'Not very many to choose from,' she said, almost to herself.

She clicked on a photograph of the Senior Adviser taken at the Holmenkollstafett relay race in 2018. A petite, slender, attractive woman stood beside a group of cheering colleagues. They had come in at twelfth place in the class *Open category, mixed, majority female* and beaten the Attorney General's office by seventeen seconds. In the picture there were only four runners, Alvhilde Leonardsen and three men dripping with sweat, so the rest of the women must have gone home.

'So she's pretty fit,' Lars said. 'Well, that's good to know.'

'We have to get the file opened,' Selma said without noticing the downbeat sarcasm. 'Considering that Jonathan was extremely troubled, plus he had hidden these files away really well, then it could be ...'

She broke off. Lars puffed up his cheeks and shaped his hands into a ball.

'I wouldn't celebrate too early,' Selma said tersely. 'I realize you're hoping this will turn out to be something really juicy, but ...'

Looking across at him, she smiled before adding: '... there are limits to how big a scandal it's possible to stir up in such a Department.'

'Boooom,' Lars said, letting his hands go off like a slow-motion bomb.

The Albums

H e did not want to visit the grave today.

Impatience was gnawing at him and he could find no peace anywhere, not even in the old-fashioned photo albums that Grethe had assembled with such care, ever since the time when they had first met. The photographs were placed in strict chronological order, with little comments and frequent dates. Here and there Grethe had taken extra trouble, such as with the memories of all their Christmases. She was so good at drawing. Little Christmas baubles at the corners, angels and elves, and in 1987 a pot of lamb ribs that looked so tasty you could almost smell the aroma.

There were thirteen of these albums but the last one was not full. It stopped suddenly after four pictures had been pasted in with no accompanying text. One of them was of Grethe. He had taken it himself and remembered the occasion well. She was going for her first course of chemotherapy on a sunny day with a light summer breeze. Leaning against the car, a ten-year-old Volkswagen. She was squinting at him with her sunglasses pushed up on to her forehead. Her reddish hair was tousled and windswept, her smile false and forced. Four weeks later she had to start wearing a wig.

He did not like that photograph.

His favourite was in the third album.

Their boy came into the world on Midsummer Eve, 1989. They used up four spools of film at the hospital. In the end there were so many photos that Grethe did not have copies printed of them all. Instead she had made an extra pocket at the front of the album with space for the negatives. They were still tucked away in there. Every time he opened the album he had to be careful they did not fall out.

The boy was unusually handsome even at birth.

All parents believe that, but this was different. The nurses had said so. Even a doctor, who had come in to check all was well following the straightforward, fast birth, had clapped his hands at the sight of the perfect infant. The baby had red-blond hair and dark, colourless eyes that opened wide at the moment of birth. He cried very little and the corners of his mouth curled noticeably upwards. Everyone laughed and clucked with delight at the serious expression and the tiny red smile that did not disappear even when he was whimpering for food.

He and Grethe had never been happier. The boy was such a welcome arrival. Their family never grew any larger and hard times would follow, but the years around their son's birth were the best of his life.

He still derived a certain comfort from that thought and that the boy had at least been able to experience a touch of the same, great love in his far-too-short life. A glimpse of the innermost kernel and purpose of life, even if it had lasted for so little time. He had asked his son more than once to tell his story. With each telling it increased in warmth and tiny details blossomed to fill out a picture of a wonderful, unforgettable weekend when his young lad had also experienced what existence is fundamentally all about.

Loving and being loved in return.

The creation of new life.

He shut the album with a muffled thud. There were important things to attend to, all planned over a long period of time, down to the smallest detail. A man of his experience and profession knew, however, that nothing could be planned too carefully. Anything could happen. The scenarios were countless. No one in this world should be content with having a plan B – you needed the entire alphabet. At the very least.

He was a thorough man. That was how he had survived despite it all.

Against absolutely all the odds.

WEDNESDAY 11 SEPTEMBER

The Reconstruction

Selma Falck was in a bad mood.

Anine had not been in touch with her since the shooting drama at Grünerløkka. Selma had waited as long as she could bear to, but the previous evening she had been unable to restrain herself any longer. She had phoned her daughter.

Who had been ill tempered and dismissive.

Who said a flat no to the idea of her paying a visit.

Who into the bargain said she had no need of a babysitter in the foreseeable future. Not in the more distant future either, as far as she could envisage. Before she broke off their conversation fairly abruptly with a 'Typical of you, Mum, getting shot at.'

Anine had at least called her 'Mum' and not by her first name as she used to do when at her grumpiest. Afterwards, Selma had slept badly. For a host of reasons. Strangely enough, her upper arm was playing up again and she had to use her sling, even when no one could see her. It was painful to roll over in bed and last night she had wondered whether she had an infection in the wound. She had not been able to take a shower either. There were still splinters of glass in the shower recess. At long last a VVS repairman was coming later that day to clear it up and install a new shower door.

What actually prevented her from dropping off, though, was an almost uncontrollable urge to gamble.

She had succeeded in controlling herself.

And as a result was in a really terrible mood.

'Will we soon be finished, do you think?'

Selma's question was wrapped in a warm smile. The female police officer shrugged with upturned hands. Probably it was both an apology and an admission that she had no idea how long this reconstruction would take.

The street had already been cordoned off when Selma arrived. Since it was already devastated by extensive road works linked to the replacement of the tram rails and pavement, the police had their hands full trying to prevent people from making their way through the barriers sixty metres up the street and forty metres south of the restaurant. The two women who had been picked out to be Vanja and Linda respectively for the attempt to reconstruct the murder of the latter, had obviously prepared well. In addition to the film Selma had already viewed in Fredrik Smedstuen's office, a digital copy had also been made that until now she had only heard of. The two officers must have watched it numerous times. They said nothing but moved at command as if they had been here last Thursday and remembered the episode second by second. As for Selma, she was given directions by a man she had never met, a young, serious guy whose dialect she had difficulty understanding.

Until now it had all taken two hours.

Everything had been filmed, photographed and documented.

The sniper had lain on the roof of Thorvald Meyers gate 49. The yellow building, built in the second half of the nineteenth century as a tramway depot and stable for the Kristiania Sporveisselskab tram company, was markedly lower than the neighbouring buildings. As early as three days ago, the police had considered the fairly flat roof to be a probable hiding place for the killer. Now they seemed absolutely certain. Selma presumed the spot had already been examined by forensic technicians. She could not understand why she had not been given the green light to leave. It was chilly. Autumn had really begun to hold its own and the fresh wind from the south sent leaves, discarded ice-lolly wrappers from summer and other odds and ends whirling through the air.

In the corner of her eye she caught sight of a figure she imme-diately recognized. Imposing, without actually being particularly tall. Erect, like a soldier, even though he was currently leaning against the wall, arms crossed on his chest. He was wearing dark jeans and a ditsy-print shirt under a brown napa leather jacket. On his head he wore an old-fashioned tweed flat cap. He smiled when he saw she had spotted him.

Birger Jarl Nilsen suited his name. There was something stately about him, almost aristocratic, combined with self-assurance so great that it had no need of demonstration. Now he strode towards her with his hand raised ever so slightly in greeting.

'Tedious?' he asked as he sat down on the chair just vacated by Linda's lookalike.

Selma took this as a sign that the session was definitely over.

'Guess,' she said. 'But necessary, of course. Good to have it in the can.'

Fredrik Smedstuen came shambling between the café tables. 'You can go now,' he said to Selma before turning to face Birger Jarl Nilsen. 'What are you doing here?'

'Just wanted to see how it was going. I assume we're sure about that roof now?'

He nodded in the direction of number 49, where the shop assis-tants in the *Godt Brød* bakery and café were standing behind the windows looking alternately out at the street and down at their watches. They had not been able to accept a single customer for more than two hours.

'We can talk about that at the meeting this afternoon,' Fredrik Smedstuen replied.

Once again he addressed himself to Selma: 'Thank you very much. As I said, you can leave the scene. Do you need a lift?'

The man must have an entire collection of identical shirts. Or else he was unusually dirty. His trousers were also the same ones as last week. Even then, Selma had noticed a grease stain at the side of his left knee. When he leaned over her to grab the water glass used during the reconstruction, as usual she was aware of the smell of cigarettes, chewing gum and Fisherman's Friends. Oddly enough, he did not smell of sweat.

'No, thanks,' Selma said, made slightly uncomfortable by the close contact. 'I'm just going up the street here.'

The Police Inspector grunted something in response and moved away.

'Are you heading up the street?' Birger Jarl Nilsen asked her unnecessarily. 'We can walk together. I'm making for Torshov. That will save you phoning me, as you promised last time we met.'

His smile was almost mocking. Selma was unsure what to make of the offer. She was intending to visit Einar Falsen, it would only take six or seven minutes to walk from here and she needed a short break from other people.

'That's nice,' she exclaimed as she set off towards the barriers at the north end that three uniformed policemen were at last dismantling.

The man followed her. Neither spoke until they had turned off into Helgesens gate at the *Espresso House*. Selma preferred not to pick her way through the busy, perpetually-dug-up Thorvald Meyers gate.

'I see you're not too keen on Fredrik!'

Birger Jarl Nilsen kept an ample distance across the pavement. One and a half metres away and slightly behind her. After a few metres he fell into step with her and only now did she notice he was not much taller than her, in fact.

'Yes and no,' she hesitated, 'I don't quite know. A little unkempt for a job with so much contact with the public. And a bit of a grouch too. He seems testy by inclination.'

'Really, he's good as gold. A smart policeman. It's just that he's newly divorced and feeling down in the dumps. Anyway, he agrees with me, even though he's not too keen to admit it.'

'About what?'

'That Linda Bruseth was the assassin's target.'

Feeling her breathing become shallower, Selma slowed down. She was annoyed at the thought of still smelling Fredrik Smedstuen's peculiar odour and she sniffed a couple of times to get rid of it. Her arm felt better, oddly enough. She twisted it out of the sling, folded up the triangle of fabric and tucked it into her pocket.

'How can you be so certain of that?' she asked.

'For many reasons. In the first place, the killer has chosen an unnecessarily arduous method of taking someone's life. That tells us quite a lot.'

Selma stopped in her tracks. 'Oh?'

'Think,' he said.

He backed away from her as soon as she stopped, almost imperceptibly. They were facing each other now, with two metres space between them.

'It was ... spectacular?' she ventured.

'Yes.'

'The killer wanted it to be spectacular. For it to ... draw attention.'

'Exactly.'

'But how does that point to Linda more than to me?'

Slowly, she began to walk on.

'Let's look at the facts in our possession,' he said. 'The gunman is good. He's used a weapon and calibre that call for experience. As far as I've understood, he's not left a scintilla of evidence on the roof, from where absolutely everything suggests he fired the shot. None of us would have been in any doubt about the identity of the intended target if it hadn't been for Linda Bruseth's sudden movement to save the glass of water from falling. If you had all been sitting reasonably still, then the shot would have quite simply been regarded as a bull's eye. Bang, right in the middle of Linda's forehead. Without a shadow of a doubt.'

'But she didn't sit still,' Selma objected. 'She moved forward like a flash! And got in my way.'

'No, actually she didn't.'

Birger Jarl looked around. It seemed as if he were studying the pavement. Obviously he failed to find what he was looking for, and instead patted his inside pocket and produced a felt tip pen. Glancing to right and left, he flipped off the lid and moved to the concrete wall between two grubby windows in the block at the corner of Bjerkelundgata. He quickly drew a large sketch of how the three women had been sitting just before Linda had rescued the glass of water and the shot had been fired. He was not a particularly talented draughtsman but had an exceptional sense of perspective. The way the sketch turned out, Selma was now standing on exactly the same sightline as the one the killer must have had. Birger took a small step back.

'Do you see?'

Selma was far from sure what he meant. She stood there for a long time studying the sketch. Two teenagers came whizzing past on electric scooters without batting an eye at the middle-aged graffiti artist. A woman in a hijab, pushing a pram containing two children, moved as far out to the kerb as she possibly could.

'He had a clear view of my head the whole time,' Selma said, blinking. 'Because this is the angle he would have had from the roof, isn't it?'

He nodded. 'If you were the one he wanted to hit, then Linda's sudden movement wouldn't have mattered at all. We're talking about an expert shot with a clear target. Linda Bruseth. The sniper registered the movement and that made it a touch more difficult for him. So the shot wasn't completely clean. He hit towards the back of the head and the bullet did a pirouette out of the skull and into your arm.'

Selma had no idea whether she was relived or disappointed by what she was now forced to acknowledge. It surprised her. After all the worry that had weighed her down in recent days, it ought to have been a huge burden off her shoulders to learn that no one had actually been out to get her. All the same she felt a stab of something or other.

'I still don't understand it,' she said as she started to walk again.

Birger Jarl scored through the drawing five or six times, replaced the lid on the pen and pushed it back into his inside pocket.

'Why did he choose such a method to kill an anonymous back-bencher like Linda Bruseth?' Selma asked. 'You said the killer must have wanted to draw attention. But in Grünerløkka on a busy Thursday afternoon ... what a place to cause such a commotion! The media would have given huge coverage to the story of an elected representative being the victim of an assassination no matter where it took place. Linda wasn't exactly an Olof Palme or Anna Lindh, but all the same!'

'But both people you mention were in government when they were killed. Not just in parliament. All the same, I do believe there's a message in this murder.'

Once again Selma came to a sudden stop as the firearms expert continued: 'If we take two steps back first of all.'

As if he meant this literally, he distanced himself again from Selma.

'Someone wants to take Linda's life. Taking someone's life is not difficult, if you really have made up your mind to do that. Not even a member of parliament. The security surrounding an ordinary member of parliament is no greater than around any local mayor. If it's true that the killer quite simply wanted her dead, he could have run her over with a car, he could have set her house on fire or he could have pounced on her in a dark alley one evening—'

'Understood,' Selma broke in impatiently.

'Overall, the possibilities are endless. The danger with such attacks is that they can be taken for sheer chance. Attempted rape. A pyromaniac on the loose. A drunk driver. Do you see where I'm going with this?'

It began to dawn on her. This policeman was good.

'The killer wants the actual intent to be overstated,' she said slowly and felt the skin on her arms contract. 'He doesn't want there to be any doubt that she was killed with malice aforethought.'

'Spot on. The question is then whether she was killed as Linda Bruseth or as an MP. In other words, whether her life has been taken as a symbol of something.'

'Does Fredrik Smedstuen know all this? Have you spoken to him about this ... theory of yours?'

'Of course.'

'It doesn't seem so.'

'He's just less willing than I am to share information with other people,' Birger Jarl Nilsen said, starting to walk off again.

They crossed Seilduksgata and cut diagonally across Birkelunden without saying anything. A tram rumbled round the bend up at the traffic lights between Toftes gate and Schleppegrells gate. The screech of metal against metal rang out and a motorist tooted angrily.

'You may well be right,' Selma said finally when they had reached the freak-fashion shop, *Scorpius*. 'Smedstuen isn't exactly communicative. In that respect he's a more typical representative of the police force than you are.'

'I don't work in the police,' he said, obviously taken aback that she could believe anything of the sort.

They had arrived at Einar Falsen's apartment block and Selma had stopped.

'No?' she asked, equally surprised.

'I work *for* the police, not *in* the force. Are you going in here?'

His eyes took the measure of the run-down, dirty building from the eaves with their loose gutters all the way down to the foundations, where lumps of dog shit lined the foot of the graffitied walls.

'Yes,' Selma answered curtly. 'This is where I'm going. What's your job, then?'

'Weapons expert. And ballistics. Didn't you pick that up when we met in Fredrik's office?'

'Yes, of course. But I mean, are you a freelancer, then?'

'My own little company and a part-time post at the college. Once upon a time I was—'

Selma raised her hand to interrupt him. 'Let me guess,' she said. 'Soldier. Or to be more correct, officer.'

Now he was laughing. The laughter was surprisingly deep but nevertheless there was a softness about it that she liked. He still kept a peculiar physical distance from her, as if he was used to moving in a milieu where women absolutely must not misunderstand his intentions.

In a way it was pleasant.

'Major,' he confirmed.

He stood aside to let Selma ring the doorbell and open the iron gate. Then he leaned forward very slightly in an almost comical gesture of confidentiality. He was still standing one and a half metres away from her.

'For a time I was a military intelligence officer,' he said in a loud whisper. 'So I followed your escapades last autumn with great interest. Well done.'

He straightened his back. It might also seem as if he clicked his heels together in some kind of military salute, before pivoting round and walking on up towards Torshov.

The Zip File

Lars Winther did not even dare try.

After spending two hours searching the Internet for how to break the code on a zip file, he had progressed no further than he had been when he arrived at work. First he had received some help from the IT team to download a program called *7Zip*. As usual, Lars did not escape the condescending comments about what kind of idiot he was when it came to the contents of the computers he was otherwise so dependent upon. While down-loading the file, the pale, skinny guy from the IT section had explained something to him that Lars in no way understood. Something about needing this program in order to create a zip file. Lars clarified that he was interested in opening something rather than generating or storing it. The muttering that fol-lowed was incomprehensible. With a face like thunder, the guy had not even said goodbye when he left and so Lars just let him walk off in a huff.

No matter how he turned it this way and that, he needed the password. On the odd occasion when he chose to secure documents with a password, he knew he had limitless attempts to open them. It was necessary – he stuck like glue to eight passwords of varying strength learned by heart and every now and again forgot which one he had used where and when.

It was not as easy as that with Jonathan Herse's file.

Lars feared it might have an inbuilt limit that locked the document for good after too many attempts. Three, for example, as with a bankcard. Or, maybe that was not even possible. He knew far too little about computers.

Lars had alternated between drumming a pen on his desk and putting it into his mouth for the last quarter of an hour. Now he had chewed too hard on it and the ink tasted horrible. He tried to look at his reflection on the darkest part of the monitor as he rubbed all the blue dye off his lips.

'Shit,' he spluttered in annoyance, freeing the memory stick and thrusting it into his pocket again.

Of course there were people who could open zip files. When he had worked at *DG* he had always used Agnes with the blue hair. She was the sharpest tech wizard in the whole *DG* building and had never turned him away. Not until he had announced his move from *DG* to *Aftenavisen* and she gave him the cold shoulder the couple of times he had approached her after that.

The police undoubtedly also had the required competence but he could not call on them either – they didn't exactly run an IT service for frustrated journalists. He knew a couple of hackers through earlier stories he had covered but he did not trust either of them. There were also programs online that promised the earth but his horror of inadvertently downloading malware was too much of a deterrent.

When all was said and done, there was only one way to get hold of the password.

The Junkie

As usual Selma Falck pulled down the sleeve of her jacket to open the entrance door from Einar's back yard without touching it with her hand. The old policeman, admittedly with plenty of help from Selma and Poker-Turk, had upgraded his apartment a little. However, the building itself was close to total collapse. Why it had to be so unbelievably filthy in addition had, of course, to do with its residents. More junkies and people with mental health problems could scarcely be gathered together in the same building anywhere outside of an institution, and none of them had the energy to argue with the building's owner.

Einar had left his door open a crack. As usual, Pussycat stood with its ugly flat face trained on the gap. Selma carefully moved the toe of her shoe towards him, pushed him back and stepped inside.

Everywhere stank of green soap. Huge quantities of it. She looked down at the still-wet floor. From bitter experience, she kept her shoes on when she walked in.

'You've been hard at work,' she said, scanning the room.

All the bundles of newspapers Einar went around stealing at break of day in the periods when he was not allowed access to the Internet were gone. Fleece blankets of the very cheapest kind were draped over the pockmarked settee. Selma felt a noticeable static shock when she sat down amidst the pale-blue splendour. The wonky coffee table had been scrubbed clean. A strong smell of ammonia wafted from the kitchen and combined with the green soap from the floors. Since the apartment was far from free of mould and rot, it all brought back memories of the cleaner's cupboard at Ullevål Hospital a few days earlier.

'I've been doing some deep cleaning,' Einar declared as he emerged from the kitchen with two cups of tea. 'A real pre-Christmas scrub.'

'In September?'

'September *is* pre-Christmas,' he said with satisfaction, motioning for her to move into the chair.

'The new sofa is for Pussycat and me. I've done everything you asked me to. Just take a seat and you'll soon see.'

'You've changed our seats around a little,' Selma said, obeying his request.

The cat's fur suddenly bristled in all directions when he jumped up on the settee.

'I'm having pork chops for dinner today,' Einar announced. 'Two for me and one for Pussycat. But there were five in the packet. Would you like to eat with us? I've got sauerkraut too. *Nora's*. The Parisian type.'

'No, thanks. I'm glad to hear you're eating properly.'

With a smile, Einar let the cat settle on his lap and, with long sweeping movements, stroked the animal. His hands looked dry and sore but still bore traces of cheese puffs.

'I'll be damned, there are a lot of people who want help from you,' he said. 'But I'm ashamed to say there aren't very many you choose to assist.'

'I don't need to. I earn more than enough for the few cases I take on. There must have been about six or seven since New Year.'

'Five. You've taken on five cases in 2019.'

'OK, it's probably only five. I've also solved them all, and earned just under three million kroner from them. With deductions for what I pay you and the expenses I incurred, that gives me an income of two and a half million. And the year's not over yet.'

'Crazy,' Einar said, shaking his head.

'That's less than I took in as a lawyer.'

'No one should earn so much money.'

'Your point of view is noted,' Selma said, sounding irritated. 'But it wasn't primarily the cases I've solved that I asked you to look at. Those clients are extremely satisfied.'

Putting the cat carefully on the floor, Einar disappeared into the bedroom and re-emerged with the folder Selma had given him. Once he had sat down again, he placed the folder on his knee and opened it up.

'Heavens above,' Selma exclaimed. 'I do declare!'

The files of concluded cases lay on top. Each and every one of them had been inserted into a separate red plastic cover. They were all neatly closed with a piece of tape and held together when he removed them and placed them in a neat pile on the table. The rest of the papers came into view. When Einar had received the folder, the no-cases had been a disorganized sheaf of papers. A few printouts but also a large number of handwritten notes. As far as possible, Selma had tried to use one sheet of paper for each case. However, some of the applications, usually ones that only comprised one phone call, were merely scribbled down on an already-existing document. Now everything had been put into order.

'Have you rewritten them all?' Selma asked, leaning across the table to take a closer look.

He used both hands to push her back.

'Yes. This was all in total chaos, Selma. Your handwriting's not too neat either but I've done the best I could. Now there's one sheet for each case, all typed up on my typewriter.'

He nodded towards the laptop, now lying at the far end of the coffee table. It had obviously undergone a thorough clean too. The silver of the plastic cover, meant to represent an idiot-proof radiation protector, had begun to flake off. Selma caught herself worrying that Einar would discover before too long that she had simply used *Bengalack* metallic paint to cover a supersonic blue *Star Wars* motif.

'It's not really washable,' she said.

'Oh, of course it is. Now let's see.'

He patted the spot beside him on the settee and Selma got to her feet and hesitantly complied. Blinking furiously, she steeled herself against the shock she knew would come as soon as she sat down on resplendent pale-blue blanket.

'Ouch!' she cried, reaching out for her cup of tea on the other side of the table.

'Don't spill it,' Einar said. 'Look here. Missing person cases are marked in red.'

He picked up a red index marker. There were three of them in all.

'Financial cases are marked in blue, infidelity cases in yellow ... by the way, you haven't accepted a single one of them!'

Selma sighed audibly. 'No. That's never going to happen either. They'd need to pay me a billion.'

'I've marked the whole kit and caboodle in black,' he added. 'A bit of everything to be found in there, from stray dogs to arguments in housing cooperatives culminating in death threats. And someone who thought he was being illegally spied on by Norway's Scout Association.'

'She was completely crackers,' Selma mumbled, pointing at a pink index marker stuck beside a black one. 'What's that?'

'There are three pink markers. Those are the cases where I think there could be some bad blood. They could be furious with you, I mean. That was what you wanted, wasn't it? For me to find a few that aspired to being that stalker of yours?'

'Staw-ker. But yes.'

'This woman here,' Einar said, handing Selma a sheet of paper. 'If the lady in the Scout Association was a mad hatter, then this one's not far behind, I'd say.'

He sniggered like a teenager, with his hand in front of his mouth and all.

'And I should know what I'm talking about,' he added, as the snigger changed to high-pitched laughter.

With a loud sigh, Selma grabbed the paper.

'Fredrikke Augustsson. The keyboard queen. I had totally forgotten that she actually got in touch with me. By phone, of all things. Good Lord ...'

She took hold of her cup and swilled down the tea.

'For some reason or other she was desperate to meet me. After having the cheek to be aggressive towards me on virtually every platform, all of a sudden she wanted my help. That must have been ...'

She held the cup in both hands as she tilted her head and pondered.

'... over a year ago? Wasn't it before I ended up on the Hardangervidda?'

'Yes. It was spring of last year, in fact. She wanted to get you to prove that Jan Herman Lie, the lawyer, was in cahoots with Facebook and Twitter, manipulating her opportunities to express herself.'

Selma shook her head despondently.

'Jan Herman is one of the country's best lawyers on freedom of expression. A fine, smart guy. That woman has been at his throat for the past five or six years. At mine, too, because I once defended him. Stupid of me. Why she would then want help from me of all people, God only knows. She's unstable.'

Putting down her cup, she twirled her finger on her forehead.

'The only consolation is that everyone's turned a deaf ear to her complaints. Almost literally. She gets hardly a single like.'

'You've just been describing a staw-ker,' Einar pointed out. 'Could it be her? Who's visiting your apartment?'

'No. I don't really think so. She's ... she's ...'

Selma struggled to picture the Loden-clad woman sneaking into her apartment in Sagene, after manipulating the security alarm, just to leave a forty-year-old packet of chewing gum on her pillow.

'No,' she repeated.

'Why not?'

'It's entirely out of character. She's like a wasp in autumn. Annoying but harmless.'

'You don't know her.'

'I know the type.'

'But—'

'It's not her. What have you got there?'

Einar took back the Fredrikke Augustsson document and gave her another one.

'You don't even know the name of this guy here,' he said.

Selma did not reply. She read the brief paragraph about the rejected client twice.

'I remember this man well,' she said slowly. 'The reason he has no name is that I met him outdoors.'

'Eh?'

'He approached me down at Myren,' she said without taking her eyes off the paper. 'I was on my way home after a long run. I'd just stopped to take a stretch when he began talking to me.'

'Didn't he introduce himself?'

'Yes, of course. Shook my hand and was very polite. It must have been some time this summer?'

'Yes. 26 June.'

'That's right. I couldn't for the life of me remember his name when I came home, but I made a brief note on him because he got so angry. Just to be on the safe side. As you've seen ...'

She raised her eyebrows and glanced at the bundles in front of them.

'... there's a lot of strange stuff among the people who contact me. And this one here was really furious.'

'It says that,' Einar commented, pointing at the text.

'Or ...'

Pussycat hissed from the floor, demanding his regular spot. He had long forgotten that, strictly speaking, he had been Selma's cat, at the time when he was called Darius and lived in a villa on Ormøya island. Selma dutifully stood up and returned to the chair on the opposite side of the table. Pussycat stretched out on his back with his front paws above his head, and began to purr when Einar stroked his belly.

'He wasn't actually so much angry,' Selma said thoughtfully as she reached out again for the teacup. 'More sort of ... completely devastated. He raised his voice and began to talk nineteen to the dozen. With sweeping arm movements and everything. A woman passer-by even came up to me and asked if everything was all right. It was kind of her, of course, but ...'

She closed her eyes and tried to picture the scene.

'I think in fact he was on the verge of tears,' she said. 'And that can be a bit scary when strange men come up to you and start talking in a loud voice, waving their arms about and then break down in sobs.'

'But what did he want? It says here only that he wanted help to sue a government department. Is that even possible, by the way?'

'Yes. Or you can sue the state through a department. I told him I no longer practised law, and therefore I couldn't help him anyway.'

'What department? And why didn't he give up?'

Selma tried hard to remember. She put two fingers on each temple as if that might help.

'He said something about corrupt civil servants. That no one wanted to listen to him. It was about ...'

She was silent. For a long time.

'You've written here that he threatened you,' Einar reminded her, obviously fed up waiting. 'That ...'

Hunched over the table, he grabbed the sheet of paper.

'..."you're going to regret this", is what you've written down. This guy singles himself out as the obvious staw-ker here. At least if we're only going to search in this bundle.'

Selma still did not answer. She was trying to recreate the dank smell of the Akerselva river as it ran quietly past the Myren industrial area. Of new-mown grass and Midsummer. One of her ankles had been hurting, she recalled: she had twisted it at the Hundremeter bridge when a stray dog snapped at her. The man had been relatively young, maybe thirty. He had been tall and slim and there was something about his clothes.

Einar was bursting with impatience now.

'Have you—'

'Shh. Shh!'

When the young man had stopped her, she now remembered, she had been ready to tell him the obvious thing, that she was out for exercise and so had no money on her.

'I thought he was a junkie,' she suddenly said. 'Because of his clothes, perhaps. His teeth. I don't know.'

'Maybe he was?'

'Yes. No. I've really no idea.'

'OK then. Maybe we should take a closer look at the third and final candidate ...'

He adopted a tone of voice that parodied a chairman at a meeting.

'... which is ...'

Selma grabbed her mobile phone from her bag on the floor. An idea had struck her. It was so weird that for once she paid no attention to Einar's phobia.

'No!' he shouted. 'Not here! Take it away!'

Selma took no notice. As her fingers raced to search for something on the Internet, she said: 'It had to do with the Ministry for Children and Families. Now I remember. He felt he was being side-lined in a child welfare case, and thought that—'

'Get that telephone out of here!'

Einar was on his feet, cowering in a corner of the living room where he stood clutching his head, whimpering.

'Two seconds,' Selma said. 'Just another jiffy.'

'No,' he squealed, about to burst into tears.

Selma glanced up. 'Sorry. I'll leave.'

She pretended to switch off the phone. Picking up her bag and denim jacket, she headed for the door.

'I'll call in tomorrow,' she called over her shoulder as she left.

The door slammed behind her. In the back yard of the ghastliest apartment block in Oslo, she lingered for a moment. It was chilly and she stopped to fasten a couple of buttons on her jacket. A movement beside the rubbish bins made her look up quickly from her mobile. The rat lurking between two of the containers, about the size of a guinea pig, boldly sniffed the air around her. Nevertheless Selma looked down again at the display.

'Child welfare,' she said under her breath.

The strange folder belonging to the deceased journalist Jonathan Herse had to do with child welfare. In no way could it possibly have any connection to the uninvited guest who had tormented Selma by breaking into her apartment. However, Einar had picked out the likeliest candidate in her archives: a man who had wanted to sue the state for injustice perpetrated by the Child Welfare Service.

No. Not the likeliest. The least unlikely, and there couldn't possibly be a connection between the cases.

But now, after reading the same text on her mobile three times in succession, she knew that Linda Bruseth, her old friend from handball days who had been shot and killed less than a week ago, had left one sole legacy behind her as a Member of Parliament.

During the spring session, Linda Bruseth had chaired the committee on one single occasion. The agenda had been a Document

8 motion about giving the Child Welfare Service extended powers to take action in cases of child neglect.

The Child Welfare Service. Again.

Concerns

There was a remarkable satisfaction in working through the night. The silence made space for reflection and concentration, increasingly difficult to find between meetings and urgent deadlines. At least twice a week he chose not to come into the office until ten a.m. After a fourteen-hour stretch, he had usually achieved as much as in an ordinary working week.

Karstein Braaten was feeling the weight of his age, even though his sixtieth birthday was still a couple of months away. He had by now had his fill of experiences and thoughts he had done his best to digest during his entire economically active life. Even though he had reason to do so in the past few years, it was not his task to instil fear. Far from it. His very title had been bureaucratized to death and no one could work out what he actually spent his days doing.

Divisional Director in the Directorate for Public Security and Resilience, DPSR.

As Head of the Division for Analysis and Data Processing, Karstein Braaten was responsible for the coordination and implementation of resilience plans for the civilians of Norway. Ever since the establishment of the Directorate in 2003, he had sat amongst his papers and rising concerns in an anonymous office in Tønsberg. He had come there straight from the Defence Research Establishment, where he had started work on the day the Berlin Wall fell. That had been his thirtieth birthday, and he remembered it down to the smallest detail.

The weather had been bleak on that historic day, with four degrees of chill in the November air. He could still close his eyes and feel the warmth of stepping into the establishment in Kjeller, outside Oslo, for the very first time. He could feel the soaring delight of that day when no one could afford to go home. He pictured the ecstatic people gathered around all the TV screens they could find. Night fell, and in reality the German Democratic Republic had totally collapsed and the whole world looked brighter.

The Brezhnev Doctrine died that night. The Soviet Union would no longer have complete control over the satellite states in the east. It was full throttle Glasnost and Perestroika, the world would be a better place, and Karstein Braaten had felt elated on behalf of future generations.

Now, almost exactly thirty years later, he sadly knew much better.

People understood nothing.

Norwegians took everything for granted.

He pushed a coffee cup further across the desk and got to his feet. Moving to the window, he gazed out over the By Fjord. Yesterday afternoon's wind had eased off and at last it was starting to grow really dark in the evenings. The lights of the town on the opposite side created nervous reflections on the water, where a fishing boat chugged quietly out of the marina, heading south.

Karstein Braaten regretted having taken on the task of committee chairman. Increasing demands, both from the parliament and international liaison bodies, called for the updating and coordination of the more or less fragmented resilience plans Norway had in place. The threat scenario was developing faster than politicians in any way appreciated. The committee he had agreed to chair was supposed to work out a strategy to incorporate NATO's seven fundamental expectations for critical functions of society into a larger national plan. At the point of intersection between the military and civilians, they were to create the basis for an effective and secure defence of life and wellbeing. Total Defence was the elegant name it had been given, something it would actually be if both politicians and the majority of the populace took genuine threats seriously.

Which they did not.

Karstein Braaten sighed. He listened to the silence. It was past midnight and apart from the security guards, he was probably the only person in the entire building. Walking back to his desk, he picked up the half-empty cup and moved to a small sink in one corner. There he emptied it out, rinsing it thoroughly under running water hotter than his hands could really bear, and then made sure to leave the basin as shining clean as before. He poured a fresh cup from a thermos flask on the tidy desk. The steam formed a damp film over his face as he carefully sipped the piping-hot coffee.

Throughout his long, anonymous working life in the service of Norwegian security, he had been receptive to the idea that most things could happen. War. Natural catastrophes. It was almost unimaginable what Norwegian infrastructure would look like in ten years' time if climate change continued. Roads and buildings had been constructed for weather as it had once been, with winter, spring, summer and autumn. Not to endure mild winters and soaking wet transitions between the seasons with floods, landslides and misery as a consequence.

He was mentally prepared for all of it. However, the most terrifying scenario of all was serious illness.

It was not a question of whether a pandemic would come. The uncertainty was attached to when it would come. Every Sunday, when he went alone to the service in Slagen church, he prayed earnestly that it would not happen before he himself had passed away. He had no children and his wife had left him years ago. The only thing he was really bothered about was the Norwegian people. If they had known of him, they would perhaps have returned the favour.

Attitudes to infectious diseases were almost a joke.

On the desk in front of him lay a brochure from the World Health Organization. Only a few days before, a committee had delivered the report *A World at Risk*. The former Norwegian Prime Minister and doctor of medicine Gro Harlem Brundtland had led the work.

The warnings about previous epidemics and worldwide pandemics positively shrieked at him from the matte paper.

Karstein Braaten was by nature an anxious man. The exposure of the NAV scandal in the past few days, in which by all accounts miscarriages of justice had been committed against a considerable number of benefit claimants, had knocked him for six, into a state resembling a depressive reaction. That was the way he was made. He was a man who had come from a humble background. His father had been an industrial worker until he had broken his back in a work accident at the age of forty-three. His mother had worked all her life as a charwoman in a primary school. Until the day she died, she had objected to the word 'cleaner'. She was a charwoman, end of discussion, and the family of three children had lived life on a paltry wage and some Social Security that made existence possible. What strength his mother had left after hard working days was spent preventing her husband from allowing his shame to make him old before his time.

Social Security was a right.

Welfare was a hallmark of this country.

Just as trust was. Belief in one another and that the authorities wish us well. That they knew what was best for us and treated us fairly. Even during the Second World War, in a completely different time and completely different general conditions, the people had closed ranks when the Nazis arrived. Some had seen opportunities for rapid profits, others had chosen to do the enemies' bidding, but the vast majority stuck together in a Norwegian, unyielding chain of resistance.

In all honesty, Karstein Braaten did not know how it would be today.

He had no idea whether the people's trust was strong enough to withstand extraordinary strain. He could hope, as the researchers did, the sociologists and political scientists and psychologists who continually wrote about the Norwegian model.

Welfare and progress, trust and growth. It sounded grand.

When the state had inflicted unfair decisions on at least 2,400 people and even put them in prison in direct conflict with law and justice, it was no longer possible to talk about either successful welfare or fertile soil for public trust.

His legs had gone to sleep. He pulled them down from the table with a grimace. Slipping his shoes on again, he stood up. His coat hung on a hook at the door, and when he shrugged it on, he felt the throb of pain in his shoulder joints.

'Foul weather,' he mumbled to himself as he cast one last glance out of the window and flicked the switch that turned off the ceiling light.

The fjord was flat calm now. No boats, scarcely a seabird to be seen. On the other side of the narrow fjord the streetlights still glittered on the water, but the traffic had turned in for the night.

In his entire career, he had dealt with administration, with planning for the worst and hoping for the best. He was equally tidy in his mind as he was in his office and in every single document that emanated from it. All the same, he could not quite shake off the thought of what the female hospital manager had said in the committee meeting on Monday.

Well, the scandal only impacts people who are generally a bit ...

The head movement that had followed had been unmistakeable. For her, the miscarriages of justice were almost OK since the victims were parasites, the ones who had travelled abroad even though they believed it was illegal. The ones who lived off her tax money without lifting a finger.

The deplorables.

The NAV scandal had become a hullabaloo restricted to intellectuals. People with principles. It was the law professors who frothed at the mouth in TV debates, it was the serious commentators who rattled their sabres and demanded for heads to roll among cabinet ministers and civil servants. Not the majority of ordinary people.

This should fundamentally reassure him, he thought as he locked his office door and padded along the dark corridor. People would not march through the streets. There would be no campaigns or petitions. No cabinet ministers would be forced to resign, and after a few weeks of upheaval, it would all be drowned out by fresh stories, yet another cycle of news. Trust in the state would hardly get a scratch.

In truth, that should calm Karstein Braaten's nerves. Instead he pictured his father before he died, scrawny and incapacitated for the last twenty-two years of his life. He had been a real grafter before he was injured. Afterwards, he could never meet anyone's eye.

This country should not be like that, neither then nor now. As Karstein Braaten nodded goodnight to the watchman in reception and exited through the heavy glass doors, he offered up his usual silent prayer.

THURSDAY 12 SEPTEMBER

The Discovery

Like the evenings, the mornings too were growing increasingly dark. The old woman liked that. She enjoyed ambling along, on her first walk with Bella, before everyone else was out and about. In the light time of year there were more people around in the well-frequented part of Marka just north of Korsvoll. The area was considered almost a public park, always swarming with children and hikers, with dogs and joggers everywhere.

But they did not like the darkness and the dawn as much as she did.

She was nearly eighty, but fit as a flea. At least she tried to appear that way. The walks with Bella kept her in good shape, and three times a day she set out from Grinda on a circular route that now and again stretched as far as the Sognsvann lake.

Bella was also getting on in years. She would be twelve in July, if she were spared to live that long. The vet had sung her praises at her last appointment, and gave assurances that there was no reason the dog wouldn't live for another year or two. Even though her sight and hearing had deteriorated and her sense of smell was also most likely not what it had been, the little poodle was healthy and had a good heart. In every sense of the word, her owner had added: Bella was the kindest dog in the world.

When the woman and her black dog were only a couple of hundred metres from the built-up area, she could not hold it in any longer. When they emerged from the forest, she still had seven minutes' walk to reach the small red house her husband had built with his own hands at one time in the late sixties. She had made sure to go to the toilet before she set off, as she always did. That extra cup of coffee around five a.m. had produced an effect all the same. If she did not empty her bladder now, she would wet her pants.

After all, it was all part and parcel of growing old. Her body was not as tough as in the past. Her knees could not tolerate hunkering down, she knew that from experience, and so she turned off the wide path she had just arrived at. Slowly she trudged up to a toppled tree trunk she knew lay only forty or fifty metres away. This was not the first time she had suddenly been caught short on a walk: she could cope with this. Sitting with her backside on the tree trunk, using it as a makeshift latrine with her trousers round her ankles, everything would be perfectly fine.

She almost toppled over a number of times. Her balance was not quite what it had been, she had to admit, and she needed to clutch at branches and bushes as she walked along the rugged terrain. Bella followed right behind her rather than scurrying ahead as she had in her younger days.

A child was hanging from a tree.

The woman stopped in her tracks. She blinked a few times, saying nothing. Bella stood calmly behind her, tired and hungry in her own deaf world.

The old wifie, as her husband had called her since the time she had been barely forty, was not born yesterday. She did not walk on. The child was hanging at the end of a rope from a tall, straight birch tree. It was a girl, the woman definitely decided, wearing red trainers and jeans. Her hair was blonde with streaks that had not been endowed by nature at any rate. Well stacked, too: in fact, the child's body looked so strange that the woman could not resist taking two more paces forward.

It was not a child. It was a dwarf. Or, short in stature as it was called nowadays. She could not fathom why all those words people had used for generations were no longer current. Darkie and Mongol and dwarf were clear, descriptive words she still used inside her head. There was certainly no harm meant by that. But times changed, and that's just how it was.

Ridiculous, all the same.

A person of short stature was hanging from a branch.

Not just any old person of short stature, she saw as the gentle morning breeze rustled through the forest, making the body rotate slightly. It was Kajsa Breien who was dangling between the autumnal yellow trees. Supreme Court Judge Kajsa Marie Breien, forty-nine years of age and the only member of that august assembly almost all Norwegians would immediately recognize.

The woman had read that she was four foot seven in height.

Kajsa Breien was among the best legal practitioners in the country. She was married to the Head of the Law Faculty and had five adopted children. In summer she liked to sail and to walk in the mountains. In winter she went ice swimming three times a week from her own jetty at her childhood home in Bygdøy. This kept her in peak health and ensured a long life, as she had said in a couple of in-depth interviews the woman had read.

Icy water had not helped her in the least, was what ran through the woman's head.

Bella was still standing like a stone statue at her back. It might almost seem as if the dog had fallen asleep on her feet. The woman drew down the pocket zip on her sensible ski jacket. Her mobile was the *Doro* brand, a phone for oldies, as her grandchild had laughingly called it when he gave it to her last Christmas. It was red and simple, with big, clear numbers. She tugged off her sports gloves and dialled 1-1-2 before putting the phone to her ear.

'My name is Anna Knutsen,' she said to the man who answered after only one ring. 'I've found a dead dwarf.'

The Handball

It had taken a couple of seconds before Selma Falck truly understood where she was.

Her bed felt unfamiliar. A stab of fear jolted her wide awake before she realized she had booked into a hotel. Of all places she had chosen to travel to Storo. Only a few years ago the area had been an unattractive, ugly and haphazard mass of buildings surrounding a retail centre. Now it had turned into an unattractive, ugly and carefully planned residential high-rise around the same centre, with a *Thon* hotel planted in the middle of it all.

Selma had actually been on her way home from a long-planned dinner with friends. The evening had been pleasant enough and a welcome excuse for not spending the evening alone at home. When she had approached the apartment block in Sagene, her legs had begun to slow down entirely of their own accord. At Arendalsgata, not far from home, she had turned off in an easterly direction without really having taken a decision about it. She walked towards Akerselva and followed the river northwards for a kilometre or so. It was not too late in the evening to drop into the *H&M* store to buy toiletries and some clean underwear.

Her sleep had been fitful and by half past five there was no longer any point in struggling. She was too early for breakfast but that did not matter. Dawn was breaking and she wanted to go home. It was strange to put on the same clothes as the previous day and she couldn't even be bothered taking a shower. She could do that at home – the shower recess had been repaired at last. The new pair of cheap underpants went straight in the bin, unused. The room had been paid in advance, and the receptionist had merely looked up apathetically from an iPad and given a brief nod when she tossed her key card on the counter and left the hotel.

Now it was half past six and she was standing at her own front door. The marks left by Poker-Turk's somewhat amateurish lock change was sufficiently embarrassing for her to decide to have something done about it before complaints came from the management committee. She almost managed to focus so intently on the disfiguring scars that she was able to suppress her anxiety about entering her apartment.

But only almost.

Slightly more elevated pulse rate. Slightly shallower breathing. She unlocked both locks and stepped inside.

Everything was as it should be. The smell was cosy and familiar. In the grey morning light spilling in through the windows she could see dust motes dancing: she should really do some cleaning. In the kitchen there was a half-full cup of tea. In the living room, her laptop was on the table where she had left it. Even a cushion she remembered having fallen from the settee on to the floor yesterday was still lying on the grey carpet under the coffee table.

Her anxiety slowly released its grip. She took one or two deep breaths in and out and strode purposefully into the bedroom. Everything was as it should be in there too. The bathroom had not been disturbed. Not that she could see, at any rate. No surprising little items beside the basin or smiley faces on the mirror.

Once back in the living room, she became aware that the apartment seemed stuffy. To tell the truth, downright dirty. Still with a phoney sense of purpose, she moved to open the balcony door.

All at once the dreadful stink of the stone shelter on the Hardangervidda caught at her nose. This phantom odour engulfed her at regular intervals, making her queasy. One evening a couple of months ago she had Googled to discover that olfactory hallucinations, more commonly than other disturbances in the perception of reality, had a physical rather than a psychological cause. Asking a doctor was out of the question, let alone allowing herself to be examined, as that would only lead to questions of the type Dr Viksfjord had asked. More than likely the troublesome attacks would go away in time.

The morning breeze wafted towards her as she opened the door. She took a couple of steps out on to the balcony where she was met by a sweet smell of rain and wet asphalt and she made sure to breathe through her nose.

The queasiness eased off. She took hold of the railings with both hands. The metal felt pleasantly cold against the surface of her skin. Two buses were struggling to negotiate a route through badly parked vehicles in Arendalsgata. A child laughed somewhere. Dog walkers were out strolling. The world was as it should be.

Her longing for little Skjalg had become a physical pain, an intermittent kind of ache. Selma had an all-consuming desire to see him, to hold him, to breathe in the fragrance of milk and nappy cream and sour baby porridge from the skin folds on his neck. She pictured his slightly squint eyes that had become increasingly brown as the weeks passed. She wanted to caress his hands and feel the strength in them when he gripped her fingers or yanked off her glasses.

She wanted more than anything else to make him laugh.

Anine had to be placated.

When Police Inspector Fredrik Smedstuen, as early as in the cleaner's cupboard at the hospital, had asked her what case she was working on at present, she had lied. 'Nothing' was the answer she had given, something that would have been true only a few minutes before she replied. At present she had nothing in particular to occupy her. She had turned down all assignments, the way she occasionally arranged things to make sure she had no commitments so that she was constantly available to look after her grandchild.

In the course of the conversation with the policeman, it had however dawned on her that she had a case. An unpaid case of great personal interest: she had to convince Anine that the shot fired at Grünerløkka had not been meant for her.

Anine would never learn anything about this mysterious stalker if Selma did not report the matter. It was only Einar and Lars who knew about the person who was dogging her movements and they had proved repeatedly that they could keep their mouths shut. Anyway, they did not know Anine.

Selma would have to take a chance that it was all over now that Poker-Turk had changed both the alarm system and the door locks. She had every reason to feel just as safe as before.

She would manage to do that. She had to.

Shivering a little, she let go of the railings. She flexed her stiff fingers slowly out and in before turning round to take serious action on her plans to launch into a cleaning frenzy in the apartment.

Her eye caught sight of something lying in the corner of the balcony, a handball.

An old, well-worn handball. The pentagonal patches of leather it was made of were more distinct than on a modern handball. The grooves between them were slightly deeper and the patches had been sewn together by hand. Several years' use of wax had rubbed out the brand name. Nevertheless, Selma knew that the ball had once been adorned with the stylized bumblebee of the German company called *Hummel*.

She was rooted to the spot. It was simply not possible. Her brain refused to take in the information provided by her eyes. Finally she managed to approach the ball. Instead of picking it up, she used the tip of her Birkenstock sandal to nudge it. The ball rolled in a semicircle.

She could only just make out the letters **SF** through the wax and dirt, written with a permanent marker, she knew, her own initials that had been freshened up once a month for as long as she had owned this ball. Vanja had given it to her as a present on her tenth birthday. It was far too good, an exceptional gift, and Selma had never been so happy to receive anything in all her short life. Every day she used it, for three years until it became so sluggish that it was no longer serviceable. She had held on to it, buried it at the bottom of her wardrobe: it was a ball she wanted to keep for her entire life. One day it was gone.

Her mother had thrown it in the bin. It was unhygienic to have it lying around amongst her clothes, she was told, and that was the end of the discussion.

Selma had rushed to the bins, turned them upside down, in floods of tears, and even used some swear words. She was thirteen and the only thing she wanted right then was to find the best, most important handball in the world. Which she had been given by the most important, best friend in the world.

She never found it again.

Not until now, almost exactly forty years later.

The Detective

Einar Falsen thought life was a real treat at the moment. Selma had been so totally preoccupied the last time she was here that she'd forgotten to take the laptop with her.

He had played his game to the very end that same afternoon but had not dared to download any others. Selma had told him about malware. If there was anything he definitely did not want, it was for the machine to suddenly crash into codes and funny business about which he did not know the first thing. It might even be dangerous for him personally as well. No one had any idea what intentions people and organizations out there had. Apart from in all likelihood being evil. Long ago, he had covered the camera's eye above the screen with a piece of sticky tape. At the very least you had to do what little you could to protect yourself.

For a while he had conducted a few random searches. Read the usual newspapers to which Selma had taken out subscriptions for him. The world out there was completely crackers, but it was important to follow what was going on. The old proverb about 'what you don't know won't harm you' was a barefaced lie. It was what you knew nothing about that was most dangerous of all. Knowledge was the way to go. The first few months and years after his breakdown, when he had still lived in institutions, he had turned to books. Einar had read round the clock. When he discovered that the old hospital library had a complete *Encyclopaedia Britannica* on its shelves, he had started at the letter A. He had still been living at Blakstad when he finished every single volume and decided that the Internet was all a conspiracy. It was a matter of reading between the lines, especially at the bottom right between the two last columns on every third page of every fourth volume. When he looked carefully, he also became convinced that the electromagnetic radiation from the contraptions with which all people surrounded themselves were instruments of evil forces.

But what a treasure trove of knowledge the Internet also was!

He had to admit this to himself. And now he had access to it day and night. Pussycat was healthy and happy, it was warm and pleasant in the apartment and there were six bags of cheese puffs in the fridge. He had a freezer full of stuffed plaice, *Kapteinen*'s brand. He had water from the tap, had remembered to take his medicines and now there was even a bundle of clean clothes on the bed.

'Things couldn't be better,' he said to Pussycat, who purred a satisfied response.

It would be fun to surprise Selma. She seemed stressed out these days. Since those hardships on the Hardangervidda, she had changed. Become more reserved. She got distracted more often than before and had taken on a new, unfamiliar facial expression that appeared a bit too often. There was something anxious about it and Einar did not like it at all.

It was probably that staw-ker. That lousy character. Every person had the right to respect for his or her own private domain – Einar Falsen knew all about that. Selma wanted her own place to herself, exactly like Einar. Sneaking in like a thief in the night like that …

'Damn and blast,' he muttered, scratching the cat behind the ear. 'Damn and blast, Pussycat.'

Selma could not remember much about that young man who had stopped her this summer when she was out jogging. But there had been something.

'One, two, three, four.' Einar stuck his fingers in the air as he counted.

'I know four things about that young lad,' he said to Pussycat as he placed the laptop on his knee before fixing the helmet on his head and fastening the chinstrap nice and tight. 'Let's see if four facts are enough for a good old policeman to make some headway.'

The Crime Scene

Following his divorce, Police Inspector Fredrik Smedstuen had been forced to make do with a rented basement apartment in Korsvoll. His wife had sole ownership of her childhood home in Langmyrgrenda as a consequence of the good sense shown by his parents-in-law when the newly married police couple had taken over the house fifteen years ago for next to nothing. Fredrik had lost count of all the hours of DIY he had invested in the property. His own friends had advised him to put up a fight about the compensation he had received at the changeover, but he could not bear to. He had obediently stuffed one suitcase full of clothes and another of tools, a laptop and a few books, before moving himself lock, stock and barrel out to a dark cellar in Øvre Skjoldvei. He was now in his ninth week there, sleeping in a bed that smelled strange and surrounded by furniture from the early eighties.

In order to be near the children, as his wife had demanded.

She was in charge of a section at Kripos, the National Criminal Investigation Service, and was able to cope perfectly well on her own. It was not so easy for him.

Of course, he had also been left with the worst car.

Today the old Kia had at least started at the first attempt. He left early: it was not yet seven a.m. when he rolled out from the parking space he had most graciously been allowed to use if he promised to clear the snow in winter. Just as he was reversing out through the gate, he had come to a sudden halt because a police car with no siren was hurtling at top speed in a westerly direction, blue lights flashing. He waited a few seconds before trying to make his way out again through the narrow gap between the gateposts. Once again he had to stop. Yet another police car in pursuit, a larger SUV this time with *Squad Leader* in black decals along the side.

In the distance, Fredrik could also hear sirens wailing.

From the time he was five years old, he had chased police cars. The urge had really never diminished, not even after twenty years in the force. He turned his car in the opposite direction from the one he had originally intended.

He did not need to drive far. After only a hundred metres, the flickering blue lights told him that the two vehicles had stopped.

He drove on and parked beside the ditch a short distance from the small parking area at Grinda.

Three men in uniform were busy setting up crime scene tape. One of them, recognizing him, made no objection when Fredrik Smedstuen lifted the tape and ducked underneath. One or two morning walkers had stopped to see what all the fuss was about. A couple of joggers emerged from the undergrowth, cursing and swearing, fifty metres east of the forest track, having obviously been forced out from somewhere further in between the trees.

An elderly woman with a grizzled little poodle stood talking in a loud voice, gesticulating wildly, to a uniformed female officer. Fredrik walked in a curve around them as another two patrol cars drove up and parked outside the cordon. He continued along the forest track until he realized he needed to take a left turn. Something was going on in there behind the trees and bushes. He calmly made his way across the rough ground and stopped just in time.

An extremely small woman was swinging from side to side, suspended from a tree. The squad leader, Inspector Roy Pettersen, must have arrived just seconds before Fredrik. He was still gasping for breath as he stood five metres from the body, talking in an undertone to two others.

It was beyond any doubt that the body hanging there was dead. If there had been the least possibility of any signs of life up there on the makeshift gallows, the woman would have been cut down. Now, instead, a photographer was walking carefully around, busily at work. Like the others, apart from the squad leader, he was wearing paper clothing from top to toe.

Fredrik knew them all.

The youngest caught his eye and said something Fredrik failed to catch. The squad leader turned abruptly and nodded only slightly when he saw who it was.

'You're quick on the draw,' he shouted.

'Not my case,' Fredrik said so softly he hoped he would not be heard.

A fleeting nod of the head in response before Roy Pettersen approached him.

'Bloody hell, it's a dwarf,' he muttered, stopping two metres away.

'Short stature,' Fredrik said.

'Yes, yes, of course. And not just any old person of short stature. It's the Supreme Court Judge—'

He broke off to bark an order at the photographer.

'Kajsa Breien,' Fredrik Smedstuen finished for him under his breath.

Fortunately Inspector Pettersen was fully occupied when four new police officers came walking through the woods. Fredrik was standing on his own, undisturbed, staring intently at the dangling body.

The woman really was small. It must have brought plenty of challenges while she was alive. He and his wife had worried when their youngest son had been closely examined the day after his birth. His arms were slightly short, according to the paediatrician, and the bridge of his nose rather flat under a distinctly domed forehead. His wife had wept buckets. Fredrik had read up on what he had believed until then was called dwarfism. His wife had felt worse and worse as time passed and they moved towards a final diagnosis. Fredrik became less concerned once he learned more about it.

And then it turned out that the boy merely resembled his pint-sized grandfather on his mother's side.

Kajsa Breien looked almost pretty, despite her stunted limbs. Her face was actually absolutely ordinary, in Fredrik's opinion, and in portrait photographs she looked perfectly fine. Well groomed. Alert eyes. Brilliant white teeth that seemed a tiny touch too big for her face. Hair always immaculate.

Now it was fluttering in the strengthening wind.

Fredrik moved back a few metres in order to avoid, if possible, anyone realizing he had no business being there. He continued to study the scene before him. Memorizing it, as he always did when he was one of the first to arrive at a crime scene. The photographers were doing an efficient job, one that was crucial for every investigation, but Fredrik Smedstuen knew nothing could replace a first impression. Not in any area of life.

A person of short stature had primarily two challenges, he knew. One was the prejudice of others. In truth, Kajsa Breien had put them all to shame, and fortunately the world was moving forward. She had never given up and had progressed as far as possible for someone in her profession. On the other hand, the physical problems were more difficult to resolve, even though medical knowledge had of course a larger bag of tools now than several decades ago. Once nature had played a nasty trick on Kajsa at conception and made her stature short, it had also blessed her with unusually good health. She had been spared the most usual skeletal problems, had exercised a great deal and kept herself fairly slim into the bargain.

'But there's no bloody way she got up into that tree under her own steam,' Fredrik Smedstuen said to himself.

Luckily there was no one to hear him.

The birch tree on which she was hanging was tall and erect. The lowest branches sprouted from the trunk a couple of metres above the ground. If she had climbed the tree unaided in order to hang herself, she would have to have used a pair of steps. Or a ladder. Something to stand on while she attached the rope and slipped the noose over her head before kicking the whole shebang away once she had really made up her mind to die. There was no stepladder anywhere to be seen. No tall chairs. Only bushes and undergrowth and scattered conifers too far from the birch to be of any assistance.

In other words, she must have climbed up into the tree like a lithe monkey and then jumped down from the branch with a noose around her neck. Fredrik Smedstuen had never ever heard of anyone being hanged like that.

This was not a case of suicide.

Everyone would soon realize that. Investigations would have to be carried out and the inquiry would take its course. All the same, Fredrik was certain the conclusion would rapidly become clear: Kajsa Breien had been the victim of a crime.

So obvious, he thought. So striking that it must have some significance. This could not be mistaken for a suicide. The killer wanted it that way. There was something demonstrative about the body dangling from that thick blue rope. It conveyed a message somehow and Fredrik Smedstuen was apparently the first to understand that. He dug his mobile out of the pocket in his leather jacket.

'That theory of yours,' he said sotto voce when Birger Jarl Nilsen answered with a terse 'Hi, Fredrik' at the other end. 'The one about the perpetrator not wanting to leave the smallest shred of doubt that Linda Bruseth was the victim of an assassination at Grünerløkka—'

'Yes?'

'I'm starting to believe in it.'

The other man did not respond. The photographers were busy finishing up at this point and it seemed as if the time had come to take the Supreme Court Judge down from the tree.

'It's possible I'm wide of the mark,' Fredrik went on, still almost in a whisper. 'But it may be that we've an intended reprise up here at the edge of the forest. We've found something that looks like a suicide, but only at first glance. Instead it's a case of murder. Without a doubt.'

'I have to admit I'm not quite following you here, what—'

'Meet me at the office,' Fredrik interrupted. 'I'll be there in half an hour.'

The Neighbours

Selma Falck knew she had to pull herself together. She was angry, scared and upset. It would have been wise to wait until she had recovered her equilibrium before visiting her neighbours on the fourth floor, but she simply couldn't. She just had to find the answer to how an old handball that had vanished when she was thirteen years old had landed on her balcony forty years later. And so she simply had to speak to her neighbours before they went out to work.

Selma stood at the front door of the apartment with the left-hand window above her balcony, as viewed from below. From inside she could hear sounds of footsteps and voices but no one came to open the door. Her finger touched the bell yet again. After a few seconds, a man's voice said hello, presumably into the intercom at the main entrance. Selma knocked on the door.

'Hi,' said the man who opened it immediately. 'Oh, it's—'

'Selma Falck,' Selma replied, smiling, as she held out her hand.

The man was carrying a little girl, probably aged about eighteen months, on his right arm. For that reason he used his left hand to shake Selma's, twisting round to grip it.

'Sorry,' he said with a smile. 'It's a bit busy here in the mornings, but would you maybe like to ...'

He glanced to one side, looking along the hallway, Selma guessed at a wall clock.

'Shit,' he said through gritted teeth. 'We're running really late, could you come back—'

'Hi,' Selma said smarmily to a woman who came into view over his shoulder. 'I'd really like to have a few words with one of you. But of course, if it doesn't suit, then—'

'Come in,' the woman replied. 'Stein-Ove needs to run, Vilja has to get to nursery and he has to go to work. But as for me ...'

The man had stepped aside. The woman's belly was so enormous that the birth should have taken place a couple of weeks ago.

'Twins,' she said, patting herself on the belly button, as if used to sympathetic looks and even anticipated them. 'But accompanied by SPD as a result. Bloody awful. I'm on sick leave. Come in.'

She introduced herself as Johanna and Selma followed her into the living room. A rumpus could be heard from the hallway as the toddler loudly protested against putting on her outdoor clothes and clearly had no plans to go to nursery. Johanna ignored it all and sat down gingerly on the settee with a grimace of pain so severe that it made Selma wonder whether she ought to leave.

'Sit down,' Johanna panted. 'It's so nice to have a visitor. I come from a small village in Hedmarken and I'm not really used to all this distance in the big city. I've seen you from time to time, a genuine superstar, and had thought it would be so lovely to ask you in for a cup of coffee some day. Just between neighbours. But Stein-Ove ...'

She nodded towards the hallway, where it sounded as if Daddy was winning a hard-fought victory.

'He's from here. Quite literally. He grew up in the building that stood here before it was demolished and this block was built. He says people mostly leave others in peace. Coffee, by the way?'

Selma did not have the heart to inflict pain on the woman by asking her to stand up again.

'No, thanks, no need. I've come straight from the breakfast table.' Her stomach grumbled at the very idea of food. 'I won't bother you for long, I've just—'

'You're not bothering me at all! I'm bored to death in this condition.' She patted her stomach with a disapproving expression on her face as if an enemy was living in there. 'I don't have very many friends here in the city and every break from Stein-Ove and Vilja is really welcome. Well, I don't mean that the way it sounds, honestly, they're the best in the whole world, but you know ...'

Johanna chattered away nineteen to the dozen. Selma was scarcely listening. Instead she looked around as discreetly as possible. The hallway here was smaller than the one in her apartment. Or the hall, as the pretentious estate agent had called it. On the other hand, the living room was slightly larger. The kitchen was hidden by a half-wall, not simply by an island as in Selma's place. From where she was seated, she could see out of the south-facing windows. There were three of them.

'Such a lovely apartment you have,' Selma said when Johanna finally stopped to draw breath. She got to her feet and walked decisively towards the windows. 'My goodness, the outlook from here is even better than from my apartment!'

'Yes, the outlook was one of the things we really fell for. And the location, of course, both Stein-Ove and I are within walking distance of our jobs. He works at Lilleborg, directly opposite the Sandaker Centre, you know? As I said, I'm not actually working at the moment, I ...'

Selma was still not listening. She had moved across to the window on the far left. According to her calculations, it should be immediately above her own balcony.

'We miss having an outside space, though.'

The panting and gasping noises told Selma that Johanna was struggling to get up.

She leaned all the way into the glass and looked down.

It was the back yard, with bicycle racks and a sandpit with a lid for protection from cat excrement. And a set of swings that had fallen apart a few weeks ago.

This was the wrong window.

As Johanna tottered across the floor, Selma realized there must be a room on the other side of the living room wall: probably a bedroom with a door leading from the hallway.

'Yes,' Selma said, flashing a broad smile at Johanna. 'I'm lucky to have my balcony. Six square metres isn't much but it's truly wonderful in the summer months. Facing south-west, it gets plenty of sun.'

Johanna nodded. She had come all the way up to the window and was using the narrow windowsill for support. 'But you can't have everything, as my father says. Anyway, it would have been a bit scary with regard to Vilja. She clambers all over the place, high and low. Especially high. She's a wee monkey, our Vilja. Look at this …'

She pointed at a device on the window catches.

'Child security. On all the windows, of course. Did you know that Eric Clapton lost his son when he fell out of a window from a great height in a skyscraper? Not Eric Clapton, his son. He was only four or something like that. The little boy, of course.'

She shuddered visibly. 'Eric Clapton was a very well-known musician at one time,' she added by way of explanation. 'American.'

Selma repressed a smile. 'He still is pretty well-known,' she said. And very British, she thought.

Johanna had barely turned twenty-five, in Selma's view, and had not been born when Clapton wrote 'Tears in Heaven'. She had probably not even heard the song, but she was certainly afraid of heights. She had hesitated to go all the way up to the window.

'The view costs extra, of course. We would really have preferred to live on the ground floor. But then on the other hand it's easier for burglars to break in. There are a lot of them here in the big city, I hear. The agonies of making a choice.'

Her laughter was not really heartfelt. Her stomach was so huge that she had to lean back to keep her balance.

'I thought you had a window above my balcony,' Selma said. 'But clearly I was wrong.'

'No, not at all! Vilja's room is in there.' She pointed at the wall. 'She's got the biggest bedroom. Quite simply because she wouldn't fall far if she did succeed in opening the window. Just straight down to you. I'm really terribly scared of falls like that.'

Her laughter was shrill this time.

'But in truth it's far enough down to there as well, so we've also nailed the whole window down. These things happen, nearly all the time, children falling. I don't know how people get over that kind of thing, I really don't. Just imagine the feeling of guilt! And on—'

'Nailed down? Have you nailed down the entire window? How do you let air in, then?'

'These child security fixtures allow us to open the windows a crack, so it's not—'

'Not here, but in Vilja's room. How do you manage it in there?'

Johanna closed her mouth, for about the first time since Selma arrived. She was a fairly small woman in all other areas apart from her belly, and now she gazed obliquely and rather sceptically up at her surprise guest. 'Why do you ask? Don't you think we make sure there's enough fresh air for—'

Selma raised her hands and took a half-step back. 'Yes, of course! It's just ...'

Once again she had to make that unwelcome little pause before launching into a lie. It annoyed her and she coughed ever so slightly before continuing: 'I'm going to apply to the management committee to have my balcony door changed, you see. It's too narrow, it's impractical. Difficult to get the furniture in and out. I store it in the basement in winter and have to take it apart first. Because of that ...'

She was out of training and felt the need to add yet another reassuring smile.

'... it might be necessary to set up a little ladder down there on the balcony. That was what I came to warn you about, in fact. So if I could take a peek, just to—'

Johanna was smiling from ear to ear. 'A ladder to change a door! On a balcony!'

Now she was laughing heartily.

'You city folk are easily fooled. You let tradesmen do far too much. The bills shoot sky-high because of that sort of thing. It's not at all necessary to use a ladder.'

She had begun to waddle towards the hallway again, one hand clutching the small of her back. She used the other one to beckon Selma.

Vilja's room was an explosion of pink. Even the floor and ceiling were rose-coloured. At a sign from Johanna, Selma crossed the floor, stepping over age-appropriate building blocks and Barbie dolls she could not comprehend why anyone would let an eighteen-month-old child play with. Once she reached the window she could rapidly confirm that Johanna was telling the truth. The window was nailed down, in a fairly amateurish way, but effective in preventing anyone from opening it. Almost certainly illegal, she also reckoned. She rested her forehead on the glass.

There was her balcony. The handball was invisible from here; it still lay in the far corner where she had found it.

'There's a ventilation system here,' Johanna said, pointing at a ventilator high on the wall close to the ceiling. 'In your apartment too, I expect. Totally unnecessary to air the room. If it gets too stuffy, we just open the hallway door.'

'Yes, of course. Good idea, that.' Selma placed her hand on the windowsill, where a huge nail had been driven through the wood around the glass and on into the wall.

'Better safe than sorry!' Johanna said.

'Agreed. But then at least now you know there might be some building work going on. If the committee agrees to it, that is. It's far from certain, of course. I should maybe think it over a bit more. Picking a fight with the committee here is ...' She put on a discouraged expression.

'I know,' Johanna said expressively. 'So good of you to let us know. Then I'll know what's going on if anything happens. Are you sure you don't want coffee?'

'Yes, sorry, but I have to go, in fact. Do you know ...'

She picked her way back through all the toys.

'... anything about the people who've bought the apartment next to you?' Selma's thumb pointed over her shoulder.

'Well, not really ... I did knock, just after they moved in. I thought ...'

Selma walked past her into the hallway.

'Well,' Johanna continued, 'it doesn't matter. They're a married couple. Older than us, but with a little boy about the same age as Vilja. I did once manage to exchange a few words with the man of the house.'

Selma had reached the front door by now.

'So lovely,' she said enthusiastically. 'A playmate in the next-door apartment!'

'If only that had turned out to be the case. She's a diplomat. The wife, that is. They're stationed in America or somewhere. Or maybe it was Australia. They were here only a couple of times before they left. I think they painted the living room. And put in a lot of boxes. Really nice people, I'm sure, but as I said ...'

Yet another grimace contorted her face.

'I think you should go and lie down,' Selma said. 'I'll leave now. But do you know if anyone looks after the apartment for them?'

'No,' Johanna groaned. 'I don't think so. At least I haven't seen anybody, and there's never any noise from in there. No sign of life, in fact. They haven't labelled their mailbox downstairs either. With their names, I mean. Just one of those little notes saying no to unaddressed advertising material. Probably don't want their box chock-full of junk mail. Oh my God ... you're right, I do need to lie down.'

Selma opened the front door. When she turned to leave, Johanna had already set off on the painful journey across the living room floor.

'By the way, do you know what they're called?'

'Heimdal,' Johanna groaned. 'At least he is. Torstein Heimdal. The boy's name is Lukas. Or Luka. Leonard? Something like that.'

Selma repeated the man's name three times to herself as she left the apartment. The door closed behind her.

'Torstein Heimdal,' she said, out loud this time, but had already forgotten what the son was called.

The Hypothesis

An unsettling spell of heavy rain had come pouring down on Oslo. Inspector Fredrik Smedstuen was soaked to the skin when he jogged into Police Headquarters in Grønland after leaving his car in a multi-storey car park in Platous gate. His space there cost three thousand kroner a month. The spluttering 2008 Kia had become his third-dearest item of expenditure, after child maintenance and the racketeering rent for the filthy basement at Korsvoll.

Birger Jarl Nilsen was already in the office and sat with legs crossed, reading a newspaper he must have brought with him.

'How the hell did you get in?' the inspector muttered as he wrenched off his leather jacket.

'It was open. Is it a problem? I've only been here two minutes.

I got you a coffee.' He pointed to a paper cup on the desk. 'Large. Black. Three lumps of sugar.'

Fredrik Smedstuen also tore off his pale-blue shirt and threw it down in the corner. He didn't bother to hold in the flesh that wobbled above his slightly-too-tight belt when he had to inch his way behind his visitor's back. From the cupboard there he produced another identical shirt.

'I should have a stash of trousers here too,' he said irritably. 'How have you managed to stay so dry? Christ, you'd think the skies had ripped open up there!'

He nodded out the window and up to the sky as he buttoned his shirt and returned to his seat.

'An umbrella and waterproof overshoes.'

'Overshoes,' Fredrik mumbled. 'How old are you, actually?'

He pulled the lid off the paper cup. Steam belched out, so the coffee was still piping hot, but nevertheless he took a great gulp.

'Bad weather was forecast,' Birger Jarl said, 'You have to keep up, you know.'

Fredrik flipped off his shoes and tugged off his socks with a faint groan. He held one up in the air and said: 'If it had rained any harder, I might as well have swum here!'

He crumpled his socks and tossed them into the corner as well. The air in the small office, already clammy with dampness, heat and coffee aroma, now also took on a hint of smelly toes.

'You asked me to come,' Birger Jarl ventured.

Straightening his shirt collar, Fredrik leaned forward, elbows planted on the desk, his hands wrapped around the cup.

'Yes. This theory of yours ...'

He hesitated, and Birger Jarl made the most of the opportunity: 'If by theory you mean that Linda Bruseth was the target for the attack at Grünerløkka, then it's not a theory. It's a fact. I've explained all my investigations, analyses and conclusions in this note.'

He took out his mobile phone and tapped his way to something. 'Sent it now.'

A ping came from the Inspector's computer. However, he made no move to open his mail.

'I was thinking more of what you mentioned here the other day,' he said instead.

'What was that?'

Birger Jarl put on a smile that seemed forced. The guy could really be very annoying. Always smartly dressed, slim and with sharp eyes, and a hairstyle that gave two fingers to people like Fredrik Smedstuen. For him it was increasingly difficult to arrange what little hair he had left in a way that looked presentable. The two sides of his receding hairline were about to meet in the middle of his crown. The tiny island of tufts just above his forehead was combed back in a fan shape to conceal the horror, but it took so much gel that he always looked untidy. Birger Jarl, on the other hand, to all appearances had a thick, youthful mane, but kept his head almost entirely clean-shaven so that the rampant growth of stubble merely outlined a hairline that a seventeen-year-old might be happy with.

What's more, the guy smelled great.

'You know what I mean,' Fredrik said crossly. 'The thing about choosing an attack ...'

He fixed his eyes on the other man's and waved his right hand to encourage him to speak. To no avail. With slightly raised eyebrows, as if he did not understand what Fredrik was asking about, Birger Jarl folded his arms across his chest.

'That ... that about choosing,' Fredrik stammered before starting over again: 'That because the perpetrator chose to be so open—'

'He wasn't open. He was very well hidden. To the best of my knowledge you haven't found a single trace of forensic evidence.'

'That's an exaggeration.'

'Oh? Have you come across anything?'

'We'll see. I didn't ask you to come here to discuss forensic evidence.'

Fredrik opened the desk drawer and took out a packet of *Nicorette*. The foil crackled as he pulled out two tabs and dropped them in his mouth. Just as he was about to replace the packet, he changed his mind and took out another one.

'Your theory is based on that, A ...'

He raised his thumb.

'... Linda Bruseth was the target. B ...'

Now his index finger was held up in the air.

'If the point was only to kill her then there were many other far simpler ways to do it. And C ...'

A third finger emerged from his closed fist.

'... there must be some kind of message in that. The perpetrator *makes a statement*, so to speak.'

Birger Jarl tilted his head from side to side with an almost imperceptible grimace.

'Well. That's more or less what I believe. Apart from A, though. As I said, it's not a theory. It's absolutely certain.'

'Nothing is absolutely certain. You'd know that if you worked in the police. Properly.'

His colleague did not answer.

'What on earth would the statement be, then?' Fredrik demanded.

'I've no idea. As you said yourself, I don't work here.'

'Do you think it's about her per se, then? I mean in a personal capacity?'

'I can't possibly know that. But if you agree with me about this theory you've more or less outlined, I can see it's most likely she was killed because she was a Member of Parliament.'

'She's scarcely spoken a word in the couple of years she's been sitting there. To tell the truth, I'd never heard of the woman before she died. Had you?'

'Yes.'

Fredrik regretted having asked. The man on the other side of the desk was a know-all. But undeniably also tantalizingly knowledgeable. Smart. Inaccessible. He was considered one of the country's unquestionably outstanding professionals in his field, but no one had ever seen him on the firing range apart from when he was working as an instructor. Now he was brushing away some invisible crumbs from his trousers, and once again it looked as if he was smiling.

At what, was impossible to say.

Fredrik had never entirely understood Birger Jarl. He was distant, though friendly in the main. While the staff at headquarters knew most of one another's business, either because they were friends or because the whole building was one vast, buzzing rumour mill, Birger Jarl gave nothing away. He came and went, according to when his presence was required, by fits and starts. A year ago Fredrik had grown so curious about him that he had taken a surreptitious peek at his personnel folder. It was held in a physical archive in the Superintendent's office. Old school, he had refused to give up on the paper files that, with their simple locks, must contravene every law of data protection. Fredrik had stolen the opportunity to read his CV one morning when he was, as usual, early for a meeting and the Superintendent had forgotten to lock the cabinet.

Birger Jarl Nilsen had started his military career in the UNIFIL forces in Lebanon at the tail end of the seventies. After that he had been a paratrooper with a number of deployments abroad, from the Balkans to Afghanistan. He rose fairly rapidly through the ranks to begin with but came to a standstill at the rank of major. In his final years in the military, it was unclear what he was actually engaged in, which probably meant the Secret Service. Three years ago he was appointed to a part-time post in charge of sharpshooter training for the police force. Such an area of responsibility, in addition to assisting the Oslo Police when called upon in cases where his professional expertise was called for, nevertheless did not make him into a policeman in Fredrik's eyes.

On the contrary. Birger Jarl was an eternal soldier.

The Superintendent's folder had said nothing about the man's civilian status, but to judge from the narrow ring on his right hand, he was married. And had been for some time: the gold was dull and worn.

There was something impressive about him, something enviable, in the way he both conducted and expressed himself. No beating about the bush. Calm, logical reasoning. Women had an especial liking for him, Fredrik had noticed, and he could understand why. At the same time there was something vaguely threatening about him.

At any rate, his immaculate appearance made him extremely infuriating.

'So what you're saying is that the assassination was a kind of ... *message*.'

Birger Jarl nodded. 'Exactly. And if anyone knew what it was all about, then a solution would be just round the corner.'

Sitting up straight in his chair, he lifted his coffee cup. Fredrik had never seen him look irritated before but now, as he glanced at the clock, his brows knitted in annoyance.

'We talked about this earlier,' Birger Jarl went on. 'On the phone you mentioned a similar case. Something about a suicide that might be a homicide. Wasn't that why you asked me to come? What kind of case is it?'

'Exactly as you said. An apparent suicide that obviously isn't one. So obvious that there might as well have been a placard hanging round the woman's neck with a message about phoning a murder investigator without delay.'

'The woman?'

'Yes. Not just any old woman, either. A judge in the Supreme Court. The best known of them all.'

'The Chief Justice?'

'Nobody bloody well knows who the Chief Justice is,' he said crankily. 'Of course I'm not talking about her, I'm referring to Kajsa Breien. She seemingly hanged herself last night or thereabouts. In Marka, just a couple of hundred metres from the built-up area at Korsvoll. Near Grinda, if you're familiar with the locality.'

Now at least the other man's interest had been really roused. Holding his chin in his hand, he ran his index finger across his smooth-shaven cheek. 'How can you be so sure it's not a genuine suicide?'

'Kajsa Breien was less than five feet tall, and disabled. Considering her handicap, she was very fit. But not so fucking frisky that she could climb up to a branch two or three metres above the ground without anything to stand on.'

Opening his *Nicorette* drawer, he produced a blank sheet of paper and a pen and quickly sketched a map of the crime scene. In a low, logical voice he explained as he drew. The birch tree. The bushes and undergrowth all around, but no other tree close enough to be of any use whatsoever to Kajsa Breien. And not a trace of anything that could have been used as a ladder.

It took him barely five minutes to describe all the details he had noted. Once he had finished, he pushed the paper across the desk. 'You see?' he asked.

Birger Jarl nodded. He turned the paper round to face him and studied the drawing. 'And this is just a couple of hundred metres from a residential area?'

'Yes, and maybe forty metres from the path. Which is really a forest track at that point.'

'Remarkable.'

'Er ... yes. That's what I'm saying.'

'I mean the choice of location for a possible suicide is pretty striking. She lived in Bygdøy, didn't she? In her childhood home?'

'Yes. As far as I remember from some interview or other, she did. With a husband and a whole heap of children.'

Birger Jarl was sipping his coffee now. 'Suicide is a fascinating phenomenon.'

'I'd prefer to call it a fucking tragic pile of shit.'

'That too. But what we don't understand, have never truly got to the bottom of, is always fascinating. People taking their own lives can come like a bolt from the blue, or it can be something the closest relatives have steeled themselves for over a long period of time. It can come as a bombshell, or obviously after a carefully thought-out plan. Travelling to the other side of the city after getting hold of a rope, sounds like the latter.'

Fredrik knew he now regretted this entire meeting. Discussing reasons people chose to end their lives had not been why he was keen to speak to Birger Jarl.

'She hasn't taken her own life!' he said heatedly.

'No. Because then she'd scarcely have done it in that particular spot.'

Fredrik opened his mouth to say something but changed his mind.

'Of all the people who take their own lives after careful planning, most are pretty considerate,' Birger Jarl continued. 'If they choose to do it at home, they usually attach a note to the door first, with a message to say don't go in, and to ring the police. Others choose to travel a great distance. To a cabin, out to sea, into the forest—'

'This *was* in the forest,' Fredrik broke in, grabbing the sketch and waving it in the air.

'Yes. But it was in a fairly busy area. As long as it's light, there are kids playing there. The people who live on the edge of the forest use the first hundred metres or so as a park. A play area. What's more, the place is full of hikers and joggers.'

'And so?'

'She risked being found by a child. I actually think a woman like Kajsa Breien would never have done that. She has five children herself. Also, she'd risk the absolutely obvious – that someone would see her and try to stop her.'

'In other words,' Fredrik gave him a quizzical look, 'you're agreeing with me?'

'Yes. Based only on the few facts you've given me here, I am, actually. And in that sense, this case has certain similarities to the shooting in Grünerløkka.'

Fredrik was aware his pulse rate had gone up a notch. He tugged at the neck of his shirt and drained what was left of his coffee.

'Two well-known women,' Birger Jarl said.

'Linda Bruseth was extremely anonymous.'

'Yes, but she was a Member of Parliament. Another similarity is that both murders, if this latest one is indeed a murder,' he nodded in the direction of the drawing, 'is that they're, how can I put it, spectacular. Dramatic. Almost ...'

While he searched for a suitable word, Fredrik beat him to it: 'Aggressive.'

'Yes, there's something aggressive, but all the same precise, about both these acts. Again, given what we were talking about—'

'Yes, yes, yes.' Fredrik interrupted him indignantly. 'You don't need to make that qualification all the time. There are only the two of us here. Anyway, you've to keep this to yourself. The dead judge isn't even my case.'

Yet, he thought. If he managed to convince his boss that the cases might well be linked, the older case would take precedence. He would be allocated both. A few random thoughts spun in cahoots with Birger Jarl Nilsen, who was not even a member of the police force, was nevertheless far from sufficient to persuade anyone to let him combine the cases. He would have to be patient.

'I need to find out if they have anything in common.'

'They're both women.'

Fredrik heaved a deep sigh. 'Along with half the population! One was tiny and the other enormous. One comes from Oslo's most patrician area, the other from a farm in Vestfold. One was an A-list celebrity and the other people had hardly heard of. One was so efficient at her job that she was strongly tipped to take over as Chief Justice when the present incumbent retires next summer. The other has, as far as I've uncovered till now, been a catastrophically bad MP. No one even knew who she was.'

He glanced up testily from his cuticle, which he had been scrutinizing intently.

'Well, apart from you, of course. But then you know everything.'

Birger Jarl did not respond. He was preoccupied with pulling on his overshoes on top of the elegant black footwear that had probably cost just as much as a month's parking in Platous gate.

'We're done now, I guess,' Fredrik mumbled. 'Thanks for coming.'

When Birger Jarl stood up and put on his jacket before grabbing his umbrella and turning round, without a word, Fredrik added: 'I mean that. Thanks a lot. You're a good conversation partner. And don't forget your newspaper.'

Birger Jarl did at least turn round again.

'That NAV scandal is really horrendous,' Fredrik said, gesturing towards the screaming headlines in *Dagbladet*. 'I'm glad I'm not the one who's been responsible for sending people to prison for no good reason. A policeman's greatest fear.'

'People are subjected to far worse injustice from the public sector than being locked up for a few months,' Birger Jarl said. 'You should have been a politician, you know. There's so much unfairness out there. Just toss the newspaper. Phone if you want me for anything.'

'How much was the coffee? I can give you the money!'

Fredrik's shout came just too late. He could hear rubber squeaking on the flooring, increasingly faint, until both Birger Jarl Nilsen and his overshoes faded into the far distance.

The Catastrophe

Selma Falck was still breathless after her run to the *Circle K* petrol station in Alexander Kiellands plass and back again. Her left arm was no longer particularly painful when she ran. Only a little pressure around it and on the wound, which was healing well. The old handball had stayed more or less firm for a few minutes after she had pumped it up down there, but by the time she got home to Sagene it was almost as limp as before. Nothing else could be expected.

The inner bladder had already started leaking forty years ago.

Selma was standing in the back yard. Someone had forgotten to replace the lid on the sandpit. The slip-up had brought its own punishment: she had spotted two lumps of cat shit already disintegrating after the heavy rainfall that morning. For a moment she had considered doing something about the mess, but then she decided there were enough parents of young children in the block to take responsibility for that sort of thing. Instead she stood a couple of metres from the bicycle racks and gazed up at her own balcony.

Viewed from below, she totally agreed with the critical voices in the locality. They had still not been silenced, almost six years since the building's construction was completed. When Selma had moved in just over eighteen months earlier, it was one of the first comments she had encountered: that balcony should never have been built. Of the twenty apartments with walls facing the back yard, Selma's was the only one with an outside space. It looked like a wart, or a fungus, an embarrassing, parasitic growth high up and splat in the centre of the otherwise smooth grey façade. No one could understand what on earth the architect had been thinking.

However, the balcony was Selma's, and a real blessing as far as she was concerned.

Lars had estimated the distance from the ground as eight or nine metres. From down here it looked more, maybe ten. But it should still be possible.

At least with a firm, well-inflated handball and if you were at the peak of a successful career. And could find the right distance from the wall and weren't also struggling with a shoulder injury. Selma Falck was a middle-aged woman who now played handball for fun once or twice a week. The next-door back yard prevented her from coming far enough out from the wall to make optimal use of the force in the throw.

Also, it was impossible to blow it up properly.

She had to try all the same. Standing as far back as she could against the neighbouring property's fence, she calculated height and distance. Tossed the ball from one hand to the other to get the feeling of it. Lifting it to her face, she breathed in a whiff of sweaty games halls and wax, of childhood and age. Letting it rest in her right hand, she moved her foot back with a slight bend of the knee. For a second she shut her eyes and tried to remember what it had been like. Fast break. The ball had just been caught. The wing had started running some time ago, she knew that, without seeing it, without having to think she could throw the ball to a point over there where her team-mate would be standing immediately after the ball had left her hand. Passing hard and with absolute precision.

This was more difficult. Far more difficult.

She opened her eyes and threw.

The ball's trajectory was correct. If the force had been greater, it would have landed on Selma's balcony. Instead it slowed in an elliptical curve to reach the top of the second floor before turning and starting to accelerate again until it hit the wall of the first storey with a quiet smack.

'What are you up to?'

Lars Winther had stopped on the footpath leading from the wide, open entryway. Sitting on a ridiculously flimsy bike with racing handlebars, he had a bag on his hip with a diagonal strap over his shoulder.

'Just a bit of fun, that's all.'

Unruffled, Selma walked forward and picked up the ball.

'Were you trying to hit your balcony, or what? If so, you're an optimist!' He stared sceptically at the ball. 'That one looks as if it's a hundred years old.'

'It very nearly is, in fact. Why are you here?'

'I've been trying to get in touch with you for the past twenty-four hours!'

'Sorry. I saw that. I've had too much to do.'

'I need to talk to you. Are you any further forward with,' he looked around, scouting in every direction, 'that you-know-what? The zip file? Have you found someone to help us?'

Selma did not answer. Instead she went back to where she had been standing when she had thrown the ball. Once again she took the measure of the wall with her eyes. Fixed her gaze on the balcony. Judged the distance and the ball's potential curve.

The conclusion was self-evident.

With a smaller, heavier and harder ball, she would have succeeded. In her active career she would most likely have hit the target with a new, fast handball. But it was not so easy with this particular ball.

She looked at it, holding it in the stiff fingers of both hands and twirling it slowly round. Her initials were carefully written with great panache, **SF**, she could remember having practised on greaseproof paper. Satisfied at last, she had cut into the paper with her father's carpet knife and tried to use it as a stencil. It hadn't worked, but in the end she managed to make her mark freehand.

'How did you know I was here in the back yard?' she called out.

'I rang the doorbell. A woman who came out must have seen which bell I was pressing because she told me you were round the back.'

Selma nodded. There were probably a good handful of people in the block who knew she was here now. Who had probably peered out in curiosity at the unsuccessful record attempt with the old, threadbare ball. No one could stand here doing anything like that without being seen.

The ball must have been dropped down from above.

Not from Stein-Ove and Johanna's apartment, that seemed clear.

'Torstein Heimdal,' she said under her breath.

'What did you say?'

'Nothing.'

She snatched the ball with her right hand and approached Lars. Without saying a word, she continued towards the entrance. She could sense him swiftly locking his bike on to the rack and before she reached the main door facing the street, he had caught up with her again. With his saddle tucked under his arm.

In continued silence, they both walked in, taking the stairs, two steps at a time. Selma unlocked her front door. She felt a touch of relief that she was not alone.

'Have you heard that Kajsa Breien is dead?' Lars said all of a sudden.

'What?'

Selma turned open-mouthed towards him as the door slid closed behind them.

'I just heard it on the radio,' Lars said, tapping his finger on one of his earbuds. 'Nothing about what she died of. But there are rumours flying that she took her own life.'

'Kajsa Breien? The judge? Taken her own life?' Selma laughed out loud, but it sounded strange even to her ears. 'To tell the truth, that's the stupidest thing I've heard for a long time.'

'Did you know her?'

'We studied together. Or more correctly, at the same time. Partially. She's younger than me, but then she also took her law exams in record time. The smartest person I've ever met. We've worked together a couple of times since. A couple ...'

She wrenched off her sports jacket and kicked off her running shoes.

'... of those "disabled health issues" things. An incredibly nice woman. And as I said: razor sharp. Full of vitality. And zest for life. She met a guy in the law faculty that she married, of average height, and they've been together ever since.'

'But you didn't really know her properly, did you?'

'Well enough,' Selma said, growing irked. 'More than well enough to be really surprised if she's committed suicide. When is this supposed to have happened?'

'This morning or thereabouts. The family, in conjunction with the Supreme Court, have just sent out a brief press release about her death. A colleague just phoned me, the tip-off phone was on the point of collapse with all the messages about her having been found dangling from a tree in Marka this morning. Very close to Kjelsås. Or Korsvoll. Up there somewhere.'

Selma, halfway across the living room on her way for a shower, came to a sudden halt. She stood for so long in the same position that Lars sat down at the table and exclaimed: 'Suicide can come as a shock even to close relatives. You can't know anything about this, Selma.'

She made no response. Something had occurred to her. Something that was difficult to grasp. A fleeting thought, a line of reasoning that eluded her. She registered Lars taking out Jonathan Herse's folder from his shoulder bag and placing the memory stick in front of him on the table. She realized that she found this annoying. She should not have let him come up with her. She did not want to help him. The only thing she had the energy to concentrate on was finding out who was bothering her. And putting a stop to it. She wanted to recover her equilibrium and the strength to persuade Anine to see that everything was the way it had been before. She had only one aim in mind: to spend time with her grandchild.

'I need a shower,' she muttered. 'It takes a while with this bandage on. Give me ten minutes.'

When she returned, Lars was on the phone. Selma was still drying her hair with a voluminous towel. When she twisted it into a turban and draped the bundle of fabric over her good shoulder, she saw that Lars's face had gone a deathly shade of pale. The hand holding the mobile was visibly shaking. Selma sat down on the other side of the table, perfectly still.

Lars finally put down the phone.

'What is it?' Selma asked. 'You don't look well, Lars.'

'Leon's been taken to Ullevål. He was knocked down half an hour ago.'

Selma felt a rush of adrenaline through her body, the same jolt of fear she had fought against so many times in her battle to survive on Hardangervidda.

'What ... could he die?' she blurted out, and regretted it immediately.

Leon was Lars's eldest son, in his second year at primary school and just turned seven the previous week. He had a Tintin quiff exactly like his father, ice-blue eyes and like his dad, was a real whizz on a bike.

'He was cycling,' Lars whispered. 'And ended up under an artic lorry. His life's in danger, Selma. My boy's life's in danger.'

Selma knew she ought to make a move. She ought to sit down beside him. Take his hand, perhaps, they were good enough friends for that, and ask if she could help him. Drive him to the hospital, possibly, or lend him her new Volvo. Something of that kind. Instead she remained seated, overwhelmed by her own fear. She was ashamed of that. It was not Leon she was thinking of. Not Lars either, despite him looking as if he could drop down dead where he sat.

Selma was thinking only of Skjalg. Of what she would have done if he had been the one who was seriously injured. She, who had scarcely used up a single calorie worrying about her own children when they were little, and far less when they had grown up, now pictured everything that might actually befall a small baby. A catastrophe-filled film flickered behind her eyelids. Cot death. Injuries through falls and various illnesses. Kidnapping. She gasped for breath and was about to say something when Lars suddenly sprang to his feet, grabbed his bag and legged it.

'I can drive you to Ullevål!' she yelled, but too late.

He was already hurtling out of the apartment and halfway down the stairs.

Frustration

Fredrik had wasted far too much time staring at the wall. By nature he was an insecure man. Now and then he could even be depressed, but right now he felt absolutely ill at ease.

It had taken him an hour and a half to extricate himself from the idiotic cul-de-sac he had been dangerously close to blundering into. It was impossible to see how Linda Bruseth's killing had anything at all to do with Kajsa Breien's murder. The fact that Birger Jarl Nilsen's imagination was running riot in that direction would have to be his problem. He did not work here. Fredrik was an experienced investigator and should really know better than to indulge in vague feelings and wild speculations. It must be frustration that had played a trick on him.

Inspector Smedstuen was a policeman of the grey type and knew this himself. He did what he had to do, no more nor less, and followed the rules to the letter. Not because he necessarily found this right, but because it was simpler that way. The colossal, curved Police Headquarters building in Oslo's east end was full of stories about men and women in the force who had got into hot water through taking liberties. One of them was due to enter his third round in the court system later that autumn with the threat of a life sentence for corruption and smuggling cannabis hanging over his head. Before Fredrik's own time in the Oslo police, a legendary couple had roamed the corridors here. The woman was called Hanne Wilhelmsen and she had managed to get shot in the line of duty. Her own fault, according to what was said. God only knew what had actually become of her after she ended up in a wheelchair. Her sidekick was known only as Billy T – Fredrik had never heard his surname mentioned, and he had gone completely off the rails a few years ago. In the end he took his own life, poor bastard.

The police force no longer had room for cowboys, and that was all to the good.

Rules were in place to make life simple and to protect both officers and public. There were no shortcuts in police work. Cases had to be built stone by stone and nothing good had ever come of empty theories. Fredrik Smedstuen never speculated about a perpetrator's motives before he had completed thorough preparatory work. He had a predilection for forensic evidence. It seldom lied. Fingerprints and DNA and weapons. Forensic science. Facebook posts and photographs. Electronic traces. Tangible, indisputable facts. If you were painstaking enough with these, in the end they would lead every investigator in the right direction. His clear-up rate was ranked somewhere in the middle, but he could live with that. The tactical part of an investigation had never been his forte, at least not the part that included interviewing witnesses. Fredrik Smedstuen was quite simply not particularly good with people, something his ex-wife had reminded him of every day without exception in the last three years before their separation had become a reality.

Firing up his computer, he logged in and located the Linda Bruseth case. The picture was from her own Facebook profile, a full-length one, taken outdoors in a field. Round face, rosy cheeks, broad smile and a lamb sucking on a bottle between her chubby legs.

Facebook had also solved the very first problem Fredrik had faced – finding out who knew the three friends planned to meet in Grünerløkka on Thursday 5 September at three p.m.

The entire world could acquire that knowledge, as it happened – at least the majority of them if they were at all interested. The woman had actually posted time and place on her own wall two days in advance. Her account was public, in common with most politicians. Admittedly, Linda Bruseth had only 769 friends and just over 200 followers, but anyone at all could peek at her cards.

If they could be bothered. She wrote about committee travels and political processes in such a boring fashion that Fredrik could not bear to read it all. What's more, she must be a dyslexic with her auto-correction program turned off, for her posts were bristling with orthographic errors. All the same, it was chock-full with fiftieth birthdays and newborn animals, cycling grandchildren, cornfields to be cut and close-ups of mother's homemade meatballs on a plate. And also quite a lot about Selma Falck.

Linda Bruseth had clearly been very proud of being a friend of the popular private investigator. A real friend, not this new-fangled expression of friendship that involved no more than having met each other once or twice. In the autumn of 2018, she had posted almost daily updates with links to the many stories about the scandal Selma Falck had wrapped up. Around the same time, Linda had pinned up four photos from the eighties in rapid succession, all with one thing in common – they showed Selma and Linda together. Three of them were taken on the handball court and one of them was from something that must have been one hell of a party. Linda double-posted in Facebook and Instagram and was fond of hashtags.

#selmaforpresident #oldbuddies #thosewerethedays

The strangest aspect of all was, however, that she intimated future meetings. Most of such manifestations of friendship on social media consisted of photos of the actual event. Smiling people around a restaurant table. On a mountaintop. Skiing. Lots of places intended to reinforce the impression of being success-ful and surrounded by friends. For Linda, this was obviously not enough. She had to announce things in advance, presumably through sheer happiness.

He caught himself feeling a bit sorry for her.

As for him, he had an absolutely dead account on each of the four major platforms. He had no need of social media apart from a handful of useful groups, most of them loosely related to his job, such as the shooting team and the police veteran car club. *Butterflies in Norway* and *The World of Lepidoptera* were the only groups he derived real pleasure from following. He had started collecting butterflies as a young lad. Admittedly, his collection had to be kept at his old parents' home, as his ex-wife had not wanted a house full of dead insects, as she put it, but he was proud of it.

Friends, on the other hand, were people he met properly. He drank a beer on Fridays with five or six old student pals from Police College. He was invited to dinner parties. It was seldom a problem to phone someone prior to the weekend and arrange a meet-up, his divorce notwithstanding. Some of his friends were even female.

Fredrik Smedstuen had *friends*.

In real life. They were not people he needed to show off or boast about. After spending a couple of hours studying Linda Bruseth's life on the Internet last Saturday, he thought he could discern the outlines of a woman who always longed for home. Who should never have come to the big city, far less let herself be elected to Parliament. Her life lay in the village, in what was known and dear to her and where her somewhat bulky appearance was regarded as a sign of physical strength and good health.

Fredrik had not yet been able to speak to Ingolf Bruseth, Linda's husband. Their eldest son had come to Oslo only two hours after the murder and asked nicely to have his father left in peace for as long as possible. Fredrik had warned him that an interview would be necessary in the near future, but had said that as long as the sons were available to the police, it would be acceptable to wait for a few days.

Those days had already gone by. The three eldest boys had given their statements, but the police were not one centimetre closer to an explanation for why anyone would want to take the life of this good-hearted countrywoman.

Fredrik had no great expectations that the widower would be able to contribute anything much to solving the case either. The information that had been gathered on him, mostly from Facebook and two or three articles in the local newspaper, drew a picture of a settled and fairly taciturn farmer, who never ventured any further than ten kilometres from home. To him, Sandefjord was a big city. The couple had married young, when Linda was still goalkeeper in the national handball team, but Ingolf had not travelled abroad with her to see a single match.

It was difficult to leave the animals, of course.

Fredrik scrolled through a number of other interviews. Three of them he had not read before, but none of these told him anything more than he already knew.

The documents from the crime scene examination were even more discouraging. The reconstruction had been successful in that it was now pretty clear what had actually happened. On the roof, where the gunman had most likely lain low, however, no significant discoveries had been made. It was also uncertain how he had made his way up there. The possibilities were numerous. The surrounding buildings were closely packed and some of them extended into the back yards. It would have been a simple matter for the killer to stroll in through the open entrances leading from the street to the back yard and then use one of the three available ladders lying conveniently beside the brick wall. He could also have moved across the roofs from virtually anywhere in the entire neighbourhood. What was strange was that no one had spotted him. At least up till now not a single person had reported any suspicious movements, neither across the rooftops nor through the warren of courtyards behind the buildings. Fredrik had ordered two new recruits to collect all the CCTV footage available in the surrounding nine blocks. He had forced overtime upon them that, strictly speaking, he had no authority to sanction and they had already gone through hundreds of hours. Without finding anything of interest.

It was as if the man were a ghost.

Fredrik opened the desk drawer to find his pack of cigarettes. He needed a break. The warning about dreadful premature death screeched at him from the label and he hesitated. He shut the drawer without even taking a piece of gum.

'Why the hell would anyone want to kill you?' he muttered to the onscreen picture of Linda.

This was the direction he had to take. Maybe he would break one of his few principles. Since the crime scene examiners and other technicians had so far come up with zilch, he should probably be a bit more modern in his approach. Searching for a motive without having anything other than the crime itself to build on was not really his style, but this was a situation he had never faced before. Exactly a week after the murder, the investigation was still directionless. The numerous interviews, abundant reports and countless forensic investigations, none of them had told him anything useful.

'Why did you have to die?' he asked again, louder this time.

By finding the reason Linda had been killed, he would find the perpetrator, no matter how clever the guy had been at concealing both himself and his tracks.

The guy.

He caught himself having decided that it was a man. He should not do that. Keeping an open mind was important. All the same, it was almost impossible to imagine a woman endowed with the physical capabilities this murder demanded: a good shot, an athletic physique, a sharp brain and the ability to plan carefully.

'Fucking gender fascist,' he mumbled as he opened the drawer.

He fished out a cigarette with half-closed eyes to avoid reading the terrifying propaganda. A moment ago he had considered going out for a smoke, but now he merely walked to the window.

Of course a woman could be athletic, smart and good at shooting. He opened the window. Lighting a cigarette was a startling breach of the rules but he couldn't be bothered doing anything else. Three mega-puffs later, his head had cleared a little.

Selma Falck was such a woman. She could have carried out such an attack. Quite apart from her having verifiably been at the other end of the gun sight, in a pavement café.

And being shot in the arm.

Without paying much heed to that. During the reconstruction she had not seemed in any pain at all. Even though she had worn a sling round her neck, several times he had noticed her take her arm out and use it as normal.

She was tough. Hard as nails. She had demonstrated that last year. She was sharp too. And really lovely as well. Age made no difference when someone kept herself as fit as she did.

He took another deep drag of the cigarette and let the smoke seep slowly out from his nose and on out the window. A warm sense of calm spread through his body. Even his clothes felt dry now. Maybe he should postpone his attempt to quit for a while. Until New Year's Eve at any rate. Another three months of smoking now and again could not possibly make much difference to his health, considering he had been a smoker since the age of sixteen.

Selma Falck knew Linda Bruseth. They were friends. If anyone could help him to find a possible motive for the murder, it was her. Maybe she was the very person. Maybe she was the *only* person, when he came to think of it. In a way she was a colleague. Previously he had disliked private investigators. Despised them, to be honest, at least if they lacked a police background. Investigation was both an education and a lifestyle and not a role that old journalists or lawyers for that matter could just jump into without so much as a by your leave.

Selma Falck, though, was one of a kind. He had to admit that. Logging out of his computer, he grabbed his mobile phone and located her number almost immediately.

It could not do him or the case any harm to ask her to join him for a coffee.

Emilie

Selma fiddled with her phone, reading the exchange of texts over and over again.

Anine, is there any chance I can meet Skjalg one of these days? A walk with the pram, perhaps? I can look after him for as long or short a time as you like. Hugs from Mum.

That bit about 'hugs' was maybe too much. When she had received no answer after an hour, she sent another one.

Hi! Did you get my message? I'd really love to see my grandson. Looking forward to hearing from you.

Idiotic, she could see that now. There was a veiled rebuke in the wording. She sounded miffed, almost condescending. When this message brought no response within a reasonable length of time, she tried again:

Hi Anine. I understand you have a lot to do and realize too that you're angry with me for some reason. I'd really like to talk to you about that. But can you please let me look after Skjalg? I can come up to your place, and then I could just take him for a walk in the pram, just in the neighbourhood. Love from Mum.

It took only five seconds for the mobile to ping.

You realize I can't let you walk around pushing my son in the pram anywhere whatsoever when someone is shooting at you in broad daylight? Honestly. Give over, Selma.

She did so. In normal families she would probably have been invited to see him in his mum's house, if present circumstances were considered so terribly sinister. Normality was unfortunately not a suitable description of the relationship between Selma Falck and her children, so she simply gave up. This was a battle she could not win.

Selma was aware of her own strengths and weaknesses. She always had been. Even as a four- or five-year-old she had understood that she could not reveal all of herself. When her parents had decided to travel home to Norway from the USA with two children and a lucrative patent in their luggage, life had changed totally. An existence balanced between the hippie era and Silicon Valley, in which the children had mainly looked after themselves, was exchanged for bourgeois, wealthy west-end living. Little Selma could no longer wander around barefoot by day with no thought for whether there was going to be time or money for a proper dinner. Her mother, who had really been the brains behind her father's lucrative patent for use in prosthesis manufacture, gave up work. Until then she had shown middling interest in her children. Once back home, the two youngsters had to be moulded into a shape she found suitable for the inhabitants of a villa in Smestad at the beginning of the seventies. When the patent also turned out to be useful in the oil industry, the regime grew even stricter.

Selma learned everything in record time. If she humoured her mother, she had peace. Even praise, on occasion. If she tried to be what she had spent four short years being, all hell broke loose. Since she really preferred her own self, she developed the art of being two people. Mummy's girl was well groomed, obedient and excelled at school. Selma, on the other hand, was an inventive tomboy, driven by adrenaline even as a toddler.

Her parents never knew her. Her brother Herman did, but he was no longer alive. Their upbringing had taken them in two different directions. Herman's disposition had been melancholy. Selma became expert in the art of camouflage. She became captivated by sport and obsessed by being best at everything. He read books. In the last years of his life, he had sat in a dusty, secluded university office at Blindern. He never finished his doctoral thesis, which was about an eighteenth-century writer whose name Selma could not even remember.

Once Selma was grown up, it grew increasingly easy to dissemble. Her mother had taught her to please others. This brought her friends and popularity. She had learned to nurture the real Selma, something that also involved never really committing herself to anyone. No one except her brother. A free person was someone who could turn her back on everything without suffering any personal loss. The strategy had proved to work almost perfectly. On only two occasions had she needed to break with something or someone. When her brother died, it was a catastrophe. She had locked herself in for two whole days. When she emerged, she never spoke of him again. When she had been forced to endure a sudden break with both her work and family life at one and the same time less than two years ago, it had felt blessedly simple. Both of these entailed a turn for the better.

Selma Falck considered herself vaccinated against sorrow and revulsion.

Now, as she sat at her combined dining table and work desk, she was overcome by despondency.

It should have been for Lars's sake. Strictly speaking, she should have gone up to Ullevål and found out if she could help in any way. There was probably nothing she could do for them right then, but Lars and his wife had two younger children. Selma could offer to pick them up from school. Maybe provide some food. She could make some coffee and take it to them in a thermos flask – there was actually a long list of things a person could do for someone else in a crisis situation. Big or small.

She just sat there.

The message that Kajsa Breien was dead had shocked her. She had difficulty taking it in. The woman had five children and a husband, and was also a treasured member of the highest court in the land. She had not yet turned fifty. It was all a tragedy, quite apart from whether or not she had really taken her own life. Selma ought to be moved, to feel something. Momentarily, while Lars was still with her and she had not yet headed into the shower, it had been as if a flicker of interest had been aroused within her. Some aspect of the story seemed odd; there was a hint of something that gave her vague associations she could not quite pin down. Since then, she had shoved it all away. Kajsa Breien had nothing to do with her. Now she let her eyes drift between the picture of Skjalg on the wall and the folder Lars had left behind in his rush. The memory stick lay there too. Selma, uninterested in either of these, pushed them aside.

Right now she had only one aim: to be permitted to see her grandson.

This was what she had to concentrate on.

Her stalker had to be exposed, her apartment made safe and Anine somehow mollified.

The police had not yet said anything officially about Linda Bruseth having in fact been the target of the assassin. It upset Selma that they were being so secretive, and it occurred to her that she should get in touch with Inspector Smedstuen. He had to appreciate the distress caused to her by everyone going around believing that an attempt had been made on her life. She could show him the messages, thirty-seven in total, she had received from the press about the incident, ten texts and six phone calls from *DG* alone. She had not replied to any of these, which did nothing to reduce the pressure.

She decided she would demand an explanation.

Anine would calm down if the police confirmed it. The uninvited guest who had left childhood mementoes dotted around Selma's apartment was fortunately a subject of which Anine knew nothing.

It was only this awful inbuilt lie detector of hers that stood in the way of a truce anytime soon. For a child who had spent less time with her mother throughout her childhood than the majority of kids, she had an astonishing ability to read Selma. She would notice her disquiet. Maybe the worst thing of all would happen and Anine would come to believe that her mother had started gambling again.

Maybe that was exactly what she should do.

Just one night on her computer would work wonders. This restless, physical ache in her muscles and joints, insomnia and sporadic lack of concentration, would all be so much better if only she could spend a few hours at the virtual poker table. Anine was refusing to see her anyway. It would almost certainly be a week or so before they met. At least. If Selma played the tables only tonight, or maybe even right now, probably enough time would have passed to allow her to deceive even Anine.

Her hands were trembling slightly as she drew the laptop towards her and opened it. Her fingers tapped in the familiar codes. The sight of the animated pack of cards on the American gambling site's home page had the same physical effect on her as always, a welcome jolt of anticipation that cleared her mind and quelled all her angst. She was about to log in when her phone rang. She jumped out of her skin, as if Anine had suddenly stormed in through the door and uncovered what her mother was up to. She slammed the lid down on the Mac and grabbed her phone.

Fredrik Smedstuen, according to the display. She waited a couple of seconds, accepted the call and put the phone to her ear. 'Hi there,' she said as nonchalantly as possible.

'Hi. Fredrik Smedstuen here.'

'Yes, I saw that.'

'I was just wondering if ...'

It sounded as if he was breathing heavily in and out. It dawned on her that he was smoking.

'Could we meet for a coffee?'

'Coffee?'

'Yes.'

'Why, though?'

'I've a couple of things I'd like to discuss with you.'

'About the case?'

'Er ... yes.'

'Is there anything new?'

'There's always something new.'

Yet another mega-drag of the cigarette, she heard, followed by a hiss of exhalation.

This was a possibility. This was exactly what she needed.

'When were you thinking of making public the fact that I was a chance bystander?' she asked. 'It's pretty annoying that everyone seems to believe I was the target.'

'You know enough about police work to know we keep our cards close to our chest in the preliminary phase of an investigation.'

'A week has already passed.'

'We ... we're at something of an impasse, to be honest. I had hoped you could help me. You've known Linda Bruseth since your teenage years. We've interviewed Vanja Vegge in great depth but nothing much came of that, unfortunately.'

'You have at least learned her name, I notice.'

'What?'

'Nothing.'

'So, what do you say? Could we meet? Fairly soon?'

Selma did not answer. All of a sudden there was something new in his voice. Something vulnerable, almost appealing. She stared at the flat laptop. Fredrik Smedstuen had saved her from a major error.

'When, then? Today, do you mean?'

'That's not possible, I'm afraid, I've to … What about tomorrow? What time suits you best?'

Selma took plenty of time, as if she had to check her diary. 'I've got a space around noon. We could have lunch.'

'Good. Great. We could find somewhere near you, so it's less bother. The *Sagene Lunch Bar*?'

It was a hundred metres away. Selma accepted and rang off.

'Saved by the bell,' she thought with an oblique glance at her MacBook. It was almost twenty-four hours before her meeting with the Inspector. She would have to find something to do in the meantime. Of course she could go out for yet another run, or go to the *Artesia* gym to exercise. That helped to relieve tension a little, she knew, but not for much more than the duration of time she was engaged in it.

Leon could be dead.

Lars was having a dreadful time one way or another. Right now. Selma sprang to her feet so abruptly that the chair clattered to the floor. She had to go to Ullevål, that idea ran through her head once again, when her eye caught sight of the memory stick.

If Leon died, the contents would mean nothing to Lars.

If the boy survived and was not too badly injured, then access to the locked zip files would mean rather a lot. She seized the red memory stick and held it in the palm of her hand, already working out methods of cracking the code. Her ideas were either hazy or strictly illegal.

She jumped to the conclusion that sometimes the simplest approach was the best.

Lars had mentioned that Jonathan had a live-in girlfriend. Even though Selma had always kept her passwords to herself, she knew couples often shared information about each other's. She made a speedy Google search on her phone and took only a few seconds to find Jonathan Herse's death notice.

♥

Our beloved son,
My best friend and sweetheart,
The kindest big brother and uncle in the world,
Jonathan Henry Herse
Born 27.03.89
Was cruelly taken from us on 17 August 2019.
Tobben and Berit
Emilie
Kasper and Julia
Liam
Friends and the rest of the family

The funeral was to take place five days later and everyone was welcome to a gathering in memory of him in the FAFO Conference Centre in Grønland.

So her name was Emilie. In common with around 3,000 others of similar age. They were not married, so her surname was not Herse at any rate. Selma began a random search. Jonathan and Emilie. Emilie loves Jonathan. Jonathan Herse and Emilie.

Bingo.

The first summer's day of last year.

Jonathan Herse and Emilie Karina Sundet were sitting on

rocks on the beach at Huk, in light clothes, with broad smiles and a disposable barbecue between them.

The announcement by *Dagbladet* that the weather forecasters were promising twenty degrees Celsius for the first time that year told Selma all she needed to know. The young girl also helpfully had a double-barrelled name. It would be easy, Selma thought, and this was confirmed by a perusal of the online phone directory.

Emilie Sundet would probably be at work at this time of day. Another search revealed that she was an administrator in the City of Oslo's Planning and Building Department. This was probably one of the busiest public services but Selma reckoned that incoming calls would be directed via a central switchboard to landlines in the various offices. In the business world it was becoming increasingly common to have all-in-one phones, Selma could not comprehend why, but it would in any case be worth taking the time to make an attempt.

Nevertheless she hesitated. This issue had nothing to do with her.

She had enough on her plate. On the other hand, this was something she could actually do for Lars. And for herself, she realized when she mulled it over again, since just sitting still was proving unendurable.

Emilie Karina Sundet answered the phone after only one ring. She had such a heavy cold that her response was a distracted 'Ebilie?' Selma did the same as always: she smiled so broadly that it could be heard loud and clear.

'Hi! My name's Selma Falck. Am I disturbing you?'

'Er … no.'

She said 'doe', in fact, and Selma hoped she was in bed, well wrapped up with cosy quilts.

'I'm at home, off work today,' the muffled voice continued. 'Terrible cold, as you can probably hear. By the way, are you … do you mean *that* Selma Falck?'

Selma laughed softly. 'Yes, yes, I'm Selma Falck. I don't know if there's anybody else with that name.'

'What do you want of me?'

Selma picked up the memory pen. It felt cold in her fingers.

'It's to do with Jonathan,' she said gently. 'About a story he was working on before he died.'

'What?' A crackling noise came over the phone as Emilie coughed violently.

'A story,' Selma repeated. 'One he never got finished. And he's left behind a memory stick I'd really like to talk to you about.'

More coughing, followed by a loud sneeze. When Emilie was finally able to talk again, Selma was unsure whether or not she was crying.

'I don't really know how I can help,' she said. 'We chatted now and again about what he was doing at work and so on, but this last while before the accident he was … a bit distant, if you know what I mean. I thought maybe … I don't really know.'

'He was working on something that might seem quite complicated,' Selma said. 'And it might be best for me to pop in to see you.'

'Now? Today?'

'Well, yes. It's fine for me, if you can put up with a visitor. Is there anything you need? I could do some shopping for you. Just a short visit.'

'Yeees …' Emilie Sundet was hesitant. 'Give me some time to have a shower, then.'

'Of course. Shall we say in three quarters of an hour? Bergensgata 4, isn't that right?'

'Yes. Right above the *Mat&Mer* restaurant. And … could you bring me a latté with oat milk?'

'I'll do that, with pleasure.'

The call was disconnected. Bergensgata was five minutes away, so Selma had plenty of time. Far too much time. Swiftly placing her laptop inside a cover, she fetched her big leather bag and peered out through the window. The weather was still fine. She stuffed the memory stick in her pocket but left the folder containing all the meaningless clippings about child welfare. Once she was out in the hallway, she shrugged on her Jenny Skavlan jacket and to be on the safe side, tucked a folding umbrella into the bag. Her arm was bothering her less and less so she took the sling out of her pocket and laid it aside. In three quarters of an hour she could manage to get herself something to eat before she paid Emilie Sundet a visit.

Yet again the thought of Lars and little Leon crossed her mind. She hoped the boy was not dead, because if so her efforts would be entirely wasted.

Piccolo

He was rarely here in daytime.

The vast graveyard was silent. Even the heavy traffic on the main road was muffled by trees and sadness, as if the huge cemetery were surrounded by invisible noise barriers. The gravestones were lined up in serried ranks, in sequence; no nonsense was tolerated in the Østre graveyard. He liked that. Christianity was a well-organized religion. He had always related to some kind of a God, even though he had rarely kept in his good graces. His outlook on life was like the rest of his existence, linear and simple. Something was right, something was wrong, but he retained the right to decide for himself which was which.

Grethe lay where she had lain for many years. Sometimes his head was filled with fantasies on his way to these meetings with his wife. He could imagine that she would be waiting there, large as life, with her shock of thick red hair and a picnic basket on the grass. They would have yet another stolen day together and the idea would be so intoxicating that his steps grew both lighter and faster. Afterwards he was always angry. With himself, for lapsing into a flight of fantasy, and with Grethe who might have been saved if only she had gone to the doctor's in time.

In daylight he hardly ever smoked.

Today he had not even brought cigarettes with him. Instead he had slipped a miniature bottle of sparkling wine into his jacket pocket, a *Henkell Trocken Piccolo* he had held on to after a flight. The size of the bottle was called the same as the wine, he seemed to recall. Piccolo, very small.

He was also carrying a folding stool.

There was no one to be seen near the grave. The violent rainstorm that morning had softened the ground. The grass must have been cut the previous day, perhaps for the last time this season. The carpet of grass should preferably have a little length before the frosty nights set in. He opened up the stool. It was small and somewhat rickety on the soft earth, but if he spread his legs and leaned forward, it was comfortable sitting like that.

He smiled at the gravestone.

'We're on our way now, Grethe. We'll soon have reached our goal.'

The bottle opened with a little pop. He waited until it had stopped fizzing and foaming over the spout before he put it to his mouth and drank.

'A little swig,' he said. 'Just a drop to slake the thirst. Not like it was that first night those two lovebirds got together.'

The thought made him smile again, more broadly now. He raised the bottle in a toast and took another gulp.

'It was so romantic. They were so in love. They enjoyed a bed-in, like the one John and Yoko had. But not for peace. For love. I'd never thought that our ... that our hopeless, strange, obstinate, handsome, beautiful boy would be able to ...'

His voice broke. He put the bottle down on the ground where it toppled over. Frothy liquid ran out over the grass, forming a circle that soaked in and eventually disappeared.

'It was love, Grethe. You should hear him talking about it. I'm so sorry you'll never get to know about it. That our boy, our ...'

He rubbed his eyes with the sleeve of his jacket. Grabbed the bottle and held it up to the sky. In the light he could spy a drop or two left. Once again he put the spout to his mouth and drank.

'I hope you'll forgive me for all I did wrong when you disappeared,' he whispered, placing his hand on the rough stone. 'At least when this is all over. When I've finished and the system has been shown in its true colours. That's important.'

Grethe was silent.

'It's important,' he repeated in a low voice. 'Those institutions must lay bare their own rotten state. Not the press. Not outsiders. The system itself must slowly come to see what I'm telling them. There's a certain beauty in that, Grethe. And deliverance.'

She still made no reply. She never did. Not here and not at night when he tried to conjure her up in bed beside him. Not at the breakfast table, which he still set for two, or on the Sunday walks when he had to stride out on his own where there had once, long ago, been three of them walking side by side.

If only she could begin to answer him.

The Zoologist

Emilie Karina Sundet lived in a brick-built apartment block that Selma presumed must have been constructed some time in the fifties. For the last half hour, she had been sitting in *Mat&Mer* on the ground floor of the building. She had eaten a boring salad while she read newspapers on her mobile. The NAV scandal once again consumed all the media – Selma was already tired of it. If she had still been a lawyer, it might have seemed different: a couple of the most high-profile defence lawyers had already insisted that no stone would remain unturned in the pursuit of justice for the people affected. That most of them had themselves been responsible for establishing the totally erroneous interpretation of the EEA regulations and thus contributed to the miscarriage of justice was something they spoke less loudly about.

Selma climbed the stairs to the second storey.

Emilie Sundet stood waiting in the doorway, wearing a yellow jogging suit that was far too big for her. The letters LSK were written in large black letters on the chest. Selma immediately assumed that the clothing had been taken from Jonathan's side of the wardrobe.

Emilie Sundet looked really full of the cold. Her complexion was pale but there were angry crimson half-moons at the sides of her nose. Her red-rimmed eyes were streaming. She sneezed emphatically as her guest arrived at the right landing, and Selma stopped abruptly.

'Excuse me,' Emilie said, stretching out her hand before suddenly withdrawing it and putting it behind her back. 'I don't want to infect you! Since you've just been shot and all that.'

'I've got the immune system of an elephant,' Selma said with a smile, stepping inside when the woman backed away. 'No danger.'

'They actually eat one another's excrement,' Emilie said, leading the way into a small living room.

'What?'

'Elephants. To strengthen their immune systems, among other things.'

'Indeed? Interesting.'

Selma looked around. The room must be about twenty square metres and it was crammed full. There was a bottle-green settee at the window, covered in colourful cushions. The coffee table, from the sixties, had seen better days: its legs were angled and there was a shelf below the dull, shabby surface for holding journals and newspapers. There had to be ten kilos of paper stacked there already. Selma noticed the *Scientific American* along with a whole heap of copies of *National Geographic*. A mountain of a magazine Selma had never heard of, called *Fauna*, was so high it had claimed space on the floor beside a mustard-coloured winged armchair. The arms were so worn that the stuffing poked out in several places. There were things everywhere. Tiny figurines of animals and buildings. Trays of jigsaws and piles of books. On a shelf beside what Selma assumed to be the door into the kitchen, she saw a collection of stones. The walls were almost blanketed in eclectic pictures, apparently entirely lacking any plan or organization other than an intention to cover ancient *Biri* straw wallpaper.

The apartment looked as if it belonged to an eccentric professor, unmarried and getting on in years.

'You take that,' Emilie said, pointing to the armchair, 'and I'll sit on the sofa over here, as far away from you as possible. And no. Jonathan was interested in his job. And in football. Not much else. As for me, on the other hand ...'

She tried to stifle a sneeze, without success. 'Sorry,' she said with tears streaming down her face. 'I'm a zoologist.'

'A zoologist? Don't you work in the Planning and Building Department?'

'Yes, I do. If you don't want to find work relevant to your studies, become a zoologist. Few employment opportunities for us in Norway. While I look, I have to earn money doing something else.'

Selma sat down.

'What are you after?' Emilie asked. 'Really, to be honest?'

Her irises were as pale a blue as it was possible to be without merging into the whites of her eyes. Normally she most likely took great pains applying makeup in the mornings, because her eyelashes and brows were almost chalk-white in their natural state. Her hair was thin and wheat-coloured. Selma scrutinized her as she went another round with the *Kleenex*.

Maybe she should quite simply give her the unvarnished truth.

'First of all I'd like to express my condolences on Jonathan's death,' she began, clearing her throat. 'Sincerely. It must be a difficult time for you.'

'Yes, absolutely, but worse for his family than for me. If it hadn't been for property prices being so insane here in the city, we'd probably have split up last summer. Since then he spent more time with his best mate than with me.'

'I won't trouble you for long,' Selma said in the hope of avoiding becoming better acquainted with this young woman. 'So I'll just spit it out ...' She raised one buttock slightly to allow her to dig the memory stick out of her pocket. 'This is something Jonathan left behind at work.'

'A USB pen drive.'

'Yes. It contains files that may be of journalistic interest to one of his colleagues.'

'Why isn't it the colleague who's asking me, then?'

'Because he's busy right now. I'm doing him a favour.'

'OK. I thought you were a detective. But how can I help you? By the way, you look more like that American actress in the flesh than in photographs. Far more, in fact.'

After Selma had finally talked in an in-depth interview on NRK just before Christmas about her physical similarity to Mariska Hargitay from the TV series *Law & Order: SVU*, it had virtually put an end to people commenting on it. Which was a blessing. Selma felt her irritation level rise.

'I guess so. What I need is the password.'

'I don't know it! We didn't talk about things like that.'

'Are you sure? Is it OK if I try some combinations?'

'For heaven's sake, go ahead.'

She grabbed a tube of *Mentholatum* from the table while Selma took out her laptop. Once she had unscrewed the cap, she squeezed out a generous blob of the transparent, ill-smelling salve and rubbed it well into the skin under and around her nose.

'What's your date of birth?' Selma asked as nicely as she could manage.

'What are you going to do with it?'

'Try a few codes.'

'23 April.'

'What year?'

'1995.'

Selma mulled this over for a few seconds before trying the most obvious.

Emilie230495

Wrong password.

Emilie23041995

Wrong password.

Selma had far more experience than Lars in coping by herself on the IT front and was not afraid of the device locking down completely or erasing the file after three incorrect passwords. She therefore continued these attempts with increasingly convoluted combinations of Jonathan's flatmate, who was perhaps not really so much of a girlfriend, and her date of birth.

'Are you getting anywhere?' Emilie asked, sipping at the oat milk latté that Selma had set down on the table.

'Not really. Has Jonathan had a dog? A cat? Any other pets?'

'Good God, no! He was terrified of animals. Scared out of his wits. No interest in animals whatsoever. That was one of the things we kept arguing about. I wanted a dog. Or best of all, a terrarium. Now the way is clear, I guess. I'm going to get myself a huge agamid lizard as soon as I can afford it. A couple, actually. So that I can have babies. Or at least, so that they can have babies.'

Selma was beginning to have a deeper appreciation of the reasons this relationship had not exactly been a resounding success.

She should never have come.

'I'm not getting anywhere,' she said, packing up her laptop. 'But it was worth a shot. Thanks for being willing to help.'

As she rose from the chair, her eye caught sight of a collection of photographs displayed on a shelf. One in particular captured her interest. She took a couple of steps closer. A velvet mourning band was draped over the corner of the frame.

'Pretty grotesque,' Emilie said from the settee. 'It's on display mostly for the sake of appearances. For the minute, at least. Jonathan's parents have given one to everyone who knew him. Well, to everyone who was … close, I suppose. In my opinion a good photo of him while he lived would be a better memento. The one walking in front on the right, by the way, is the guy I just told you about.'

'Who?'

'Allan. Allan Strømme. Jonathan's best pal since they were at nursery together.'

The picture had been taken while the coffin contain-ing Jonathan's remains was carried out of the funeral chapel. Considering it from a photographic point of view, it was excel-lent. The angle was slightly low, bringing the pallbearers' faces into focus. All of them were men.

Emilie had got to her feet. Fortunately she refrained from approaching Selma and stayed a couple of metres away from her.

Selma paid no heed. She concentrated on the man at the front right: she was sure she had seen him before. Somewhere or other, fairly recently, but she could not recollect where.

'Allan Strømme,' she repeated softly. 'So where does he work, then?'

She did not need to ask. She suddenly remembered where she had seen him. It had been a picture in a newspaper. In *Aftenposten*, she thought for definite, when she and Lars had been searching for information about Alvhilde Leonardsen, Senior Adviser in the Ministry for Children and Families. The woman had been celebrating, surrounded by three perspiring men, members of the team that had taken twelfth place in the Holmenkollstafett relay race in the class *Open category, mixed, majority female*. It had beaten the Attorney General's office by seventeen seconds and was manifestly proud of it. Allan Strømme had stood on the outside edge of the group with a bottle of *Gatorade* in his hands.

'Allan?' Emilie said. 'Allan's a lawyer and sociologist. He works in the Ministry for Children and Families. Jonathan and Allan were thick as thieves. Since last summer they hung out nearly all the time, as I told you.'

She sneezed yet again before adding: 'It was almost as if they shared a secret.'

Lunch

It was certainly a lucky day. Despite the date.

Leon Winther had survived his dramatic encounter with an articulated lorry. By the skin of his teeth, according to the clear impression Selma got when Lars phoned her that morning at half past five. Since she was finally enjoying a good night's sleep, he could really have waited until later, but good news is difficult to bottle up, as we all know. He had sobbed on the phone and given her more details of the tense hours they had spent than Selma was really interested in hearing. As he had already woken her, she attached her earphones to her mobile and got out of bed as they talked.

While *he* talked, more correctly. And that he did. Kept going. Told her about a fractured pelvis and an operation that had taken seven hours. About a near-cardiac arrest and about his wife who had fainted in the end. About fantastic doctors and how much coffee he had poured down his throat. Finally she had to pretend the connection was broken. She immediately sent a text to prevent him from calling back: *Dear Lars, wonderful news! Use your energy now on your family and we'll talk later. All the very best in the world to you and yours from Selma.*

Leon was alive, so the visit to Emilie Sundet had not been a waste of time.

Soon Lars would be back to his usual self. This morning, fleetingly, Selma had been tempted to interrupt him and tell him about yesterday's stroke of luck in Bergensgata, but it would probably have been too early. He actually had more on his mind.

When she entered the *Sagene Lunch Bar* at five minutes to twelve, she almost regretted having agreed to meet Fredrik Smedstuen. She had spent the morning ascertaining that Allan Strømme still worked in the Ministry for Children and Families and that he lived in Mortensrud. Selma's initial impulse had been to phone the guy, something she quickly realized would be a stupid move. All logic suggested that he had been Jonathan's source in the MCF. It might even be that the sound recordings stored on the zip file on Jonathan's memory stick were his. If that were the case, then it opened up the possibility of obtaining the files without having to crack the password.

However, it was far from certain that the man would be willing to cooperate. A plan would have to be hatched and Selma would have to do that on her own. First of all, though, she had to go through with lunch as agreed.

She scarcely recognized him.

The Inspector was also early and already seated at a window table. The restaurant was practically empty. He had cropped his hair. Completely. His head was clean-shaven, leaving only a vague shadow outlining a pattern that revealed little fertile ground for his few remaining locks. His bushy mono-brow had been trimmed into two fairly sharp eagle's wings. His shirt, always light blue and crumpled, had been swapped for a freshly ironed white one. It looked good with the chinos she caught a glimpse of under the table. When Selma sat down, she noticed that he smelled as if straight from the shower, without as much as a hint of cigarette smoke or Fisherman's Friends.

'You're looking great!' she exclaimed. 'Really cool hairstyle.'

'Thanks,' he muttered, beckoning to the waiter. 'How's your arm?'

'Oh, that,' Selma said casually, touching the gunshot wound, on which she had changed the bandage that morning. 'Soon won't notice it any more. Healing up nicely. I'll have to get the stitches out soon.'

He pushed the menu towards her. 'Lunch is on me,' he said. 'Have whatever you like. Beer too, even though it's early in the day.'

'I don't drink,' Selma said.

'No. Right. I did know that.'

'I'll have a chicken salad, please. And a Pepsi Max, preferably with ice cubes. What was it you wanted to talk to me about?'

'You certainly get straight to the point!'

'That's probably best for us both.'

The waitress, a slender woman with pink streaks in her hair, approached them and Fredrik ordered the food and drink.

'Well,' he said when they were alone again, 'as you appreciate, it's about Linda Bruseth.'

Selma could not even be bothered nodding her head.

'We've reached the conclusion that she was definitely the one the killer had in his sights. Quite literally, so to speak.' His smile seemed almost sheepish and he quickly grew serious again. 'If it can stay between us, it's also about the only thing we seem to know.'

'No leads?'

'We're still at an early stage in the investigation.'

Selma leaned forward a little. 'That hackneyed phrase means only one thing,' she said sotto voce. 'That you don't have a damn thing. You should really find something new to say when you draw a complete blank.'

'Indeed. But ...'

He wriggled around in his chair as if he did not feel entirely comfortable in his new clothes. Or with his hairstyle either, since he kept running his hand over the unfamiliar bare scalp.

'To tell it as it is,' he said finally, 'we're really struggling to find a motive for killing Linda Bruseth. She honestly was an innocent country girl.'

'Well, she wasn't really as innocent as she looked,' Selma said, 'but I know what you mean. She really wouldn't have hurt a fly.'

'If you'll excuse the hackneyed phrase, it really *is* early in the investigation. We're going through her whole life. Finances, disputes, hostility ...'

He hesitated for a moment.

'... and politics. We've only just begun. But so far ...'

Now he spread out his arms in resignation.

'Everything seems shipshape,' Selma finished for him.

'Yes. At least in the private sphere. Emails, texts, social media accounts, call lists ... we've gone through them all. She seems to have had a very solid marriage. Her sons are pleasant and have turned out well, and the eldest has just announced that he wants to take over the farm. Exactly as his parents have always wished. Linda and Ingolf lived simply and there's nothing to put a finger on in their finances. Quite the opposite, they've saved some money. Not exactly a fortune, but enough to do up a house for their retirement when that time comes, with a reasonable sum left over. In their home village, she's not only popular, I'd say she was ...'

He smacked his lips as if tasting the word.

'... loved. Treasured. Very well liked.'

'Not so well liked in Parliament, though.'

'Well. I don't think there was anyone who genuinely disliked her. Not from what we've gleaned so far. It's more that she shouldn't have been there in the first place. Parliament was too big for her. I've spoken to two of her colleagues from Vestfold and they both say she wasn't going to be re-nominated.'

The waitress had returned with Pepsi Max and water. Selma

and Fredrik waited in silence for her to fill their glasses and make herself scarce.

'She didn't want to be either,' Selma said softly. 'In fact we talked about it last Thursday, just before she died. She really regretted having allowed herself to be seduced into a dead cert of a seat.'

Fredrik nodded. 'That's my impression too. The strangest thing of all is that ... you know, politicians in this country are subjected to lots of smears and all sorts of shit. On social media, in emails, texts, all over the place.'

'But not Linda.'

'Yes, she was.'

Selma realized she felt slightly flummoxed. 'No, we've talked about it a few times and she said she wasn't bothered by anyone.'

'But she was. Not much, and the messages she received were not among the worst I've seen. But all the same.'

'What were they about?'

'She was the spokesperson for a Schedule 8 proposal.'

He gripped his glass and drank half the contents before continuing: 'To be perfectly honest, I don't really know what a Schedule 8 proposal is, but—'

'Actually it's called a member proposal,' Selma said. 'It can have to do with the budget, legal issues or other things, but is moved by one or several members of Parliament. So it doesn't come from the Government, which would be the norm. Exactly like the major propositions, it is sent to the relevant committee, which later gives a report on it to Parliament. It's as if ... never mind.'

She was already sensing that the lunch had been worthwhile. That Linda had been spokesperson for a proposal to extend the opportunity for urgent decisions to be taken with regard to care orders by the Child Welfare Service was something she had already discovered last Monday. The information had allowed her to detect a very slender line of connection between Jonathan

Herse's unfinished journalistic work and her dead friend. At that time she had rapidly tried to dismiss it all as a coincidence. Now she felt less certain.

'In any case,' Fredrik said, 'these came to her in connection with that.'

He tapped his mobile for a few seconds before handing it to Selma. Taking it from him, she saw a Word document that quoted seven text messages.

We'll never forgive you for what you're doing, read the first one.

Not so bad, Selma thought, reading on.

The Devil will come for you. We know where you live.

Vulgar and comical was what ran through her head.

This proposal will lead to a further entrenchment of a policy that already contravenes both human rights and the children's convention. Watch your step.

'These can't really be regarded as threatening, to be honest.' She held the phone so he could see what she was pointing at before skimming through the last four messages. 'I've seen worse,' she said, returning the phone to him. 'Far worse.'

He nodded. 'Me too, as I said. Believe me. But ...'

Putting his thumb and index finger to each eye, he rubbed them hard. It looked as if he was desperately trying to wake himself. When he looked up again at last, his eyes were red.

'You've heard that Supreme Court Judge Kajsa Breien is dead?'

'Er ... yes! Yesterday's news, Fredrik. In both meanings of the phrase.'

'She seems to have taken her own life.'

'I don't believe that for a minute.'

He met her eye. 'You neither?'

The woman with the pink-streaked hair was back. She placed the salad in front of Selma and the hamburger with Roquefort cream before Fredrik, wished them bon appetit and departed.

They still had not relinquished eye contact.

'No,' Selma said finally. 'I don't.'

'I don't either. As soon as this case has been allocated to our patch, it'll be investigated as murder. It's so obvious it would make you laugh. If it wasn't so serious, that is.'

Neither of them touched the food. They did not even pick up their cutlery.

'Did you know her?' Fredrik asked. 'Judge Breien?'

Selma gave a slight shrug. She touched her gunshot wound, but let go almost at once.

'According to today's definition of the words "knowing someone", then yes. Definitely. And even though a surprising suicide is far from an unknown phenomenon, I was extremely sceptical, to put it mildly, when I … heard the rumours.'

'I've never met the lady,' Fredrik said. 'But I have seen the crime scene.'

He peered down at his food. Picking up his knife and fork, he warily cut off a piece. He got only a small morsel of the hamburger bun. Selma planted her elbows on either side of her plate and used her fist to support her chin.

'Dare I ask why you mention Kajsa Breien's name in relation to this?'

Slicing off a larger piece, he stuffed it in his mouth, chewing well for a long time. He popped in yet another piece and chewed some more before laying down his implements and wiping his mouth with a napkin.

'You may well ask, yes. The answer is a bit more …'

His right hand was raised level with his face, flat and palm down. He let his plump fingers teeter quickly from side to side.

'I don't quite know what to say,' he went on. 'But I'm walking around with a feeling there's something.'

'That's a bit vague, I'd say.'

'Yes.'

Selma knew exactly what he was struggling with. When she had first met Inspector Fredrik Smedstuen in the cleaner's cupboard at Ullevål Hospital what, unbelievably enough, had only been a week ago, he had been a stranger. Nevertheless she knew the type. She'd come across people like him throughout her career as a lawyer.

Fredrik was a passive policeman.

He wanted to stay on the safe side. Always. He never did anything wrong but just as rarely anything spectacular. Slowly and surely, he would tread carefully all the way to retirement age, a big, heavy brewery horse who never deviated from his regular route. He also knew it off by heart.

There was nothing wrong with such police officers. On the contrary, Selma's experience with them had been better than with the sharp-witted, eager beavers. In their defence, they were usually younger than Fredrik and as a rule envisaged such a bright future for themselves that they had neither the time nor the energy to concern themselves with boring investigations.

Very many police investigations were boring. All the same, they had to be tackled.

Behind facades such as Fredrik Smedstuen's there lay, every now and then, pure gold. That dogged patience and willingness to spend time could result in a fairly unique fund of experience. The man was obviously not lazy. He had a certain curiosity, even though he had used a great deal of energy in killing it off. When she had met him at the hospital, she had disliked him practically on the spot. Now she was not so sure how she felt. Something new had entered his gaze, something sharp and quick and appraising. He had plucked up the courage to ask her out but had not yet decided whether she was to be trusted. The way he sat there, with his cutlery alternately in his hands and on the table, she also saw a nervousness that was not entirely professional.

It was clear that Fredrik had realized a little too late that it was embarrassing to order an enormous hamburger when Selma had made do with a small salad. Now he was not quite sure how to devour it without emphasizing his excess weight. He took another piece and stuck his fork carefully into a roast potato.

'Come on,' Selma said, unfazed. 'This stays between us. What is it you ... feel? As far as this case is concerned, I mean.'

'These cases,' he corrected her once he had finished chewing. 'You remember Birger Jarl Nilsen?'

'Of course. I've met him twice.'

She smiled and added, 'For that matter, in your company. Both times.'

The policeman pushed his plate to one side.

'He thinks there's something strange about Linda Bruseth's murder,' he said, folding his napkin. 'Something apart from the fact it's incomprehensible. Something theatrical, as if the point was ...'

He licked his lips. His head had become shinier; he was sweating.

'It almost seems as if the killing in itself conveys a message,' Selma said.

Now he looked up in astonishment, gazing straight at her. His eyes were a little too close-set and practically piss-yellow: a cloudy shade of pale brown.

'I've spoken to Birger Jarl about this,' she said. 'Just after the reconstruction. I'm familiar with his theory.'

'Do you believe in it?'

'Do you?'

'Yes and no. I'd probably have let it go as pie in the sky if it hadn't been for this business with Kajsa Breien. Because the way I see it, Birger Jarl's theory also applies to her.'

Selma suddenly felt hot. She had not yet touched her food. Now she sat bolt upright in her chair and placed both palms on the table.

This was exactly what had struck her, she realized. Yesterday, before Lars had received the terrible news about Leon and while she herself was on her way to the bathroom for a shower. There had been a pregnant pause, but she had not been able to grasp the significance of it.

'Is everything OK?' she heard his voice ask, but it seemed very far away.

'Yes,' she replied, forcing a smile. 'I've actually thought something of the kind myself. Without quite being able to grasp it. But you're right. If Kajsa Breien's death really was a criminal act, then the perpetrator, by staging it as a suicide, absolutely made ...'

She froze for a second before shoving the untouched plate even further away and picking up her mobile phone. Just as she was about to Google something, Fredrik reached his hand out across the table and placed it over hers. She looked up in surprise, almost in shock.

'You don't need to Google it,' he said quietly.

His skin was warm and dry, strangely enough. He released her as if he had scalded himself. Then he leaned towards her and said: 'Norway has had three judgements against it in the Grand Chamber of the European Court of Human Rights in the past year.' He was speaking so softly that he might as well have been whispering. 'It's fucking serious, even though it hasn't created a huge stir here at home. There's a whole queue of similar cases waiting. As I understand it, the Norwegian Attorney General stands to lose most of them. Norway, Selma! Europe's self-declared beacon when it comes to children's rights is about to fall flat on its face in the international arena! And can you guess who was first to deliver a verdict when the two most controversial of these cases was decided by the Supreme Court?'

It was not necessary.

'Holy shit,' Selma said. 'That was what I was just about to Google. Whether she had been a judge in one or other of the most central children's rights cases.'

'I realized that.'

'So there's something about ... child welfare here?'

Now he was the one to smile, though he did not look particularly happy about it.

'Exactly. Maybe. And if that's the lie of the land ... those people out there, Selma, the ones who've had their children taken from them and have embarked on a crusade against the system, they are absolutely, completely ...' He tapped a curled finger on the side of his forehead and rolled his eyes.

'Do you mean that they might have—'

'I don't mean anything. Not at present. But there's some kind of connection here. Perhaps. A possible connection. I don't know. All the same, it's—'

'Shh.'

'What?'

'Shh,' Selma repeated pointedly as she closed her eyes. 'Wait a minute.'

Bright green dots danced before her pupils. She tried to relax and let her thoughts fall into place of their own volition. She must not exert herself. Not make any effort to be logical. She let her lips pucker slightly and took a deep breath through her nose.

'The three estates,' she said in the end, opening her eyes wide.

'What do you mean?'

'Linda was spokesperson for a Schedule 8 proposal that would expand the Child Welfare Service's powers. She did support the change but the findings of the committee were negative. The proposal was never carried. In other words, Linda doesn't have too much to answer for when it comes to child welfare. She could have been more of a ... symbol.'

'Of what?'

The waitress reappeared without either of them having noticed her approach. 'Don't you like the food?' she asked, sounding dismayed.

'Yes, of course,' Fredrik mumbled without looking at her. 'Just leave it, please.'

As she withdrew, slightly offended, Fredrik repeated: 'What would she have been a symbol of?'

'The Parliament. The first estate, the first branch of government.'

There was total silence. Selma picked up her glass of Pepsi Max and raised it to her mouth. Her throat was dry but her arm felt powerless. She had to lower it again.

Fredrik put both hands on his head and left them there. 'The courts of justice, where Kajsa Breien was a central figure, is the—'

'The third,' Selma interjected. 'The courts are the third estate. If Kajsa was murdered, and for the same reason as Linda, it doesn't have to be because she was first to bring in a verdict in some of the cases that have now been thoroughly condemned in Strasbourg. She too could be a symbol. Of the third estate.'

After a brief pause, she added: 'The Government, incidentally, is the second, as I'm sure you know.'

'Does that mean ... does that mean ...'

Fredrik could not get any further. Selma nodded all the same.

'Yes, she said. 'This means that if we're now on to something that has even a scintilla of substance, it's pretty risky to be walking about as a member of the Government right now. Considering the value of symbolism, which this killer is obsessed by if we really *are* on to something, I'd suggest that the Minister for Children and Families is in the greatest danger.'

Fredrik had visibly paled. He was still holding his head and dark circles had appeared in the armpits of his shirt in the last few minutes. His lips were moist and his voice quivered when he finally let his hands drop as he exclaimed: 'But what the hell are we going to do with this, Selma? *What the bloody hell do we do if this is actually true?*'

'Nothing. Absolutely nothing. It's all castles in the air. Figments of the imagination. We're just guessing, Fredrik, we don't know anything for certain. I'm afraid we can't do jack shit.'

As for her, she knew precisely what *she* was going to do, but there were limits to what you would be willing to share with a policeman.

Especially one she barely knew. What's more, she was busy.

The Interview

'What do you mean, you've "already done it"?'

Selma had walked so fast to Einar Falsen's apartment in Toftes gate that she was sweating. Now she sat in an armchair with a reasonably clean tumbler filled with water. It was not particularly cold, because Einar never had the patience to let it run for long enough through the dilapidated building's more than likely rusty and corroded plumbing system before he filled it. She pushed the glass away after a little gulp.

'You forgot to take the laptop from me when you were here last,' Einar grinned with satisfaction. 'And so I thought I'd make myself useful. And I have done. In the search for this staw-ker of yours, you could probably do with a helping hand.'

He looked like the cat who stole the cream as he sat with the laptop on his knee, using both aluminium foil and the grey-painted *Star Wars* cover for protection. Amazingly enough, he had not put on his helmet. Selma assumed he was too eager to remember his genuine fears about radiation.

'But what have you ... I mean, how ...'

Selma shook her head. When she had arrived five minutes earlier, she had asked him to try to find the young man who had made contact with her this summer. She had been out running, it had been 26 June, and the man had been outraged. He had looked like a junkie, his name had slipped her mind, and his story seemed nothing but tiny fragments of information that made the possibility of finding him absolutely minuscule.

'Have you really found out who he is?'

'Well, sort of ...' Einar hesitated slightly and his smile was no longer so broad. 'I don't really have his name as such, but I have ... come here.'

As usual, he patted the seat beside him on the settee. As always, Selma tried to chase the cat down on to the floor, but today the animal was unwilling to cooperate. Pussycat stayed put, lying between them, purring loudly.

'I've read in the newspapers that there are these child welfare groups on the Internet,' Einar said in a remarkably calm voice. 'They all have similar experiences of the Norwegian child welfare system being an abomination, that they're a bunch of chancers with one aim in sight, to damage other people. To steal children from decent folks. They use words like "child welfare industry", "human trafficking" and suchlike.'

'Yes,' Selma murmured, 'there are groups like that.'

'So I looked into what you'd told me about this man. There wasn't very much to go on. But there *was* something.'

He still hadn't opened the laptop. He was not using his hands as energetically as he usually did when he talked. It was as if he was trying to be what he had been such a very long time ago, a well-liked and respected policeman.

'The info I had to go on was that he was relatively young, so I thought under thirty. Also, he wanted to sue the Department. He also claimed he had been a victim of corrupt civil servants—'

'Don't they all?'

'Wait a second. You also said you thought he was a junkie who was going to ask for money. In other words, I knew four things about this guy.'

Nodding, Selma stared impatiently at the laptop.

'What I then thought,' Einar said, becoming increasingly enthusiastic, 'was that when he had the guts to flag you down like that in the middle of the morning, and got so agitated into the bargain, then maybe he'd already tried most other avenues? And maybe even contacted one of these groups I mentioned. It's obvious they gather online. Most of them have set up closed Facebook groups, but many of them have also got their own sort of … webpages. I've even managed to become a member of some of those closed Facebook pages, you know.'

Once again that grin. Selma had at long last got him to the dentist's last spring. Which had not been easy, and in the end she had been forced to use a specialist in dentist phobia in Sandefjord. For Einar, it was not the pain but the apparatus that was frightening. After a two-hour attempt at therapy, Einar had been anaesthetized. Three visits and fifty thousand kroner of Selma's money later, he was able to smile again.

'Finding them on the Internet,' Einar went on, 'is easy. You just Google "child welfare" and add a couple of negative words, such as "unjust" or "thieves" and they pop up. I must have found twenty webpages, each one crazier than the next. Apparently.'

'Not just apparently.'

'The picture is not completely black and white, in fact, if you read with an open mind. As of course you should.'

Finally he opened the machine that lay on his lap.

'I concentrated on three of the groups,' he said, bending down to the floor to pick up his helmet. 'The largest ones. And most professional.'

He fastened the strap tightly under his chin.

'Now let's see. The webpage *childrennotwelfare.no* seems to be the most serious of them. It looks like an online newspaper. It links to cases in the mainstream media but goes over the score in the comments section. It's not even a normal comments section, it's more of an invitation to write your own articles. There's a lot of weird stuff. A lot of anger. And an incredible number of spelling mistakes. There was one lady, from Stavanger, I think ...'

He burst out laughing and looked as if he was about to close the laptop already.

'Don't stray off the subject,' Selma said firmly, forcing the screen up again.

'No, not at all. Not at all. I'm not going off at a tangent here. Never.'

He pushed the helmet further down on his head.

'I concentrated on the period before and just after 26 June.'

'And?' Selma asked when he did not continue.

'I found nothing of interest.'

Selma gave a heavy sigh and swallowed audibly. She gingerly placed her hand on his. 'Can we skip all the webpages where you didn't find anything? And go straight to what you found instead?'

'Sure. Good idea.'

Using his index fingers, he stabbed at the keys to find a page called *theftofchildren.no*. It too looked trustworthy. At the top there was a link to an article written by a respected lawyer in the field of human rights. Immediately underneath was an interview with the Oslo City Council's Child Welfare Department.

'Let's see,' Einar said, and the eagerness had returned to his voice. He hit the keyboard so hard that the whole machine shook. 'Here we are!'

Now he tapped his fingers on the screen, equally hard. Selma was afraid for a moment that it might break.

'What's that?' she asked.

'An interview with an anonymized young man. Who does at least strongly resemble the person you described. It was published on 21 June, that is five days before you were contacted on that run of yours. I think I've read a hundred similar stories. This is the only one in which all four aspects are present.'

Selma lifted the laptop over to her own knee. This was almost unbelievable. She had come to Einar to get him started on a project that was practically doomed to failure: finding the nameless man who had reached out to her one summer's day nearly three months ago and to whom she had not given a single thought until relatively recently.

Right now she seemed to come across the topic of child welfare wherever she turned. Strictly speaking, she was devoting her time to three cases. The first was the story Lars had inherited from Jonathan Herse, which neither he nor Selma understood much of. The second was the one Fredrik Smedstuen had dragged her into, the mystery of finding a motive for the murder of the kind-hearted Linda Bruseth. The third, and in her opinion the most important case by far, was finding out who had sneaked uninvited into her personal territory and tormented her with little teasing signs that he had known her all her life.

She couldn't care less about Lars and Fredrik.

They were adults, each with a task here in life, and there was not much prospect of any recompense for all her bother. Normally she would have turned her back sharpish on Fredrik. It was not her job to help the police. As a rule she was happy to play ball with Lars, in the way they had assisted each other now and again in the past. She had helped him more than the other way round, so she could choose to shut that folder as well if she really wanted to. Deep down, she already had.

But there was a peculiar pattern here.

'Are you just going to sit there?' Einar said all of a sudden.

'Yes, just another minute. Just hold your horses for a second.'

Einar got to his feet and padded out into the kitchen. Pussycat jumped down and followed him. Selma concentrated hard on completing a train of thought that kept eluding her. It had to do with a potential client, inconsolable about child welfare, but obviously also furious with the child welfare system's overarching Ministry. The workplace, seemingly, of the chief characters in a strange, locked computer file left behind by a dead journalist. Linda for her part, killed in an apparently motiveless assassination, was a member of the Parliamentary Committee with responsibility for the cases the Ministry for Children and Families took it into their heads to send to the national Parliament.

Everything just kept whirling round and round.

'A dead journalist,' Selma said into thin air.

'What?' Einar asked, stopping in the middle of the room. He was carrying a bowl of cheese puffs for himself and a Pepsi Max for Selma.

'Nothing,' Selma said, shaking her head, more to clear her thoughts than to brush Einar aside.

The discovery of Kajsa Breien the previous day had further complicated the picture Selma was trying to uncover. It had all become like one of those images in which you had to run the pencil from dot to dot to see what was hidden within the pattern, but without anyone having numbered the dots. The Supreme Court Judge also had a connection to child welfare, and all indications suggested she too had been killed. In a very conspicuous fashion, to put it mildly.

'Honestly,' Einar said, almost brusquely. 'I've been working like a Trojan here, and now you're just sitting there!'

'Sorry.'

Selma was reading the interview. The man had been given the fictitious name 'Ola' and was thirty years of age. More than eight years earlier, he had fathered a child with his girlfriend. The relationship proved of short duration. For somewhat imprecise reasons, it seemed his pregnant partner had been ill and Ola had disappeared out of the picture. She was more established and Ola himself had plans to study abroad. When the child was three, the mother died of the same illness she had suffered from all along. Ola was not even informed at his address abroad. When he had finally headed for home in 2018, he learned of his ex-girlfriend's tragic demise. And of course was keen to take care of the child, his own flesh and blood.

It turned out to be impossible.

Ola's son was living with his grandmother and her new husband, who had made life hell for Ola ever since. They were in the process of adopting 'little Phillip'; probably that too was a made-up name. The Child Welfare Service showed no appreciation of the importance of a real father. They had picked his life apart in their pursuit of shortcomings, defects and reprehensible conduct.

There was always something to be found in a young man's life, as the author of the article vaguely alluded to. For a period he had used drugs. He had not always had a fixed abode. Now and again he had been short of money, the writer admitted, before moving on to describe Ola's numerous virtues, including being kind and intelligent. He now had steady employment, at least almost, and a place to stay as well.

Selma had heard this story before. Many of them. Far too many at the time when, as a young lawyer, she could not be fussy and had still accepted child welfare cases. A desperate mother or father, either together or separate, full of optimism at the idea of looking after a beloved child. As a rule it took no more than a little careful prodding at the veneer they had laid over their existence before it all unravelled. The living quarters were extremely temporary. The drug use was far worse than claimed. The job they cited was a stopgap and usually non-existent by the time the case came up in front of the Regional Social Welfare Board.

However, Ola went further.

He claimed the child's grandmother was employed by the Ministry for Children and Families. She had fiddled the paperwork and told lies about him. Submitted information that was untrue. Falsified documents to show he had scarcely known that little Phillip had even been born. She was able to do all this because she was part of a system that could not care less about a child's need to be loved and part of his biological family.

Selma gave a discouraged sigh.

'The boy *is* living with his biological family, though. With his grandmother. And with all the inconvenience that accompanies such a custody battle, I expect she must love her grandchild to the moon and back.'

'True enough,' Einar said. 'But I do feel sorry for the man, all the same.'

'That's the point. This story is concocted with that sole aim: to reinforce the impression on the reader that the Child Welfare Service is the work of the devil.'

'But it could still—'

'Why hasn't his lawyer been interviewed?' Selma asked rhetorically. 'If it really is true that there was reason to suspect forgery of documents and perjury from the highest level, then the journalist ...'

The quotation marks she drew in the air were gigantic.

'... should have asked him or her how the case was progressing. And most likely been served up an entirely different story. If it weren't for the lawyer having a duty of confidentiality, which means we're back where we started.'

'If I'm right, and this guy is identical with the one who wanted you to help him, he had no lawyer. He wanted to have you!'

'Exactly, then. But in the preceding wrangle, he must have had some assistance. He has a right to that. I'd bet he's in such straitened circumstances that he would have received free legal advice too. His lawyer has just got fed up with the case. Whoever it was has realized there was no point in continuing.'

'You're not allowed to bet at all,' Einar said with a smile. 'You've sworn off it.'

Selma put the laptop on the table and was again lost in thought.

'A dead journalist,' she muttered once more.

'What are you babbling about?' Einar asked, sounding annoyed. 'I've been working here like a madman to track down this stawker of yours, and then—'

Selma flashed a smile and put a reassuring hand on his arm.

'Thanks, Einar. I agree with you, this really could be the young man I'm looking for. Sadly, I still don't have a name to follow up.'

'No, but you have the name of the journalist. Ask him, why don't you?'

Einar gave her a note with a meaningless name written in capital letters. He had even found a phone number on top of everything else. Glancing at the piece of paper, Selma shoved it into her back pocket.

'Thank you,' she said. 'You're an angel. And you've become a real hot shot on the Net.'

She rose to her feet. Disappointment was clearly etched on Einar's face when she looked at him.

'I mean it,' she insisted. 'I'm over the moon that you've found this ... Ola. Of course we don't yet know if you're right but maybe we're a step further to finding who's been bothering me. But how a guy like this could have sufficient know-how to get into apartments in such devious ways and also have knowledge of my childhood secrets, is really something of a mystery, but ...'

When he still looked down in the dumps, she flung out her arms and raised her voice. 'Thanks, Einar. I came here to ask you to do this and found you'd already done it! Thank you, I really appreciate it. And I do mean that. It's just that ...'

The estates, the branches of government, crossed her mind.

'The estates,' she said.

'Eh?'

'There is a *fourth* estate.'

'Er, yes. The press.'

There was something about the order, Selma thought. Standing absolutely still, she did not even notice that Pussycat was on the point of peeing on her bag.

'Good grief,' Einar said sternly as he managed to avert the catastrophe.

'First Linda was killed,' Selma went on, unmoved. 'She's a representative of the first estate, the first branch of government. Then Kajsa Breien, the third estate.'

An hour ago Selma had been sitting in the *Sagene Lunch Bar* outlining the appalling idea that it could be the turn now of the second estate, in all likelihood a member of the Cabinet.

There had been a certain logic to that, she had thought. But the order did not make sense. The first one first, and then the third. Shouldn't it have been the second, if the entire project was intended to be a demonstration? A message? First, second, third. That would be the clearest manifestation, if the killer's intention were for everyone to see it. Something was impossible to figure out.

'Jonathan Herse died as early as 17 August,' she said, catching Einar's eye. 'He belonged to the fourth estate.'

'Now I don't understand anything at all,' Einar said.

Selma slowly sat down on the settee, perched on the edge of her seat. She stared blindly out into the room with her elbows on her knees and her hands folded while she continued at a leisurely pace: 'Maybe Jonathan Herse didn't die in an accident after all. Maybe he was the very first one to be murdered.'

She turned to face Einar who stood gaping at her.

'You're not the only one,' she said. 'You're certainly not the only one of us who doesn't comprehend anything about this at all.'

The Resilience Meeting

Karstein Braaten was in the habit of coming early to the twice-yearly meetings with the Resilience Minister. He was a punctual man and it was hit or miss whether the Vestfold train would be running to timetable. On two previous occasions in the past three years he had been forced to take a taxi home from Tønsberg station at the very last minute to pick up his car in order to reach the capital in time.

Today the train had not only departed, it was also on schedule. Karstein had so much time to spare that he had taken the subway from Jernbanetorget to Nydalen and strolled all the way up to the Maridal lake and back. He had never walked along the footpath flanking the winding Akerselva river, and it was slightly longer than he had envisaged. On the way back he had jogged the final stretch.

Karstein Braaten was a slim and fairly fit man for his age. In the time it took to negotiate security clearance and be escorted up to a large conference room in the Ministry's suite of offices, his pulse had returned to resting rate.

He took the seat he had been allocated for many years. That had been in 2012, the year after the government quarter had been blown up by an extreme-right-wing terrorist and the Ministry had been forced to find temporary office space. For eight years the government's various ministries had been spread throughout Oslo. Even at the first meeting, Karstein Braaten had been a veteran in the Directorate for Public Security and Resilience. Behind his back they called him Smiley, he knew, even though he was neither short nor stout and did not wear heavy-rimmed glasses. The nickname, after John le Carré's famous intelligence agent, had probably been given to him because he looked as if he always harboured weighty secrets.

And indeed he did, but there were not so many who knew that.

The assignment he had been given in 2012 was somewhat ambiguous, at least in his opinion. He had to continue in charge of the anonymous office at the Directorate in Tønsberg, working on analyses and writing reports. In addition he now had to probe more deeply. He had been noticed, he was told by the then Minister of Justice from the Labour Party. From his very start in the Armed Forces' Research Institute at the exact time the Berlin Wall fell, his superiors had noted Karstein Braaten's unusually observant eye for social trends. By education he was both an economist and a political scientist. He did not draw attention to himself and rarely spoke without being asked. The figure he cut was just as grey as the clothes he always wore, an anonymous, childless divorcé who lived his life through watching others and analysing the behaviour of the populace.

After 22 July 2011, the Norwegian state of readiness had been completely exposed. Although it had no significant consequence for anyone other than the families of the slaughtered and all the young people forced to go on living with the deep after-effects of trauma, in Karstein's view. As usual he said nothing, however. The Justice

Minister had given assurances that a range of measures had been initiated. *Across the board*, as he had put it. One of the measures involved Karstein Braaten. Thereafter, every six months, he had to provide a judgement of the level of trust between the Norwegian people and their Government. Ever since the war linkages had been strong and good, he was reminded. The Norwegian model was built on trust and depended upon that. New times brought new challenges and both the Government of that day and subsequent ones had to know approximately where they stood. Here too, the Cabinet Minister had come up with a statement that Karstein had picked up on: *We have to know how much elastic we can rely on. In case it snaps some day and we need to resort to crisis laws.*

At the initial meeting, Karstein had scarcely said a word beyond accepting the assignment. In the following twice-yearly meetings in which he had watched Justice Ministers come and go at an accelerating speed, he had not raised his voice to do anything other than go through the main points of the written report he had provided. Just over six months ago, in January, there had been yet another reshuffle in Solberg's government. In order to make room for all four parties in the new conservative coalition, the Ministry for Justice was divided in two. Karstein would now report to the Cabinet Member with special responsibility for resilience. They had only just met in March, but by then she had spent so little time in the post that the journey to Oslo had felt virtually pointless.

This time she rolled up with a whole entourage.

Karstein recognized both the Justice Minister and the Minister for Work and Pensions. He had also previously met the Permanent Secretary in the Ministry for Justice and Resilience. In addition to the main person and these three, two other men and one woman followed them through the door, shook hands with him and smiled, and then sat down.

'There's quite a crowd of us today,' the Resilience Minister said with a smile, having taken a seat at the curved end of the table. 'I hope you got all the names?'

Karstein gave a brief nod, even though it was not true. He had taken in their titles and that was the most important thing. Anyway, he assumed minutes would be taken. One last man, a bit younger than the others, had just entered and sat at the foot of the large, elliptical table with a laptop open in front of him.

'The reason is that your last report was a little more worrying than before,' she said. 'As usual, I'd like you to give a short account of the principal points in it. For that matter, you may as well begin. Water, by the way?'

'Yes, please.'

Karstein helped himself from a jug of iced water in the centre of the table. The others observed him in silence.

'As you're aware,' Karstein began without opening the report he had placed on the table, 'we were able to conduct an evaluation of public trust following the winding down of the *Rugged/Stormscarred* operation in November last year. The results of that can be found at the back here.'

He tapped the paper with his fingers.

'It was, as you also know, disturbing. Some would probably have called it disheartening.'

Karstein took a couple of deep breaths and then a gulp of water before spending ten minutes giving a presentation of his last report. It was longer than the ones he had written previously. And more sombre in tone. Only now and again did he have to open the report to retain the thread: in fact he was so well prepared that he knew most of it by heart. Finally he placed his palm on the bundle of papers in front of him and rounded off:

'The hope was that the Norwegian people's trust in the authorities would eventually rise again once those guilty in the RS case were caught and punished. That did happen, in fact. The problem, however, is that we never succeeded in returning to the old level before the NAV case broke. The next evaluation of trust will be undertaken in a fortnight and I fear we will receive yet another setback, given the large number of miscarriages of justice that have occurred. When we now, because of a mistaken interpretation by our own regulations, set up in contravention of our EEA obligations, have let down several thousand benefit claimants and thrown many of them in jail without actual legal authority, I believe a limit has been reached. We should really—'

'In the strictest sense, it's mostly the press that has reacted,' the Resilience Minister interrupted. 'Just as they always get worked up about so many things. I'm not complaining, of course, far from it, but isn't the smart tactic just to wait it all out?'

'The NAV case is being very thoroughly dealt with,' said the Pensions Minister, silent until now, leaning across the table. 'We're pretty certain it will be handled adequately and the mistakes that have potentially been made will be corrected as soon as possible.'

'Exactly,' the Resilience Minister said, nodding. 'Up till now we've seen plenty of angry reactions from lawyers, specialists and political commentators, but from the majority of people ...'

She gave a slight shrug before going on: '... we hear very little. The people affected can't exactly speak too well for themselves, if I can put it that way. After all, nearly all of them have defied the orders and bans placed on them. The idea there was any chance it was unlawful was unknown to them. Or what do you think, Karstein?'

He felt hot. Sick. He grabbed the glass and drained it. Swallowed the water down and moistened his lips. He was buying some time.

'I'm not a politician,' he finally said rather curtly. 'My judgements are professional and express the opinion I've arrived at. I restrict myself to that.'

'Yes, of course, but all this kerfuffle about breaching trust and consequences, that comes primarily from those I call professional critics. Commentators who would be redundant if they didn't always take a negative view of things. They also have a tendency to use lots of big words.'

All of a sudden she raised her palms towards the others.

'But heavens above! I am of course a supporter of both the press and freedom of speech, anything else would be out of the question. I can't however see that there's really any evidence for these ... pessimistic prognoses you've given in this document.'

'As I said, I'm not a politician. It's up to all of you to decide how to make use of my assessments.'

Karstein wanted to leave. He had to get out of here. The jug of water was empty. He was tempted at least to put the cold glass to his forehead, but dropped the idea.

'We're nearing a conclusion,' the woman at the end of the table said lightly, lifting the bundle of papers up in the air. 'But first, about this other point you've brought up for the current half-year. You just touched on it in your verbal summary. It has to do with ...'

It was so quiet in the room when she broke off that Karstein could hear the rustling of paper as she riffled through the report.

'... these child welfare cases. Can you say something more about them?'

One of the men whose names Karstein had not caught stole a march on him: 'As far as the paragraph about the ECHR's treatment of the decisions made in the Norwegian Supreme Court is concerned, I can assure everyone that this will not be a problem. Not in connection with what we've been discussing here.'

'We've already been roundly convicted three times,' the Pensions Minister said, sounding slightly irritated. 'Surely Norway breaching human rights has to be regarded as a problem?' Of a certain magnitude, shouldn't we contend? And as far as I can see from this ...'

Now it was his turn to wave the report about.

'... we can expect to lose a whole heap of other cases that are queued up right now to be dealt with in the Grand Chamber.'

Karstein noted that the Pensions Minister was far more eager to see the problems in the child welfare system, for which he had no responsibility, than in the NAV scandal, which was a considerable headache for him.

'I wouldn't say that at all,' the other Minister said. 'It's far too early to say anything about the results. Anyway, we have an ace up our sleeve. If it ends up that some new verdict or other is in process, then we have a very secure tactic in mind to stem any criticism here at home. The Child Welfare Service has always borne the brunt of the storm. It's part of their purpose for people to easily feel hard done by. That doesn't mean I'm saying it's justified. In Norway we have a strong tradition of always placing the child's best interests first.'

'Yes, of course,' the Minister for Work and Pensions said drily. 'But if our idea of placing the child's best interests first actually breaches human rights, as they are formulated in a convention we have been bound by since 1953, then *it could well be ...*'

Drawing this out with an almost shrill sense of irony, he leaned even further across the table and looked straight at his colleague.

'... that we have a tiny problem.'

'As I said,' the other man replied stiffly, 'we have complete control of this. The Ministry for Children and Families has good ongoing contact with the Government's legal office, which conducts these cases for us in Strasbourg. An extremely reassuring contact, I would add.'

Karstein felt his jaws about to lock. He concentrated on not clenching his teeth so tightly. The meeting would soon be over.

He would take his leave politely, make his exit from this bleak office building in Nydalen, take the subway to the city centre and then the train back to Vestfold. Once home he would have a bite to eat and then saunter down to the marina and chug out into the fjord to do some night fishing. If he were lucky, he would catch a pollock or two, the best fish he knew.

This would soon be over.

It had gone quiet. Only the faint noise made by the secretary's fingers on the keyboard at the very end of the table could be heard. The Resilience Minister opened her mouth to say something when the man from the Ministry for Children and Families started speaking without asking for permission.

'To make things crystal clear,' he said, 'so that no one leaves this room without being convinced that these child welfare cases will not have any impact whatsoever on what is discussed in Braaten's report: the criticism of the service is oversimplified and built on lack of knowledge. I actually wish our Divisional Director, Braaten, would also appreciate that.'

At last Karstein looked straight at him. He had been chewing on a little lump on the inside of his cheek. The mucous membrane tore and he was aware of the metallic taste of blood when he swallowed and spoke: 'Excuse me, I didn't catch your name.'

The man got to his feet and extended his hand theatrically across the table once again. Karstein rose slightly and shook it.

'Director General Horatio Bull-Pedersen,' the bureaucrat said. 'I'm in charge of the Child Welfare Department in the Ministry for Children and Families. And you have nothing to worry about. Absolutely nothing, I can assure you of that.'

The Colleague

Fredrik Smedstuen could not stand Saturdays.

Every other weekend he had the children. It was always unsuccessful. They were eleven, twelve and fourteen years old and generally had their own plans. In the basement apartment he had to make do with, there were only two small bedrooms. The youngest, still short and tubby and quite a shy lad, had to sleep in the double bed with his father. The girl of twelve then had to share a room with her big brother and she found it necessary to complain loudly about this every time the three of them peevishly lugged their bags and baggage out to his car every second Friday at five p.m. In the initial phase of being divorced, Fredrik had insisted on the children spending the first evening of each contact weekend with him. Eating tacos like everyone else. Watching a film together, maybe, or playing board games. All three of them insisted they must be the only kids in the whole world being forced to do that. He gave up on the third occasion.

The contact weekends had been reduced to a chauffeur service, with him dropping the children off at get-togethers, sports practice and birthday parties before picking up the churlish, grumpy youngsters who then went straight to bed in the basement they all four hated with a passion.

Last weekend he had been forced to interview Selma Falck while the children were at McDonald's with his bankcard. They had gone wild. This weekend, Fredrik was on his own.

To be honest, it was better. He missed the children and the normal, good life when he had been a full-time dad and they could come and go without him feeling he was losing out on something, but it was easier to bear when he did not have responsibility for them. It was worst when they were within reach and yet not really. The most difficult aspect of the divorce was still having no grip on his children's daily lives. When he had dropped a hint that Eivind, Marie and Mikkel might put up with staying week about with each of their parents, like most of the other children of divorce he knew, his wife had merely laughed. Loudly. And said he was totally free to go ahead and ask the children if that was a good idea.

Since he knew what the answer would be, he had let it lie.

Today at least he could go to work, even though he had a day off.

The press had started grumbling.

More than a week had passed since Linda Bruseth had been killed. Even though she was neither known nor admired by anyone other than the people in her home county, she was nevertheless an elected representative. In the first few days, when everyone believed Selma Falck had been the target of an assassination attempt, the screaming headlines had fleetingly put even the NAV scandal in the shade. Eventually the leaks from Police Headquarters grew so numerous and unambiguous that even the media understood that Linda Bruseth had been the intended target.

Fredrik hated leaks but had long ago given up the fight against them. Individual journalists, especially a pair from *DG*, enjoyed an almost symbiotic relationship with a few handpicked criminal investigators. They exchanged information the way young girls in the old days had swapped scraps. *Something for something* and a perpetual battle for titbits. Fredrik Smedstuen sometimes had to admit that such cooperation could be beneficial, especially when it involved entering into agreements on what should *not* yet be mentioned. All the same bargaining with journalists conflicted with all his principles. He could work himself up into a real rage when he came across details in the media that clearly stemmed from one of his own detectives, but which had not yet even reached his desk.

In the course of the last three days Linda Bruseth, according to the media, had become a prominent politician, which was untrue. She was deeply loved in her home constituency, which *was* true. She had become a casualty of political fanaticism as a result of her strong support for refugees in the autumn of 2015, something that was most certainly sheer nonsense. The woman had not uttered a cheep about immigration policy since she entered Parliament. The idea that a sniper hostile to immigrants had waited four years to bump Linda off when there were plenty of vocal liberals to choose from nowadays was quite simply unbelievable. The problem was the same as always: for lack of anything more specific to go on, journalists would begin to speculate.

The only tiny glimmer of light he could see as far as the media were concerned was that they had still not started to work out a connection between Kajsa Breien's death and Linda's. It still seemed as if the editors believed in a self-inflicted death in the case of the Supreme Court Judge. This meant the story was handled in a more low-key tone than it otherwise would have been.

For the moment at least, Fredrik thought despondently. He looked at his chaotic desk. They were supposed to work paper-free.

Opening his dark-blue thermos flask, he poured the coffee into a mug. It was white, with a summer photo of all three children on one side. On the other it said *Best Dad in the World* in rainbow lettering. He gulped down some boiling-hot coffee and heaved a deep sigh.

It was four years since he had received that mug. When he put it down again, he turned the text away.

Pictures. He was drowning in them. It was sometimes to the benefit of the police that absolutely everyone these days snapped away non-stop with mobile phones. Since, in addition, the number of CCTV cameras downtown had exploded in the last decade, a shortage of photographs was seldom the problem when a crime was committed in the city centre.

It was the abundance of them that was the challenge.

Often it was impossible to see the wood for the trees, and it all took a ridiculous length of time. The police did not have access to all the mobiles that had been in the vicinity of the café in Thorvald Meyers gate when Linda Bruseth had been shot, but it looked at last as if the telecomms companies would assist them.

Whether that would help was another matter.

He had hardly slept. The meeting with Selma Falck in the *Sagene Lunch Bar* churned around in his brain continuously. Especially the last part of it. The notion that a Government Minister was in danger of being murdered was so terrifying it was impossible to keep it to himself. Selma was a freewheeler who had few commitments but his mission in life was to prevent injustice and clear up crimes. When he returned to Police Headquarters after lunch yesterday, he had most of all been tempted to circumvent all lines of command and march straight up to the sixth floor and confide in the Chief of Police.

But what would he say?

What on earth would he say? Selma's train of thought had been so nebulous that he was scarcely able to express it in words. Far less be able to convince anyone that it had to be banged on a big drum to sound the alarm in the Norwegian Government.

He had dropped the idea.

Fredrik got up awkwardly. With his mug of coffee in his hand, he headed out of the office and moved four doors down the corridor. The door was open.

'Hi,' he said to his colleague sitting there.

'Hi,' she answered, glancing up. 'No Saturday off for you either?' She let go of the computer mouse and signalled for him to sit down.

'Will I get you a cup of coffee?' he offered. 'I've got a thermos with me.'

'No, thanks. I drink tea.'

Only now did he see that there was a proper porcelain teacup, complete with saucer and everything, half-hidden behind the monitor. Fredrik produced his mobile from his back pocket and placed it display-down on the desk in front of him before slumping into the chair.

'Are you getting anywhere?' he asked, stifling a yawn.

Inspector Sylvi Mobakk shrugged. 'So-so,' she said. 'You were at least right to say it's not a suicide.'

'I thought that.'

'In the first place it's a mystery how she got up there if she went of her own accord. There's no car parked in the area that can be linked to her. No witnesses have seen her arrive on public transport. But her ... unusual appearance means someone should have noticed her.'

'She was also widely known. Almost famous, I mean.'

'Yes. If nobody drove her up there, rope and all, and then drove off as if everything was hunky-dory, then the woman must have been done away with. Unless she could fly, that is. To get up there and then up into that tree, I mean. The post-mortem report is probably not complete yet, but last night I got some preliminary conclusions. The woman died of strangulation, but the marks and injuries are not consistent with hanging herself. The imprints from the rope look as if they were made after death. To sum up, this is a homicide. Sadly.'

'When did she disappear? Had she even been reported missing?'

'Yes. Only just. In a sense. We haven't made much progress, it's ...'

She pulled up her sleeve and cast a glance at her watch.

'... only about fifty hours since we found her. But as far we know she was at home on Wednesday night. Made dinner for the family – apparently that's a fixed routine. The children are busy, especially at weekends, but Wednesdays are seemingly holy. Four of her five kids still live at home. Her husband was away. He's the head of the legal faculty and was in the USA at a conference for university leaders. At twenty-five minutes to midnight Kajsa was observed by a neighbour while out in the garden with the dog. A little Jack Russell. She stood there for about ten minutes according to what we've worked out. The dog, which is actually also *called* Jack Russell ...'

For a second Fredrik thought he saw her smile before she drank some tea and became just as serious as when he had arrived.

'The mutt was bedded down for the night. In some sort of utility room. Water and food were left out. By this time all the children were asleep. Since then no one has clapped eyes on the woman.'

'No sign of her having gone to bed?'

'So far not. The bed was unmade but her oldest son says that was normal. It's difficult for such a small woman to make up a king-size *Hästens* bed with double quilts, he says. And as I told you, her husband was away.'

'He's the one behind it.'

Now Inspector Mobakk flashed a genuine smile.

'Believe me, we're keeping that option open. From a purely statistical standpoint, he's the one we should put our money on. In that case we must be talking about a hired killer, because the man was verifiably in the States.'

She drank some more tea before stretching her arms above her head and giving a protracted yawn, struggling to avoid opening her mouth more than a chink. Since her face was already long and narrow, she now reminded him of a horse. A fjord pony, with the bleached fringe on her forehead and the rest of her hair gathered into a high ponytail she was at least fifteen years too old to wear.

'Anyway ...'

She cracked the knuckles on her left hand.

'The youngest child, a girl of twelve, discovered her mother gone about five a.m. The girl had got up to go to the loo and passed her parents' bedroom door. It was open, which it never usually is at night. Also the ceiling light was on. So the girl started to search. She couldn't find her mother anywhere and so she woke her seventeen-year-old brother. He rang their father, who's in Houston, who then called the police here in Norway. The formalities to do with a missing person report hadn't even been sorted out before a wee wifie up on the hillside ...'

Her hand flapped lethargically in the direction of the window. In the completely wrong direction, Fredrik noted.

'... rang up and reported having found a dead dwarf.'

Now she was laughing. It sounded like a little, lively whinny.

'Not nice to laugh,' she said, collecting herself. 'At least the ship is sailing now. The forensic examination of the crime scene is not yet finished. Witnesses have been interviewed, all traffic in the relevant time frame has been checked, and I've even got one of the young lawyers to voluntarily go through all the verdicts Kajsa Breien has handed down in the last two years. To see if there could be something there. The one with the black curly hair, you know.'

Fredrik knew that Sylvi Mobakk would have said 'the darkie' a couple of years ago, but the Police Chief had given her a serious dressing-down after she had used similar language on TV.

'He's smart, but I doubt anything will come of it. This case has something ... something ...'

'Odd about it?' Fredrik suggested.

'Yes! I mean ...'

She lowered her voice as if she had a secret she was deciding to share. Sylvi Mobakk was a countrywoman, even after two and a half decades in the capital city. She had spent years fighting her way up to her position as an inspector in charge of investigations, but it was far from undeserved. Fredrik knew that behind her unsophisticated appearance and slightly coarse language – not until recently had she learned not to swear like a trooper in every second sentence – lay a sharp mind. And what's more, the tenacity of a fighting dog. Sylvi never gave in.

She would not this time either. He was less sure whether that would help any.

'What do you mean?' he asked guardedly when she seemed at a loss.

'I mean, what would the point be? In hanging her up on that birch tree like some Christmas bauble? The woman who found the body jumped to the conclusion that it was a suicide, of course, but it would take even the average first-year police student only five minutes to see that didn't add up.'

Fredrik nodded but chose not to say anything.

'Dressing a murder up as a suicide must be one of the oldest tricks in the book,' Sylvi went on thoughtfully. 'But then it's got to be convincing, surely! More than just a rope, I mean! And dangling her up there. The perpetrator has done bugger all to imitate a genuine wish to die by her own hand. Or her own rope, to be more accurate. At the same time he ... yes, or of course she ... at the same time the person in question has been extremely careful not to leave behind a single trace. You'd have thought the bloody guy was invisible.'

'There must be loads of traces up there. It's crawling with people all the time.'

'Yes, of course. But you know what I mean. We can't find any damn thing that seems suspicious. Or out of place. Or that could tell us anything about what happened. On the other hand …'

Once again she began to crack her knuckles, this time on her right hand. The noise was nerve-racking.

'… we've only just got started. Slow and steady wins the race, as my mother always used to say.'

She hesitated for a second before adding, so softly that it was probably meant mostly for herself: 'But I'll be damned if it isn't the strangest murder I've ever come across. It's exactly as if …'

Suddenly she looked up and met Fredrik's eye. 'It's as if the killer is making fun of us,' she exclaimed. 'It's as if he's mocking both us and that poor victim!'

'Or maybe he's trying to tell us something instead,' Fredrik spoke up.

'What do you mean by that?'

Fredrik Smedstuen did not answer. His mobile growled at him, a push alert from *DG*, he heard, and grabbed his phone. He glanced at the display.

'Is everything OK, Fredrik? Hey, Fredrik, are you ill, man?'

Not until she was standing beside him, leaning over with her hand on his back and an expression of deep concern on the face that was too close to Fredrik's for comfort did he take a deep breath in what sounded like a sob. He pushed her carefully away and picked up the phone again. Sylvi tried to see what he was reading. Yet again he gave her a nudge, without looking up.

'I'm fine,' he muttered. 'Just sit down.'

The person who was not fine, however, was the Norwegian Minister for Children and Families. He had died last night, *DG* said, aged only forty-two.

Almost exactly six hours ago.

The Excursion

Selma Falck was ashamed of what her apartment looked like. The stovetop was spattered with stains and there were crumbs all over the kitchen. It had not been vacuumed for at least ten days. If the bathroom did not exactly smell rank, it was at least not very hygienic in there. She had not even removed the paper labels from the new shower door. To top it all, the whole place stank of dust and stale bedclothes.

For a week she had blamed her sore arm. Then an attempt at cleaning had been interrupted when she found the old handball on her balcony. She had almost decided to pay no attention to the ball, at least for the moment, and her arm was more or less better. It was time to have the stitches and drain removed.

And get down to some scrubbing.

Slipping her mobile into her back pocket, she made a start. Of course she could have put down the phone and listened to the radio through her earbuds, but experience had taught her that the connection between the devices had a tendency to drop off. Especially in the bathroom. When she decided to pee, she forgot about it. The mobile fell into the bowl when she pulled down her jeans. Since P4 was just then broadcasting an unusually noisy Aerosmith track, she failed to hear the clink of metal against the porcelain. Only once she had finished and stood up again did she notice her howler. Abhorring the idea of sticking her hand down the toilet, she took too long running around in confusion looking for rubber gloves.

Her mobile phone died.

She was put out about it for all of five minutes. Then it dawned on her that she had actually been meaning to buy a new one for ages. The old one, after all, was only a 7 and the iPhone 11 would come on the market in no more than a week or two. In the meantime she could swap her sim card over to one of the old phones she had lying in a drawer in her storeroom.

The sim card did not fit any of them.

The knowledge that she had no mobile phone at present felt strange and slightly scary, but also pretty liberating. No one could get hold of her without physically looking her up. There was a certain tranquillity in that, something that made her scrub down the rest of the apartment with the radio on full blast. While she was busy, it was at least possible for her to displace the idea that had struck her when she was with Einar the previous day: that the death of the journalist Jonathan Herse had not been a genuine, unfortunate accident.

When she was done, the restlessness returned. A shower did not help. She could not phone Lars. No one else either. Her pleasure in being without a phone did not last long. For a moment she contemplated not bothering to wait for the 11 and just going for an iPhone X. She could pop up to Storo and arrange that on the spot. Just as she was about to leave, her eye fell on a note on the dining table, tucked halfway under her laptop.

Allan Strømme, Granebakken 3F, Oslo

Along with a telephone number. By yesterday morning Selma had, however, decided against calling Jonathan Herse's best friend. If he really had been the one who had given Jonathan the memory stick, and it was also true that the zip file was locked because it contained compromising material, then it was far from certain that the guy would be cooperative. She risked him slamming down the phone on her the minute he knew what she wanted and thereafter making himself unavailable. Somehow or other she had to engage him in conversation without there being any immediate opportunity for him to cut her off.

That was where she would go. To Granebakken 3F in Mortensrud.

Seventeen minutes later, her new Volvo was parked at the kerb in an area of detached houses in the most southerly part of Oslo. It was now half past ten and children had been sent out to play. Just like earlier in the week, the morning had brought heavy showers, and it had been cold that night. Now her dashboard showed an outdoor temperature of fifteen degrees Celsius. The clouds were scudding northwards and the asphalt was drying. An elderly couple, hand in hand and dragging a wheelie shopper behind them, sauntered slowly past her. Two ten- or twelve-year-olds whizzed past on BMX bikes before one of them stopped at the corner fifty metres away and executed a nifty pirouette, balancing on his back wheel. Taking a deep breath, Selma made up her mind and stepped out of the car.

The pale-ochre timber house looked as if it had been built some time in the eighties. Sensible, solid and boring, little money seemed to have been spent on it since. A wooden house with vertical panels and bars added to the windows, located between other timber houses of exactly the same type and age. The garden was tiny, at least what Selma could see of it from the road. It was enclosed within a picket fence the same colour as the house. The hinges on the low wrought-iron gate squeaked noisily when she lifted the latch and pushed it open.

A dog suddenly began barking. It sounded small but all the angrier for that. Selma continued anyway to the front door, where a plastic plaque confirmed that here indeed lived 'Allan Strømme and'. A precise length of blue masking tape covered the second name. The tape was relatively new. Yet another broken relationship, Selma thought as she rang the doorbell.

The barking increased. The mutt was right behind the door now: she could hear the sound of claws scratching the wood. After a few seconds she heard a muffled voice approach. The dog calmed down and the door swung open.

'Hi,' Selma said cheerfully, reaching out her hand. 'I'm Selma Falck. And I believe you're Allan Strømme, is that right?'

The question was superfluous; she recognized him at once. Both from the picture in *Aftenavisen*, where he had stood with his colleagues from the Ministry for Children and Families, having just beaten the Attorney General's office in the Holmenkollstafett relay race, and the pallbearer photo in Emilie Sundet's apartment. Admittedly his hair was a little longer than in the photographs and the stubble that spread all the way down to his neckband gave him a slovenly look. As if he had been ill or on a very long trip to a cabin in really bad weather. He was unusually pale. On his arm he held the smallest chihuahua Selma had ever seen.

Her hand was left hanging in mid-air and she let it drop. 'And hello to you too,' she said to the poor creature: it bared its teeth in response.

'Er ... yes. I'm Allan. What do you want?'

'As I said, my name's Selma Fa—'

'I know who you are. My question is: what are you doing here? What do you want of me?'

'I'd really like to talk to you about something,' Selma said as she desperately struggled to come up with a plan B.

Normally she reaped the rewards of her celebrity status: people frequently invited her in and accepted her at face value. This man was just as hostile as the mini-monster he had on his arm.

'About what?' he said, making no sign of letting her in.

Selma made a show of looking at her watch in an attempt to give the impression of being short of time. And that she would not bother him for long.

'Listen,' she said in an undertone. 'I know you've given confidential information to Jonathan Herse. Information about your employer. Breaking your duty of silence could, for a start, cost you your job. Unless you qualify as a whistle-blower in the eyes of the law.'

Selma had staked everything on one card. This time she had chosen the truth, which was so unfamiliar that she suddenly had no idea how to continue. Her opening gambit at least had the desired effect – the man turned even paler. Even the chihuahua seemed perplexed as it stared at her with big, shining and slightly prominent eyes.

'As you've probably picked up,' she added, in even more of an undertone, 'I'm now a private investigator. However, I also have years of experience as a lawyer. I can help you.'

He drew back a few centimetres but still kept his free hand on the door handle.

'It was you who gave Jonathan the memory stick before he died. With sound files you've recorded of conversations within the Ministry.'

She was still speaking softly, but now she had also dialled down the speed. As she went on speaking about what she knew and also what she guessed, she did not take her eyes off his face.

'It would probably be best to let me come in,' she suggested.

The man thought it over. For an age, Selma felt, and she was about to make yet another effort to persuade him when he finally took a step to one side and let the door swing wide open. Without saying a word, he put down the dog and shooed it into an adjacent room before closing the door. Selma followed him into a spacious, bright living room. It was only semi-furnished. A beige corner settee was placed beside the large window facing on to a terrace, but there was no coffee table in front of it. Between the settee and the open-plan kitchen, marks on the parquet revealed where there had once been a dining table and six chairs. Here and there on the walls, she could see pale rectangles suggesting that pictures had recently been taken down.

She made no comment on any of that.

'Sit down,' Allan Strømme snapped, pointing at the shortest part of the settee. 'I don't have much time. Get to the point.'

It was too warm in there and Selma felt the need to take off her denim jacket. Afraid he might change his mind and throw her out, as he presumably wanted to do more than anything, she refrained.

'Jonathan was your best friend,' she ventured.

'Yes,' he said. 'He was indeed.'

'You trusted him.'

He said nothing.

'You trusted him so much that you talked to him about something you were worried about. At work. Something that ... was possibly against the law.'

Still he remained silent, staring at her. Did not nod. Uttered not a word. His eyes seemed to sink into his head, but it was probably just a result of the light from the window.

'It's obvious this information also made Jonathan nervous,' Selma continued to speculate. 'He had worked on the story for a fairly long time before he died and he had not dared to say much about what he was working on. Not even to his editor.'

The tiny dog began to bark. Allan Strømme did not blink.

'This is a story that has major ramifications, Allan.'

'You have to leave.'

He got to his feet. There was something stiff about his movements, as if he had been sitting locked in one tense position, even though it had only been two minutes since he sat down.

'I really need to know how to open that zip file,' Selma said. 'And if I don't get the password from you, I'll have to ask the police for help. I can of course just go ahead and do that, but then I'll no longer be able to protect you in the same way.'

'Why would you protect me?' He had not resumed his seat, but did at least remain standing.

'Because I think you deserve it. Because I'm convinced something has happened in the Ministry that could have a connection with something even bigger.'

'You can't know how big this is, so you're not in a position to judge.'

Selma nodded calmly. 'I'm sure you're right about that. But let's not split hairs. My offer to you is as follows: you help me open the file and I'll move on from there on my own. And keep you out of it all, as far as that proves possible. If you won't help me, I'll go to the police, who have equipment and expertise to break the password. You can choose.'

He stood so long without moving a muscle, without even blinking, that Selma began to worry that he was suffering from some kind of seizure. She had heard of silent epilepsy, but had no idea whether you could have an attack while still standing upright.

'Are you OK?' she asked.

'You have to go.'

Selma rose from her seat. The dog was yelping like mad from the other room where it was shut inside. It felt as if this room was becoming stuffier and warmer.

'You're making a mistake,' Selma said, heading for the hallway without waiting for further requests. 'The next person to stand at the door will be wearing a uniform.'

'I haven't done anything wrong.'

'Maybe not. As I said, I could have helped you obtain whistle-blower status. That provides strong protection. Very strong. In cases like this ...'

At the hallway door she turned to face him again. In the harsh light from outside he had become a dark silhouette against the window. He seemed to have shrunk, almost like an old man, as he stood there.

'... it's a matter of making sure you emerge unscathed from the brink of disaster,' Selma continued. 'But you can choose for yourself.'

'Does last night's death have anything to do with this?'

Selma frowned and pulled her head back in surprise. 'What death?'

'The Minister for Children and Families. It was announced on the radio just before you rang the bell.'

'Er ... what did you say?' In confusion, Selma rummaged around in her pocket for her mobile phone.

'Børre Rosenhoff. Of the Christian Democrats. He died during the night. They didn't say of what. I thought his heart: as far as I know he's not been suffering from cancer or anything. I saw him as recently as Monday. But then you came barging in, and I thought—'

'Shit,' Selma said. 'I don't have a mobile. Can I borrow yours?'

She had to almost shout – the little bastard of a dog was flying off the handle.

'Does the death have anything to do with me?' he replied, dissolving into tears.

Now he was breaking down completely. Selma slammed the door shut and took a couple of steps back into the room.

'How should I know?' she hissed. 'I haven't a clue what it says in those files! What do you think? Is that how everything hangs together?'

Slowly he slumped down on to the settee. 'I don't want this,' he sobbed. 'Go away.'

'Yes, I'll go. But first I have to borrow your phone.'

'Get lost.'

Selma saw that this was all a waste of time. Not entirely, of course, since Allan Strømme's behaviour confirmed at least that the zip files contained sound files right enough, as she and Lars had guessed. Since the man was in the midst of a total breakdown in front of her eyes, the contents must also be far from insignificant. If, to crown it all, the Minister for Children and Families really was dead, she could only pray to the high heavens that it was all nothing but a coincidence. And that Børre Rosenhoff, a forty-two-year-old father of three who neither drank nor smoked, who cycled from Trondheim to Oslo every year and was even a veteran footballer far up in the second division, had simply passed away peacefully as a result of sudden but natural heart failure.

These things happened.

'Good God,' she whispered to herself as she turned on her heel and made for the door.

She had to get a new phone. Whether she would then phone Lars Winther or Fredrik Smedstuen she did not know, but at least she would not be on her own in this. As soon as she reached her car she began to puzzle over where the nearest shopping centre was situated. Hesitating, she closed her eyes and came to the conclusion that the Manglerud retail centre was her best alternative, if not the nearest. Also, she would then be already halfway back to the city centre. She yanked the car door open and clambered in. As the engine fired up and she was signalling to move out on to the road, she saw Allan Strømme come haring after her. Selma stamped on the brake and let the window roll down.

Inclining towards her, he showed her a memory stick. 'I don't know the code on Jonathan's one,' he said. 'But these are the original recordings. This file is not password-protected.'

He gave a sob, as if convulsively struggling to pull himself together. 'They've already been here.'

'Who?' Selma asked.

'The others. They took everything. Except for this, which I had hidden. I just want to get away. I don't want all this. Keep me out of it, OK? Please, keep me out of it.'

'I promise,' Selma said. Her heart was pounding so hard when she took the memory stick from him that she did not even get as far as thinking that, all things considered, it would probably be impossible to let the guy escape anything at all.

The Friends

This was exactly how Karstein Braaten liked things best.

The bureaucrats and politicians in the capital were forgotten. The outer reaches of the Oslo Fjord were smooth as glass, as if it were the height of summer. The night chill still hovered in the little breaths of air, but he was wearing a woollen sweater. It was old and smelled of diesel and bonfires and tar. The almost forty-year-old two-stroke engine chugged faithfully and noisily, preventing all conversation between the two sailors aboard.

Just as he wanted things to be on his day off. Even though they spotted the occasional leisure craft on the waters around them, it was far quieter than it had been only a couple of weeks earlier. The cabin owners had long ago travelled home to the towns. Even though the most enthusiastic of them extended the season into the weekends all the way through to October, it was more pleasant to be a permanently residing boat owner out here once the school holidays were finally over.

This vessel was not fast but it ran smoothly.

They were heading to Stauper – that cluster of small islands and rocks scoured smooth by the tide far out in the Tønsberg Fjord was Karstein's favourite spot. When he acquired his first boat at the age of eighteen, a ten-foot timber dinghy his grandfather had built and attached a four-horsepower outboard motor to, Stauper had been strictly forbidden. It was too far out, his mother said. Stauper was a fair-weather destination only; it was too dangerous when the weather turned nasty. The weather could certainly turn quickly at sea, and his parents never learned that Karstein Braaten had got to know the spot out there among the reefs like the back of his hand as early as that first summer in his own boat.

They were going ashore. Just as friends, the way they had been ever since the two of them had taken part in the Armed Forces Russian course at one time in the eighties. They were both in the same mould. The man who sat in the bow with one hand round the gunwale, staring southwards, was also weighed down by anxieties and silence. His working life had brought him greater mental challenges than Karstein. More external drama. Nevertheless, they had both chosen to serve the good of the community. They protected those who had no understanding of their own need for protection.

They looked after Norway, Karstein Braaten and his best friend.

They had both also suffered a good measure of sorrow. Karstein with his childlessness, which he had never got over and which in the end had driven his wife away, leaving him to his introspection and self-chosen isolation. Birger, with his extreme experiences as a soldier and silent losses on the home front, that bound them together.

On the way out, they intended to pull up a couple of crab pots. The shellfish were at their best now and Karstein had landed six big ones last weekend. On deck they had a sturdy steel pot and a waterproof bag that held birch firewood, lighters and all the trimmings for the crabmeat. Even though Karstein Braaten was a careful man in every aspect of life, he had also added a couple of bottles of pilsner to the bag.

They were approaching the first pot now. The orange buoy was marked with Karstein's name and address, as the regulations stipulated. Without asking, his friend got ready to haul in the buoy with the boathook. Neither man uttered a word: both the boat and the two men knew exactly what had to be done. Once the pot was on board, they could count three large and one smaller crab. The last of these did not comply with the minimum size permitted and had to be thrown back again. Karstein let the engine idle to take a few minutes to release the shellfish.

As he grabbed the largest by the back of the shell, the crab waved its huge claws.

'This'll be tasty,' Karstein called out with satisfaction, holding the crab up to his friend. 'This is bound to be the best lunch of the autumn, Birger Jarl!'

Birger Jarl Nilsen did not reply but he did join him in a broad smile.

The Cabin in the Woods

Selma Falck stood by a window looking out over the lake at Movatn. The opening was small and low and she had to crouch down. The cabin, barely thirty square metres in area, was built of notched rough timbers and belonged to Fredrik Smedstuen. He could scarcely have lifted a hammer in here since he inherited it from his grandfather more than twenty years ago. Outside toilet and paraffin lamps. Furniture from the fifties. The beds in the tiny bedroom they had passed on the way into the living room could not have been more than 180 x 60 centimetres. There was a travel radio from the sixties on a small table beside the settee, obviously battery-operated. Fredrik had not splashed out on as much as a solar panel.

But the cabin was in a beautiful location and it took less than half an hour to drive there from Oslo city centre. Fredrik had insisted on taking her with him when she called the minute she had obtained a new mobile phone.

'Isn't this a bit paranoid?' she asked, straightening her back.

'No,' the policeman replied. 'Or maybe it is. I'm out in deep waters here, Selma. You are too. Oslo makes me feel slightly claustrophobic. Out here, I've always found a sense of peace.'

He groaned as he ran his hand over his obviously unfamiliar bare scalp. 'Not that it's helping very much this time. Christ, I should have sounded the alert about these suspicions right away.'

'Suspicions about what, though?' Selma said, sounding discouraged, as she crossed to the rough-hewn dining table that took up most of the living room.

She sat opposite Fredrik but changed her mind at once. Her laptop already lay between them. She turned it round and moved over to his side.

'All we did yesterday was to toss out a whole series of loose thoughts and ideas,' she said, sitting down. 'There was nothing in what we knew that proved anything whatsoever. Very far from it. We had loads of ifs and buts, mixed together in a potful of fantasies with a couple of cups of conspiracies for good measure. You'd have made a fool of yourself if you'd sounded the alarm. What's more, we've no idea what Børre Rosenhoff died of. It could have been his heart. Or a brain haemorrhage. Anything at all.'

'Healthy forty-two-year-olds don't die of just anything at all,' Fredrik pointed out irately. 'And certainly not less than twenty-four hours after you and I sat in a café wondering about whether he was next on the list of this ...'

He took a deep breath without exhaling.

'... this bloody cryptic killer we're faced with!'

Selma turned her chair to make it easier for her to look at him. Leaning forward slightly, she placed one hand lightly on his thigh for a few seconds.

'Fredrik,' she said as calmly as she could while trying to catch his eye. 'Now we really must take things steady here. You've taken a giant leap to conclusions in a case we're not even sure really *is* a case. Right now there are three. Or in actual fact only two.'

She sighed in dismay and ran her hand gingerly across the worn surface of the table.

'If anyone suspected that Børre Rosenhoff had been killed, you'd have known it. It's sheer routine for the police to be informed of his death. You know that, of course. Doctors have a duty to report sudden, unexpected deaths without a known cause. When the deceased is a Cabinet Minister, the threshold for reporting it must be even lower. But there's been no hullabaloo, Fredrik. You'd have heard about it. "Died suddenly in his home during Friday night" means one of two things. A sudden illness, such as a heart attack. Or suicide. If he'd taken his own life, for example, the police would have been all over the place in five minutes flat. And you'd have known about it, Fredrik. You've had those assignments far too often.'

Once again she tried to catch his eye, but his gaze was nailed to something far beyond the cabin.

'In other words, last night's death is not even a case. At least not at the moment. When it comes to the murders of Linda Bruseth and Kajsa Breien, we don't have anything tangible there either that points to the same person being behind them. Just feelings, associations. We're bumping into these child welfare issues everywhere we turn but we have to remember that there's a difference between correlation and causality.'

He was still staring out through the window. Selma still had no idea what he was looking at. Probably nothing. She ploughed on: 'The fact that Linda, Kajsa Breien and Børre Rosenhoff have all had some connection or other to child welfare doesn't have to mean it's of any relevance to how all three of them died. It could well be that all three of them liked pancakes. That's equally irrelevant.'

At last he looked at her. 'That's complete drivel,' he said, on the verge of losing his temper. 'You'd have failed a beginner's philosophy exam with that reasoning of yours.'

'Possibly. But you get my point.'

He growled something indistinct and got to his feet. 'I need some air,' he barked as he headed for the door.

Selma followed at his heels. The door was so low that she had to dip her head. Outside, the sky had grown dark and the wind had turned. Now it was coming from the north, with a hint of impending night frost up here in Marka. From the little yard in front of the cabin, a grassy hill sloped down to the water. It was usually swarming with hikers around here, especially in winter, but now everything was silent. A heron took off from the woods on the other side of the lake, gliding ponderously southwards only a couple of metres above the surface of the water.

Fredrik straightened his back and raised his face to the darkening sky. He could not have had a smoke for a while: there was no smell of tobacco or Fisherman's Friends from him.

'I once saw a she-bear with her young over there,' Fredrik said, indicating a stand of trees only thirty to forty metres to the north. 'Two little growling balls of fur. When I was eleven. I was petrified.'

'My goodness,' Selma said, smiling, enjoying both the fresh air and the break from their chaotic thoughts. 'Bears so close to people?'

'Yes. But no, I must have been mistaken, nothing else.'

'Er ... is that right? How do you know?'

'It was between Christmas and New Year.'

'And so?'

'Bears mate in early summer. The egg doesn't attach itself to the womb before she hibernates in autumn. The cubs are born from the end of December until maybe February, while the mother is still hibernating.'

'She could have woken up, though? Isn't that possible?'

He shrugged. 'I don't know. But what I do know for sure is that between Christmas and New Year, the cubs would be about half a kilo in size and totally helpless. If they're even born at all, of course.'

His hands measured the size of a bear cub at around fifteen centimetres.

'I must have got it wrong, that's all. But they're just as vivid in my mind's eye today as they were then. The she-bear came waddling out between those two pines ...'

He used both the index and middle fingers of his right hand to point.

'They were smaller then, of course. The mother came first and the cubs came tagging along behind her. One was a bit braver than the other, but got a smack from the she-bear to stay in line. I stared at them for quite a while, completely mesmerized. Then I ran in but didn't dare tell anyone. Not until a year or so later, when I confided in my grandfather.'

Fredrik sniffed and ran his sleeve under his nose. 'He laughed at me.'

Selma smiled.

'Bears do wander into Nordmarka,' Fredrik said. 'That's conceivable. But that they might turn up at that time of year is highly doubtful. They're asleep then. That they could have a couple of cubs of that size with them ...'

Now his palms were just over half a metre apart.

'... is totally impossible, in fact. I must have seen a vision. Or dreamt it. Something of that kind, but I most certainly didn't see that fucking bear. Even though I could have sworn to it even today.'

'The Mandela effect,' Selma said, drawing her jacket more snugly around her.

'What?'

Now he canted his head and looked at her. For a moment he seemed really curious.

'We humans have a fantastic ability to deceive ourselves,' Selma said. 'The expression "he lies so convincingly he believes it himself" is not so far off the mark. The point is that we're not really telling lies. We're misremembering. We believe we've experienced something that never took place.'

'Yeees ...' Fredrik nodded, digging his hands into his trouser pockets. 'I've come across that phenomenon now and again,' he said. 'But where does Mandela come into it? Is it Nelson Mandela you mean?'

'In a sense. But he wasn't the one who misremembered. It was someone else.'

'What?'

'A slightly crazy lady, I've forgotten her name, was sure she remembered Mandela dying while he was in prison. She could describe his funeral down to the last details. Which in that case must have happened while he was still a prisoner on Robben Island. Before 1990, that is, not in 2013.'

Selma was shivering in the chill of the evening and was desperate to go back inside again, but Fredrik showed no sign of feeling the cold. On the contrary, he seemed, for the first time since she had met him in a cleaner's cupboard at Ullevål, pretty relaxed. His breathing was deep and even and he closed his eyes from time to time as he stood there.

'She could have been written off as being off her head,' Selma continued, 'and it's true she was overly interested in paranormal powers. The interesting thing, though, is that she shared this false memory with quite a lot of other people.'

'Eh? People are nuts.'

'You could say that. This bear experience of yours could have been like that. You say yourself you didn't mention it until a year later. Your memory could have been playing you a really serious trick.'

'Maybe,' he said. 'I suffer more often from forgetting things that have really happened, to be honest. What's the explanation for it all?'

Selma gave a lopsided smile. 'It depends who you ask. The woman who was the originator of the expression believes it's to do with parallel universes that sometimes brush against each other.'

Fredrik laughed. Selma could not recall having heard him laugh before. The laughter was deep and easy on the ear.

'If you ask the conspiracy theorists, they have a lot to offer. That it's about the manipulation of information by evil-minded governments experimenting on our brains, for instance. Psychologists and psychiatrists, on the other hand, think more in the direction of things we might be able to believe in.'

With a yawn, she added: 'Not exactly my field of expertise. If I were to make a guess, I do at least believe that some things are so difficult to live with that our subconscious sometimes hoodwinks us. We embellish reality, plain and simple. So that it becomes easier to live with.'

'But I did see those bears. And there was nothing difficult about it, other than that I got scared. For no reason. Since they can't really have been there.'

'Exactly. You got scared. It could have been something else you were really afraid of. An anthill, for that matter.'

Fredrik did not respond. He glanced down at the ground, where tufts of grass were forcing their way up through the paving stones. Using the tip of his toe, he tried to kill the stubborn remains of a dandelion that had withered long ago.

'I really can't work out what to do,' he said softly.

'Nothing,' Selma said. 'For the moment you mustn't do anything except investigate Linda's death.'

He stood in silence, kicking the ground.

'Why have you brought your laptop?' he asked all of a sudden.

'Just from habit,' Selma lied. 'There's probably not even any power up here. Or Internet connection, for that matter.'

The machine was fully charged and if a Wi-Fi connection was required then she could connect it to her new mobile and use 4G. Originally she had thought of opening the zip files in the policeman's company. Now she discarded that idea. She would not risk him seizing the memory stick in evidence and taking it with him to Police Headquarters. Then the case would be entirely beyond her control.

A short time ago that had been precisely what she wanted. To get rid of it all. To put it behind her, make peace with Anine and get to meet little Skjalg.

That was no longer true.

The complex case was motivating her. At last. It was utterly thrilling. Last night she had slept like a log for the first time in ages. She had woken rested enough to clean her apartment and she had been resourceful enough to pay a visit to Allan Strømme. Since then everything had simply grown increasingly complicated.

Life had become a game, a challenge with no certain outcome. Her thoughts had not touched on poker for thirty-six hours. This was better. What was at stake here was her relationship with Anine, the risks were high, and she would need loads of luck in order to win. But also skill.

Selma felt on top of the world again for a brief moment and wanted to keep the memory stick to herself. At least until Lars could tear himself away from his son's hospital bedside.

'By the way, there's one thing you could maybe do,' she said.

'What's that?'

'On 17 August, there was an accident at the Bislett roundabout. A young man on a bike collided with a taxi and died. Could you check whether it was really an accident?'

He stared at her doubtfully.

'Which it most likely was,' Selma quickly added. 'But if you could just take a quick look at it, to make sure it was beyond doubt a real and unintentional crash, I'd be really grateful. The victim's name was Jonathan Herse.'

'Does it have anything to do with all this?'

'Probably not, in all seriousness. But can you just have a look at it?'

'On one condition.'

'Which is?'

Turning to face her, he crossed his arms over his chest. Out here in the wilds, in his old Wellingtons and Icelandic sweater and with his new shorn hairdo, he looked more handsome than she had ever noticed before. Not exactly handsome, to tell the truth, but attractively masculine. In a slightly mournful way, as if there was too much in life that he had already given up. Birger Jarl had said that Fredrik was recently divorced. That often meant they had not come much further than a separation order, and Selma had noticed he still wore his wedding ring. It was so deeply embedded in the flesh of the ring finger on his right hand that it had possibly proved impossible to remove it.

'If it turns out that Børre Rosenhoff has been killed,' Fredrik said solemnly, 'then we have to go further. To my superiors. With all these thoughts of ours.'

He nibbled at a loose flap of skin on his lip. 'All those thoughts of *yours*,' he corrected himself. 'Do we have a deal?'

Selma could smell the scent of a bonfire far in the distance, an almost imperceptible trace of smoke combined with wet, dead leaves and something she could not quite identify. She squinted at the ridge of a hill on the other side of the lake. It had almost merged into the sky now. Just behind them there was still a narrow strip of daylight left. It would sink down into the west in a few minutes and disappear.

'Yes,' Selma said at last. 'We have a deal.'

Eureka

Pussycat had once been called Darius after a fabled king of Persia. His territory at that time had been vast and even though he was an expensive pedigree cat, he enjoyed most of all roaming through the gardens around the villas on Ormøya island, hunting for mice and small birds. Despite his noble antecedents in the Middle East, he had never stayed indoors for more than a few hours at a time. Whenever a collar had been put on him, he had come home without it. No one had ever discovered how he managed to get rid of them. Darius was a free spirit.

Now he was called Pussycat and lived in an area of fifty square metres with a man who took him out for fresh air, on a leash, in a park, a couple of nights a week.

Pussycat had never been happier.

He was living with a true cat lover. The animal was always cleaner than his human owner and usually his stomach was fuller. He was fastidious about keeping his coat sleek and seeing to his toilet needs, though never too fussy. His food arrived in a bowl four times a day – he had become a plump cat. He was on the receiving end of more than enough hugs and cuddles in that little apartment and they were both all the happier for that. He was even allowed to sleep in the human's bed, something he had never done before he moved house.

His owner was kind. His voice was soft, just like his hands when they stroked his back. Sometimes the man changed, something that no longer confused the cat. Pussycat just withdrew a little. Stayed in the bedroom during the day or took up residence on top of the big heaps of newspapers that regularly piled up at the front door. In these strange periods, the man talked to himself, not to Pussycat, and his voice was different. Fortunately these spells were increasingly rare. It had been a long time since the last one.

Right now Pussycat stood in the middle of the living room, arching his back and hissing in confusion.

The man had abruptly leapt up from the settee, stretching his hands up in the air and shrieking. The sounds that emerged from his throat were far too loud, far too piercing. His face was almost twisted and it looked as if he were boxing with some invisible entity just below the ceiling.

'Eureka!'

The cat snarled and slinked off into the hallway.

'Selma needs to know this!' the man shouted at the top of his lungs as he raised his fists in the air in a gesture of triumph.

SUNDAY 15 SEPTEMBER

The Sound Files

The first thing Selma noticed when she woke unexpectedly was that it was still pitch dark outside. At this time of year, dawn came creeping in at the back of five. She turned over in bed to sleep on. Fredrik had driven her home from the little timber cabin in Sørbråten around ten the previous night. He had a rattle-trap of an old Kia and the rubbish littering the car bore witness to his unhealthy diet. Before Selma could sit inside, he had swept out a considerable number of McDonald's containers and cola bottles from the passenger seat.

Her new phone used facial recognition that she had not yet mastered. She scrabbled around a bit before she could see what time it was.

03.47.

Admittedly, she had been so tired when she arrived home that she had only eaten a slice of bread before having a shower and collapsing into bed, but she had hoped to be able to sleep longer than this. Just as she was about to put down the mobile, she saw that Einar had called.

That almost never happened. He was terrified of the phone and she could picture him muttering as he used a whole roll of aluminium foil to wrap the device for protection. In other words, something important must have happened, especially since he had plucked up the courage to make as many as six attempts. Selma had shown sufficient presence of mind to turn the phone to silent. For a moment she lay looking at the mobile before deciding to call him back.

No. His last attempt had been made at ten to twelve. Now he was almost certainly fast asleep. In his healthy periods he was dependent on fixed routines far more than the average person, not least including getting a good night's sleep. She would try tomorrow. Or today, in fact. In a few hours' time.

There was no point in trying to fall asleep again. She was already so wide awake that she could not stop thinking about the password-less memory stick Allan Strømme had handed her the previous day. Last night she had managed to resist the temptation to take a closer look at it. Or more accurately, to listen to it. She had wanted to be at her best when that happened. Even though she both needed and wanted to sleep for a few more hours, the thoughts whirling around in her head made that impossible. Instead she got out of bed and shrugged on a college sweater and a pair of joggers before slipping her feet into her Birkenstocks and padding out into the kitchen.

She helped herself to that week's ration of sugary soft drinks from the fridge: one can of full-fat cola. The first mouthful always tasted best. Packed with sweetness and caffeine, she immediately felt even more wide-awake. From a drawer she produced a packet of rough oatcakes before settling down at the dining table in the living room.

Her laptop lay where she had left it the previous night, the memory stick already inserted in the USB port. Starting up the machine, she chewed down half an oatcake before everything was ready. The faint tingle of anticipation in her body felt almost like falling in love. Or like sitting with a brilliant hand in her fingers, waiting for the last card to be turned. She was tense, expectant, nervous and really pretty scared.

The list of contents on this memory stick was the same as the one belonging to Jonathan Herse. First of all Selma opened the document called simply *A.docx*. From memory the sequence of weird codes was identical to the one she had perused with Lars. She sent a message to the printer in the hallway to give her a copy and moved through to pick it up. On her return, she placed the sheet of paper on the left-hand side of the laptop and closed the document.

As she placed the cursor on the zip file, the anticipation and tension heightened.

Click. The file opened. As expected, they were sound files, eight in total. The first recording was more than an hour and a half long, she saw from the counter.

Selma pressed *play*.

The noise of chairs scraping across the floor and an unnerving beeping was the first thing she heard. The volume was a bit too high so she turned it down a little. A voice began to speak when the beeping stopped, a man who did not introduce himself. So it seemed to be a meeting whose participants knew one another so well that introductions were unnecessary.

'Damn cold today,' the voice said. 'I forgot my gloves.'

Small talk for a couple of minutes. The sound of at least one more person on the way in. Clearing of throats, coughing, sneezing. If Lars and Selma had interpreted the codes correctly, it was January and the first working day after the Christmas holidays. The alternating mild and icy weather throughout the festive period had obviously caused several of them to suffer from colds and chills.

The first quarter of an hour was boring. Office chat. A photocopy machine needing service. Discussions about a proposal that had to be completed as well as the follow-up to a strategy memo concerning the management of Child Welfare's first-line service. Selma impatiently spooled forward, ten seconds at a time. Still nothing of interest to outsiders.

She glanced down at the printout beside the computer.

1. 02.01.19 CFAD HBP Cnr 1, doc 2+3, Sf archive.zip 01.13.14

When she and Lars had looked at the sequence for the first time, they had guessed that the last group of three numbers was a time code. She let the cursor move the recording on to 01.12.00.

'... enough for today,' said the same male voice that had opened the meeting by complaining about the weather. 'Take care on the ice, all of you.'

More scraping of chair legs on the governmental linoleum. General chit chat, a door opening with a thud. Nothing of any particular note and the meeting definitely seemed to be over.

'Allan,' the same voice said so loudly that it crackled through the loudspeaker. 'Have you got a minute? Shut the door, please.'

The general chatter was silenced as the door closed with a click.

'Sit down,' the voice said cheerfully.

It sounded as if Allan did as he was asked.

'What's the situation? Did you spend Christmas taking a closer look at it all?'

'Yes, at least some of it.'

'And?' The voice already sounded annoyed.

'I definitely think,' Allan said – Selma thought she could hear a touch of nervousness in his voice – 'there's a clear dichotomy between several of these cases and the decisions we can anticipate if they come up in the EEA's Grand Chamber.'

'What do you mean?'

Rustling of papers. Some kind of harsh tapping that Selma immediately guessed was Allan's fingers on his iPhone, which he had probably hidden in his pocket.

'We're going to be found guilty in a number of cases, Horatio.'

Now the voice had a name. A name that concurred with the initials on the numbered list she had on the printout. The Director General in charge of the Ministry's Child Welfare Department.

'Exactly how many,' Allan continued, 'we don't yet know. But some of those lawyers out there have tasted blood, you know.'

'I see. That's detrimental. Extremely detrimental. We're finally in the process of rolling out this strategy ...'

A strange sound could be heard, perhaps the movement of air. It was possible he was waving something. Quite angrily.

'More knowledge – better child welfare,' Allan read out.

Smart. He was the only one who knew the conversation was being recorded. The young man was well prepared and on the alert.

'Skills development in local authority child welfare services,' he read on.

'I know what it is,' Horatio said irritably. 'And according to plan, this fairly comprehensive Child Welfare Reform will come into operation as early as 2022. The last thing we need now is a drubbing from the Human Rights Court.'

His final words were spoken in a distorted tone. It might almost be thought that the guy disapproved of the very concept of human rights.

'We are Norway,' he added sternly. 'If anyone can boast when it comes to human rights, it's us. Not to mention children's rights.'

Selma heard a sliding noise she could not quite figure out.

'Well,' Allan said. 'I've done a lot of reading. I've spoken to a lot of people. Including some of the lawyers involved on the side of the complainants, but also with people connected to the court in Strasbourg. Based on that, and the more dubious signals I've managed to interpret, as well as the seemingly pretty eager willingness to take a closer look at our cards in this area, the Grand

Chamber of the ECHR is going to give us a right good drubbing. And then some.'

Horatio Bull-Pedersen coughed. 'We have to do something about it.'

'What?'

'You heard what I said.'

'Yes. No. At least I didn't really understand.'

'These cases are quite varied, aren't they?'

Rustling of paper. Selma could not imagine that they would have specific individual case files in the Ministry and assumed this must be some kind of summary. Legal opinions, hopefully anonymized.

'Well,' Allan Strømme hesitated.

'All child welfare cases are different,' he said. 'Nonetheless there is reason to believe that the main focus will be on our practice in the area of access and adoption. As you know even better than I do, some people out there feel we are too trigger-happy when it comes to removing children at birth from disadvantaged parents. And if they, especially the mothers, are in fairly hopeless life circumstances, we have to admit that from an early point, our work is predicated on their adoption by strangers being the most likely outcome. As a result, access to children by their biological parents is a rare event. And very time-limited. And thereafter even rarer, and in the end non-existent.'

'Out of concern for the child! The child's best interests guide our action, a principle that's always been the force behind Norwegian child welfare provision.'

Horatio Bull-Pedersen could hardly have had a peaceful Christmas. Now he seemed absolutely desperate. His voice was totally different from the one he had used throughout the previous hour when many people had been present during a meeting of extremely convivial character.

'I agree,' Allan said, surprisingly unruffled. 'But you have to admit we have a problem if our decisions contravene the European Convention of Human Rights. That's just the way it is.'

A bang, like a fist on the table.

'What else can we expect, when there are judges down there in Strasbourg from cultures that scarcely bat an eyelid if people slap their children? Who regard children as ... as property! Albania! What do they know about children's rights? Judges from Armenia? The Ukraine? Eh?'

'Horatio—'

'I want a list of the statements given by these complainants.'

'They're mostly contained here in this ...'

The noise that followed sounded like paper being pushed across the table.

'I mean *really* specific,' Horatio Bull-Pedersen said, somewhat calmer now. 'I want to know quite specifically what the lawyers believe has been done wrong and should be undone, and what has not been done that according to the ECHR ought to be done.'

'I don't entirely understand. If and when we are convicted in the ECHR, the Norwegian Supreme Court will then discuss—'

'There must be things here that can be fixed.'

'Fixed? You mean—'

'I mean exactly what I say. You understand me. If not, the two of us have a problem. I expect an overview by Monday. Of real cases and with suggestions as to what can be fixed.'

More scraping of chairs followed by a beeping noise.

Silence.

The tape had ended. Selma must have heard it wrongly. Drawn erroneous conclusions. She must have put more into what Horatio Bull-Pedersen had said than there was any basis for.

That must be how it was.

She sat for several minutes, deep in thought. Staring at the screen, on which the file was now just a grey, broad line with the round cursor resting at the far right. It was so quiet she could hear the cola fizzing in the can.

Her eye finally fell on the sheet of codes. Or the list, maybe the menu, she had not quite made up her mind what to call it.

1. 02.01.19 CFAD HBP Cnr 1, doc 2+3, Sf archive.zip 01.13.14

This was the first sound clip. The date was the second of January this year. The location was the Ministry for Children and Families. Selma guessed the case was the first in a series. But *doc 2+3*? She already knew what the file name that followed meant. The final numerical code was definitely an indication of time.

Documents two and three.

These could be documents in a particular case. Horatio and Allan had not discussed any specific cases.

Once again thoughts whirled through Selma's mind, but nothing would stick. It was as if she continually came close to a conclusion so terrifying that her head simply refused to cooperate.

Horatio had said that the cases could be 'fixed'.

Fixing something could mean repairing something. You could not 'repair' a case that had already been dealt with by the Norwegian justice system. In order to be considered for processing by the Court of Human Rights in Strasbourg, all Norwegian avenues must already have been explored.

There was nothing that could be 'fixed'.

Unless they were talking about it as it was meant in the world of sport.

Where 'fixing' involved rigging something. Cheating.

Selma grew hot and cold by turns and grabbed the can of cola. She drank all that was left. Drawing her chair even closer to the table, she picked up a Post-it block from the corner and took a pen from her bag.

Then she listened to the other seven recordings.

Two and a half hours later she knew more than she ever wanted to know. She had a strong urge to turn back time to yesterday and pay no attention whatsoever to this case. As a matter of fact, she wanted to rewind all the way back to Thursday 5 September at five to three in the afternoon. That was when she had been on her way to Grünerløkka for a late lunch with her good friends Linda Bruseth and Vanja Vegge. She could have turned round. In the middle of Olaf Ryes plass, where she recalled catching sight of the other two on the opposite side of Thorvald Meyers gate and they had waved at her. She could have put on a sorry face, thrown out her arms in apology and gone a different way.

Or just sent a text.

Then her life would have looked different and she would not be sitting here on a Sunday morning in September with no idea where she should take what she thought had just gone through her head. Most tempting of all was simply to burn the memory stick, break off all contact with Lars Winther and maybe even move abroad. Flee from such a gigantic scandal she manifestly had no wish to have anything to do with.

But that was impossible.

The Cleaner

Seven-year-old Leon would recover with no permanent injury. Nothing serious at least: the doctors thought he might be bothered a little by stiffness in his hips and lower back in the years ahead. With good follow-up care and hard work from both the boy and his parents, however, everything would go well. First he had to stay in hospital for at least ten more days and then ideally attend an institution specializing in intensive rehabilitation. One of his parents would be able to go with him, in that case.

The boy's head was intact.

Lars had been terrified when he had seen his son only an hour after the accident, the small body hooked up to all kinds of tubes, pipes and machines – what little he could see of his face with all the equipment was hardly recognizable.

His head, had been Lars's immediate thought. His brain must not be damaged.

Lars would be happy to put up with anything, almost anything at all, but Leon had to wake up as the boy he had been before the accident. He had to have that same inquisitive attitude to life, he had to retain his love of mathematics and the films of Hayao Miyazaki. Lars could get a trike for him if the boy could no longer keep his balance. Maybe even a power-assisted one. They could move house if Leon was dependent on a wheelchair, he and his wife had already agreed on that, and he could carry the young lad on his back to the woods to go fishing in the Marka lakes if that proved necessary. They could sort it all. They could live with all that.

As long as his head was undamaged.

God must have heard him, Lars mused as he walked through the doors of the *Aftenavisen* offices in Akersgata in the middle of Oslo city centre. Not that he had thought too much about an omnipresent power prior to this, but in the last few days he had prayed often and wholeheartedly to a God who perhaps did exist after all. This morning his boy had been able to eat by himself for the first time since the accident and had asked for food from Burger King. Since none of the fast food outlets were open at seven a.m., he had promised his son a Whopper with all the trimmings for lunch instead.

And so it suited him to pop into work and do some checking. To get the sense that there was still some kind of normality in the world. And, if Lars were to be entirely honest, to escape from both the hospital and his wife. Their two younger sons had grandparents and good neighbours to take turns looking after them and if he were to be completely honest, he had to admit he did not miss any of them. They were fine.

These last few days had been a living hell and he needed to breathe in the smell of a newspaper office.

It was Sunday-quiet in the building. Having no desire for questions about how things were with his son or himself, he steered clear of the few people sitting around, most of them glued to a monitor, some wearing headphones. He negotiated his way through the open-plan office and into one of the quiet rooms without anyone having actually noticed him.

With a sigh of relief, he took off his cap.

He logged in on one of the two computer monitors while trying to phone Selma. The call went straight to voicemail. This was the third time he had attempted to reach her this morning and he was becoming irritated. A couple of days had passed since the accident before it dawned on him that he had left Jonathan's papers, with the memory stick and everything, at Selma's apartment when he had raced out the door in his dash to the hospital. It did not really matter: in the best-case scenario, she would have moved on a bit further with the story.

All the same, he could not stand the idea of her making herself unreachable.

Actually he had nothing to do in the office.

Leaning back in the swivel chair, he clicked into various online newspapers. The door opened behind his back and he noticed the skivvy come in. The cleaner, he should say. Lars mumbled a hello. She gave him a shy 'good morning' in return. Lars was reading an article about the previous day's drone attack on two oilfields in Saudi Arabia, in which the Energy Minister expressed regret that production had been halted in both fields. He also noted that Bernie Sanders had cancelled a number of election rallies to spare his failing voice.

'Old fogey,' Lars muttered.

'What did you say?'

He saw that it was the dark-skinned woman with the black chador who had worked there longer than he had. It must feel hot in that clothing. And pretty impractical, too, since the generous fabric fluttered around her as she wielded the brush.

'Nothing,' he said, clicking on through the news.

'Excuse me?'

Once again he looked up, more annoyed than surprised.

'Yes?'

'I don't mean to disturb you, but could I ask you something?'

'Er … yes.'

'You knew Jonathan Herse, didn't you?'

Lars put down the mouse and finally looked her straight in the eye.

'Yes. He was a colleague. We weren't … friends or anything. Did you know him?'

'Yes.'

She gave a faint smile. Her teeth were white and well cared for. Her eyes were large and angled down a little at each side, which made her look a bit sad.

'I was helping him. And he was helping me.'

'Oh? With what?'

'With the Child Welfare Service.'

Now she was almost whispering and moved closer.

'Jonathan was working on a very big story,' she said. 'And I have a lot of problems with the child welfare people myself. They took my girl. She was just newborn. Jonathan listened to me more than my lawyer ever did.'

264

Lars drew out the other chair, turned it round and signalled for her to sit down. The woman threw a glance at the door.

'No one's coming,' Lars said. 'Anyway, you're not doing anything wrong by talking to me. Just take a seat. My name's Lars Winther. What's your—'

'Aisha,' she broke in, placing her hand on her heart and nodding a little. 'Aisha Mohammad. I know who you are. You're working on Jonathan's story, aren't you?'

Slowly and carefully, she sat down, as if afraid the chair would not bear her weight. She perched on the edge, obviously ready so spring up at once if anyone came in. It made Lars feel uncomfortable that she was so obviously ill at ease.

'Yes, in a way I am. But what ... how did you and Jonathan—'

'You all don't see me and don't hear me either. But I hear everything you say and do. I know who's working on what and what everyone thinks about the new editor.'

Again that quick, sad smile: her face was divided into a happy mouth and mournful eyes. Swallowing audibly, Lars found himself feeling slightly ashamed. They had shared the same workplace for more than a year now and he had never spoken a single word to her.

'Jonathan had got something from a friend,' she said in an undertone. Something very com-pro-mis-ing. About child welfare. I knew that. I hear everything, you know.'

Shaping her hand into a bowl, she placed it behind her fabric-covered ear.

'So I took my case to him very late one evening. He was very kind, Jonathan. Very kind and capable.'

'I see. So ... so one of the cases in Jonathan's folder is yours?'

'Yes. It was five years ago now, you see. I was only sixteen when my daughter was born. I was living in a foster home myself, and it was not good for me. They said things wouldn't go well.'

'Who?'

'Child welfare. They decided. I was allowed to stay with her for nearly a fortnight. With my daughter. Sayneb. At the Mother and Baby Home. Or, it's called something different now, but everyone still calls it that all the same. But you know, no matter what I said or did, everything was wrong. They didn't give me a chance. She was placed in a foster home. I was allowed to see her sometimes at the beginning. But then a decision was made by the Welfare Board and after that I got access twice a year, you know. Now Sayneb is no longer mine. I'm not allowed to see her. She's been adopted and I don't even know what her name is.'

Her eyes, that seemed even larger now, were shining with tears.

'Even though I did what they said. I've gone to high school and taken exams. For four years, and I've worked really hard. I'm good at maths and science, but I'm not so good at Norwegian. Just level 2. In maths I got a 5, even though I took an advanced course. That is difficult. I want to be a nurse, but for that I need to have better marks in Norwegian. At least a 3. So now I'm taking more tuition and will re-sit my Norwegian exam.'

'Impressive,' Lars mumbled half-heartedly, though she paid no attention to that.

'I did exactly what they said. I pulled myself together. The whole time they said I would get Sayneb back if everything went well. But now ...'

Her head shook gently and tears spilled from her moist eyes.

'Now I live on my own. I take care of myself and I work very hard. I'll succeed with that Norwegian language too. And become a nurse. But I'll never be able to see Sayneb again.'

Lars was at a loss for words. He felt uneasy beside this young woman. Uncertain, and that felt uncomfortable. He started thinking that maybe she should not be in the same room as a grown man, all by herself. He did not really know. The woman must be a devout Muslim, wearing clothes like that. At Ullevål one of the nurses had worn some sort of hijab, but that was white and only covered her hair. Apart from that she was like the others, in white trousers and shirt. The garment Aisha wore would never be accepted as work-wear in a hospital. He glanced at the door, which was closed. It was too warm in the room and when he ran his finger under his nose he realized his top lip was damp.

'They had falsified my papers,' Aisha said.

'What?'

'I found out, you see. I've read all the documents in my case file many times. Then suddenly there were more papers in it. Two documents that said they had tried to help me many times. That they had given me lots of chances. That I had been allocated a support worker at the Mother and Baby Home. That I was offered an apartment where an assistant would come every day. That was a lie. All of it. They said I had been violent towards a staff member. That's nonsense. My lawyer was going to take the case to Strasbourg, to the Court of Human Rights, but all of a sudden everything looked different. He said ...'

She broke off and stared in alarm at the door. Outside they could hear at least two people walking past, talking loudly and starting to laugh, but they eventually disappeared into the open-plan office.

'I gave Jonathan all my papers,' Aisha went on. 'And he talked to my lawyer. Jonathan had some kind of folder with many cases and many cuttings: I gave him a lot of what I had seen on the Internet. I wanted—'

'Was it you?' Lars interrupted when a sudden thought struck him. 'Were you the one who put a new article into the green folder after Jonathan died? The one about leaks from the ECHR that made the Attorney General so angry?'

'Yes, I heard you'd been told to take over the story. You didn't want it. You begged to get out of it. I wanted to make you a bit curious and I wanted ...'

Dimly, far back somewhere in his memory, Lars could recall a cleaner coming in to empty the editor's bin during their first conversation about Jonathan's folder. This girl was sharp as a tack. It was exactly the presence of another news clipping, obviously inserted after Jonathan's death, that had ignited Lars's first little spark of interest in the story.

Aisha suddenly fell silent when someone knocked on the door. Lars was tempted to sit completely still and ignore it, but thought it necessary to answer.

'Come in.'

A woman in her fifties in a simple hijab and a floral tunic over polyester trousers opened the door and stood in the doorway with her hand on the doorknob. She gave Lars a brief nod before launching into a tirade that made Aisha jump up out of her chair. Lars assumed the language to be Somalian.

If there was such a thing as a Somalian language: he did not really know, to be honest. On further reflection he did not even know if Aisha was from Somalia.

He sat there without saying anything, without defending Aisha and without making any effort to smooth over the situation at all. He merely watched as the young woman grabbed her cleaning implements and followed the older woman out as she continued, albeit at lower volume, her reprimand.

And it occurred to him that he could scarcely remember what she looked like, only seconds after she had left. Her clothing got in the way of her personality. She was a bright and probably sweet woman, with all kinds of opportunities, if only she dispensed with that impractical, horrible garment. Not that it was really any of his business, people could wear whatever they liked for that matter, and Lars Winther was far from being a supporter of any kind of ban, but it was ever so slightly more difficult to feel sympathy for people who found it absolutely necessary to wear that kind of religious clothing.

In all likelihood he would not be able to help Aisha. It was not up to him to do so either. Her story, on the other hand, was something he needed. If the young woman was right that the Child Welfare Service had committed flagrant forgery of documents in order to embellish their case, then it was a scandal of considerable proportions.

Lars Winther knew all about scandals and now he really *had to* get hold of Selma. He would just pop into Burger King first.

The Post-Mortem

When Selma Falck emerged from her apartment block in Sagene, a small crowd of young couples had gathered in front of the entrance, waiting for something. At least she guessed they were couples, they were huddled together loosely in pairs, four heterosexual and two women holding hands. A man of around her age, formally dressed and with cropped, slicked hair, was setting up a display board advertising a public viewing. As she passed, he looked up and smiled.

'Hi,' Selma said automatically and it crossed her mind that this was the same estate agent who had dealt with the sale of her own apartment.

Unfortunately, he took this as encouragement to engage in conversation. 'Happy with your apartment?' he asked, straightening up.

'Absolutely. You're still selling in this building, then?'

Luckily she had not come to a complete halt and within a few seconds she would be beyond his reach.

'Yes. People like estate agents to have local knowledge, you see. I've had extremely good results for this entire area.'

'That's good. Isn't it a bit early for a viewing, eleven o'clock?'

By now she had moved past him, so he was talking to her back when he almost shouted: 'Not at all! This block is popular. People would come during the night if I asked them to. Contact me if you're ever thinking of selling, won't you?'

Selma did not reply.

She nearly stopped again. Fredrik's dented Kia was parked immediately across the street. He obviously spotted her in the mirror because his arm emerged from the window and waved at her to come across. She approached the car, though she was on her way to see Einar and should really have been heading in the opposite direction.

'Hi,' she said, bending down towards him once she had reached the car.

'Get in,' he said.

Selma hesitated for a second and glanced at her watch. 'Why didn't you phone? I'm on my way to—'

'Please get in.'

Shaking her head a little, she skirted round the vehicle and did as he asked. This time at any rate the seat had already been cleared for her.

Fredrik himself looked as if he had been through a tumble drier.

'Have you slept at all since you drove me home last night?' she asked, sniffing the air with a theatrical flourish.

He had obviously succeeded in stopping smoking, but now he stank of stress.

'No, I've been working. When I dropped you off last night, I couldn't face going home. So I went to work. And a few things had happened there, to put it mildly.'

'Did you go to work so late on a Saturday night?'

'Criminals have no respect for either the clock or the calendar.'

Selma put on a smile. 'What did you find out, then?'

'That Børre Rosenhoff may have been murdered.'

'Oh ... I see? *May* have been? We could well have said the same yesterday, surely? That he *may have been* murdered.'

'We can say it with far more certainty now. He was *probably* killed. Or ... I don't entirely know. His death was at least far more dramatic than we thought at first.'

Letting go of the steering wheel, he put his head in his hands. He rubbed his face for a long time and then sniffed loudly several times before shaking his head vigorously and opening his eyes wide.

'Christ, I'm so tired. But I had to talk to you. And not on the phone. As I told you, I'm totally paranoid about those things.'

For the second time in twelve hours, Selma laid her hand lightly on his thigh. 'What has happened?' she asked calmly before pulling it away again.

Fredrik grabbed a paper cup of coffee from the centre console and gulped down the contents, swallowing loudly.

'Rosenhoff had felt unwell for a couple of days, as it turns out.'

Fredrik stretched his arm to the rear seat and grabbed a thermos. The contents were not particularly hot – there was not the least sign of steam when he took the plastic lid off the flask to pour out the black liquid.

'The guy was fit as a fiddle until last Wednesday morning. He got up at his usual time, half past five. Went for his usual run, five kilometres. Then made his regular breakfast for himself, his wife and children, oatmeal porridge. And then he was picked up by his daily transport, the government chauffeur service. Later that day he felt under the weather. It grew steadily worse and on Thursday he left work early because he could scarcely manage to stand upright.'

'Why didn't he get help?'

'His wife was away at the time. She says she nagged him on the phone, but he wouldn't do as she asked. He thought he had influenza or something like that. Pains in his body, diarrhoea. General debility. Of course, his whole image was about being fit and sporty. Men of his age have a remarkable delusion about their own immortality.'

'But ... what happened?'

'God knows. In any case, his wife had taken the children on Thursday morning to visit her parents in Hemsedal. He insisted they should go. It would give him peace and quiet and there was less chance of infecting her and the children. He was in touch with both his work and his wife on Friday but after that he did not pick up the phone. Through the night his wife sounded the alarm. The doctor who was called was told where the spare key was kept, but he brought a police patrol with him to be on the safe side. The Cabinet Minister was dead. They all thought it must have been his heart, of course, and there was some discussion of that. Our boys insisted the body should be taken for a post-mortem. Taking no chances.'

'Wouldn't that have happened anyway?'

'Bloody hell, never mind that,' Fredrik said crossly. 'The point was that when the body was undressed up there in Pathology, it turned out that he had underpants on beneath his pyjama trousers. And inside the pants he damn well had ...'

Selma saw he was struggling to suppress an inappropriate smile.

'The guy had three sanitary towels lumped together inside his underwear. Side by side or ... whatever. He was bleeding from his arse.'

'What?'

'There was blood coming out of his anus! Apparently he'd been embarrassed. Too embarrassed to tell anyone.'

'You're joking,' Selma whispered. 'Are you pulling my leg now?'

'No. He was laid out on the table late yesterday afternoon. At the pathologist's. I don't know what that kind of doctor envisages when sudden unexpected deaths arrive in that way. But I expect they're thinking in the direction of heart attack or brain haemorrhage, just like all the rest of us. So that was out of the question. When people's intestines bleed, apparently it can be due to a whole lot of things, from Crohn's disease via ulcerative colitis to ... cancer, for that matter. But when they cut him open, what a surprise they got. His internal organs were completely disintegrating. His intestines were bleeding. His liver had virtually given up the ghost. His kidneys were destroyed. The pathologist raised a red flag long before he had finished.'

'Why was that?'

'He began to fear it was some kind of virus. Or possibly poison. Some kind of bacteria for that matter. Then they have to take special precautions.'

'Did he already suspect that the Minister had been murdered?'

'Could be. I think doctors in those situations are fairly deductive. They feel their way forward with the most obvious hypotheses. Such as illness. If they're rejected, they move on. And on. Anyway, the conclusion they came to was that something really serious must have happened to that poor corpse. While it was alive, I mean. When I phoned them late last night, they'd raised the alarm to the police only minutes earlier in accordance with the protocols they have for such instances.'

'And are you mentioned in those protocols?'

'No. But I spent half an hour partly bluffing, partly overdramatizing, and got a clear signal from top brass to go and talk to the doctors. In such cases, forewarned is forearmed. We could be talking about a haemorrhagic virus, for example. That can be extremely serious and highly contagious into the bargain.'

'Hemora—'

'Haemorrhagic. Ebola, for instance.'

'*Ebola*?'

'Yes. Since Rosenhoff has never been to Africa and has not even been abroad in the last two months apart from a flying visit to Sweden, it was more likely to be nephropathia epidemica. That's a scary disease you can pick up in an ordinary Norwegian cabin. One of the ways the virus spreads is by mouse droppings.'

For a man with the limited capacity to remember people's names, Fredrik was impressively confident when it came to viruses. Selma had to ask him to tell her everything again from the very beginning; it was so surprising that she found it difficult to take in.

'In the meantime they'd embarked on comprehensive damage control up there. Or ...'

Annoyed, he scratched the bristles on his face, which had begun to resemble a dishevelled beard.

'Potential damage control, is what I should really say. They still didn't know what they were dealing with. But in such cases whole areas have to be cordoned off, people isolated ... to sum up, a fucking uproar.'

'But how on earth could Børre Rosenhoff have contracted such a virus?'

Fredrik groaned and hammered both fists on the wheel. 'We've no idea! Isn't that the very point, Selma? It could be a matter of poisoning, of bacteria, of all sorts of things!'

Now he leaned his head back on the seat and rolled his eyes towards the roof.

'Until further notice, the family are in quarantine,' he said. 'And it seems there's a real furore at the Ministry. They have to secure themselves against a possible virus without creating panic. Now they're standing up there in Pathology with these spacesuits on, wondering what the hell has hit them, I think.'

There was a prolonged silence.

'So all this could be down to a case of poisoning?' Selma asked when the pause had become painfully long. 'It doesn't have to be a virus?'

'Yes! It could be thousands of things!'

'Poisoning could be murder.'

'Or an accident.'

'Or murder,' Selma said.

One shot, she thought. One hanged. One poisoned.

Possibly poisoned.

She touched her temples with both hands. A throbbing pain pulsed behind her eyes. She opened them wide and moved her head from side to side. In the mirror on her side she could see increasing numbers of people streaming past to view the two-room apartment on the first floor.

'You must come to a meeting this evening,' Fredrik said, with a long-drawn-out yawn as he emptied out the rest of the coffee. 'At the Police Chief's office. I've been given permission to have you there. It's difficult to give an account of other people's ideas. And you were the one who started thinking in this ... direction.'

He waved his hand by way of illustration.

'What direction?'

'All this about the estates, the branches of government. If someone has done away with Rosenhoff, using poison or a virus or whatever kind of devilment we know nothing about, then ...'

Now he was massaging his sweaty scalp with the fingertips of both hands.

'We have to be one step ahead here. Things are happening so bloody fast. An unmarked car will come and pick you up at half past six. You'll be brought into HQ through the back door. Fortunately the press are still going around believing that Kajsa Breien killed herself and that Børre Rosenhoff died of an acute illness.'

'That won't last long.'

'No. That's why it's important that ...'

Selma was no longer listening. Her gaze was fixed on a faded Pride flag. It had been hanging from a window in the old building on the opposite side of the road for years. The bright colours of the rainbow were almost washed away. The purple patch had become pink. Things were not always as they looked.

The three branches of government. And maybe the fourth.

'Have you found out any more about Jonathan Herse's case?' she interrupted him in the middle of his argument.

'What?'

'Jonathan Herse. The journalist. The one who died in an apparent accident at Bislett. Have you had time to take a look at the case?'

'No,' Fredrik said, irritated. 'When the hell would I have had time for that?'

Shot. Hanged. Poisoned.

And then a road traffic accident, Selma mused. A tragic but everyday occurrence. A collision that had come first and that did not seem to be connected to the others in any way.

No. Maybe. Yes.

Shot, hanged and poisoned. There was something in that. Selma was just unable to grasp what on earth it could be. For the past quarter of an hour she had quite simply been bombarded with so much information and so many surprises that nothing in her head would stack up properly.

'See you, then,' she said instead, tersely, and stepped out of the car to pay a visit to Einar Falsen.

The Change

The man was at the graveyard again.

His visits had become more frequent now; he had more to say than usual. Grethe had never been very interested in his job. That was probably how she had learned to live with it. When he was at home, they talked about their boy and relatives and the weather, about holidays that lay ahead of them and garden projects they needed to make a start on. Never about what he was doing. After she died, he had tried to respect that. He kept things to himself. Anyway, there was not so much to say, but that did not matter. The most important aim of these visits to the cemetery was to find some peace. That was not easy to achieve and in these years he had found on many occasions that he had left the place more depressed than when he had arrived.

Now he was longing to go there.

Grethe was his comrade-in-arms, the only one who knew and the only one who would really have understood if she had still been alive. Now he was in high spirits, almost happy. The weather was cold and fresh, with a south wind driving the light cloud cover northwards at great speed. Dead leaves had swirled around him on his way to the grave. Down here in the one corner of the graveyard, however, it was quite snug. The gravestone was beneath a large elm tree and he put down his folding stool in such a way that he could lean his back against the rough trunk.

'It's all progressing just as it should,' he said, settling more comfortably.

He had brought with him a small pot of heather. Grethe was so fond of that colour, which she called lilac even though to his eyes it was clearly pink. She had so many names for colours, Grethe. To her purple was never just purple, it was violet or indigo, reddish-blue or bluish-red. The pot was sitting a bit crookedly and he had to lean so far forward to straighten it that he nearly fell off the stool.

'Like so,' he said, regaining his balance and brushing his hands together. 'That's better.'

Everything had gone so amazingly well. Actually he should not really be surprised. Through a long life he had learned by experience that nothing could be planned too carefully. The devil was in the detail. He had tried to get the boy to understand that when he was still living at home. Again and again he had hammered it into the boy, trying to get him always to remember:

'If you're thoroughly prepared, you'll never have any reason to be nervous. Nervousness is for the careless. The ones with no plan, goal or conviction.'

'It's gone better than I could ever have dreamed,' he said. 'And I don't even feel drained.'

He had planned for that too – the vacuum, the restlessness following a completed assignment, the urge for fresh, immediate challenges. As this had been the riskiest thing he had ever undertaken, he had also expected the ensuing sadness to be more profound than usual.

It was not.

Quite the opposite. When the assignment was over, he was filled with something that most resembled euphoria. Last night he had sat in the conservatory with one of the photograph albums. The third one, from the time when their son was a baby. For a while he had considered opening a bottle of *Hennessy Paradis*, the cognac that had been a gift from his colleagues for his fiftieth birthday – it had remained unopened for eleven years now. Fortunately he had dismissed the idea and contented himself with a cup of tea with a spoonful of honey added. The evening had been so beautiful. The darkness enfolded the glass walls as he sat there, nice and warm, and around midnight he had gone out into the garden for a stroll.

'Those gigantic verbenas of yours are still flowering,' he whispered with his eyes trained on Grethe's name on the bronze plaque. 'Even though we're into September. They're so lovely. Pink. Or purple. Or lilac, if you insist.'

He smiled. As usual, Grethe did not answer. It did not matter. She was here, all the same. Her garden was a wonder, comprising plants that flowered from Easter until far into autumn. The plot was like a living carpet, with colours and blooms that imperceptibly moved through three seasons. He had taken care of it all to the best of his ability, without ever entirely succeeding.

That did not matter either.

He remembered it the way it had been. Here, in the corner of a far too large and almost deserted graveyard, the only thing that meant anything was that he had carried out his plans.

Only one detail remained.

They had to understand what had happened and why. If they could not do that off their own bat, then he would need to help them. Making them realize what had really taken place, without them twigging who he was, would be a challenge.

'Look at that,' he said to Grethe, with a smile. 'Another assignment already. Not at all strange that I feel so satisfied, my darling.'

He stood up, aware that he would soon be able to attach the second plaque to the gravestone. The one the stonemason had wanted to put on as soon as the urn was in the ground, but that he himself had wanted to postpone until the whole enterprise was accomplished.

Now it would only be a matter of days.

The Disappointment

Selma Falck had not seen Einar so excited since the time when he had been at his most unwell. Now he was so happy to see her that he was jumping up and down on the floor. Selma stared at him in fascination. His arms were at an odd angle from his body, with hands alternately balled into fists and then all his fingers stretched out stiffly in time to his leaps.

'You look a bit like a really crazy old woman,' Selma said from the hallway door. 'Or like a five-year-old on Christmas morning.'

He stopped abruptly. His grin, however, did not disappear. Pussycat was nowhere to be seen and Selma assumed he had taken refuge in the bedroom amidst all the commotion.

'I've found your *staw-ker*!'

'Yes, you said that. In six voice messages last night and five texts this morning. Are you no longer afraid of the phone?'

'Well, yes. But I just had to get hold of you. You're hardly ever here!'

The last comment was spoken in an almost pathetic tone of voice.

'You silly old thing,' she said.

It sounded almost tender, and she quickly added: 'Sit down. I don't have much time.'

'No, no, no! Now we have to go through everything I've found. Thoroughly, Selma, very thoroughly. You'll be impressed. I guarantee that. You'll be really impressed. You can certainly chase old, mad Einar Falsen out of the police, but you really can't chase the police out of Einar Falsen!'

Once he had deposited the familiar tray wrapped in aluminium foil on his knees and lifted the laptop into place, Selma noticed that two of the letters on the keyboard had fallen off. The E and the G. It did not seem to affect Einar in the slightest once he had put the helmet on his head, tightened the strap under his chin and begun to hit the keys. It was not so good when parts of Darth Vader's mask could be clearly seen under the flaking paint on the cover.

'I think you might soon be needing a new computer,' she said. 'And you'll have to learn not to be so hard on the keyboard.'

'The first thing I did was to search some more on that webpage where I found the interview with "Ola",' Einar said without paying any attention to her offer. 'With particular focus on the guy who interviewed him. He calls himself a journalist, but he's really more of an activist.'

He froze, with his fingers stiff like claws above the keyboard. 'Do you know, Selma, I think we have a problem.'

'Who has a problem?'

'We. Norway. Now that I've dug into all this, and even though there are a lot of crazy people in there, it's really awful if we do actually take children away from their parents without having permission to do so. We really do have to take these human rights seriously, Selma. Yes, yes, true enough. The more cases like this I delve into, the clearer it becomes that the Child Welfare Service has a tendency to decide matters in advance. People don't really have a chance, you see. To turn over a new leaf.'

'Yes, I see,' Selma said, pointing at the screen. 'But now let's concentrate on "Ola", shall we?'

The claws attacked the keyboard again. 'Yes. Of course. "Ola". Where was I? The activist. Here!'

A photo of a man appeared on the screen. He could be in his early forties, with a receding hairline and an intense, almost obstinate, gaze. He was so skinny that his cheekbones seemed abnormally sharp and high.

'Sjur Vending!' Einar announced triumphantly, pointing. 'Father of two. Of children he has no access to.'

He glanced up with a grin. 'That rhymed!'

Selma gave him a look she hoped would force him back on track.

'They were taken from him and his wife in 2015,' he said hurriedly. 'He's fought with tooth and claw against the Child Welfare Service ever since. Or ...'

He cocked his head.

'... really since long before that. That was part of the problem, I assume. He was hostile towards them from the very beginning. Refused any kind of help. That's what I presume, though, because his version, the way he writes about it both on *theftofchildren.no* and other places is of course different. Well, I sent him an email, as you do. Made out that I was very much on his side, and that I was interested in all these cases that are headed for Strasbourg and suchlike. And then I would get the information and take it further ...'

All of a sudden he leaned back on the settee and folded his arms over his chest.

'Do you know, Selma, you can learn such a lot from the Internet. Just think, I've lost out on so many years of knowledge when I was wandering around as a down-and-out, sleeping under the Sinsen bridge. It's almost unbelievable, and I—'

'Einar. Stop it.'

He looked at her, taken aback.

'I understand you've done a lot of work and a good job,' she said.

'Yes! I'm going to show you how I discovered that staw-ker of yours! Once I'd found out more about that journalist, that led me on to—'

'Einar.'

He shut his mouth and placed his palm over it. 'Sorry,' he whispered through almost clenched lips.

'Even though you're clearly a brilliant detective, it's not necessary for you to give an account of every single step you've taken. I can take your word for it that you've made a Herculean effort.'

'You've no idea! A computer is like a ... detective machine! If you follow the clues through social media and webpages and back again and cross them with other names you find and then—'

'Einar!'

Her voice was too harsh. She was struggling to concentrate anyway after her conversation with Fredrik Smedstuen. When Einar was in such an excitable state, he was a real trial. She tried to take the edge off her irritation by flashing a smile.

'Let's go straight to "Ola",' she said as gently as she could.

'He's not called Ola.'

'No. What's his name, then?'

'Endre. Endre Cappelen.'

Einar stared at her, still with his hand over his mouth. When she carefully took hold of his arm, she noticed how tense he was.

'Do you have a picture of him?' she asked without releasing her grip. 'Can't we have a look at it while you tell me, slowly and steadily, who he is?'

Einar still sat as if rooted to the spot.

'I'd be really happy if you would do that,' she said in a near-whisper. 'It's so exciting, all this. Let me hear.'

His shoulders seemed to sink a little. He removed his hand from his mouth and took a deep breath.

'I just wanted to show you what a genius the Internet is.'

'I realize that.'

'And that I've learned how to use it.'

'You have indeed. I know that too. Let me hear about Einar.'

At last he moved his fingers to the keyboard. Selma had tried for a long time to get him to use a computer mouse, but since he preferred to sit on the sofa with the laptop on his knee, he had to use the track pad. He had also become skilled at managing that. A picture appeared on the screen.

'That's him,' Selma said brusquely. 'That's the man who stopped me.'

'Endre Cappelen,' Einar said.

'Endre Cappelen,' Selma repeated. 'I certainly don't remember the name, but it *was* him.'

The photo had been taken in summer. The young man was wearing a dark hoodie emblazoned with text she could not make out, across the chest. He had a faint smile and his blond hair had blown to one side. His teeth were conspicuously bad for his age, as they sometimes were in drug addicts. He was slim and fairly tall. It was difficult to tell for sure: he was standing beside a tree that gave no particular point of reference.

'What do you know about him?' Selma asked without taking her eyes from the photograph.

'Not very much. It's not so easy when only one side of the story is told. To summarize ...'

He looked almost roguishly at Selma, who smiled back.

'To summarize would be good,' she said.

'... he has fought for custody of his son since the child's mother died. Illness, I believe. The problem is that he doesn't know the youngster. Again, that's my interpretation. When you read the story about him online, you would feel terribly sorry for him. When you fill out the picture with some of the things we already know ...'

He gave a little snort.

'... then the picture looks a bit different, I think. As it always does. Fault on both sides is probably the norm.'

Selma felt dizzy and closed her eyes. She should not have let Einar loose on all this. It was not really good for him. At the same time she knew the pleasure he derived from helping her. Of seeming to help her, she should perhaps say. The stalker, whose identity until a short time ago it had been so important for her to find out, had dropped into the background for her now. The last time she had thought about it had been this morning. The fact that the handball was on her balcony probably meant he no longer had access to her apartment. Whether he had by some miraculous means managed to throw it up there, or whether he had dropped it out of the window in the empty apartment beside the one where the heavily pregnant Johanna and her family lived, no longer meant so much to her. All of this other stuff was far bigger. Far more important.

So endlessly more complicated.

'By the way, he's dead,' Einar told her.

'What?' Selma asked, opening her eyes again; she had almost dozed off in her seat.

'He died in July.'

'Er ... what?'

'Yes,' Einar said with a sudden upswing in enthusiasm. 'He seemed to disappear from all this stuff in here. Sometime in summer. Completely gone. Vanished. Then it struck me that I should have a look at the death notices. But I didn't find one.'

'No?'

'And then I began to think about what it was like in the police, what we did about these lone wolves. The paupers and the homeless and the petty criminals who didn't have anyone. Sometimes the council put in death notices for them. They're totally cheerless, too. Other times they might have a relative somewhere that we'd manage to get hold of. Some of them chose to skip the whole business of an announcement. But ...'

He stuck his finger triumphantly in the air.

'... on the webpage *lawcourt.no* ...'

The keyboard was complaining loudly.

'... they have a list of deaths reported for the whole of Norway. In alphabetical order and everything. Really excellent. The list is not complete there either, sometimes relatives reserve the right, but that's rare. And so ...'

Einar was about to point at something, but brought himself up short.

'Are you going to put in a death notice when I die, Selma?'

'Yes. What did you want to show me?'

'What are you going to write?'

'Einar!'

'There,' he answered quickly, pointing at the list of the dead. 'Endre Cappelen, Oslo. Born 23 June 1989. Just think, Midsummer's

Eve. Died 10 July 2019. Look at that! I've now found out everything there is to know about your staw-ker, Selma!'

He did a little drum roll on his helmet, making the silver paper rustle.

'You've done a brilliant job,' she said evenly. 'But he's not my stalker.'

'What? Surely we agreed ... you said I was to find out everything there was—'

'He's dead, as you say. He died in July. That makes it a bit difficult for him to come into my apartment in August and September.'

It was as if Einar suddenly deflated. Slowly, he slumped into his seat, his thin legs sliding so far out that the laptop threatened to tumble to the floor.

'Shit,' he said plaintively. 'Why didn't I think of that?'

His faint whimpering noises made Selma wonder if he was crying. She got to her feet.

'Don't take it so hard,' she said, forcing a smile. 'In the first place, nobody's really bothering me any more. I've got new locks. And secondly, you should be proud of the fabulous job you've done. You've become shit hot, Einar. In fact, you're my most important colleague.'

And strictly speaking, the only one, she thought. If 'colleague' was even the appropriate description.

'Are you crying?' she asked in astonishment when he did not answer.

He looked up. Big tears were hanging from his stubby eyelashes: one droplet had already broken free and was trickling down his cheek to rest on the stubble.

'Such a rookie mistake,' he said bitterly. 'Such a huge blunder. Sorry.'

'No need to apologize.'

He looked like an illustration of sorrow and disappointment.

Pussycat finally made an entrance from the bedroom. Soundlessly he stalked across the floor and jumped up on to Einar's lap. That made him sit up a little, but he still seemed just as crushed.

'Actually, I need you to help me find out something else,' Selma said.

'I'm an idiot.'

'No, you're very capable and I need you. I'd like to know as much as possible about a man called Torstein Heimdal.'

Now at least Einar looked up. 'Who's that?' he asked in such a quiet voice that she could hardly hear him.

'My neighbour. Above me. He's married and has a little boy. I don't know the names of the other members of the family. But he should be easy to find – his wife works in the Diplomatic Service. Of course, I could do it myself, but I don't really have time. Are you OK with that?'

Pussycat had rolled into a ball on his knee.

'Is it important?'

'Yes,' Selma lied. 'Very. I need to know as much as possible about both him and his wife. Could you also write a brief resumé on them?'

'Like a special report, you mean?'

'Yes. Exactly like a special report in the police. Torstein Heimdal. Are you writing it down? He has the same address as me, unless they've already notified their move. They're posted somewhere abroad.'

Einar had already moved Pussycat to a spot by his side on the settee. The last thing Selma heard when she opened the front door to leave was hammering on a damaged keyboard and Einar's voice muttering:

'Torstein Heimdal. Torstein Heimdal. Plus wife and small child.'

Ricin

A senior doctor at the infectious disease isolation ward in Ullevål Hospital had just arrived at work. In common with many others in his professional field, both in Oslo and other places, he had received an emergency callout. He had been halfway to Bjørnsjøen from Skar on Friday when his mobile rang, compelling him to turn back. While other experts in infectiology at Ullevål and other hospitals chose to collaborate, this man preferred to work alone. At least for the moment. He was now seated in his office in old, worn chinos, deep in concentration as he perused three documents.

This time they did not refer to a patient in critical condition.

About three kilometres away, at the National Hospital, however, lay a dead Cabinet Minister who was of steadily increasing interest to him as he read. The preliminary post-mortem report was unusually detailed, but could really be summed up in two words: total collapse.

Liver, kidneys, bowels, heart, multiple organ failure.

Sadly, the doctor had seen this before. With major intestinal bleeding, a patient would suffer hypovolemia sooner or later. Excessive blood loss. The pulse rate would soar and blood pressure plummet. Thereafter circulatory shock would follow. Blood vessels would narrow and internal organs would no longer receive sufficient blood and oxygen. Followed by unconsciousness and death.

It was regrettable that the poor man had not gone to see a doctor at the onset of the very first symptoms. It had all happened so suddenly and progressed very rapidly. From feeling unwell on the Wednesday, he grew worse on the Thursday and then died late on Friday night. Probably the bleeding from his anus had made him quite literally shut his eyes and hope for the best. The infectious disease specialist's wife was an oncologist and continually tore her hair out over embarrassed patients. By the time they at long last sought help for pain and bloody stools, the colon cancer had usually spread. For Børre Rosenhoff, it had also at some time through the night become too late to sound the alarm – he had seemingly lost consciousness some time before his death.

The senior doctor picked up another document. His colleagues at the National were keeping all possibilities open, he read. They were right to do so. The Cabinet Minister's internal collapse was consistent with a number of causes, virus, bacteria, cancer, but it was impossible to determine what had taken the man's life without conducting more exhaustive analyses. Which was tedious, because they could take time. In addition, the National Hospital was now in an extremely critical situation: the infectious disease specialist knew that extensive control measures had been initiated.

Some clear head had sent him a third communication.

A member of staff at the Institute of Public Health had written it and she must be unusually quick off the mark. In the time between midnight and eleven a.m., she had managed to put together a description of the deceased's movements in the past six weeks, which would normally have taken several days to reconstruct.

Lots of people must have had their night's sleep disturbed.

The infectious disease specialist read the three-page document repeatedly. All the papers had been sent to him in digital format but, being old school, his powers of concentration worked best with paper copies.

Børre Rosenhoff, Minister for Children and Family Affairs, had not been abroad in the past six weeks, with the exception of a one-day visit to Stockholm. That had been seventeen days ago, when the man had participated in an inter-Nordic meeting of Cabinet Ministers at a hotel close to Arlanda Airport. The return journey had occurred the same day.

None of the other participants at that meeting had shown any sign since of serious illness. Nor before that, either. On the domestic front, Rosenhoff had gone on one trip to Bergen in the course of the same period as well as two visits to Trondheim. Until now, the woman at the Public Health Institute had found no potential sources of infection or other illness along these routes either.

Apart from that, the Cabinet Minister had remained in Oslo.

Excluding cases of head colds and one instance of lumbago in a political adviser, Børre Rosenhoff had moved in a normal, healthy environment the entire time.

The doctor smacked his lips, leaned back in his chair and clasped his fingers at the back of his neck. 'Virus,' he whispered experimentally into the room.

He had served in Mali during an Ebola epidemic. When he returned home four months later, he forced himself to remember the knowledge he had gained and suppress everything else. It had been difficult. Not until six months afterwards had he been able to sleep right through a dreamless night.

Ebola's incubation period was from two days to three weeks. In other haemorrhagic viruses, such as nephropathia epidemica, it could take up to six weeks from infection to outbreak.

Unceremoniously he let go of his neck and placed his hands flat on the table.

Of course, the deceased could have been infected by a virus. The extensive injuries were pretty much consistent with, for example, an Ebola viral infection. All the same it was most unlikely. Quite the reverse, in fact. You could always construct theoretical possibilities for an individual being infected by an extremely serious viral illness in a geographical area where the virus had not been detected in anyone else. However, it was bordering on inconceivable as long as the patient had not been travelling.

The simplest answer was often the best. This also applied in the field of infectious diseases.

The Ebola virus did not exist in this country. In 2014, a Norwegian woman, infected in Sierra Leone, had been brought home to Norway for treatment. That had gone well. He himself had been the medic who treated her. The patient had made a good recovery and no one else had been infected. Admittedly, nephropathia epidemica was a virus that did exist in Norway, but only one person had ever died of it here. Besides, that had been as far back as 1998.

Of course it was correct to instigate infection control measures. The public health authorities had a duty to be on the front foot. The idea that a potentially fatal virus had infected and killed one person within an extremely large circle of associates, in which no one else had demonstrated any symptoms of the illness, nevertheless seemed improbable. So much so that the senior doctor, at least for the moment and as a working hypothesis, preferred to overlook that possibility. Others could concern themselves with that scenario.

Poison, on the other hand.

There were countless kinds all around us, all the time and everywhere. You could ingest them by accident. It happened once in a while, sometimes with fatal consequences. It was one thing that a number of medications in overdose could prove fatal, but entirely another that there were also poisonous substances in every well-equipped garage.

Furthermore, nature was full of poisons, completely natural poisonous material, in the sense that they belonged there and were not artificially manufactured. He himself had grown up hearing his grandmother's repeated warnings about the plants in the garden: foxgloves, laburnum and yew. She had been so afraid of an old castor oil plant beside her wrought-iron gate that it had been dug up and thrown away when his little sister was born in 1969.

Castor oil plant, he lingered on that.

All at once he stopped and grabbed the post-mortem report again, letting his finger run down the first page. The pathologist had, along with his technician, as usual conducted an external examination of the body before opening up the corpse. He had also been very punctilious on this point. The report described a man of average build. He had a small scratch on his thumb and a scar from having his appendix removed. Both knees had undergone meniscus surgery, approximately ten years previously.

In addition Børre Rosenhoff had a small puncture wound on his leg, described as about three millimetres in diameter, and it was not too deep for a natural, circular scar to have formed over it. Presumably fairly quickly. The description could fit a little jab of some kind, possibly an insect bite.

Pushing the papers aside, he drew the keyboard towards him.

Castor oil plant, he thought once again, as he tapped the keys to summon the pictures the pathologist had attached to the provisional post-mortem report. For a few seconds, he studied the photograph of the almost imperceptible but strikingly circular wound on the deceased's leg. All of a sudden he closed the email from the National Hospital and logged in to something completely different.

Ten minutes later it dawned on him that it had not mattered one jot that Børre Rosenhoff had not gone to the doctor's soon enough. No one would have been able to save him, at any rate. There were no medicines. No antidote. Not if the specialist in infectious diseases was right in his assumptions. He hesitated yet again as, with eyes firmly shut, he followed his train of thought. In the end he lifted the phone and dialled the number for the pathology section at the National Hospital, where he was immediately transferred to the right person and introduced himself.

'I assume you've tested for virtually everything up there now,' he said after a few introductory phrases. 'And of course that's all to the good. Since you've asked me for advice, I'd like all the same to request you look for traces of ricin.'

'Ricin?' the voice at the other end repeated, slightly taken aback.

'Yes. The pathologist's findings are consistent with ricin poisoning in every respect. Astoundingly consistent. You would probably have come to that conclusion sooner or later but I do think sooner would be best in every way possible.'

He paused briefly but the other person found no reason to comment.

'Ricin is certainly a hypothesis worth considering for several reasons,' the infectious disease specialist finally went on. 'Firstly because the substance is incredibly toxic, in fact a thousand times more toxic than cyanide. In other words, extremely small amounts are required to produce a fatal outcome. The deceased has a wound on his leg that reminds me of another fairly famous case of ricin poisoning. A murder. Another place and another time, but believe me, eerily similar.'

Once again he hesitated.

'And secondly, the raw material can be found in Norwegian gardens and outdoor spaces,' he added, 'in the seeds of the ornamental castor oil plant. The poison itself can be extracted by ... practically anyone at all.'

Terrifyingly enough, he thought, shivering a little as he rang off.

The Meeting

The first thing Selma Falck noticed after being picked up by an unmarked police car, ushered in through the back door of the Police Headquarters building and upstairs to a conference room on the sixth floor, was the flip chart.

She caught herself smiling at the rickety, archaic easel. The pad of paper was brand new and there were three marker pens on the metal runnel at the front. Angled a metre and a half from the end of the long table, it seemed to have been placed there for the occasion. Selma could not remember seeing such an ancient contraption for a very long time.

She was first to arrive.

The room was completely deserted and Selma felt a bit disorientated to be left there on her own when the officer who had accompanied her pointed out a chair. 'The others will be here in a few minutes,' he said before disappearing.

Which turned out to be true. Five minutes later, all the participants were present and correct. Selma was introduced to them all in turn by the Police Chief, with the greatest of solemnity. Beside the Chief of Police, Kjersti Sprang, the Head of Intelligence and Investigation was also there. Per-Arne Svendsen disliked his long and cumbersome title and insisted on using the good old 'Head of CID' tag. Fredrik Smedstuen had paid a visit home, Selma saw, and was now wearing a pair of light denim jeans she had not seen before, a white shirt and a blazer. Even his brown, shiny shoes were new, in her opinion. Until now she had never seen him in anything but running shoes or clumsy wellingtons. He had arrived in the company of a woman whose handshake was far too brutal and drawn-out, Inspector Sylvi Mobakk. Selma understood she had the same rank as Fredrik and was in charge of the inquiry into Kajsa Breien's death.

'Well,' the Chief of Police began, with a nod in the direction of Inspector Fredrik Smedstuen. 'You're the one who requested this meeting. I am, as you know, sceptical.'

She looked it too. She had not met Selma's eye as they shook hands and now sat with her shoulders thrust forward in a sullen, dismissive pose.

'This is highly irregular,' she said caustically, 'but so is the situation we face, for that matter, so I'll give this no more than an hour. Max. I assume Selma Falck has signed the necessary declarations of confidentiality?'

The Police Chief still did not look at her. She was talking as if Selma was not really there.

'Yes,' Selma replied all the same. 'The officer who escorted me arranged that. They should now be on your desk.'

'OK,' Kjersti Spang said, once again nodding in Fredrik's direction.

This was obviously a good enough start to the meeting. The Inspector placed a palm on the iPad in front of him, without turning it on.

'First I'll just run over, in broad outline, where we stand as far as Linda Bruseth's murder is concerned. Then Sylvi will do the same for the case we now assume to be the killing of Kajsa Breien. Then I'll give an account of developments in the last twenty-four hours concerning Cabinet Minister Rosenhoff. And finally we ...'

He looked up.

'... Selma Falck will present a theory you could say we developed in tandem.'

'I'm looking forward to that,' the Chief of Police commented tonelessly, quite literally wrinkling her nose. 'You're certainly staking much of your reputation on this,' she went on. 'But fire away. I'm all ears.'

A slight flush had crept up over Fredrik's cheekbone. He cleared his throat and prodded the iPad screen with his fingers.

'First of all,' he said, taking a deep breath, as if getting ready to jump, 'we're now as sure as we can be that Linda Bruseth was the sniper's target. At this point I'll simply make brief reference to the report I sent to you all this afternoon. We are, furthermore, reasonably convinced about the sniper's location when the shot was fired, and this is also described in detail in that report. As far as the forensic examinations are concerned, these all suggest the perpetrator used a ladder lying in the back yard in order to access the roof.'

'Any other forensic evidence?' the Head of CID asked. 'Fibres? DNA?'

'DNA from several sources. A number of fibres, textiles as well as metal and wood. Painstaking work is ongoing, sorting them all out. There had been recent repair work on the roof, which was also the reason three ladders had been left in the back court. In fact, a whole set of scaffolding had just been taken down. DNA is of no help to us in isolation, though, if we don't already have the profile on file. But of course we're doing further work on that.'

There was silence for a few seconds before the Chief of Police asked abruptly: 'Weapon?'

'The bullet was totally deformed,' Fredrik said, nodding once again towards Selma, who automatically touched her arm. 'But metallurgical and other tests have been carried out. Several more will be done. Provisionally we think it was a .222 Remington. We're not yet absolutely certain. If we're skilful and lucky enough, continued analysis will come close to identifying what ammunition we're dealing with, in the best case scenario even the place and time of production.'

'And what kind of weapon are we talking about, then?' the Head of CID asked.

'A lot of weapons still use this particular ammunition nowadays, even though .223 has become the more usual bullet. We're talking about a rifle intended for hunting game up to the size of roe deer. It's high velocity and the smaller the bullet and higher the velocity, the more likely it is to become deformed when it hits the target. We have little to no chance of linking a specific gun to this particular bullet even if we should stumble upon it. The barrel grooves are missing.'

'And how many such rifles are there in Norway?'

'Many. We're working on it.'

Fredrik's eyes had taken on a grim, almost irked, look. It seemed he was not really interested in continuing to speak. As if the lack of concrete evidence pointing in a particular direction after ten days of intensive investigation was mortifying. Selma knew that was far from true.

'Now, Selma Falck will explain a more ... general theory a little later. So I suggest we let things lie with this case for the moment, and move—'

'What about the victim?' the Head of CID broke in. 'What do we know about her?'

Fredrik used his right hand to rub his face before running the same hand over his bald head.

'If the woman had been a Catholic, she would've been in the running for beatification.'

He sighed audibly.

'A thoroughly decent person, Linda Bruseth.'

The glance in Selma's direction made her give a faint nod.

'Kind and adaptable. Well liked. A conscientious worker. Her home district's Mrs Fixit. A caring woman with five handsome sons, a solid marriage and finances in apple-pie order. Good friends. A less than successful half term in parliament, but that's scarcely reason to kill her. It's simply a mystery that anyone would bump her off. Something Selma will also come back to in her theory, which ...'

He let the unfinished sentence hang in the air. The Police Chief took the hint and held up her hand in invitation to Sylvi Mobakk, who picked up a glass of water and drained it before she began to speak.

'First and foremost it has now been established that Kajsa Breien did not hang herself. Some of us, of course, had realized that already, even at the scene where she was found. The marks from the rope were caused post-mortem and she was strangled before being hanged. Between three and six hours before the old wifie up there in Korsvoll came across the body, the pathologist suggests. So we're talking about a time of death between midnight and three in the morning. The last time anyone saw her alive was in the half-hour before midnight when she was in her garden with her dog.'

Sylvi Mobakk adjusted her ponytail before she went on: 'We do have a little geographical problem in this case. From Admiral Børresens vei in Bygdøy, where the deceased lived, to Grinda, where she was found, the shortest route is 11.7 kilometres. Outwith the rush hour, such as at night, that still takes just under twenty-five minutes to drive. At the moment we've discounted any transport other than car. The question is firstly, where was she killed? At home, en route or in the forest? Second, why there in particular? Why the hell, of all places, did this perpetrator choose to hang her on the other side of town?'

The question was left unanswered until Fredrik spoke up: 'We'll leave that question there until it's Selma's turn to speak. Then we'll get a possible explanation.'

'OK,' Sylvi Mobakk said, nodding.

She scratched the side of her nose before continuing: 'We know Breien went back into the house after stepping out for a blow of air, because the dog had been bedded down for the night. It didn't make a racket any time after this, as the children slept on undisturbed. Considering it's a terrier, that's puzzling. We're holding open the idea that the perpetrator may have been an acquaintance or a friend of the victim. Someone the mutt didn't react to.'

'Quite apart from the idea,' Fredrik began speaking again, 'that if he followed closely behind Breien and the dog into the house, the terrier may have thought he was a guest. Or it could have been too well trained, or tired, even. Or something.'

Sylvi Mobakk shrugged.

'Yes, of course. But at any rate ... either Breien has gone out again after putting the dog to bed, or else the killer has ent ... er ... possibly killers, plural, have entered the house. Since, for the time being, we assume Breien *did* actually go out again, it's not only because of the dog keeping its mouth shut. There's honestly no sign of any struggle inside the house. Our investigations are far from over yet but when we found a hidden flowerpot filled with cigarette ends under the steps outside, that opened things up for a different explanation.'

'Smoking on the sly,' the Head of CID suggested in an undertone.

'Exactly. Kajsa Breien was a secret smoker. None of the children knew about it but her husband confirms the judge was in the habit of having a fag at bedtime. Along with the dog, sort of thing.'

'Why didn't she do that this time, then?'

The Head of CID posed the question. He had already loosened his uniform tie and opened his top shirt button.

Sylvi Mobakk gave a lopsided smile. Her face was unusually long, Selma noticed, and her teeth were far too big.

'Because the neighbour was there,' the Inspector answered. 'Presumably. Her husband told us she was embarrassed about smoking and since the neighbour was outside, she might have been reluctant to light up her night-time cigarette. And then went out again once he was gone. The butts have also been sent for analysis, to confirm, if possible, that they really were hers.'

Now she suddenly leaned back in her chair and put both palms flat on the table. Her hands were as long and narrow as her face.

'To sum up: We're working on it. As far as the investigations into Kajsa Breien as a person are concerned, we're also continuing with those with undiminished vigour. Until now we've found nothing that seems of immediate relevance. It looks as if her marriage was absolutely fine. Perfect finances. No threats, either in real life or online. Not a single one, in fact. She's been a judge for so long that we can't overlook the notion that there could be a hate motive resulting from some judgment or other, of course, but the honourable gentlemen in the Supr ... the ladies and gentlemen of the Supreme Court feel the wrath of convicted felons only in exceptional circumstances. That sort of thing is left to the poor souls further down the pecking order.'

'To sum up, then,' the Police Chief repeated – Selma could not really read whether her tone was sarcastic or not – 'you don't actually know whether Breien was killed there and then transported or carried off and then killed somewhere else, or even if she quite simply went willingly and was later disposed of. And you haven't detected any forensic traces in the area around the tree where she was hanged. Not a thing on transport used either. Nothing whatsoever: in fact, we have very little?'

Sylvi Mobakk nodded, her lips clenched.

'But we're working on it.'

'You're working on ...'

The room went utterly silent. Selma was gazing at Police Chief Kjersti Spang. She could be just under sixty. Run-of-the-mill attractive, run-of-the-mill ten kilos overweight. Greying hair and eyes that disappeared behind a pair of heavy glasses. Her mouth was tense and there was a network of wrinkles around her lips that made her mouth look overly pronounced on her anonymous face.

'Then we have the Cabinet Minister,' she said. 'What news there?'

'A great deal,' Fredrik said, straightening up.

'Be brief.'

'Of course. Three quarters of an hour ago I had it confirmed that Børre Rosenhoff was poisoned with ricin.'

Selma forgot herself.

'What?' she exclaimed, leaning across the table to make eye contact with Fredrik.

Their eyes met for just a second or two too long.

'Yes,' the Inspector said finally. 'Ricin.'

'The umbrella murder,' the Head of CID exclaimed with a touch of excitement in his voice. 'Some time in the seventies, wasn't it? A Bulgarian in London became extremely ill and died a few days later. The autopsy showed he had a microscopic ampule of ricin in his leg. It had been placed there using the spike of an umbrella, stabbed into him while he was waiting for a bus. A trivial incident he nevertheless managed to mention before he died, isn't that right?'

'Yes,' Fredrik said with a nod. 'It happened in 1978 and the victim's name was Georgi Markov. A comedian and BBC journalist. Originally from Bulgaria, as you said. The ampule wasn't even two millimetres in diameter but it contained enough poison for him to die after being seriously ill for three days. The homicide has still not been completely cleared up but strong suspicions have always pointed in the direction of the KGB.'

He paused as if the very thought of death by poisoning perturbed him. Selma fiddled with her mobile under the table, hoping no one would notice.

'Ricin is obtained from the seeds of an ornamental bush called the castor oil plant,' Fredrik went on when the Chief of Police cleared her throat. 'Which can be found in certain Norwegian gardens and parks. In 2011 there was a guy in Tromsø who was keen to produce ricin in order to kill himself with it. He succeeded in both intentions.'

He shuddered visibly, Selma saw.

'It's quite a method,' he added in a mumble, raising his voice before going on: 'A truly *horr-en-dous* two or three days before you die. But back to Børre Rosenhoff – the post-mortem showed he had a minuscule, relatively recent puncture wound on his leg.'

'With an ampule inside it?' Per-Arne Svendsen asked, becoming more and more interested. 'Of the kind they found on Georgi Markov?'

'No. It must have fallen off. If that was in fact the method used to poison him. That remains to be seen. However it's now certain that he *did* die of poisoning. Ricin can be detected in the urine. Rosenhoff was extremely dehydrated and his bladder was more or less empty. But there was enough. Quickly done, and all kudos to the National Hospital for lightning-fast work. They've been able to call off all the virus prevention measures up there now and everyone's pleased about that. His house and family are being thoroughly checked for traces of ricin, so from that point of view the danger is not entirely over with respect to his surroundings.'

'All the same that's far better news than a virus,' the Head of CID murmured before looking up in Fredrik's direction. 'Anything more?'

'Not really, for the moment at least.'

Kjersti Spang nudged her glasses into place on the bridge of her nose and peered at Selma over the rims. 'So now we come to you, then.'

Selma's sense of not being particularly welcome moved up a notch. The way Fredrik had presented the situation, she had been given the impression that the Chief of Police had practically insisted on Selma's attendance. Now the woman's eyes, squinting slightly and fairly aloof, made her want to walk out.

Selma Falck had something to offer but she was certainly not under any obligation to hand it over.

'Absolutely,' she said with a faint smile. 'Fredrik earnestly entreated me to come. I found that somewhat strange, even more so now, and I'm happy to leave if you prefer.'

Kjersti Spang hesitated and before she had time to reply, the Head of CID protested:

'Come on. Every little bit helps, and you've solved a couple of mysteries for this country in the past. It won't take too much time, will it?'

'No, of course not,' Selma said, rising to her feet. 'May I use that flip chart, or is it just there for decoration?'

Without answering, Per-Arne Svendsen sprang up and arranged the easel so that everyone could see it. The Police Chief herself, who to begin with had been sitting at the head of the table with her back to the flip chart, turned her chair round, making her inconvenience obvious to all.

'Three victims,' Selma began, drawing three consecutive red circles on the oversized sheet of paper. 'None of them especially controversial. Linda Bruseth least of all – she's hardly hurt a fly all her life. She demonstrated great commitment during the refugee crisis of 2015–16, but then mostly to show care and humanity to the people who arrived. But that's quite a while ago now.'

She drew a heart inside the first circle, accompanied by the initials LB.

'Kajsa Breien was something as unusual as a household name, despite her rather ... elevated position. She was open about the challenges of being disabled and was both admired and popular for that very reason. In addition she was an uncommonly smart lawyer. Well liked by everyone in the profession. Admittedly, she was on the young side when she was nominated to the Supreme Court and competition between our prominent legal beagles can be both fierce and tainted by jealousy, but we can safely discard that as a factor here.'

'Strictly speaking, it's for us police to decide that,' the Police Chief interjected.

'Yes, of course. My point in this connection is that Kajsa Breien had no adversaries either. Much less enemies.'

The second circle was now also given a heart with the initials KB.

'When we come to the Minister for Children and Family Affairs, the situation might be a bit different. After all, he's a top-drawer politician. Politicians do at least attract opponents, often adversaries and sometimes even enemies. It's no Sunday School picnic, even though he represented the Christian Democrats.'

No one smiled. Selma was aware the old-fashioned flip chart made her feel more secure and it was easier to concentrate with a pen in her hand and something specific to fix her eyes on.

'Abortion law – during this government's tenure they've managed to haggle their way to a tiny amendment and that's always a touchy subject. On the other hand ...'

She turned away from the paper chart and looked at Fredrik.

'If anyone had wanted to kill a politician, I don't think the Minister for Children and Families is the first one you'd guess at.'

No reaction.

She wrote BR inside the last circle, but instead of a heart she drew a question mark. For a moment she stood with her back to the small audience. All of a sudden she wheeled round.

'The first estate, the first branch of government,' she said, using the marker to tap the circle with Linda's initials. 'Parliament. The second estate – the Government itself.'

The pen pointed at the Rosenhoff circle.

'And here,' she said, outlining an extra circle around the initials KB, 'we have a prominent representative of the law courts. The third estate.'

Now the silence was deafening.

'The three branches of government,' she said tentatively, uncertain whether the other participants in the meeting were really with her.

'We realized that,' the Police Chief said scathingly. 'But what's the meaning of it?'

This woman annoyed Selma. If you had agreed to a visitor then you should really show good manners. It was Selma who was doing her a favour, not the other way round. She decided now to go for broke.

'These three murders have something spectacular about them,' she said hurriedly. 'Linda was shot in broad daylight in circumstances we would normally regard as safe. Kajsa Breien's death is like a mystery taken from a bad movie. Why hang her like that? When it obviously wasn't the intention to make it look as if she had really hanged herself?'

To make time for a brief pause, she drew a noose above the judge's circle and a very stylized gun above Linda's.

'Before I came here, I didn't know Børre Rosenhoff had been poisoned. I'd a theory, and since it has now been confirmed, it slots very well into my narrative.'

Above Rosenhoff's circle, she sketched a pill. It looked more like a Paracet tablet than something capable of killing an adult male in a quantity approximating to a grain of salt, but it would have to suffice.

'As we know, I've never worked in the police,' she said, putting the lid on the pen. 'But I *have* brought criminal cases to court for a number of years. That means I know you should look for motive, method and opportunity.'

Tearing off the first sheet of paper, she let it drop to the floor and wrote the words at the top of a blank sheet.

'As far as method is concerned, we know most about that. Linda was quite simply shot. Kajsa Breien was, as far as I understand, strangled to death …'

She looked at Fredrik, who nodded in confirmation.

'… while Børre Rosenhoff was murdered using poison. Even better, we know exactly how the two last murders were committed. That is to say, how the Cabinet Minister was poisoned and how the judge was strangled. For the purposes of my account, we've sufficient knowledge to put a …'

Taking the lid off the pen again, she marked METHOD with a big √.

'… tick on that point. As far as OPPORTUNITY goes …'

Little dots appeared around the word as she smacked the marker against the paper.

'… then that's a huge, gigantic, open question. If I was forced to answer that today, I'd venture this assertion: "Everyone" could have done it. As a starting point. If the three killings are not connected, then—'

'Connected?'

Kjersti Spang met Selma's eye for the first time. Her gaze was sharp and critical and now she turned her back.

'What do you mean by "if they're not connected"? Of course they're not. There's nothing here to suggest anything other than that we're dealing with three unconnected cases.'

'Well,' Selma said, unfazed. 'If you'll give me five more minutes, I'll hopefully be able to set you on another way of thinking.'

Teaching your granny to suck eggs sprang to Selma's mind. There was more than a hundred years of combined police experience around the table. She swallowed audibly and spoke even louder when she continued:

'If these are three unconnected killers, then Linda's assassination demands experience with guns. And skill. The two others? Not so much.'

'I don't know how to make ricin,' Sylvi Mobakk protested.

'I do,' Selma said with a joyless smile. 'I learned it just a few minutes ago. By Googling it, no less, when Fredrik told us we were dealing with ricin. In other words, it doesn't require any special expertise, just extreme care. And strangling someone demands nothing. Apart from a certain degree of strength, and in this case the victim had less than most to offer by way of resistance. In other words ...'

Now she stood with her hand on the left arm that had started to ache for the first time in several days.

'For lack of obvious motives and groups of suspects, it might be an idea to make a detour to the actual methods.'

'What?' Sylvi Mobakk asked.

'The motive could well lie in the methods,' Selma elaborated. 'We're faced with shooting, hanging and poisoning. Each of the victims represents one of the three branches of government – the law-giving, the judging and the practice.'

The room fell silent. Even the unsettling clicking of Fredrik's pen had stopped. Sylvi Mobakk stared at the Head of CID, who looked down at the table, eyes askance, as if concentrating really hard. The Police Chief for her part stared straight ahead with a gaze that was impossible to interpret.

'Do you see the same thing as me?' Selma ventured at last.

'Ritu ... ritual murder?'

It was the Head of CID who came up with this. Slowly and almost warily, before adding: 'Shooting, hanging and poison. Three common ... methods of suicide.'

Selma barely nodded.

'Used on the three branches of government,' the Head of CID continued tonelessly. 'In other words, against Norway itself. A symbolic, theatrical and fairly … aggressive attack on Norway. As a country. Can this whole series actually be some kind of … demonstration?'

'No,' the Police Chief said, having finally torn her eyes away from a point on the wall somewhere behind Fredrik. 'This is sheer speculation. Fanciful speculation, totally without foundation. That's not how we work in the police. If this is all you have, Selma Falck, then I think we'll draw a line right here.'

Selma looked at Fredrik in despair. He formed his lips into a word she could not make out. The Head of CID raised his hand – for a moment it looked as if he were about to put it on the Police Chief's arm. He caught himself in time.

'That's fine,' Selma said with a smile, replacing the pen on the metal runner. 'Even though I'd prefer to distance myself from the description "wild speculation". This is a theory. It's also quite a good one and developed by Fredrik and me as recently as Friday morning. In other words, twelve hours before any of us knew that Børre Rosenhoff was going to die. We did, however, fear it would happen. That he would be the very person to die.'

Walking back to her place, she picked up her bag and slung it over her good shoulder. No one said a word, even though the Head of CID still looked as if he wanted to raise objections to her departure.

At the door, she turned and looked directly at Kjersti Spang.

'As far as I can see, you've very little to go on. If I were you, I'd spend a couple of days on the idea that this could be a symbolic attack on the institutions of this country. And then I would start to ask Fredrik what it might all be about. If you do that, he'll give you the answer "child welfare". Thanks for seeing me.'

She opened the door and marched out. In her pocket she could feel the memory stick Allan Strømme had given her. She had brought it from home at the very last minute to afford her the opportunity to support her hypothesis if anyone turned out to be willing to listen. Fortunately she had not been tempted. The door slid shut behind her. The young officer, who had waited in the corridor outside, began to walk towards the elevator without speaking. Selma followed him obediently but turned down the offer of a lift home.

She had stolen a march on the police, she realized. She made up her mind to retain her lead. The way the meeting had developed, she had entered into single combat against Oslo's Chief of Police.

Selma was on the offensive and also a clear favourite.

It was like sitting with a very promising hand just before the last card was played.

Family History Research

Einar Falsen was unable to recover from that morning's setback until he had demolished two bags of cheese puffs and a *Kvikklunsj* chocolate bar. Contrary to all routine, he had then put Pussycat on a leash and taken a stroll through the Sofienberg Park in broad daylight. Pussycat had been even more terrified than him of the stray dogs and sprinting youngsters and Einar had been offered drugs for sale three times in succession. He had not even dared to answer and merely drew back, dragging a reluctant Pussycat behind him. Quite literally, as the animal lay down on his side and had to be hauled across the grass as if he were dead.

After this, they would confine themselves to outings at night.

Einar had made a fool of himself by not considering that a stalker necessarily had to be alive. Now he was eager to re-establish Selma's belief in him. The assignment she had given him was, sadly, disappointingly simple and not the kind to impress anyone.

It took him less than ten minutes to discover that Torstein Heimdal, Selma's upstairs neighbour, was a car mechanic. Normally he worked at the Økern branch of *Bilia*. However, he was married to Anna Lisa Knoph. At present she was a secretary in the Norwegian Embassy in Washington and had taken her husband and son, little Lennart, with her for a spell in the American capital. Torstein came from Bomlø, had three siblings, and his mother had died last year following a brief illness.

The Internet was truly exceptional and right now Einar felt like a researcher for *Tore på Sporet*, the Norwegian TV version of *Who Do You Think You Are?*

A fantastic programme. He had watched every episode without exception several times over. All that driving around in foreign countries, rounds of questions with neighbours in Bogota and Lagos and Beijing to find vanished fathers and biological mothers, rummaging through handwritten records in Afaristan – Einar knew it was all mere window-dressing to generate vivid TV footage. The real job was done in a backroom office in front of a computer in Trondheim's Tyholt district.

In actual fact it was amazing that the presenter did anything more than sit behind computer screens. It was spookily simple to find facts about other people within this fascinating, frightening World Wide Web. As a policeman a whole lifetime ago, Einar had been used to piecing together scraps and fragments of information to make complete pictures. He was doing the same thing now at the keyboard. It was just that everything was easier and progress much faster. He was convinced that TV producers and the CIA and Mossad and MI5 and Uncle Tom Cobley and all scarcely needed to get off their arses these days.

This thought made him get up from the settee as fast as his wonky knees would let him to run into the kitchen in search of an extra piece of tape to cover the camera. Once back at the laptop, he drummed up a message to Selma. Yet another letter flew off the keyboard. B, but that was of no consequence. The note was about Torstein Heimdal. About who and where he was, what phone numbers he could be reached at, along with information that he collected *Matchbox* model cars. His collection was really impressive and Einar had been spellbound by Torstein Heimdal's homepage, *matchboxshowoff.no*. He had even spotted a miniature copy of Selma's old car, a bright red Volvo Amazon 123 GT from 1966. Unfortunately hers had literally gone up in flames on the Hardangervidda last autumn and the sight of the little model car made Einar shed a few tears. Some for the demise of the beautiful vehicle, some for having made such a fatal blunder earlier that day and even more because it had been so creepy in Sofienberg Park on a Sunday morning.

He refrained from mentioning that Torstein's mother had died. That, he decided, would be unlikely to have anything to do with the case.

Selma would not want to be bothered by another phone call, so Einar sent her an email. That would certainly do. He was loath to use the mobile except in extremis and he did not want to disturb the woman needlessly. After that he had more than enough to occupy him on the computer Selma had once again forgotten to take from him.

He would strike while the iron was hot.

The story about Endre Cappelen kept niggling him. Especially now, when he knew the boy had certainly not been following Selma. Only thirty years old, the poor guy, and already dead. Gone in a puff of smoke, sort of thing. Einar had not found the cause of death anywhere. Everything suggested the young man was or had been a drug addict, so perhaps an overdose. However, it could also have been cancer or all kinds of misfortune – sometimes people died young. Awful, but that's what life was like.

Einar dissolved into tears again. Now it was his daughter he was thinking of.

She was the one to whom he should never let his thoughts stray. That was the ultimate limit of what he was able to cope with. She had taken her own life at the age of eighteen, after having been abused by a paedophile for the majority of her childhood. Einar himself had killed the perpetrator. With his bare hands. And gone stark, raving mad afterwards.

Don't think.

Don't think about her.

It was such a shame for Endre Cappelen: Einar rushed to turn his thoughts to him. He tried to picture him, to form an impression of the boy from what he knew about him. And the photograph he had unearthed, of Endre standing beside a tree, it could have been taken anywhere at all. His hair was a bit wispy; he would have been bald in five years' time if he had lived. Selma had made a fuss about his teeth. Just like Einar, Endre had let his mouth go to rack and ruin. Stupid. If the careful smile in the picture did not exactly uncover rotten stumps, it definitely did not look good in there. His top left canine was missing and the gums had visibly receded.

All the same, the lad had once been good-looking. Slim, with fairly broad shoulders, even though he looked skinny in the photo. His thighs appeared almost as thin as his calves, but the boy had deep dimples and a mouth that Einar's wife would once, in a prehistoric time, have called sensual.

If you overlooked the teeth, of course.

There was something about the lips – such a lovely curve to them at the corners, as if the boy was actually always smiling.

Einar wondered how Endre Cappelen had ended up in such a difficult situation. Where he really came from. The identity of his parents who had been forced to endure such a painful loss.

A couple of days ago, in his search for information, he had come across a page called *myheritage.no*, where you could delve into more than twelve billion historical documents. He had entered his own name into the search field, just for fun. A dialogue box had popped up, promising the moon and stars, but required payment.

He had not gone any further. There had to be limits. Einar did not want to be one of the idiots who left a trail behind them here, there and everywhere. If you gave them an inch, they took not only a mile, but also the whole road.

Selma had got him a bankcard.

He had an account. Einar Falsen was honestly and fairly in receipt of disability benefit. He received a tidy sum of money from the government each month. Since he never ventured any further than a couple of hundred metres from the apartment, no one could take him to task for benefit fraud, either. That was a dead cert. In addition, an envelope containing thousand-kroner notes came from Selma around the twentieth of each month. She gave him cash, since she was not keen for his disability benefit to be docked. To hell with the tax, she always said when he got scared – she had already paid tax on the money herself. Gift-wages, she called it, and Einar should certainly not fret over it. What's more, they were keeping the money outside the Internet, which Einar had to admit was a good thing. The token sum he paid Poker-Turk for the apartment, along with electricity payments and Internet access, were taken care of by Selma. In the bedroom cupboard, in a cigar box behind a loose plank right at the bottom, there was now so much money that he could almost certainly have gone to Hawaii and stayed there. Almost, that is.

That family history homepage was very tempting. Maybe he should take a chance.

The problem was that he had no idea how to pay with his own card. Selma's details were already in the machine but Einar

313

knew that would not be sufficient. He needed some kind of code. Numbers and a gizmo from the bank. They asked all sorts of weird stuff when you wanted to buy something on the Internet, so he had never done so. Since he enjoyed computer games, Selma bought the occasional HOG for him, but otherwise he gave it a wide berth.

He sat looking at the enticing site.

Then an idea struck him.

It might not have been particularly good, but it was at least his own.

The Bullet Hole

'It's Sunday. What are you doing here?'

Fredrik Smedstuen glanced up from the provisional post-mortem report on Børre Rosenhoff when someone rapped lightly on the doorframe. Birger Jarl Nilsen flashed a smile from the doorway.

'I lend assistance to other people in this building, you know,' he said. 'I've been taking a look at an investigation on the third floor. How's it going?'

Fredrik muttered in response. He had picked up a photograph he must have been studying for the past ten minutes or so.

'I'm guessing the story about this Rosenhoff guy is far more dramatic than the media are making out,' Birger Jarl said. 'For a fit forty-something-year-old to die so suddenly is bad enough in itself, but there's more to it, isn't there?'

'Who have you been talking to?'

'Oh, I pick bits up here and there, you know.'

'Rather too much, it sounds like. The folk in this building need to learn to keep their traps shut.'

'Agreed. But what's done is done. Can I help you with anything?'

'No.' The answer was drawn out in a lengthy yawn, and Fredrik shook his head vigorously. 'I've been up all night,' he said. 'And this must be the thirty-somethingth cup of undrinkable coffee I've put away today.'

He downed the rest of the contents of the *Best Dad in the World* mug and banged it back down. The handle broke and he stared dumfounded at the damaged Christmas gift for a second or two. Then he tossed both mug and handle into the bin.

And then changed his mind.

'Look at this,' he said, grabbing the photo and handing it to Birger Jarl.

'What is it?' The former officer took the picture and examined it as he sat down. 'Børre Rosenhoff?' he asked.

'You don't need to know that. But what do you see?'

'A wound. On a man's thigh or maybe his calf. Upper arm?'

'A lower leg.'

'To judge from the millimetre ruler beside it, the wound is really tiny. And remarkably round. Some kind of puncture wound?'

Fredrik scrutinized the man opposite him. As usual, he looked well groomed. Fresh, as his wife would have said. Ex-wife. He would have to get used to the new designations in his family. The guy's gaze was alert, as always. Now there was a frown between his eyes, and Fredrik was not sure whether this was because he had been asked a question or because he was unsure what the photograph depicted.

'Could it be a gunshot wound?' Fredrik asked.

Birger Jarl burst out laughing. 'In that case it would have to be a peashooter! How deep is the cut? One millimetre or two? Was there a bullet lodged inside, since you ask?'

Fredrik did not answer. He had begun to realize that his own slight animosity towards Birger Jarl Nilsen was down to sheer jealousy. Fredrik would have given almost anything to look like that. To act like that. With some effort he might well be able to lose some weight but no matter what he did, he would never have the same effect on the female sex as Birger Jarl. When the guy had swaggered off with Selma Falck after the reconstruction on Wednesday, he had almost run after them and knocked him to the ground. In that department at least Fredrik had an advantage: he probably had thirty kilos more than the former military man to pack behind a punch.

'Stop,' he mumbled.

'What?'

'Nothing. What about an airgun?'

Birger Jarl chewed his bottom lip and tilted his head as he brought the picture closer to his eyes.

'Difficult to say. An airgun pellet has an exit velocity of let's say ... from well under 100 metres per second to around 500. The pellet itself can be anything from tiny balls to pretty advanced ammunition. They extend from maybe half a gram or even less to ...'

Lifting his backside a little, he dug into his pocket.

'... ones like this. It's an *Exact Jumbo Beast* from *JBC*.'

Between his thumb and index finger, he held a bullet reminiscent of a squat little mushroom.

'This weighs more than two grams. But you can get them even heavier. They require a powerful weapon, of course. It needs to have an impact energy of 40 Joules or more.'

Fredrik probably looked slightly confused because the man then added: 'I'm training my neighbour's boy at my own shooting range in the garden just now. And if this were fired from an airgun ...'

He stuffed the bullet back in his pocket and peered down at the photograph again.

'... then we'd be talking about a small, low-power weapon.'

'But is it possible? That we're dealing with a gunshot?'

Birger Jarl pushed the picture back across the desk.

'Why do you ask? The man can't possibly have died of that wound there? It's scarcely even bled!'

Fredrik gave a heavy sigh.

'Could you please just answer what I've asked you? Could this wound be the result of an airgun shot?'

Birger Jarl crossed his arms over his chest. His eyes narrowed. With a faint sniff, he ran a finger under his nose and eventually replied:

'Yes. A low-power weapon, light ammunition, some distance. And someone who's a good enough shot to deal with the challenges all that entails. The pellet could have struck this …'

'Calf.'

'… this calf, maybe even through a trouser leg. It has subsequently made this puncture wound and presumably then fallen off. Or remained in place for a while: I'd expect a hit like that at best to feel like a bite from an angry insect.'

'At best?'

'Yes, from the point of view of the person who fired the shot. Not for the victim. I assume the intention has been for the victim not to pay much attention to the pain? I don't understand why and as I told you, it would demand great skill to do the calculations. The injury, as I said …'

He nodded at the photo of Børre Rosenhoff's leg.

'… is hardly anything to write home about.'

You think, Fredrik mused.

The sniper could have fired off a special bullet. Coated in ricin. Or preferably filled with the poison, as had been the case with the ampoule that had once killed the Bulgarian journalist in London. Just as tiny, just as unremarkable. That time a jab from an umbrella, this time a shot from a small airgun.

While the victim was out running, for example, as Børre Rosenhoff had done every Wednesday and Saturday morning, like clockwork. Just as he had done last Wednesday, a few hours before he collapsed. The pinprick had probably stung a little. The pellet might have been brushed off inadvertently. While the man was running or when he took a shower.

The damage had already been done seconds after he was hit.

'Thanks,' Fredrik mumbled. 'I have to go home.'

'Yes, you look as if you could do with forty winks.'

What he needed more than sleep was a chat with Selma Falck, thought Fredrik Smedstuen, and he did not even say goodbye when Birger Jarl Nilsen got up and left.

Bedside Vigil

Lars Winther was so angry he had difficulty thinking straight. That Selma was sometimes hard to get hold of was a truth he had eventually learned to live with. Her conduct now was unacceptable, however. He had rung her six times that day. Straight to voicemail every time. Nor had she answered the four texts he had sent. In the end he had made an attempt on Messenger: there he could at least see if Selma had received the messages. Each time he checked, that bloody chevron sign was still there. The message had not even been read.

She had things belonging to him. A folder of papers and a memory stick with a sound file he still did not know if it was even possible to open. Admittedly, he had been the one to make the mistake of leaving them behind at her apartment, but that did not mean she could keep it all and then enter into total radio silence. If it had not been for him being alone at Ullevål Hospital with his son, he would have headed to Sagene to demand his belongings be handed over immediately.

If nothing else she could at least have shown some interest in how Leon was doing.

The very thought made him even more furious.

Fair enough that their relationship was more of a partnership than a friendship. All the same, they had gone through so much together that she could have shown some empathy. Selma had never appeared to have any particular love for her own children, strange to say, but she was crazy about that wee grandchild of hers. She must understand what he was going through.

The mobile display lit up.

A colleague from *Aftenavisen* wanted to get hold of him, Lars saw. He grabbed the phone, accepted the call and whispered a hello as he ran to the door.

'Hi there. What's that pal of yours doing at the cop shop on a Sunday evening?'

'What do you mean?'

'Selma Falck. I happen to know she's just had a meeting lasting more than half an hour with Kjersti Spang.'

'The Chief of Police?'

'Yep. The Head of CID was also present, as well as a couple of inspectors. The guy in charge of the Løkka attack was one of them. Rumours are flying all over the shop now. That suicide of Breien's is seemingly a murder. And up in the National Hospital a full-scale virus alarm was sounded last night. Things have calmed down now, I think, but it all had something to do with Børre Rosenhoff's death. Tip-offs and info are pouring in. Three prominent public figures killed in less than a fortnight. Fucking bizarre, you have to admit.'

'Eh ... maybe.'

'But no one can tell me what Selma Falck was doing at Police HQ.'

Lars was struggling to gather his thoughts. 'It probably had something to do with Linda Bruseth's murder,' he answered on autopilot. 'An interview or something.'

'Does the Police Chief herself normally interview witnesses? Or the Head of CID? It must have been something brand new.'

'Er ... maybe. Or ... I really haven't a clue. I've been trying to get in touch with Selma for a couple of days now, without success.'

'Come off it. I know you can't work right now when your boy ... is he doing OK, by the way? Your son?'

'Yes, much better, thanks.'

'That's great. And of course you have to be with him just now. But if you know of something that could be a story, you can't just sit on it right up until—'

'I know nothing,' Lars broke in brusquely. 'I really have no idea. And if you're trying to breathe life into something, then you could always put out a short piece about Selma having been at such a meeting. If your sources are good enough, that is. And if you also ask somebody in charge at Police HQ what it's all about, you'll most likely get "no comment" as a response. That means something's going on. Worth a short piece, I'd say. And an article like that can quickly generate more tip-offs. After all, that Police HQ leaks like a sieve.'

There was crackling on the line. A hissing sound betrayed that his colleague was opening a soft drink can. 'And you don't know anything?' he asked, gulping something down.

'Nothing,' Lars said. 'Believe me.'

'OK. I'll have to do some more work. Hope your lad's better soon, then.'

'Thanks.'

The connection was cut. Lars was so agitated that he started to pace the floor. There was not very much space around the bed with all the apparatus, but he simply could not keep still.

Leon had fallen asleep long ago.

Probably he would not wake for a long time. Lars could therefore take an hour off and pop down to Sagene. It was now ten o'clock on a Sunday night and Selma would almost certainly be at home.

He gazed at the boy in the bed.

He was so small. So incredibly vulnerable when all was said and done. He was breathing and eating well now and the medication kept the worst of the pain at bay. All the same, Lars would have given everything he owned to change places with the poor lad. Slowly he sat down again and stroked the young boy's fringe from his eyes with a tentative finger.

If Leon woke up, one of his parents had to be there.

Tomorrow evening, however, it would be his wife's turn for the bedside vigil. He would give Selma another twenty-four hours. If he hadn't heard from her by then, he would kick up merry hell.

In the meantime, he would keep hounding her, and then hound her some more.

The Secret

Everyone looked like a criminal on FaceTime: the light was always wrong, the picture quality poor. The transmission was often choppy and if you forgot to sit at the right distance from the camera, your face became distorted in the wide-angle lens.

To top it all, people were able to see how you lived.

Fredrik Smedstuen had not yet been inside Selma's home and for some reason she could not quite explain, she had arranged to sit in such a way that the window facing the balcony was the background for the onscreen image. No pictures or ornaments to be seen. Also, she had used a piece of sticky tape to mark the correct distance on the table to make sure she stayed far enough from the screen. And placed two coffee table books under her Mac to avoid being filmed at too low an angle.

Fredrik had not thought of taking similar measures.

He looked really fat as he sat there, so close to the camera that his crown was sliced off like a Sunday boiled egg. Now and again he leaned back suddenly and then Selma could see something that had to be a cross-stitch embroidery of an elk at sunset. As well as a five-armed candlestick on a mantelpiece with no fireplace underneath.

Odd.

'Did you manage to explain yourself any further?' Selma asked.

'Not really. I had to give some explanation of these child welfare ideas of ours, since you'd already mentioned them. It wasn't particularly successful. Put nowhere near as cleverly as you, and the Police Chief just grew grumpier and grumpier.'

'What was needling her, anyway?'

Fredrik shrugged outside the scope of the picture, making his double chins even more prominent.

'Kjersti Spang is obsessed with two things,' he said. 'A high clear-up rate and as much harmony as possible, both within and around the force. What you put forward was astounding, to put it mildly. That might be why the Head of CID became so inquisitive. He's a man for the limelight. Much nicer guy too, for that matter.'

'What was the upshot?'

'The cases will not be combined. The Police Chief quite simply didn't believe any of our theories. Especially the subject of child welfare – she was very dismissive of that. I'm sure I wasn't as clear in my presentation as you would have been. Even though I think I was pretty explicit that the only thing the three victims have in common, without a doubt, is some sort of accountability for child welfare. And even though Sylvi thought I did well.'

'I guess Sylvi Mobakk probably thinks you're good at most things.'

Ignoring that, Fredrik said: 'All the same, the Head of CID managed to cajole a bit more out of her. I've to follow up the

Rosenhoff case in addition to keeping the sniper attack at Løkka. Since Sylvi is totally on board with you and me, I think we'll be able to set up some double bookkeeping. At this point in time, anyway, there are still a lot of boring but necessary routine investigations to carry out.'

'What about you?'

Fredrik drank something from a glass. The picture was too dark to see what it was.

'What do you mean?' he asked.

'Do you believe this theory of ours? Really and truly, I mean?'

He slurped a little. Sucked his teeth for a second and put his hands in front of him. They looked gigantic in the picture.

'That doesn't really matter,' he said at last. 'What I believe, I mean. The point is that these three cases, taken individually, are so conspicuously outlandish that it almost seems impossible for them not to be connected. I mean, what are the odds, eh? Someone from each branch of government, shot, hanged and poisoned ... completely bizarre. On the other hand, it conflicts with everything I've learned about police work to build such castles in the air without having anything more tangible to go on.'

'Have you heard any more from the National Hospital? Have they come up with any theories about how Rosenhoff ingested the toxin?'

'Not that I know. But they're working to capacity up there. In cooperation with us, of course, we have people checking his office and home as well as the hospital.'

'What about you, then? Do you have any theories?'

Fredrik stood up without saying a word. Now Selma could see the picture behind him quite clearly. It really was an *Elk in the Sunset*. Embroidered in cross-stitch. Never in her life had she seen anything like it. Or anything so ugly. She heard loud noises followed by a hollow thud.

He popped up again. Straightened the iPad – its position was so crooked that she could now see only half his face.

His voice was lowered as he stared into the camera: 'I broached a theory with Birger Jarl this evening.'

'Oh? Where did you run into him?'

'At HQ. He was in about another case.'

'What theory did you discuss?'

'The good old umbrella method, but using an airgun.'

'What?'

Selma began to laugh. The story of Georgi Markov was tragic but so farcical that she had chortled the first time she'd heard it years ago.

'Birger Jarl thinks it's far from impossible that the guy was actually shot. With an airgun. In which the bullet, or the pellet, I suppose, was either impregnated or filled with ricin. The last bit he didn't know, of course, because we're keeping that nugget of information to ourselves for as long as we can. There were a lot of ifs and buts and whys and wherefores, but when all was said and done, it seems a person who knew a lot about weapons could have managed something of the sort.'

'Shot?' Selma said in disbelief. 'How could he have been shot without noticing anything? And when on earth could that have happened?'

Once again the picture became unsteady – it seemed as if the iPad was sliding away from whatever it was leaning against. Suddenly Selma could see the ceiling in his apartment. The brief glimpse told her he had a chandelier in the living room, made from antlers, with little lampshades covered in red and white tartan. Selma vaguely recalled seeing something similar one time in a mountain cabin.

If Fredrik had succeeded in tidying up his own appearance in recent days, he was still pretty far behind the times when it came to interior décor.

'He went running on Wednesday morning,' Fredrik said, moving back into the picture again.

'Wednesday—'

'A few hours before he got sick. Or … we don't know exactly when he started to feel under the weather, because the guy seems to have been what you might call an inverted hypochondriac. But some time through the day on Wednesday he looked decidedly green around the gills.'

'How much ricin did he actually ingest?'

'I don't know yet. But Christ, Selma, next to nothing will do it, if the poison is pure enough. What a fucking poison. Just a couple of salt grains and you'll be dead in 72 hours. No antidote. No treatment.'

He took a swig from his glass, so modest that Selma thought it must be an alcoholic drink. For some inexplicable reason she found it gratifying that he had poured himself a wee dram to talk to her.

Despite the farcical subject.

'Do you know,' he said suddenly, moving closer to the screen again, 'premeditated murder is still fairly unusual. I've been working on murder cases for seven years now and have only come across one previous case in which the perpetrator had really planned to kill someone. Pretty thoroughly, in fact, but we caught him all the same.'

'Because he was in the victim's close circle,' Selma said with a smile.

Fredrik smiled too. He should do that more often. His eyes softened, even through the dreadful picture quality.

'Exactly,' he said. 'If we find a body, we start with the spouse, move on to the lover and then the children. That hits the mark in nine out of ten cases.'

His smile grew even broader.

'It's not quite so simple,' he corrected himself. 'But you do have a point. The nightmare is the premeditated murder in which the killer is not related to the victim in any way. Like that novel by Patricia Highsmith, *Strangers on a Train*. Two passengers on a train, unknown to each other, both with someone they want dead. So they swap murders.'

'Isn't that a film?' Selma asked. 'By Hitchcock or something?'

The alcohol was obviously having a positive effect on the usually dour Police Inspector. Now he laughed. 'Films are often based on books, Selma.'

'Yes, of course,' she said in a rush. 'And if this theory of ours is correct, we could be facing something similar: a killer with no personal relationship to any of the deceased. To be honest, he doesn't even need to dislike them. If we're talking about some kind of symbolic act, I mean.'

She hesitated for a second before adding: 'The Child Welfare Service in Norway at any time has responsibility for the care of around 15,000 youngsters. In principle that adds up to 30,000 parents and 60,000 grandparents. Even if forty per cent of the cases are based on voluntary action, we still don't get down to fewer than around 40,000 adults affected. Who could bear a grudge against the Government, I mean.'

'Yes, there you have it. Too large a group of potential suspects, I'd say. Hopefully there aren't many of them who believe it's easy to kill someone. Because we don't generally, we humans.'

'What do you mean?'

'Exactly what I say. It might be scarily easy to come up with a well-planned murder. But such homicides rarely happen. We're reluctant to kill. We can murder in the heat of the moment and in particular situations, in war or by accident. But planned murder? Really systematic, planned murder? You find very few of those. Whether it's conditional on culture, "thou shall not kill" and all that stuff, or whether it's ingrained, I've no idea. It doesn't bother me much, either. I just catch the slobs. No matter what.'

Grimacing as he drained the rest of his glass, he changed the subject.

'If I could wish for something right now, it would be some more meat on the bone. That child welfare bone, I mean. What we have is so vague. Nothing specific. If there's anything to our theory, that's where the answer lies. In my opinion.'

For the first time in the course of the conversation, Selma was grateful for the clunky connection. She felt hot and it was touch and go whether she would tell him all she knew. The sound files from the Ministry for Children and Families were as specific as you could get.

The memory stick lay beside her laptop.

She looked at it. Held it between her thumb and forefinger, careful not to bring it into camera range.

If she gave this up, she would be out of the picture entirely. The contents of the files were a scandal so enormous that the case, regarded in isolation, would also run through Selma's fingers. Fredrik would have to move on with it. He would get the attention he needed from his colleagues.

And no longer need Selma.

At some point she would have to tell him what she knew. Even if the recordings turned out not to have anything to do with the murders at all, there were still good grounds for involving the police. Selma was safeguarding a secret that could be absolutely detrimental to many individuals.

And a vast Government Department.

The information in her possession could also offer redress to people who had suffered great injustice.

She really should speak up. From where she sat, she could gaze straight at the large portrait of Skjalg when she raised her eyes. She could give the memory stick to Fredrik and bow out. She could make up her mind to forget the existence of her stalker. The very fact he had left the handball on her balcony proved that he could no longer gain access to her apartment.

It looked as if Skjalg was smiling in the huge photograph. It must have been one of his first happy expressions when he was almost newly born. Missing him was beginning to become a tolerable part of her existence, like a chronic illness she simply had to make the best of.

If she told Fredrik what she knew, she would be able to concentrate on what really meant most in her life.

'We'll have to work on that,' she said instead. Sudden, almost breathless. 'Isn't that what you say down there at Police HQ?'

'Yes,' Fredrik said, yawning. 'Tomorrow we'll keep going in pursuit of a fucking brilliant sharp shooter who has some reason to hate the Child Welfare Service, who knows a lot about biological warfare, and who can make himself totally invisible into the bargain.'

'From that point of view, Birger Jarl Nilsen would seem a good candidate.'

Fredrik smiled again. The man was far less humourless than the impression he gave.

'You're spot on there. If he had children, that is. He's childless. I asked him a couple of years ago. What about me, then? I've got kids, and their mother doesn't exactly make it easy for me to spend time with them. I have to undergo regular training in shooting. I'm pretty good, even if I say so myself.'

Now it was Selma's turn to laugh. 'I can just imagine you crawling around with a gun on a rooftop in Grünerløkka.'

'Well, you shouldn't underestimate me. But now I really need to catch some sleep.'

'Me too,' Selma replied. 'Goodnight, then.'

And with that she logged off quickly to avoid changing her mind and giving the Police Inspector even more to think about.

MONDAY 16 SEPTEMBER

The Fury

Even though it was only seven a.m., more than a hundred people had already wished her Happy Birthday on Facebook. Heaven alone knew how she would find time to mark them all with a heart. Most people with multiple followers normally wrote a thank-you message to them all that evening or the next day, but Selma Falck was not most people. Every year she laid aside a couple of hours to provide a personal thank-you to every well-wisher without exception, with a few extra words for the ones she had met once or twice.

She had seldom been on social media since she was shot. On Thursday it would be a fortnight since then. A couple of her real friends had started to post her missing, at first as a joke on her page, then more seriously via text messages. Vanja Vegge alone must have sent her five texts in the past week, plus an email to do with Christmas celebrations.

Selma would have to sit down and answer sometime soon.

But not today.

When she had pulled on her college sweater and joggers, she shuffled out into the kitchen. There was one more can of real cola left in the fridge but she resisted opening it, though it would have done her a power of good and she would, after all, turn fifty-three in precisely five hours.

Her father had always made a huge point of the fact she had been born at twelve noon on the dot. It was a stroke of luck, he felt, something to smooth her way through the path of life. He had been a physicist who scoffed at astrology and had no leanings towards any other obscure creeds, despite the five years he had spent in his youth as an American hippie. Why then, of all Selma's distinctive features he should latch on to the idea of the time she had entered the world being something so special, she failed to figure out. On the other hand when, as a thirteen-year-old, she had played competitively for the local team, he had things to do rather than come and watch. Selma was the only one of all her teammates with no parents on the sidelines. Only her brother had turned up, one hour before the match, and even waited patiently for her afterwards to accompany her home.

Selma had played the best game of her life up till then.

The other girls drove home with their families. Herman and Selma took the train from Lillestrøm and then the Østbanen tram home. They paid the train tickets with their own money and skipped the other fare.

Selma banished thoughts of her brother. No good would come of that. The phone rang.

No one should be phoning her before half past eight in the morning: everyone who knew her was aware of that. Not because she was in the habit of sleeping late but because she needed time to wake up properly. It had to be a journalist. Or a telesales person, she thought in annoyance as she picked up her mobile, lying display-down on the kitchen worktop.

Lars Winther.

No. She could not be bothered talking to him. The very thought of Lars gave her a pang of conscience; he had phoned her a thousand times in the past few days. To tell the truth, she had more or less impounded his belongings. He had no idea she had gained access to the sound files, either. Since she was busy following a lead he had no idea about, she had thought it best to keep it secret.

She left the phone and headed into the bathroom.

Actually she should go back to the hospital to get her stitches removed today. It would be a waste of time and involve a tiny chance of bumping into Lars Winther. When she had showered, once again with cling-film wrapped around her arm, she saw the wound was dry and had healed well. Not the least sign of redness, apart from a scar that looked fairly recent, understandably enough. The drain, a little plastic tube in the middle of the five-centimetre-long operation scar, had already come loose by itself. After holding a lighter flame for a sufficient length of time under a pair of tweezers and nail scissors, it took her only two minutes to detach both the stitches and drain. She washed the wound in Pyrisept and placed a new sterile gauze pad over it all.

Once she was dressed and back in the living room, she noticed that journalists from *DG*, *Dagbladet* and *NRK* had phoned her. Slightly troubled, she sat down at her laptop and logged on.

The danger of imminent war in the Middle East was growing in the wake of new drone attacks on Saudi Arabian oilfields. The price of oil had shot sky-high and Donald Trump was lumbering around in the midst of it all like a crazy hippopotamus, making everything steadily worse. A Latvian had also died following an accident at sea outside Averøy, according to *Aftenavisen*.

Selma Falck at Secret Police Meeting.

'Shit,' Selma spluttered. 'Shit, shit, shit.'

Damn Lars Winther.

The byline was not his, but no one would have written anything about Selma in *Aftenavisen* without first talking to Lars. She read the article twice. It was not long and really contained very little. There was speculation that Selma had been appointed as some kind of special adviser to the Chief of Police, with particular reference to the two high-profile criminal cases that had occurred within a short space of time. Fortunately, Børre Rosenhoff's death was not mentioned. The police could easily have extricated themselves but the police spokesperson had committed the cardinal sin of refusing to comment.

Just the same as begging the journalists to delve deeper.

People should learn to lie more, Selma thought, in fury. Far more. Life would be so much simpler that way. Indignant, she picked up the phone and found Lars's number. He answered after one ring and before she had even managed to say a word, she heard him almost scream at her:

'At last! Where the fuck have you been? I've been calling and sending messages and—'

'Where have *I* been?' Selma broke in sharply. 'I'm the one who should be asking you – what the hell is that headline in *Aftenavisen* supposed to mean? When did you start writing things about me without even talking to me first?'

'Me? Christ, I'm at the hospital with a son who's only just escaped with his life from a serious accident. I haven't written anything at all!'

'We have an agreement, Lars.'

Selma had to pull herself together to avoid roaring at him.

'You and I scratch each other's back. Last year you got a real gift-wrapped package from me. That led to SKUP prizes and all sorts of other honours and distinctions. You lend me a hand when I need it, and—'

'*Lend a hand*? What the hell kind of language is that? I'm not your fucking servant!'

Selma's anger fizzled out. She could not understand why he was so furious. Making themselves inaccessible to each other was hardly a new tactic for them. Their entire partnership was founded on the kind of reciprocity that also included the need to keep some distance on occasion.

'What's going on with you?' she said, slightly less aggressively.

'Going on with me? *Going on with me?* My family and I are in a real crisis situation, and you not only make yourself scarce, you have to—'

'We talked for a long time on Friday,' she interrupted him. 'And I sent you a text when we were regrettably cut off.'

'Friday? Today is Monday! My boy's life has been hanging by a thread and—'

'Stop it. Honestly. Things were OK, you said so yourself on Friday. Of course I was pleased to hear that. I've been thinking a lot about you and your family. Naturally I have. But I didn't want to disturb you.'

Something sounded like a groan at the other end. Lars had been annoyed with her before, sometimes even with good reason. Selma had to admit that. But this tongue-lashing was overstepping the mark.

'There's no point in talking to each other when you're so angry,' she said with as much equanimity as she could muster. 'We might say things we don't really mean.'

'You've got my stuff, Selma! My folder and memory stick! Have you done anything with them?'

'No. They're lying here, as they have been the whole time. Of course I don't rummage around in your belongings. I've done sweet FA.'

Lars did at least seem a bit more subdued when he said: 'I want it all back. Now.'

'Now doesn't suit, Lars. I've other things to see to. Other commitments.'

Lars muttered something she could not catch.

'Where are you?' she asked.

'At the hospital. But on my way home now. Just leaving.'

'Can't you just concentrate on looking after Leon? Your papers are safe here with me. You don't have the opportunity to do much work right now, anyway. If I have time, I'll ask a couple of IT people I know if they could possibly help you with that locked file. I don't have very high expectations, but I'll try.'

Now he did not answer. She was bringing him round.

'Can't we meet … let's say tomorrow? Tuesday. Here at my place. We can pencil in nine o'clock in the evening. Leon will probably be asleep by then.'

Still Lars said nothing at all.

'Then we'll firm that up,' Selma said. 'Bye.'

'Wait!'

'What is it?'

'What were you actually doing at Police HQ yesterday evening?'

'I went in to see Fredrik Smedstuen, Lars. Fairly straightforward. There were some ambiguities in my witness statement regarding Linda's murder. They're stressed out down there now and I did him a favour by dropping in. Plain and simple. There's absolutely nothing in the article in that rag of yours but now you've set the whole of the Norwegian media on me. For no good reason. And on my birthday, of all days.'

A faint 'Happy Birthday' could be heard at the other end.

'Now I'm going,' Selma said as she hung up.

Quick as a flash, she took out the coded memory stick, which neither of them had managed to open. Taping it to the inside of the green folder, she put it all into a plastic carrier bag from the *Rema 1000* supermarket.

And laid it on the sideboard in the hallway, ready for collection.

Just like that. Lars was no longer angry and they would soon be friends again. She would return the calls from the other media outlets as she walked and tell them exactly what she had said to

Lars. Everything and everyone would cool their jets. Right now she wanted to see Einar. She had given him a senseless assignment yesterday: to find data on Torstein Heimdal. It had probably taken Einar only minutes to arrive at the details he had then assembled into a comically formal report he had sent her by email. Selma had decided to pay no attention to her upstairs neighbours and heaven only knew what Einar would be using the computer for now.

This business with Lars had at least been solved for the present.

Selma undid both locks on the front door. Once again it crossed her mind: if only people could learn to resort to untruths now and again, the world would certainly be a far better place.

For everyone.

The Coffee Connoisseur

Today he had once again brought flowers.

The potted heather he had left a few days ago was dry. The grave might be too much in the shade of the elm tree: at any rate, the occasional heavy cloudbursts had not kept the compost damp. Heather was a hardy plant, accustomed to poor soil conditions high in the mountains as it was. Fortunately it had not died off. He had brought a bottle of water and used it to soak the earth in the plantpot.

He had cut three stalks from the colossal verbena in Grethe's favourite flowerbed that same morning. They were so tall they had to be put in a vase with pebbles at the bottom to prevent the spartan flower arrangement from toppling over.

The colours were well matched, shades of purple. Lilac. Dark pink. Whatever Grethe would have called them.

'I love you,' he said quietly once settled on the folding stool. 'And soon everything will be fine again. We can find peace, all three of us.'

Slowly, with customary unhurried movements, he opened a thermos of coffee. He poured the steaming liquid into a wooden cup with a handle and took a sip. It did him good. He never drank really bad coffee. His quota of that sort of thing had been filled long ago. Some of the large chains could brew a decent cup, no more than that. Filter coffee was like dishwater. A French press was acceptable at a pinch, but when he had time, it was steeped coffee that did the business. It was an art. You had to take everything into consideration, quite literally. Steeped coffee was a tradition among mountaineers. Up there you boiled the water to 95–96 degrees so that the chance of burning the coffee was eliminated. For that reason, he always waited a few minutes after boiling the water before pouring a precise litre over 73.5 grams of freshly ground coffee from beans he had also roasted himself.

Storing it in a thermos degraded the product, but it would have to do.

He raised the hiker's cup, which gave the coffee a vague hint of pine, to the gravestone in a little toast and drank.

'I have only one worry,' he said as he put down the cup.

Producing his mobile from his inside pocket, he found an article online and read it aloud.

'Do you understand?' he asked, looking at the bronze plaque. 'Do you remember her from last year when I sat here and read it out to you?'

Grethe, as usual, did not reply. There was a strange absence here today. He suffered from neither stupidity nor dementia and was well aware that his long-dead wife could not really hear him. All the same, being here usually brought him peace. It was as if they were still together when he sat down for a chat. As if she was there, somewhere hidden inside the rough little stone, and saw him.

'I don't like it,' he said sternly, waving the still-lit-up mobile phone. 'She might be no more perceptive than the police. But last year she showed she has far greater stamina. And better instincts.'

Abruptly and angrily, he stuffed the mobile back in his pocket and grabbed the cup from the grass. The smooth wood felt good in his hand. The coffee aroma calmed him down as he raised it to his face. He drank deeply and straightened up the verbenas.

'Selma Falck was a setback. I absolutely should have anticipated that. You can never be too well prepared, Grethe. Never.'

Someone came walking along the rows of gravestones a hundred metres or so off. An elderly man, with a dog that was presumably meant to be white. Its fur was tangled, long and dirty and it began to whimper when the man stopped in front of a grave that did not yet have a stone.

'I did know she would be there,' he whispered. 'It was OK, I thought. More fuss that way. Hitting her was a damned accident. I'm too competent to let things like that happen. She's starting to take this personally, I think.'

A younger woman approached the other grave. She put her arm around the old man, who was weeping. An unwelcome disturbance.

'They thought I was aiming for Selma Falck. Fortunately they've thought better of that. But now she's helping the police ...'

He shook his head and drank more coffee.

'If I have to take care of Selma Falck,' the man said almost inaudibly as he got to his feet, 'then I'll do it. You can rely on that, Grethe. I just have to keep an eye on her and this will go the way we want it to.'

When he had packed the thermos and cup back in his rucksack and attached the stool to the straps on top, he hunkered down. Effortlessly this time: his knee had been behaving this past week or so.

Carefully forming his mouth into a kiss, he put his lips to the ice-cold marble. It tasted of earth and minerals and the autumn dampness.

'No one will stand in our way, Grethe.'

When he stood up again, he felt a stab of pain in his knee.

'Not even Selma Falck,' he added as he began to walk.

The Birthday Present

This was simply unacceptable.

When Selma finally stepped into Einar Falsen's apartment, it stank of death and destruction. She had rung the bell, rapped on the windows from the street and tried to phone him. The latter, seldom successful in the past, did not work now either. For the second time since Einar had moved indoors, Selma was forced to use the spare key she kept on her own key-ring.

It was in fact a mystery how Pussycat could shit so much in such a short time. That Einar could fail to notice that the animal had for once defecated in lots of places other than his sandbox in the hallway, was however even worse. That it must be thirty-five degrees Celsius in the apartment and some *Kapteinen*'s stuffed plaice had been burnt to a crisp in an oven that was still switched on was downright dangerous.

'In God's name,' Selma exclaimed from the living room doorway.

'Happy Birthday,' Einar called out enthusiastically, without looking up from the laptop. 'I've got the most wonderful present for you.'

It took her more than an hour to make Einar's quarters reasonably liveable. The most difficult thing was forcing the man himself into the shower: he had once again taken it into his head that Zyklon B could spray out of the shower head if he as much as touched the mixer taps. The solution was a story so complex and imaginative that even Selma had difficulty keeping a tight rein. Her lies shot out in all directions. The explanation as to why the Oslo waterworks definitely had no access to what was left of the Nazis' poisonous gas reserves was in the end so absurd that Einar believed it.

'So,' Selma said at last, when the small apartment had become somewhat habitable again, 'if you're going to go on like this, Einar, then you can't have a computer when I'm not here. That would be silly, don't you think?'

His reply disappeared in the roar of a lorry driving past the open windows. Selma had felt compelled to air the rooms, but whether it was any better to fill the apartment with exhaust fumes rather than the stink of cat excrement and male sweat, she was not entirely sure. She moved to close them. All the frames were warped and she was warm from exertion by the time the place was tolerably quiet.

'I've become a genealogist,' Einar announced proudly.

He had been into the bedroom to collect a rectangular, fairly flat parcel, wrapped in newspaper and gaffer tape.

'Had no gift wrap, sorry. Didn't want to go shopping. It's for you.'

'Thank you,' Selma said, sitting down in the armchair. 'There was no need. Have you had any sleep, Einar?'

'I couldn't sleep at a time like this. The Internet is incredible. I've become a family history researcher. Did you know your great-great-grandfather was Danish? And that your surname comes from the life-saving service he founded in Copenhagen in 1906? *Did you know that, Selma*?'

'No,' Selma replied. 'I certainly did not. What's this?'

'Open it! Please!'

Selma looked down at the parcel and began to rip off the tape. 'You've certainly used enough tape, my goodness!'

Finally the newspaper and silver tape lay on the floor. Selma was left with a booklet, sewn together at the margin with red woollen yarn. The front was a blue background with her name and date of birth written in big pink letters.

'I don't have a stapler,' Einar said by way of apology. 'But one of my sweaters has unravelled a bit. The red one, you know. And then I found one of these big needles. A darning needle. Doesn't it look lovely?'

'Yes, it does,' Selma nodded as she carefully opened the booklet.

A family tree opened up. At the foot of the page, the trunk, her own name was written inside a frame, beside Herman's. Out along the increasingly narrow branches Einar had tracked down her parents, grandparents, great-grandparents and three of her great-great-grandparents. Most of the names were totally unknown to her.

'Really splendid,' she murmured, leafing through the pages.

In a way that was true. Einar had done an impressive amount of work in a short time. This would have been a very nice gift if Selma had felt the least iota of interest in her origins.

Which she absolutely did not.

The red yarn tore easily through the paper and she had to make a fold a couple of centimetres in on each page to prevent it all from falling apart. The next eleven pages in the booklet contained further descriptions of her forebears' history. Marriage and career, titles and children. It was certainly true that a Sophus Falck had founded the company with the red logo of a falcon with outstretched wings at the beginning of the last century. Whether he really was her great-great-grandfather was something she could not be sure of, however.

'What have you actually done?' she asked carefully.

'Researching family history! I got some help from Petter, the guy across the landing, you know, the one who's only awake at night.'

Selma stared at him in incomprehension.

'The one who howls,' Einar continued impatiently. 'Everybody else complains, but he doesn't bother me. And he's a wizard with computers, Selma. When he was well, he was an electrical engineer.'

'I thought you didn't know your neighbours?'

'I don't *know* them. But I do bump into them now and again. At the bins and so on. Petter is sometimes out and about when I take Pussycat out for a walk at night. He sits down at the bins then and counts rats.'

He pointed eagerly at the booklet.

'These genealogy websites cost money to use, but they have a free trial period!'

He clapped his hands with excitement. Pussycat shot like an arrow into the bedroom. Suddenly Einar grew serious.

'Petter had to fill in his account details, though. On three websites. But I've promised him not to let it transfer to a full subscription. And then I gave him a thousand kroner for his trouble. From the cash box in the bedroom.'

'A thousand kroner? How long did it take?'

'Ten minutes at least. Three Internet sites, with a total of a million billion public documents from five whole centuries! Exceptional, Selma.'

'A million billion, really.'

She diffidently continued to thumb through the contents. The setup at the side was as messy as the apartment had been when she arrived, but the material seemed thoroughly enough worked out. The family tree on the first page was obviously a stencil.

'Really beautiful, Einar!' She closed the booklet cautiously. 'Thank you. But how did you come up with something like this?'

Einar began to trot around the floor. His hair was like a shaggy cloud surrounding his head and he had become far too skinny again. With his excessive calorie intake and almost no movement, Selma could not understand why he was not as round as a barrel.

'I made a fool of myself yesterday,' he said pathetically. 'A dead man can't stawk anyone, of course.'

'Forget it,' Selma answered with a smile. 'I've made up my mind not to bother with that any more. Since I've had the locks changed, no one has been inside my apartment.'

'He was so vulnerable, you know.'

'Who?'

'Endre. Endre Cappelen. So thin and strange and had such a lot of problems and is dead even though he was just a young lad.'

'Thirty years old.'

'That's no age to die, though!'

'No, that's true. Won't you sit down?'

'He reminded me of my daughter, Selma. Of ...'

The tears streamed down his face and now at least he stood still.

'You mustn't think about her. We've agreed on that for years now.'

'Don't think,' Einar repeated, slapping his forehead with his palms. 'Don't think about her.'

'Sit down.'

'I wanted to know more about him. On the Internet you can find everything. So I made his family tree too. After Petter had helped me with those expensive search sites. Which I haven't paid anything for, by the way. Not yet.'

He sat down on the settee and folded his hands. 'Endre had parents, Selma.'

'As have we all.'

'But no siblings.'

'No. As I said a minute ago, I've decided to forget all about that stalker business. I've sorted it. Poker-Turk has sorted it.'

'Poker-Turk sorts everything for us.'

Smiling, Selma laid the booklet down on the table. 'Yes. We're lucky.'

'Endre was not so lucky. Even though his father founded Stockholm, you know.'

A faint smile played around his mouth at last.

'Well, this was a beautiful present, at any rate,' Selma said, rising from the chair. 'Thank you. I really have to get going now, but I'll come back tomorrow. In the meantime it would be best if I take your machine. You need to sleep, Einar.'

'Wasn't he the one who unified Sweden too?' He gazed at Selma with a look of wonderment.

'Who?' Selma asked, oblivious. 'I think the family history book should stay here just now. It'll get crumpled in this bag. I can take it with me another time.'

'Birger Jarl!' Einar cried, pretty annoyed by now. 'Birger Jarl was the Swedish Harald the Fair-haired, so to speak. Or ... now I'm getting mixed up, I think. I read a book when I was in Blakstad, one by that Swedish guy. You know, Jan Guillou. He—'

'Birger Jarl?' Selma stiffened mid-movement. 'Who's that?'

Einar gave a histrionic sigh: 'I don't remember all of it. He founded Stockholm, but did he also unite Sweden into one kingdom?'

'What has all this got to do with Endre Cappelen's life?'

'It's his father! Endre's mother's surname was Cappelen. They thought Cappelen was nicer than Nilsen, I suppose. For their only child. I completely agree. My name's Falsen, just like one of the founding fathers of the Constitution, but unfortunately I discovered last night that I'm not related to him. Names make people, you know.'

'It's clothes that make people. But why are you bringing Nilsen into this?'

Einar looked at Selma as if she were a bit backward. 'I just told you! But Endre's son, the poor soul, he's called something else altogether. He's called David Connert, and was adopted by his mother's mother, exactly as we found out a few days ago. The grandmother's name is Ewa Connert. Ewa with a w. Maybe she's Swedish too?'

Selma sat down for a few seconds. She produced a half-full bottle of Pepsi Max from her bag. Opened it and drank.

For a long time. All of it. Then she stood up and walked to the other side of the coffee table. She crouched down in front of Einar. Took hold of his hands. He peered at her in alarm.

'Einar,' she said solemnly. 'Now you really have to concentrate. And then you're going to answer what I ask you. Only that. Nothing else. You must answer exactly what I ask you, OK?'

Einar gave a quick nod.

'What's the name of Endre Cappelen's father?' Selma asked, exaggerated and slow.

'He's called Birger Jarl Nilsen,' Einar said in an anguished voice, as if he thought he had done something terribly wrong.

The Fire Service

The funeral for Karstein Braaten's mother had taken place at last.

It had been exactly the kind of service she would have wished for if she had still had all her marbles. Four years had passed since she had last been able to recognize her only son and in the death notice Karstein had announced that the funeral would be private. Which meant he was there on his own. With the pastor, of course, and a couple of other churchmen, but in the complete absence of friends or acquaintances.

The Head of the Division for Analysis and Data Processing in the Directorate for Public Security and Resilience had driven into the *Circle K* petrol station after the ceremony and eaten a hotdog before heading back to the office to continue his working day.

He had grieved for his mother for many years now. Today what he felt most of all was some kind of doleful relief.

Freedom, perhaps: being spared having to think about her and able to do exactly as he pleased. Although he had once had two female cousins, they had died in an aeroplane accident in Nigeria before families had come along.

Karstein Braaten now had no relatives and found that acceptable in many ways, taking his work into consideration. Nothing would be personal for him. Everything could be judged with a cool, calm and professional distance.

Today he had received a letter by courier. That worried him.

Karstein Braaten could not bear irregularities. Much of what he himself worked on was, admittedly, far from regular, in the sense that it was top secret. Evil tongues would probably use expressions such as 'avoiding democratic control', but in his opinion that was wrong. He wrote his reports and kept the Minister of Justice orientated. The Department's creative solutions to circumvent the Freedom of Information Act were moves that all democracies had to resort to from time to time to ensure peace, freedom and democracy itself.

Unfortunately, according to both Karstein Braaten and others, his task was too important to be the object of modern transparency. At least fully.

The letter he read had also evaded public scrutiny. It was a note from the Attorney General's office to the Justice Department, with a copy to the Prime Minister's office, containing a short but precise account of the challenges involved in the forthcoming cases to be raised in the Court of Human Rights in Strasbourg.

Karstein was less concerned about the legal aspects. He was not a lawyer, even though all these years had given him knowledge of the subject that made him far more skilled than the average person. He relied on the Attorney General having a complete overview. That the verdicts being complained about conformed to Norwegian law was beyond all doubt. That the judgements were good from a purely substantial point of view, that is to say that the circumstances of the children in question had improved as a consequence of the decisions made for them, was also unquestionable. That the same interpretation of the law was 100% in agreement with Article 8 of the Human Rights Convention with regard to the right to respect for private and family life remained, however, to be seen. The Attorney General's office were very confident of acquittal. And felt that if the outcome proved to be the opposite, then they would simply have to live with one or several negative decisions; there were excellent rules governing how the Supreme Court and legislators should respond to that sort of thing.

Moreover, the number of people who would really be interested in the welfare of children was limited. Most people gave the entire service a wide berth.

Oil on troubled waters, Karstein thought when he had read the letter for the fourth time. That was what this was: a dry, reassuring account of a legal problem over which you thought you had complete control. It was not only the letter itself that worried him.

The covering letter, which neither the Attorney General, the Justice Minister, nor even the Prime Minister's office knew of, was far more concerning. It had come to him in the post, encoded and seemingly completely innocuous. To his home address, in fact, in an unmarked, anonymous envelope. The missive was from a section in the Police Security Service. This too had a neutral designation, just like the division in the Directorate of Public Security and Resilience of which Karstein himself was in charge. The difference was that while none of Karstein's subordinates really knew what he worked on, the Security Service's minor subsidiary was a group of fixers.

It did exist. It was described now and again in annual reports from the Parliamentary Oversight Committee, Parliament's controlling body for the secret services, but then only for some of the paper activities they were involved in. Only eleven people knew about the additional work they undertook. Those eleven had their own name for the group.

They called it the Fire Service.

They put out fires that could cause dangerous unrest. Not ordinary, democratic debate and argument but deeply detrimental scandals. Not all, not even most of them, but when the barometer of trust was plummeting and yet another drop in the cup would threaten the delicate balance a society such as Norway depended upon, they had both their methods and their strategies.

It was not always enough. The NAV scandal had been a predictable catastrophe, though the Fire Service managed to do nothing about it. It was too immense. Far too many people knew. You could see the consequences now – a commentariat in uproar, lawyers screaming blue murder and thousands of people happy to come forward with their stories of state-sanctioned assault on entire families. Many of them deeply tragic.

This case was smaller in scope but would potentially have an extremely unsettling effect if it became common knowledge. A young man, employed in the Ministry for Children and Families, had leaked internal information to a journalist a couple of months ago. Including certain sound files that, if they went astray, would be decidedly damaging to the Government. Karstein had never learned explicitly what it was all about. All the same, he had formed an impression.

It was about the falsification of documents, no less.

By the public sector.

The Attorney General obviously had no idea about it.

Hardly anyone else did either, but this Allan Strømme apparently had proof. Fortunately he no longer did, following the Fire Service's visit out there at Mortensrud. The story was disturbing all the same.

The NAV issue revolved around the fact that no lawyer in the whole of the huge state apparatus that comprised the Norwegian state had any inkling that the law had been misinterpreted. That was bad enough. That an institution such as the Child Welfare Service, with power to encroach hugely on the lives and rights of individual citizens, might resort to outright manipulation of their cases was even worse.

Allan Strømme should of course have invoked whistle blower status and gone to the appropriate authorities. The Fire Service would then probably have fallen short. He had instead chosen a different strategy, running to the fourth estate and telling tales. A couple of weeks later the journalist had gone out and got plastered before his regular nightly cycle trip in Oslo city centre. He collided with a taxi and died that same night.

With no intervention from anyone.

Tragic for him and his family. A stroke of luck for the Fire Service. Allan Strømme himself had been compliant, according to the covering letter. Which to all appearances meant scared out of his wits. He swore that no one had received copies of the sound files; he had only had a chat with his friend from *Aftenavisen*. The man had voluntarily surrendered his own IT devices in exchange for new replacements and was obviously shaken by the thought of the consequences it would have if he did not faithfully follow the instructions they gave him.

The danger was over, at least as far as could be hoped. As far as you could go within a set of rules that *did* exist despite it all and that ultimately should prevail in a modern democracy. The Fire Service was not illegal in that sense. The group did not resemble the illegal forces wound up last autumn, real defence organizations that took the crassest of liberties they deemed necessary.

The Fire Service was more like a discreet servant, someone who cleared things up, washed things away and swept them all under the carpet.

Karstein Braaten could still taste the hotdog from *Circle K*. It had been a bit rancid and the ketchup vinegary. The mustard had also been far too sweet – he should really have passed on it.

'Irregularities' was what the Fire Service had called them.

A cautious word, to put it mildly, for state-sanctioned forgery of documents, if Allan Strømme's claims were correct.

That was something Karstein Braaten could not know for certain. No one should ever know.

And that was all to the good.

The Questions

Selma Falck had run twenty-four kilometres.

When she left Einar, again without remembering to take the laptop with her, she had gone home to Sagene in a daze. It was as if her head were stuffed with cotton wool. With ants crawling around in it. Her brain was simultaneously empty and overactive: she did not know which way was up. It felt physically painful to sit down when she got home. Completely unable to decide what she should do now, she had changed into her running gear, tied on her best running shoes and rushed off.

Aimlessly. Her feet took her in an eastwardly direction, towards Torhovsdalen, where she followed the paths, the bridges, the underpasses and the tracks that led her to Alna, all the way through the huge industrial estate to Karihaugen before she turned around. When she arrived home, she had taken two hours and twenty minutes to wear herself out.

But it had not cleared her head in the least. Her arm was also aching now, a dull, throbbing pain.

A shower helped a little.

She stood there under the cascade of slightly too hot water until she felt the shared minds of everyone in the entire building must soon be blank.

And finally came to a decision.

A provisional one, but the only one she could live with. What just one person knew, nobody knew. That had been her maxim for as long as she could remember and this was certainly not the occasion to change that.

Her hair was still so wet it clung to her back when she pulled on clean clothes. She draped a towel over her shoulders and used her hands to flick her hair over it without bothering that her shirt was already soaked. The first thing she did was to compare the birth dates of the Birger Jarl Nilsen in Endre Cappelen's family tree with that of the Police College's sharpshooting instructor and lecturer in ballistics.

They were identical.

There could not be two Birger Jarl Nilsens in Norway. At least not born on the same day.

She took the last can of real cola from the fridge, opened it, took a swig and sat down at the dining table with her mobile in one hand and her thumb on the display.

After one ring, Fredrik Smedstuen answered.

'Hi, Selma. I'm a bit busy here, could I call you—'

'No. You have to answer a few questions for me. Please.'

'I can call you back in half an hour or so, I just have to—'

'Please, Fredrik. It's really urgent.'

He made no reply but Selma could hear the sound of his breathing. Slightly laboured, as if he were moving. His footsteps were also audible. He must be outdoors.

'What's up with you?' he finally asked.

Selma thought she could discern some kind of anxiety in his voice and struggled to subdue her own pulse. Breathe in through the nose, out through the mouth.

'Everything's fine with me,' she said. 'I just need answers to some questions.'

'About what?'

'Who was it who first suggested the idea that there was something ... demonstrative about Linda Bruseth's murder? That there could be a message in it?'

'Er ... wasn't it you? At the *Sagene Lunch Bar* last Friday?'

'No. Think it over, Fredrik. Think it over very carefully.'

Once again she could hear footsteps. His breathing disappeared for a moment, as if he were moving the phone from one hand to the other.

'Hello?' Selma said.

'I'm trying to think here. You're right. It wasn't you, but Birger Jarl Nilsen. First of all in my office. It must have been last Monday. Or Tuesday? Anyway, I thought about what he'd said when I happened to be one of the first on the scene where Kajsa Breien was found hanged.'

Yet again he took a brief pause before exclaiming: 'In fact, I phoned him. From the crime scene. Early on Tuesday morning. He came to the office at my request and we tossed a few balls in the air. My belief was strengthened there and then. Enough to follow it up by asking for a meeting with you.'

Selma had to stand up. Her feet had gone to sleep in a way she had never experienced before. Her hands were tingling, and she got up, shifting her weight from one foot to the other and shaking her free hand as she continued: 'You told me yesterday that Birger Jarl had no children. How do you know that?'

'Why are you asking me all this?'

'Just answer. Please.'

He did something with his mouth – whatever it was sounded like loud bangs in her ear.

'We were chatting about my children a couple of years ago,' he said, sounding slightly dejected. 'Things had started to go wrong between my wife and me and the kids took her side in everything.

It was extremely frustrating. I mentioned it over a beer after a workshop at the Police College. That's where Birger Jarl is really employed, as you know. Yes, a part-time post, I think. Training in sharpshooting.'

'Did he say specifically that he had no children?'

'How am I supposed to remember that?'

Fredrik Smedstuen had given Selma more than just a feeling that she had a lot to go on. Now, however, he seemed a bit annoyed.

'Try. Please.'

There was silence for a few seconds. And then a few seconds more.

'Well,' he said at last, long-drawn-out and doubtful. 'I seem to remember he said something like, "I've been spared problems like that. I don't have children." Yes, it must have been something along those lines.'

'I see. Thanks. One last question. Does Birger Jarl have access to guns?'

Now Fredrik burst out laughing.

'Yes, what a question. He's an old member of the military elite, Selma! He teaches sharpshooters. There's scarcely a conflict in the world in the past thirty-five years where he hasn't been present on the ground. The guy has his own shooting range on his property. Whether that's legal, I've no idea, but he mentioned it to me as recently as yesterday.'

He had started walking again, Selma could hear.

'But why are you asking me this?'

'Later, Fredrik. Later. By the way, one very last thing: have you had time to look at Jonathan Herse's file? The journalist who died in an accident?'

'Yes, actually I have. I didn't have more than an hour to spare, Selma. To tell the truth, not even that. That case looks absolutely clean cut. Nothing that doesn't stack up. To crown it all, there's video footage of the first part of the crash. It looks completely legit. No history on the taxi driver, either. Norwegian-Pakistani who has lived here since the eighties, clean record, nothing fishy. The lad was unquestionably far too drunk to be zipping around on a bike. In addition, it's far from the first time there's been an accident at that particular roundabout. To be honest, I can't understand why people dare to cycle in this city. It's real kamikaze—'

'I have to go,' she broke in and disconnected the call.

She sat staring at the picture of Skjalg. On Wednesday, during the reconstruction in Thorvald Meyers gate, Birger Jarl had turned up for no good reason. He had joined Selma on her walk through the area. He had sketched the shooting scene for her on a concrete wall and convinced her that Linda was the target of the fatal bullet.

What's more, he had pointed out how curious the killing had been.

As if it contained some kind of message.

At first Selma had thought it a strange thing to say but the man had been really convincing. Without being too insistent. There was something matter of fact about him. A professional, explaining to her in a friendly manner what had actually happened.

Not at all odd, since it must have been Birger Jarl Nilsen who had murdered Linda Bruseth and injured Selma's arm. He had left a message the police had not been able to see until then.

So he helped to steer them in the right direction. Not only the police, but also Selma, whom Birger Jarl had undoubtedly noticed Fredrik had his eye on and would most likely listen to.

That is how it must have been.

But it simply could not have been like that, Selma thought, confused, as she held the fizzing can of cola to her ear.

Nothing made sense. It was incomprehensible. The hanged Supreme Court Judge and the poor Cabinet Member who was killed with ricin. The sound recordings from the Ministry. Einar's family tree that showed Birger Jarl really did have a child, something he had denied two years earlier.

'Chaos, chaos, chaos.'

She sprang to her feet so suddenly that she dropped the can. A stream of cola ran out, greyish-white foam on the beige carpet. She stared at it for a couple of seconds before deciding to ignore it. In a glimpse of common sense she had realized where she had to start to bring some order to the chaos. She applied her makeup at record speed and before she went out the door she had found a phone number she had never rung before.

The Trick

'Selma Falck,' Fredrik Smedstuen said by way of excuse as he stuffed the mobile into his jacket pocket.

'What did she want?' Sylvi Mobakk asked.

'Something or other. I didn't really understand what. Where were we?'

They were standing in the small clearing where Supreme Court Judge Kajsa Breien had been found hanging from a birch tree limb four days earlier. The police cordon with yellow and black crime scene tape had been removed that same morning. Here and there, trees and bushes were marked with orange spray paint, already faded from the rain, which would be completely gone in a week or two.

'He fooled us completely,' Sylvi said, not without a trace of admiration in her voice.

'You're still sure we're dealing with a man?' Fredrik asked.

'At least at the moment,' Sylvi said, with a slight whinny. 'He must have carried the woman all the way from the Sognsvann lake, you know!'

Even Fredrik was a tad impressed. For more than four days, the police had fine-combed the area around the birch tree. They had gone through all the traffic cameras to be found and all other CCTV surveillance in the entire network of streets leading up to Grinda. Even though it should not have been the case, the crime scene technicians had concentrated on the forest area between the birch tree and the road.

They should instead have gone into the woods. Away from the road.

At six o'clock this morning, a message had come in reporting a vehicle on fire in the car park at Sognsvann. It was immediately below the edge of the forest, and by the time the fire crews had reached it, there had not been much more than a burnt-out chassis left. The possibility of finding DNA was absolutely minimal. However, what made the police show particular interest in the car was a black and sooty steel knee brace in the boot with parts of elasticated textile burnt away. A quick-witted officer had discovered the metal support and found that it had been specially made. He rubbed it to uncover a serial number and brand name and it had taken only two hours to establish that the support had belonged to Kajsa Breien. The car, a BMW 3 series sedan, had been stolen from a garage in Løchenveien in Bygdøy, only a couple of hundred metres from Kajsa Breien's home. The owners had been on holiday and knew nothing until the police phoned them in the Bahamas that morning. Since their son intended to borrow the car from the following Friday, the key had been tucked away on top of the tyre inside the front right-hand wheel arch.

'So he *did* drive here with her,' Fredrik said in amazement. 'And then carried the body to Grinda through the forest. In a rucksack or something, maybe?'

'Presumably. The poor mite weighed only thirty-eight kilos. Heavy enough, but not for a very fit person. And especially not for a very fit man. It's no more than one kilometre through the woods.'

'One and a half, maybe?'

'Something like that. The perpetrator has certainly not been anywhere between the birch tree and that road down there.'

She pointed south.

'This explains why he hanged her up here and not anywhere near where she lived. Bygdøy is a peninsula, with only one way in and out by road. It would've been difficult for him to avoid cameras and suchlike. Here, on the other hand, you have the fringes of the forest all round the city to disappear into. From that point of view, he could have parked anywhere from Bærum to Nittedal. If he could be bothered walking so far, that is.'

She let her long ponytail slide through the fingers of one hand.

'Not so damn strange we didn't find anything. But that the guy had the nerve to just leave the car over here at Sognsvann until he came back last night and set fire to ...'

Sylvi Mobakk shook her head.

'First he tricks us into wasting valuable time. Then he completely covers himself by setting fire to the car several days later. And then he's probably gone back into the woods again and reached some other mode of transport so far away from here that we've no chance of finding out about it. Bloody smart, I must say.'

'A mistake with that knee support, though. He should really have got rid of it somewhere else.'

'I don't think so, no.'

Sylvi gave him a bitter smile, making her long chin look even broader.

'He wanted us to find it, you know. He's playing with us, just as you and that woman Selma tried to explain to Kjersti Spang yesterday. There's a message here, Fredrik. You're right about that. I just can't understand what it is.'

They stood there looking at the tree for a few seconds before Sylvi Mobakk exclaimed: 'A horrible death, though. I don't want to jump the gun here, but with this car and stuff it looks as if the bastard has just ... helped himself to the woman. I mean ...'

With a sigh, she swatted away an intrusive butterfly. A *vanessa atalanta*, Fredrik noted, a really large, beautiful example of the type. He grabbed Sylvi's arm to stop her and instead the insect landed on his forefinger, where it sat for a silent second until it took off and danced away.

Sylvi, unimpressed, went on to say: 'I mean, he must have carried out pretty thorough surveillance work in advance,' she said. 'Not least to find out about all that with the car. And when we've learned that the lady had the same evening routine more or less every day, that secret smoking time of hers was put to good use. And she was so tiny, you know, he could probably just cover her mouth and stuff her into the car. It'd be like picking up a kid, wouldn't it? He probably strangled her in the car, I think. An easy thing for a grown man. Soundless and fast.'

A thought struck Fredrik but then slipped his mind.

'He was lucky the neighbour appeared the first time she went out,' he said instead, slightly amazed. 'If Kajsa Breien had been smoking while the dog was still on the scene, there would have been more of an uproar taking her away.'

'Well, yes. Luck. Or else the guy had a plan for that as well. We're not exactly talking about an amateur here, Fredrik. We're certainly not.'

She sighed loudly and shivered.

'What about that poor guy up at the National, then? Any more on that?'

'Yes. Chemical analysis takes a nerve-rackingly long time, but they're rushing it as much as they can. They're searching for traces of metal in the tiny wound on his leg. The working hypothesis is currently that he was somehow hit by a projectile that did not cause him any great pain. So he just ran on. The projectile later fell off, we don't know where, but it stayed in his leg long enough to supply him with sufficient ricin.'

'Christ.' Sylvie muttered a few more expletives as she began to walk towards the parked car.

'Shall we swing past Sognsvann and take a look at the wreck?' she shouted. Fredrik was already ten metres behind her.

He was actually just walking around waiting for a whole heap of forensic analyses, so he picked up speed and decided to go with her.

Ewa

Ewa Connert, eight-and-a-half-year-old David Connert's grand-mother and adoptive mother, was an unusually beautiful woman of almost seventy. Her figure was slender and despite her age she wove her way gracefully and quickly between the restaurant tables. Selma knew the woman would recognize her but stood up all the same at the table at the far end of the spacious, bright premises of the *Nedre Foss* restaurant as she approached. It was half past three in the afternoon. Too late for lunch and too early for dinner and Selma had confidently banked on the place having few customers at this time on a Monday afternoon in September.

She offered a handshake and a smile that were both reciprocated.

Ewa Connert slipped off a trench coat that the waiter imme-diately suggested he could hang up for her in the cloakroom. She accepted with thanks and also gave him her dry umbrella.

'You never know at this time of year,' she said after a few intro-ductory pleasantries, and sat down. 'When I left home the sky was dark and threatening. Now the sun is shining.'

Once again her face lit up in a dazzling smile. Her hair was light silver-grey and she must have been at the hairdresser's recently. Ten minutes ago, seemingly: her newly shampooed hair was full-bodied and sat in a sharply cut bob almost exactly three millimetres above her level, narrow shoulders.

'I don't really know what this is about,' she said, looking Selma straight in the eye. 'But to be honest, it's the nicest invitation I've had since I retired three weeks ago. Thank you. Selma Falck in person. Happy Birthday, by the way, it was in *Aftenavisen*. I'm a great admirer of yours, just to let you know!'

Her laughter was full of the joys of summer as she picked up the linen napkin from her plate and smoothed it out over her lap.

'So let's hope I'm equally enthusiastic when I find out what this is all about. You sounded a bit cryptic on the phone.'

Selma sent up a silent prayer to all the gods in existence. Until now in this lamentable case she had not derived any benefit from her celebrity status at all. It had been more of a drawback. However, this woman had been delighted when Selma rang her. She was an old handball player herself, she had said, and had derived great pleasure from following Selma through *Shall We Dance?* a few years ago. She was finding life as a pensioner a trial and a late lunch in a good restaurant was something she definitely did not want to miss.

She really did look like an ageing angel. Her eyes, almost green, had faded with the years to a glassy shade of early spring. Her skin was exactly as it should be at her age, a little loose around her face and with a sprinkling of fine lines. Her rimless glasses were balanced in the middle of her straight, narrow nose and gave her an appearance of alertness and curiosity.

'What would you like?' Selma asked, nodding in the direction of the menu.

'Let me see,' Ewa Connert said, pushing her glasses further up as she opened the booklet. 'There are a lot of goodies here. What about ...'

She ran her narrow finger down the page. Her nails were manicured and newly varnished. One stopped beneath something Selma was unable to see.

'It's probably still the lunch menu that's on offer,' Ewa said. 'Then I'll push the boat out and go for a steak tartare. With all the trimmings.'

She raised her eyes above the rim of her glasses. 'And you?'

'The same,' Selma said with a smile. 'Where you're safe to eat a tartare, then you eat a tartare. Without a doubt.'

'Could I have a small glass with my meal? David's at the cabin with my husband. I'm all alone in the city and when you don't even have to go to work, I'm sure a few liberties are acceptable.'

'By all means. What would you like?'

'What do you think? Maybe some ...' She hesitated and her smile disappeared. 'Sorry, you don't drink. I'll make do with a glass of Farris, then, thanks.'

'Not at all,' Selma said genially, waving politely to the waiter before ordering their food, a Pepsi Max for herself and a glass of whatever red wine the waiter thought suitable to go with the steak.

'Now I'm excited,' Ewa said, straightening the napkin on her knee.

'I understand,' Selma said. 'I'm going to ask you a few things that might be difficult for you. I apologize in advance.'

Ewa's green eyes narrowed. 'Is this about my daughter?' she asked.

'Yes, and about David's adoption.'

Ewa's face closed down. Her eyes darkened and they no longer met Selma's. Her mouth tensed, even though Selma could still see that the lips had been unusually full in the woman's youth.

'OK.'

It looked as if she were considering leaving. She had still not made a decision. She put down her glass of water and folded the napkin once too often before setting it down on the edge of the table. But she stayed in her seat.

'Dare I ask why?' she said. 'Why do you want to talk to me about Victoria?'

'Actually this is not about her,' Selma said as quietly as she could without starting to whisper. 'This is more about what happened when David was born and the process you've recently put behind you. The adoption.'

'I see. And why are you interested in that?'

Her voice was different now. Snappier and sharper. More bureaucratic, as if her pensioner status were suddenly lifted and she was back in a department where she had spent thirty-five years of her life.

'Because I …' Selma put her fist to her mouth and cleared her throat. 'I'm involved in a project for the Church City Mission,' she said.

She had to moisten her lips before continuing. 'Actually it's more of a feasibility study. The City Mission is thinking of opening a kind of children's home in Oslo. Copying the model of the SOS Children's Villages. Not quite the same, but something similar. So they're interested in learning more about how untraditional families work in Norway. In many places around the world it's not at all uncommon for children to grow up with older relatives, most often grandparents. In this country it's more unusual.'

'I had the distinct impression you now operated as a private investigator.'

'That's correct.' Selma looked down to avoid the scrutiny of those green eyes. 'But since the universe has been kind to me and my finances, now and then I take pro bono assignments,' she said, unfazed.

'There's something I really can't work out here,' the older woman said, equally unfazed. 'And that's why you're sitting there telling me lies.'

Selma opened her mouth but shut it again quickly when Ewa Connert raised her palm.

'I sit on the Board of the Church City Mission,' she said. 'And we have no plans for any children's village.'

From the opposite end of the restaurant, Selma could hear the clinking of glasses and rattling of plates being stacked. A young couple several tables away suddenly burst out laughing. Selma felt her pulse climb a notch or two.

No one could lie like Selma Falck.

'Then you've probably not been informed of it yet,' she smiled, taking out her mobile phone. 'Which isn't at all strange. This project, as I said, is at a fact-finding stage. Slightly hush-hush and the Board hasn't been informed yet. It's possible nothing will come of it. There's a lot of clamour about private child welfare initiatives at the moment. Politically sensitive. So I'd just like to show you ...'

She had gone into her own mailbox while speaking.

'... this.'

She turned her phone around and pushed it across the table.

'What's this?' Ewa asked in consternation.

'An email. From Anne Grønnern. She's Operations Manager of the Church City Mission's Services for Children. There, in that email, you'll find a description of the assignment I've taken on.'

Ewa leaned her head back to see more clearly through her varifocal lenses. She held the phone away from her face and had to squint to read the text. Or skim through it, to be more precise, and she handed the phone back after only a few seconds.

'I'm really sorry,' she said candidly, pushing her glasses back into place. 'That I could ... sorry. Really and truly.'

'No worries,' Selma replied, with a strained smile. There was still a possibility that Ewa Connert would insist on phoning this Anne Grønnern.

In that case, the game would be up.

'That I could—' Ewa Connert mumbled.

'As I said, it's fine. People ought to be more sceptical. Scepticism is a good thing. Can't we just move on from here?'

The woman looked up. A distinct blush made her features even more prominent. Then her face broke into a wide smile.

'You're one of a kind, Selma Falck. Thank you so much. Of course I'll answer your questions. Victoria was very determined that David's existence and life should not be kept secret. He's too young to know all about it now, of course, but eventually, whenever he asks, he'll be given honest answers. No child should be forced to build their life on lies and shame, was his mum's firm belief. My husband and I agree totally. So in principle I'm always open to answering questions about this topic. Even if I'm not particularly happy to do so. It's been … difficult.'

'I do understand,' Selma said. 'And if you like, we can bring this to a halt right here and now.'

'It would be a shame to let what's probably going to be an outstanding steak tartare go to waste.'

'Agreed.'

The waiter arrived with the wine and Pepsi Max and poured. The two women sat in silence, watching. When he disappeared again, Selma said:

'However, I haven't been entirely honest with you.'

'What do you mean?'

Ewa Connert no longer looked like an angel but she listened, at the very least. When their eyes met again, the green of hers had turned almost grey. Selma began to speak slowly. She had planned this and for the moment everything was going as it should. All the same, this woman was far from stupid and a lot could still go wrong.

'In this project for the City Mission … this feasibility study, the experiences you and your husband have had with David are of great interest.'

363

'I understood that.'

'But I also have a personal interest in this. An interest that's difficult to explain without breaking my duty of confidentiality.'

Strictly speaking, Selma was not bound by confidentiality, but it sometimes worked like a magic word.

'Oh, OK, then. What's it about?'

Selma moved her knife and fork a few millimetres further in on the table before glancing up.

'Fundamentally it has to do with the attack on my friend Linda Bruseth. It might also have to do with several murders – I'm not sure.'

'What? What does my grandchild have to do with all this? Not to mention my daughter? She died in 2014!'

'Neither of them have anything to do with this. Not directly. It's information about Endre Cappelen I'm after.'

The name had a staggering effect on the older woman. She stiffened visibly. Her eyes flickered, as if she were suddenly afraid anyone in the restaurant might be listening to them. She opened her mouth a couple of times without uttering a word.

'You don't need to answer my questions. I'll understand if this gets too difficult for you. Endre Cappelen was David's biological father, I know that.'

'He died this summer,' Ewa said, her voice far more strained now. 'He can't possibly have anything to do with that attack.'

'No, but ...'

Selma lifted her knife and fork and held them above the empty plate on the table for a few seconds before putting them down again.

'It's a very long story. And complicated. But I can guarantee that nothing you tell me is going to damage your daughter's reputation. Or impact David in any way.'

The waiter arrived with the food. He placed a plate in front of each of them, wished them bon appetit and disappeared just as quietly as he had arrived. Selma raised her glass and said, 'It's a lot to ask. Maybe we should just—'

'Fine,' Ewa said curtly, raising her own stemmed glass. 'In the light of what you did last year, and after following you for as long as I can remember, I choose to trust you. Anyway, I'm starving. What do you want to know?'

She put her mouth to the rim of the elegant red wine glass. Sipped slowly and then nodded in acknowledgement. Selma felt so confused by this sudden accommodating attitude that she fired off the first and best question that entered her head.

'How did David come into being?'

Ewa Connert nodded as if the question was expected now that the subject had been broached.

'That's also a long story,' she said, cutting a piece of steak and putting it into her mouth. 'It all began when Victoria got ill.'

Even when eating, Ewa Connert was beautiful. She chewed with small movements and took her time. Her wrists only just touched the table, and the cutlery was held horizontally, slightly above the white tablecloth.

'Or more correctly, when *I* got ill. I got breast cancer at the age of thirty-two.'

Although Selma did not really understand where the story was now heading, she said nothing.

'It turned out I had a mutated gene that leads to far greater risk than usual of that kind of cancer. I had to have both breasts removed. The whole lot. Victoria was only nine at the time. She's always known she ran a considerable risk of meeting the same fate. When she grew up, I begged her to undergo gene testing.'

She sliced off another piece of food and it dawned on Selma that she ought to eat too. The yellow egg yolk broke and Selma felt a strange sense of nausea. Nevertheless she looked up attentively at the other woman and put a piece of meat into her mouth.

'But no,' Ewa said, sounding brusque and slightly cold. 'Victoria refused to be tested. Wouldn't hear of it. And she was very far from accepting the radical idea of having her breasts removed prophylactically. As some women actually do. And as I would have done. Victoria was too vain. Too … optimistic. Time went by, and hey presto …'

She shrugged her narrow shoulders.

'… Victoria also had cancer. She was thirty-seven then. She hadn't yet found a husband, which I was very pleased about at that time. We all wanted her to concentrate on getting better. Which she did manage to do, apart from …'

Now her eyes were bright green again. And moist. She lifted the white linen napkin to her mouth a couple of times.

'Victoria had no children,' she said in an undertone. 'And was in the midst of a battle for her life. All the same she arranged to get pregnant.'

Selma thought Ewa Connert was shaking her head, almost imperceptibly, as if she didn't think it respectable to distance herself from her daughter's choice, but all the same couldn't quite resist. When she went on eating without saying another word, Selma tried to prod the conversation on.

'How?'

'With a … casual passer-by. A young boy who helped her one evening. To get home after a slightly too boozy night in the city. It was all a clinical affair. Artificial insemination, no less. A kitchen table conception, so to say. Victoria knew nothing about the young man apart from him being good-looking, kind and …'

She laid down her cutlery and wiped her mouth carefully again. Drank some water. Then some wine, before giving a dejected sigh and continuing:

'… gay, into the bargain. Not that it should be held against him in any way, but this … arrangement carried a certain risk of infection, I assume. HIV, I mean. She woke up the next day with a headache, a touch of remorse and the realization that she didn't even know the man's name. And a child came of it. Exactly as she'd wished, in her heart of hearts. The problem was that the battle against cancer grew steadily harder. When David was three years old, she died. Pretty worn out by then.'

'How do you know this was how he was ... created?'

'Victoria told me. She also wrote it all down. She began on a book for David while she was pregnant. Even then both she and we knew that her chances of staying with David until he grew up were minuscule. I've to give him the book on his eighteenth birthday. I intend to do that.'

'I don't mean to ...' Selma pushed her almost untouched plate over the table a little. 'This is difficult for you, I'm sure, but do you know that this is true?'

'What do you mean?'

'That it happened the way you just described?'

Ewa Connert fixed her eyes on Selma's. 'My daughter was an honest soul. She did not tell needless lies. On the contrary, it was extremely important for her that David should know everything. Moreover ...'

Selma began to eat again so that she could look down without it seeming conspicuous.

'She told the whole story to her best friend the day after it all happened. This friend has provided testimony about it under oath at the Social Welfare Board. She's a judge herself by profession and doesn't resort to lies lightly.'

Selma kept chewing.

'To cut a very long story short,' Ewa Connert said with a sigh, 'we were given custody of David. Victoria had stipulated that in her will. As I'm sure you know, such things are not binding on the authorities but some weight is attached to them. The Child

Welfare Service agreed to that arrangement and we became foster parents. My husband and I. Gunnar is not Victoria's father – I'm married for the second time – but he's loved David ever since he was born. Everything went well. Up until …'

Now she was clearly on the verge of tears. She raised her napkin to her right eye and dabbed it gingerly. A little fleck of mascara was left hanging right under her eyelashes.

'The Child Welfare Service, which was formally in loco parentis, agreed with us that it would be best for David to be adopted. By us. It seemed absurd not to have complete responsibility for a child whose care we would undoubtedly have for the rest of his childhood. It should have been a simple case that no one disputed. But then …'

Now the tears spilled over.

'Then Endre Cappelen turned up,' Selma said slowly and quietly. 'The child's father. And demanded custody of David.'

Ewa covered her whole face with the napkin. Her shoulders were shaking.

'Sorry,' she said sotto voce. 'I haven't talked about this since summer. I thought … I don't quite know …'

'Shall we go?' Selma suggested, leaning across to the other woman. 'I live only a short walk from here. Then we can talk undisturbed.'

Ewa Connert nodded as far as she was able to.

'Let's do that, then,' Selma said and rose from the table.

The Observer

He saw them come out together.

This was worse than he had thought. He drew in further beneath the maple tree he was leaning against and held his mobile up to his face in case they looked his way. His skip cap was pulled far down on his forehead.

Selma Falck put her arm around Ewa Connert's slim shoulders. They were walking slowly, making their way up towards the footpath that would lead them north along the Akerselva river.

Maybe they were heading to Sagene.

To Sagene, and Selma Falck's home, he assumed, as he began, at an ambling pace, to follow them from a distance of fifty metres.

Video Evidence

'At last,' Fredrik Smedstuen bellowed, making a triumphant gesture with his fist. 'Show me!'

He was with the two young officers who had been given the thankless task of collecting and going through all the CCTV footage within a perimeter of nine blocks from the crime scene implicated in Linda Bruseth's murder. They had now been working on this twelve hours a day for more than a week and a half. Fredrik firmly believed that one of them was starting to get square eyes.

'The problem was,' the young recruit began, 'that as usual we were trying to follow one particular person from several angles. We start some distance from the crime scene, a given time before the murder, and follow that person's movements through a certain timeline. It's a demanding jigsaw, especially because we're dealing with the city centre on a busy afternoon. Crowds of people.'

'I know what you're doing,' the Inspector grumbled, 'just show me what you've found.'

The fair-haired young man's fingers raced expertly across the keyboard. Suddenly he pointed at the middle screen of three on the desk in front of him.

'There!' he said.

A man came walking down Thorvald Meyers gate from the north. The film was in black and white, so his clothes could be grey, blue or some other dark colour. He wore a greyish baseball cap with no logo and was carrying a duffle bag. His eyes were trained on the ground.

'You'll see he avoids looking at the cameras all the way along,' said the officer. 'He must have done some solid prep work to chart where they all are.'

The film cut to another angle, further south. Here too the figure's eyes were downcast. The duffle bag also had no logos or any other distinguishing marks.

Yet another film clip. The officer stopped the film and pointed.

'Notice the time code,' he said. 'Here he's going into the entrance at Thorvald Meyers gate 49, and the time is 15.24. So it's just over three quarters of an hour before the shot is fired. It's so far in advance that we didn't get to these recordings until a couple of days ago. For the first week or so we were mostly focused on the minutes before and after the shooting, since snipers aren't usually in the habit of hanging about at a crime scene, if you get my meaning. What everyone had assumed, including you ...'

He looked straight up at his superior officer.

'... was that the perp had arrived just before he fired the shot, and made himself scarce as fast as possible afterwards. In all the chaos, you see.'

Fredrik made a rotating motion with his finger. The officer obeyed and continued.

'We've studied the film from this camera for more than five hours forward in time, but the guy never comes out again. Not from here, anyway.'

'But maybe he does from another spot?' Fredrik mumbled with his eyes fixed stiffly on the screen.

'Yes, that's right.'

He set the film rolling again. It had been taken with a camera on the other side of the road. The time code showed 17.59. The figure was wearing the same hat and the same clothes and was equally careful not to look in the direction of the camera. He emerged from the *Godt Brød* bakery – the building from the roof of which he had fired the fatal shot. In his hand he held a paper cup of what Fredrik assumed was coffee.

'One minute to six!' he exclaimed. 'That's nearly two hours after Linda Bruseth was killed! And where's the duffle bag?'

The officer stopped the film yet again.

'One and three-quarter hours,' he nodded. 'We don't know where he's been for all that time. He could have hidden in the back yard and then gone into *Godt Brød* a while before this image was captured. All the businesses in the area were shut for an hour after the shooting, and the customers inside had to stay put. So either he sneaked in before we managed to close it, that is about half past four, or else he's been somewhere else and gone in after half past five.'

He reached out for a bottle of cola and drank it loudly.

'And as far as the duffle bag is concerned, you're quite right. It's vanished into thin air. That was one of the reasons I asked you to come. We should probably send out a group as soon as possible to search through all the back courts around that block one more time? Stairways and basements? Storerooms and garages?'

'Give me an overview image,' Fredrik ordered. 'Of the block between Thorvald Meyers gate, Grüners gate, Markveien and Helgesens gate.'

The officer did as requested. The aerial photo appeared on the largest monitor.

'I've prepared this for you,' he said, stretching out for the documents. 'I thought it would be of interest.'

Fredrik picked up the documents and began to leaf through them. 'What is it?'

'A timeline. From when the shot was fired. The first patrol arrived on the scene three minutes afterwards, in fact. I've marked everyone who came to the scene, including you, according to time codes and movements. And if I now do like so ...'

Once again his fingers tapped the keyboard at lightning speed. 'Then it looks like this.'

He pointed at the aerial photo, which was now divided into coloured codes and fields.

'Here you see exactly when each of the shops was closed, which areas were cordoned off, when they opened again, how far into the back yards we searched on that first day. This row here' – he pointed at a detailed list along the edge of the image – 'links the map with the footnotes of interest contained in your documents.'

'My goodness,' Fredrik exclaimed. 'Where did you learn to do this?'

'Modern police work,' the young man replied.

Fredrik chose to overlook the ill-concealed sarcasm. Instead he leaned forward and squinted at the map.

'Of course we'll send some bodies to conduct another search,' he said. 'For example here,' his stubby finger drew a half-moon over the north-west corner of the block, 'since that area obviously wasn't searched on the first day.'

'It's too far away,' the officer said.

'For us, maybe. Not for the killer. At a guess, I'd say he went all the way up here.' He pointed at the back court just beside the intersection between Helgesens gate and Markveien.

'Then he'd have had to jump a few fences.'

'Fences are the least of this guy's problems. Up here he's hidden the duffle bag that obviously contained the gun. He'd scouted a place out in advance. Maybe he stayed there for a while himself, or else he came back here ...'

Now he was pointing to the outside tables behind the *Godt Brød* bakery café.

'... almost immediately. There's a back door. For staff and deliveries, admittedly, but he must have used it. And then he's just sat there, along with the other bewildered witnesses to the murder. Had a cup of coffee, perhaps. Or two, since he took one out with him as well.'

'Shouldn't we send someone out right away? To search for the gun across a larger area?'

Fredrik puffed out his cheeks and straightened his back. He let the air out again with a snort as he struggled to hoist his trousers up around his waist.

'Yes. But they won't find anything. The bag, presumably with the gun inside, will have been removed ages ago. Three or four days after the murder, I'd think.'

'How do you know that?'

'Because this guy here ...'

Again Fredrik leaned forward to the screen with the picture of the assumed killer as he was leaving the premises of *Godt Brød*. It was difficult to say anything about his age. His height could be between five foot seven and five foot nine – they would be able to establish that through painstaking measurements. In other words, an average Norwegian man in ordinary clothing. With no noticeable characteristics, other than that Fredrik had a vague and slightly uncomfortable feeling that he had seen him before. There was something about his gait, when the young officer, on Fredrik's command, let the image become film again. Lithe and confident, but ever so slightly off-balance.

'... is shit hot. He fooled us all with a similar stunt up at Marka. He lets the gun lie there, while everyone in the area carrying larger bags is checked. Then he picks it up when things have calmed down. But I agree. Send somebody out. At once.'

He slapped the young man on the shoulder.

Muttering, 'Great work,' he walked to the door.

'How can you know we won't find anything?' the young officer asked before the Inspector reached the door.

'Old-fashioned police instinct,' he answered, without turning round.

The Confidences

Ewa Connert was a bit tipsy. In Selma's apartment, there had been a stash of three expensive bottles of red wine and a bottle of Limoncello for over a year. When she had embarked on a passionate affair with a young celebrity chef the previous year, he had refused to let her drink Pepsi Max with her meals. Farris mineral water or plain tap water was acceptable, but when he had stood for hours over the stove, he insisted that the food he produced should be enjoyed with the correct accompanying drinks. He used the Limoncello to make a spritzer for sipping out on the balcony on warm days, which even Selma had to admit looked good. When the chef had been suddenly thrown out of Selma's life, the little store had been left to gather dust in the wardrobe.

Now there were only two bottles of red wine left. Ewa had agreed to a small glass but the bottle was nearly empty. Her lips had taken on a transparent purple coating and her eyes were swimming.

'I've said too much,' she said under her breath.

'No,' Selma replied. 'I'm incredibly pleased you did. Thank you.'

She was still struggling to digest it all. The story was both tragic and distressing. Viewed from both sides, of course.

Victoria Connert had chosen her fairly unorthodox method of becoming pregnant for two reasons: she was short of time also and she did not want anyone she knew as the father. Even at the moment of conception she had realized David would be brought up by others. She had chosen her mother and stepfather. Despite her drunken state, the pregnancy had been planned and, Selma had to admit, pretty well thought out.

When Endre Cappelen returned to Norway in the summer of 2018 after several years of a fairly hazy existence in Bali and Thailand, he had voluntarily checked in to a detox clinic. He was in a dreadful state and would probably have died in Southeast Asia had he not been picked up on the beach one day after something bordering on an overdose. The Norwegian backpacker had recognized him from their schooldays. She bought him a one-way ticket to Norway and made sure her mother, who worked for the Blue Cross, a Norwegian charity tackling alcohol and drug abuse, took care of him the minute he set foot in his homeland.

Six weeks later, he was clean.

That was the only thing to be said in his favour. No education, no money and now also infected with HIV. The Norwegian backpacker's mother felt sorry for him and tried to help him obtain both a job and a place to stay. It was only a partial success. He fell by the wayside again but when he came across Victoria's name by chance on the Internet, it was as if something happened. Since then he had pulled himself together. It had not taken him long to find out that Victoria was dead.

And that she had left a little boy behind her.

The arithmetic was simple. He was certain the boy was his. For reasons no one could quite understand, Endre had actually taken note of Victoria's name. Following a clinical deal one night in May 2010, he therefore turned up on the doorstep of the house Ewa Connert shared with her family just over eight years later and demanded what was rightly his.

'We should never have given that interview,' Ewa had repeated over and over again when she reached this point in the story. 'Never.'

She and Gunnar had appeared in a series of articles in the *We are Sixty* oldies' magazine the summer Endre came home. Its subject was unusual family constellations and what modern grandparents might mean for their grandchildren.

Endre Cappelen did not exactly belong to the target readership for the magazine, but he could still use Google. Connert was an unusual surname and finding the article had not posed any problem. Accompanied by a picture of David, laughing on the lawn as he played croquet with his ageing adoptive father.

In the beginning, Ewa and Gunnar had taken it all very calmly.

Of course a young man with serious problems, with no support network and scarcely a place to stay, would not be allowed to assume responsibility for a son he had never met. Ewa had turned him away then and there and told him to contact the Child Welfare Service. And he did so.

Then things began to happen.

It was as if the thought of his son gave Endre new strength. When his paternity had finally been established through a DNA test, Ewa and Gunnar became more doubtful. Especially Gunnar, who found it difficult to sleep at night. Ewa tried to keep a cool head – she had herself worked in child welfare for the whole of her economically active life.

The child's best interests were central in Norwegian child welfare law.

Tearing David away from a secure existence with guardians he loved and had known all his life was not in his best interests. Ewa Connert knew this and tried hard to let that knowledge keep her calm.

But it proved impossible.

Endre Cappelen refused to give up. He got a job as a refuse

collector in the local authority. Cut out all stimulants. Rented a two-room apartment in Romsås and signed up for evening classes to complete his high school education.

The Child Welfare Service, which until then had been Ewa and Gunnar's faithful and appreciative supporters, then informed them that the adoption process would not be as simple as they had previously anticipated. Endre had sought the help of *Juss Buss*, a free legal aid clinic, and they had referred him to a child welfare lawyer who had made a habit of scaring the hell out of employees in every child welfare office.

The Child Welfare Service and David's family still had a good hand of cards. Endre Cappelen had no family or support network at all. His mother was dead. He had not seen his father since he claimed to have been thrown out of his home at the age of seventeen. He refused point blank to involve his father in the case. He would do this by himself.

So his lawyer was of the angry kind and did two things simultaneously. He brought a court action and also pursued a claim for the transfer of parental responsibility and custody of David with the Social Welfare Board.

As a general rule, children should grow up with their biological parents.

'That's the law,' Ewa whispered into her empty wine glass. 'We were so afraid of losing our boy.'

Selma poured the last dregs of wine into her guest's glass.

'This case would have resolved itself,' she said calmly. 'You would have been allowed to keep David, but would probably have found it difficult to prevent Endre from having some type of access. I can understand that would've been a challenge, but not a catastrophe. No?'

Now Ewa put down her glass. 'Probably that's how it would have turned out. A bit different from what we'd envisaged, but of course we could have lived with it. The problem is that you feel so insecure.'

She was lost in thought. Her eyes became distant and she fiddled for a long time with her wedding ring before she finally composed herself.

'There are a lot of good things about the Norwegian Child Welfare Service. But by God, there's a lot wrong with it too. We've certainly experienced that in recent days, with the reprimand from the ECHR.'

Selma's eyes narrowed. 'So you've worked in that system for a lifetime, but still don't believe it's good enough?'

'It can never be good enough. But we must always keep moving in that direction as our aim. A lot needs to change – not least we have to achieve more. Know more. Be better, quite simply, at what lies at the heart of child welfare.'

A faint smile tugged at the corners of her mouth when she made eye contact with Selma again.

'The Norwegian Child Welfare Service has been founded to a large degree on realism. Which has a lot going for it, but it must never tip over into cynicism. What the European Court of Human Rights is telling us now is that it should also build on hope. That the value of family life in itself is so great that we must never lose sight of the fact that people can change for the better. In many ways I'm happy to be out of it all. Big changes have to come and I'm getting old. I know the system, but it's evolving. For my part, and for David's, it terrified me far more than there was really any need for. It's so strange ...'

She swallowed audibly and looked around the room. Picked up her napkin and put it down again.

'I haven't spoken about this since it was all ironed out,' she said in the end. 'Not to Gunnar. Not to friends. And certainly not to David. We've protected him from it as much as we could.'

378

'But you're speaking to me,' Selma said.

'Yes. I can't really understand why.'

'I'm a stranger. But all the same you know me in a sense. Now and again I have that effect on people.'

Ewa took a handkerchief from her handbag, licked her lips with a thin, pale-pink tongue, and then rubbed them carefully. It helped a little.

'We asked our lawyer to do everything in his power. To tell the truth, he wasn't our lawyer, in fact. He was the Child Welfare Service's lawyer. As foster parents you have hardly any rights: that was one of the reasons we wanted to formalize the adoption.'

She snorted slightly, as if trying to show anger but found herself unable to quite manage it.

'Foster parents are not even part of the case, in normal circumstances. But we asked him to do everything. And he did.'

Selma had for once poured her Pepsi Max into a glass with ice cubes. Now they had melted and the pale-brown liquid was almost tasteless. Nevertheless she drank it: it was important to give Ewa some natural pauses when she obviously needed them in order to continue.

'Endre was totally taken apart,' Ewa whispered, 'when they met up at the Social Welfare Board, the case that was scheduled first. In May. Gunnar and I sat in a nearby café – we weren't even allowed to be present. But we got information and reports from our caseworker at every break. The Child Welfare Service's lawyer destroyed Endre on the very first day. Dug up all the mud there was to be found. Endre's own lawyer tried all the counterattacks in the book, but he had very little to go on. When they came back after lunch, Endre was under the influence of something. Apparently it was obvious to everyone. The Chair of the Board curtailed the meeting and asked the participants to allow for more time the next day to compensate. He took Endre aside when the others left. I expect he gave him a stern warning.'

'Oh? And what happened next?'

'Endre Cappelen arrived forty minutes late the next morning. So stoned he could scarcely stand up. Even his own lawyer was raging. The case was postponed until the end of summer. Before that time came round, Endre Cappelen was dead.'

She was clutching her glass of water but did not drink.

'That's my understanding,' she whispered. 'We drove him to suicide. The way the Child Welfare lawyer demolished him, he had no chance.'

'But was it true? What was said about Endre?'

Now she looked up.

'True? I assume the lawyer wasn't lying! The boy was a wreck. I've been able to read all the papers, and they don't look good. It's out of the question to think that Endre Cappelen could have taken care of a child. It was a daydream. He spun fantasies about him and Victoria being in love. That they had created David deliberately. That they were to be a family, the three of them, and that they had a most amazing, beautiful weekend together when all their plans were made. Pie in the sky! All of it! Downright lies!'

'Maybe not lies,' Selma said, far calmer than she felt. 'It's possible he believed his own story. That it was just such a fiction that made it possible for him to live with it all.'

Ewa stared sceptically at her.

'The kind of false memory I've read about?' she asked, knitting her brows to make three distinct wrinkles.

'Maybe. Or another type of psychic distortion of a story your subconscious refuses to accept. We all embellish our own lives, do we not?'

'Sure, but there must be limits. And even though he had

smartened up over the winter, he collapsed like a house of cards after only half a day in front of the Social Welfare Board.'

Finally she drank some water. Drained the whole glass. Again she dabbed her mouth carefully with the handkerchief. And looked up.

'By the way, it isn't absolutely true that I haven't spoken to anyone about this matter since Endre died,' she said.

'No?'

Selma felt an instinctive sharpening of her faculties, though she could not entirely understand why.

'Endre's father sought me out. While I was out for a walk, in fact. On my own. How he knew I was in the habit of walking that particular route, I've no idea, and I became a bit scared.'

'Er ... Endre's father?'

'Yes. His name is Birger Nilsen. Birger something or other Nilsen. Endre got the Cappelen name from his mother. As I said, she died long ago.'

'What did he want?'

Ewa glanced at the empty water glass. Selma got up immediately.

'Farris?'

'No, thanks. Plain water will do.'

Selma filled a carafe with ice cubes and water. While she ran the tap, she noticed her hands were trembling. The information she had received in the last twenty-four hours was so revolutionary and so terrifying that she could do nothing except go with the flow. Take in as much as possible so that she could then spend time making up her mind what to do with it all.

She filled Ewa's glass and sat down again.

'A severe guy,' the older woman said. 'Well groomed. Not as tall as his son but you could certainly see the family resemblance. Which you can't see in David, though.'

Selma thought she heard a muttered 'Thank God', but she could not be sure.

'What did he want?'

'You may well ask ...'

She stared unfocused into the room. Her eyes narrowed.

'You could well believe he might be angry. But he wasn't. A bit upset, presumably, but he seemed to be a man with the ability to keep a stiff upper lip. First and foremost he wanted to ask if I knew Endre was dead. I could confirm that. Then he said he'd like to meet his grandchild. That's when I got scared.'

Her gazed focused at last and fixed on Selma's.

'Would we have to go through it all again? I mean, this Nilsen character was not going to demand custody of David in any way, but would we have to go through a battle to keep yet another unwelcome person out of David's life? As Victoria's crystal-clear wish had been?'

'So did you say no, then?'

'I didn't dare to. I said he would have to contact the Child Welfare Service. That was the system, I told him. There were rules about how these things should be done. The Parliament made laws and the Government put them into practice. If he felt unfairly treated, he could take us to court. Those are the three branches of government, that's the way democracy works. Order and rules. That's how things work in this country.'

Selma felt an uncontrollable urge to open the balcony door. It was now far too hot in the apartment, as if someone had turned up all the thermostats in the whole building.

'I wanted to walk away,' Ewa continued, 'but he followed me. In the end I grew so irritated that I confronted him with the fact that Endre had not wanted his father in his life in any way whatsoever. Then he changed his tune. If he had been a woman, he would have wept.'

'What do you mean by that?'

'He got really incredibly upset. Controlled, and not really frightening for me, a mature woman weighing fifty-two kilos, getting stopped in the woods some distance from people, by an obviously strong and very agitated man. He moved away from me a little, to emphasize he wasn't dangerous. But his mouth was trembling.'

'Did he say anything else?'

'Yeees ...'

She half-closed her eyes again, as if trying to recapture the scene from summer.

'He said he had made some terrible mistakes after his wife died. That had been when Endre was only fourteen, he said, but I knew that already. From the case documents. Which of course I really shouldn't have been allowed to read, but we'll draw a veil over that. He said he'd been a dreadful father who drowned in his own sorrows and that he completely lost control of the boy. But that Endre had got in touch with him after his first suicide attempt.'

Aware her hands were perspiring, Selma folded them round the glass of Pepsi Max. The ice cubes clinked faintly.

'The first?' she asked as gently as she could.

'Yes. It happened two days after that catastrophic meeting at the Social Welfare Board. He tried to shoot himself. I don't know any details. But he didn't succeed. After a short stay at Ullevål Hospital he was transferred to some other psychiatric ward.'

'But you said "the first"?'

'Yes.'

Ewa Connert shuddered and ran her slim hand through her hair. She had faded. Her skin was no longer so dry and seemingly silky smooth: there were sticky furrows of sweat in her wrinkles, which had become deeper. Her mouth was tighter and her shoulders, if possible, even narrower than before.

'Endre Cappelen tried to kill himself three times before he succeeded,' she said in a quivering voice. 'And I can't feel anything but awfully sorry for him. For his father too, who has obviously gone through a bad time. Then he just walked off, in the opposite direction from where I was heading.'

'But ...'

Selma could not contain herself any longer – she got to her feet, moved to the balcony door and opened it wide.

'Thanks,' Ewa said, 'it's really hot in here. He mentioned Strasbourg.'

'Who? Endre?'

'No. Birger Nilsen.' She touched her forehead, as if she had to concentrate all of a sudden. 'Birger Jarl, that was it. Birger Jarl Nilsen. He said his son had wanted to take his case to Strasbourg. To the European Court of Human Rights.'

Once again that little snort.

'Strasbourg!' she repeated loudly. 'A young man who couldn't even stay clean for the duration of a piddling Social Welfare Board meeting! His father obviously believed all that nonsense. About love and promises about a future together for Endre and Victoria. She was seventeen years older than him and met him for only a few hours of her life! In a drunken stupor! Also, she was seriously ill at the time.'

Her earrings jingled.

'By the way, could I use your toilet, please?'

'Yes, of course.'

Slightly disconcerted, Selma tried to remember whether it was reasonably tidy in there before pointing to the hallway.

'The guest toilet is immediately opposite the front door,' she said.

Grabbing her handbag, Ewa stood up, her movements not quite as smooth as when she had been in the restaurant. As soon as Selma heard the toilet door lock, she snatched up her mobile, moved out on to the balcony and rang Fredrik. He took her call at once.

'I need to meet you,' she said so quietly that he asked her to repeat it. 'I need to meet you! I've got lots of news, so much that—'

'Sorry, Selma, we're starting to get a handle on this over here. There's no chance today. I don't think tomorrow either, we've—'

'It's important! I've spoken to ...'

She realized he had moved the phone away from his ear. His voice sounded distant as he barked out a couple of orders. There were several people present, she could hear, and she glanced anxiously at the hallway door.

'Can I call you back?' Fredrik asked. 'Later. Or some time tomorrow. We're beginning to get the picture here. Talk later.'

The call was abruptly disconnected. Selma just managed to tuck her mobile into her back pocket before Ewa Connert returned from her toilet visit.

It had done her good.

Her skin was dry again, and her hair just as shiny as when they had met three hours earlier. Her smile was back in place and the last remnants of the red wine stain were concealed by a flattering application of a discreet, subdued lipstick.

'I should really go,' she said without sitting down. 'Thanks for listening to me. It's amazing ...'

The angelic demeanour was back. Her eyes were smiling as she thanked Selma again.

'It was almost like going to a psychologist,' she said. 'I feel easier already. You're lovely to be with, Selma. You're a person who instils confidence. Nothing of what I've told you will probably be any help in your ... study, but I realized that from the very beginning. I just had such a desperate need to—'

She broke off with a smile.

'However that may be, thank you anyway.'

'No trouble,' Selma said, forcing a smile. 'I'm the one who should say thank you. But if you could just answer me one more thing—'

'Yes?'

Her eyes were sparkling green again. Her silver-grey hair sat perfectly and newly combed just above her shoulders and her posture was erect.

'You said Endre tried to take his life three times before he succeeded.'

'Yes, that was what his father told me.'

'Do you know how?'

'How he tried to commit suicide?'

'Yes.'

Ewa Connert patted her hair. A diamond ring glittered in the light from the ceiling lamp.

'First he tried to shoot himself, as I said. There was something wrong with the gun or something. His father wasn't clear about that. Then he hanged himself, also without success. The nurses at the hospital discovered it and got him down in time. Then, after they had to discharge him from the hospital – there was no longer a legal basis for forcibly keeping him there – he took a heroin overdose.'

'And died,' Selma said, almost losing her voice. 'After having shot himself, then hanged himself, and in the end used poison to kill himself.'

Farewell

Weeks, perhaps days. Then it would all be obvious. The police had begun to work it out. He knew that because he had called in there earlier that day.

Days, maybe only hours.

It was almost midnight as he approached Grethe's grave. His knee was sore now. It was probably worn out at last. Throughout these weeks it had behaved well, giving him relief from the worst of the pain and letting him regain a lot of the suppleness of his youth.

By God he had needed that.

It was only a question of time before they understood what he had told them. Norway would at last come to see itself in the mirror he had held up. In days or hours the contorted image of corrupt authorities would come into sight for the entire world. The apparently orderly and fair Welfare State Norway would be revealed in all its repulsiveness. Everyone would see what he was directing the spotlight towards: a lawgiving power that sanctioned the destruction of families. A government that sanctified the devastation caused by the Child Welfare Service. A law court that blindly endorsed these injustices, with no thought that their actions contravened human rights.

He had given them a distorting mirror.

He knew it was closing in now. A promise was held in the breeze through the treetops, wafting around the graves as he limped past.

Tonight he wanted to be with her for a while. He had brought his folding stool and coffee, and also the name plaque it was now time to put on.

'Hello, my darling.'

Maybe he did not say it out loud. It was not easy to tell, talking to Grethe was a stream of thoughts and words over which he did not always have control. She still understood him, just as she had always guided and helped him when the nightmares became too violent after an excessively long and brutal period spent abroad.

It was cold tonight. He had gone down to the basement and looked out his sheepskin jacket for the coming season. When he sat down on the flimsy stool, he drew the jacket more snugly around him. He took the plaque from his pocket and opened out the tissue paper in which it was wrapped.

Endre Cappelen

b. 23.06.89 d. 10.07.19

The metal felt cold on his palm. The copper gleamed in the darkness. He let his thumb slide gingerly over the letters before taking out screws and a screwdriver from the small zipped pocket on the stool.

The stonemason had prepared everything. All Birger Jarl Nilsen had to do was to turn four screws. They were made of brass: copper was too soft to last. It did not matter, the colours were similar. When the plaque was in place, it was as if the natural world came to a halt.

The wind suddenly abated. The magpies had gone quiet for the night long before. No rustling of leaves could be heard, only a distant, insignificant thrum of traffic. He felt warm. The coffee in the thermos tasted freshly brewed. His breathing was even and soundless and light.

'I'm free,' he said, his voice sounding almost amazed.

He had once been given much and he had messed up even more. All the same, he had lost most of all.

When Grethe died, Endre turned into a boy he did not know. His son became an eternal, repellent reminder of a loss he found unendurable. When he left, there was no room for any more pain in Birger Jarl Nilsen's life. He let his son go, in the numb knowledge that the boy would never be able to cope on his own.

He had been a useless father. However, Endre had returned. When all was dark and no way out was to be found, his son had come home. It was too late, but he had come.

Endre had confided a wonderful story to him, about love and hope and about a young child who was his. A beloved and welcome child, just as Endre himself had once been. A child who was his, who belonged to them both, a child of Endre and Birger Jarl's family, but who had been taken from them.

Everything was already too late by the time Endre came back. Nothing could be changed. They both knew that, in the three weeks they had spent together before Endre succeeded in being unable to take any more. He had gone to pieces long before that and it was his father's fault. The child was the only thing that could have put him back together again. David could have filled Endre's life with a meaning that had disappeared when he was only fourteen and his mother died.

David would have changed everything, but other people had taken him.

With the help of Norway.

'I let our boy down,' he said, dropping to his knees in front of the rough marble stone from Italy. 'But now I've made up for it. I've punished the system the way they punished our boy. Please. Say that I've made amends.'

His knee ached but he paid no heed. Grethe was saying something. At long last and for the very first time. Her voice was firm and gentle, with the little hint of a smile she always added to everything. Leaning his forehead on the copper plaque and placing his hands on the stone, Birger Jarl whispered:

'Thank you, dearest Grethe. I can go on now. At last I can go on without the two of you.'

The Report

The day was unbearable.

Selma Falck had lost count of the number of times she had tried to get hold of Fredrik Smedstuen. He had only answered her once and then with a text message in which he asked her to send him an email if she had anything to tell him. The investigation had taken off, he wrote, and he would be difficult to contact in the next few days.

Email, Selma had thought despondently. The information she had was so voluminous, so robust and so spectacularly astounding that it could not possibly be sent electronically. She had paced around the apartment, completely at a loss.

For a while she had considered talking to Lars Winther. A bad idea, she eventually decided. He was to drop in one evening for his folder and the locked memory stick and Selma knew she would have to find some excuse to keep the meeting as short as possible. Lars was a journalist through and through. He was always on the hunt for a story and the one Selma now sat on was far too juicy for her to be able to depend on him. Far too elaborate.

So elaborate she would have to write it down.

It would make time pass. And ensure she had not forgotten any of what Ewa Connert had told her.

It took an hour. To be on the safe side, she had disconnected her laptop from the Internet. It should not be able to be hacked. Also, she took a printout of what she had written and slipped it into a yellow plastic folder. Finally she put the document, the machine and the memory stick she had received from Allan Strømme at the bottom of her wardrobe, under the box of fancy shoes she had never worn.

It was now three o'clock in the afternoon and she sent one last text to Fredrik Smedstuen.

Fredrik. You MUST MUST MUST get in touch with me. I've sensational news for you. Please! S

Waiting was impossible, so she packed a bag of swimming gear. A couple of hours at the *Bislet Bad* swimming pool would at least help the time to pass.

And also curb the temptation to play a round of poker.

Or fifteen.

The Observer

He saw her as soon as she appeared inside the glass doors on her way out. There was something about the way she was walking. Determined, almost masculine, but nevertheless graceful. He had noticed the way she walked when he had joined her on the way up through Grünerløkka and he had taken the opportunity to convince her that she had not been the target of the fatal attack. Linda Bruseth's sudden movement just as the shot was fired had almost spoiled everything. An inferior marksman would have missed. The doubt that arose about the intended target would have botched the message.

It would have ruined his revenge but he had persuaded both Selma Falck and Fredrik Smedstuen to go in the right direction. Just a little nudge to set them off and they were on their way.

Now she was coming out. She looked preoccupied. However, she stopped after about twenty metres and stood still for a second before changing her mind and walking in the opposite direction. Just as quickly.

He stood watching her until she disappeared round the corner of a building. Then he waited for another five minutes before moving casually towards the block where she lived. Just in time to arrive quite naturally behind a heavily pregnant woman who was rummaging in her bag for a bunch of keys. As she opened the door, he kindly held it open for her. With a groan of thanks, she waddled towards the elevator while he stood studying the mailboxes in the foyer.

Soon after he was alone in the stairway and began to climb the steps.

The Break-in

'You can't stay,' Selma Falck said.

She realized she sounded far too brusque but she was too exhausted to be friendly. Having swum for an hour and a half, she had called in on Vanja and Kristina. Not because she felt the need of meeting them, but to avoid going home. Her friends had been visibly annoyed when she kept checking her phone and after a couple of hours Selma had thanked them for their hospitality and gone to see Einar. He wanted to play cards. Casino. It meant absolutely nothing to him that Selma could not concentrate and lost every game without exception. On the contrary, he was equally delighted with each victory.

When a text message finally arrived, it was from Lars.

He reminded her of the appointment they had made for him to pick up his folder and memory stick at nine p.m. It was only half past six when the message ticked in and she had asked him to come in half an hour instead.

It was just as well to get it done and dusted. She was dreading the fuss he would make and had cooked up a cock and bull story to get him to leave as soon as he had collected his belongings.

Lars stood waiting outside the entrance when she arrived home.

His restless body language was almost aggressive, his hands thrust deep inside his trouser pockets. His arms were stiff, making his shoulders rise, as if he were a sulky teenager.

'You can't stay,' Selma repeated when he did not react.

'Why not?' he asked crossly.

'I have plans,' Selma replied, opening the door. Strangely enough, she could not be bothered using the story she had concocted.

'OK,' he said sourly, 'but I need to collect my things. Have you managed to open my memory stick?'

'No. That gizmo is not really my problem, to be honest, Lars.'

They walked up all the stairs without speaking. When Selma was about to insert the key in the door of her own apartment, she stiffened.

'What is it?' Lars asked.

Selma fiddled with the lock. The key would not go in. She twisted it and nudged it a little and after a bit of coaxing, it slid into place. She turned it round. She could feel an unfamiliar stickiness in the cylinder case, but she could hear that the bolt had slid out of the strike plate. She pulled the key out again and crouched down.

'What is it?' Lars repeated impatiently.

'Shit,' Selma whispered. 'My stalker has been here again. This time he's picked the lock.'

'What?'

Lars bent down to take a look.

'I can't see anything.'

'You weren't the one trying to unlock the door,' Selma said angrily. 'I could feel at once that there was something wrong. And look at this ...'

Still hunched over, she stared at the doorjamb and pointed.

'Only one lock has been used. I know I used both. He's picked them open but only gone to the bother of closing one.'

She put her hand on the doorknob.

'Don't go in!' Lars shouted. 'He might still be in there!'

'Then he wouldn't have locked the door again,' Selma said, opening the door.

'You must phone the police,' Lars said.

'No.'

The bag – Selma saw it the moment she stepped inside. The *Rema 1000* carrier containing Lars's folder and memory stick. It had been lying on the sideboard since yesterday morning. It had still lain there when she went out swimming. She remembered that for definite, since for a second she had considered hiding it too in the bedroom wardrobe. But had not done so – she had lost all interest in the package. However, it had distracted her enough to forget to switch on the alarm. She glanced up at the ceiling, where she knew one of Poker-Turk's little devices was attached. Now it was missing.

'Then *I* will,' Lars hissed, still standing out on the landing.

'*You will not!*'

Startled, he stuffed his mobile back in his pocket. When Selma walked on into the apartment, he followed her warily.

'Anybody here?' he asked meekly.

'No. Nobody but us.'

Selma advanced into the living room and looked around. Nothing had been touched, at least not as far as she could see. With mounting anxiety, she ventured into the bedroom, opened the wardrobe and looked down at the box of shoes.

It was still there, but the laptop, the document in the yellow plastic folder and Allan Strømme's memory stick were all gone.

Unable to understand any of it, Selma instead dissolved into tears.

Slagentangen

'There must be something you can do,' Birger Jarl Nilsen said. 'Isn't this a typical case for the Fire Service?'

He was seated at a kitchen table in a small house in Slagentangen in Vestfold, following less than an hour travelling at excessive speed on the E18 motorway. An untouched cup of tea sat in front of him. Karstein Braaten, shaking his head, held his cup in his hands.

'The Fire Service puts out fires,' he said in an undertone. 'We don't set things alight. Scandals are something we prevent, not something we stir up. You found that out when you turned down the opportunity to enlist, Birger Jarl. We've never been, and never will be, anything like the antidemocratic groups that were exposed last year. We are … friendly guides. Discreet mediators. Fixers, you could well also say, but our methods are limited. Letting people … disappear, is not one of them.'

'It's a major scandal that the authorities have routinely forged documents to put lipstick on a pig before the court in Strasbourg slaughters it. Damaging, Karstein. Extremely damaging for Norway's international reputation. And even more important: for public trust. Isn't that what you're supposed to safeguard?'

Karstein nodded.

'Yes, you're right in that. But the situation is now under control, apparently. It's regrettable that Allan Strømme had hidden a memory stick that he then passed on to Selma Falck. But you've sorted that out, as far as I understand. I'm grateful to you for that.'

He gestured towards the end of the table, where Selma's laptop lay, with a memory stick taped to the lid.

'All we can do now,' he said, 'is trust that there are no more copies.'

'But she knows about it, Karstein! She's listened to those tapes!'

'Knowing something is quite different from being able to prove something,' Karstein said calmly. 'She'll never dare to publicize such claims without proof.'

'But what about the journalist, then? This guy Lars Winther?'

'We don't know if he also knows. If so, he works for *Aftenavisen*, a responsible media outlet that won't put undocumented claims into the public domain. No ...'

Yawning behind his clenched fist, he shook his head slightly and said: 'Thanks, Birger Jarl. As I said, you've done me a favour. But from here on we'll just have to keep our fingers crossed.'

'About what?'

'That it goes well, of course. That the barometer of trust will show an upswing. And that the country is not affected by any particularly challenging ordeals in the next few years. I honestly don't know if we're equipped for that yet.'

Birger Jarl let Karstein's words hang in the air. He looked out of the window, where it was growing dark. The wind was blowing from the south and even the tallest pine trees were swaying visibly. Far out there, behind the darkness and beyond the huge peninsula that bulged out into the Outer Oslo Fjord, lay the sea.

Maybe he should travel. Flee.

Now he should really move on. Embark on the final chapter of his life, without both Grethe and Endre. Everything was accomplished. His duties fulfilled. There could still be contentment to be found in the new life that began when he got up off his knees from Grethe's grave having made up his mind never to come back again.

He had felt so carefree, but the thought of Selma Falck had been like a stone in his shoe on the way home.

The document in the yellow folder still lay in his car. Karstein had not seen it. No one should be allowed to see it. It would have to be burned, just as he would take the laptop and destroy it as soon as the tea was drunk and he could leave his old friend.

Selma Falck knew everything. She had seen the message that lay in the shooting, the hanging and the death by poison. That was the point. Everyone should see it. The triple murders were a message and messages should be understood.

Unfortunately, she also knew that Birger Jarl was behind it all. He could not live with that. Meticulous planning and extreme care on his part would make it impossible for the police to track him down. If they knew who to look for in the first place, then that would be a different matter.

Quite a different matter, sadly.

Luckily, Selma Falck's document also revealed a number of details. Reading between the lines, it was clear she had not confided in anyone. She was alone with her knowledge.

Selma Falck held his life in her hands.

She could let it drop to the ground at any time.

Birger Jarl came to a decision. It had never been part of his plan. He was a man who took everything into account. He had not included Selma Falck in his equation. His mistake. His error. He was the one who would have to put things right.

He carefully set down his teacup on the kitchen table and stood. 'All the best, then,' he said softly as he took hold of the machine.

'I'll keep that,' Karstein said, looking up.

'No. You can take this.'

Birger Jarl put down the memory stick with the sound files from the Ministry for Children and Families on the table and tucked the laptop under his arm.

'I'll take this.'

'Are you going to destroy it?'

'Yes,' Birger Jarl replied, limping out of the kitchen with unfinished business on his mind.

Not even the Fire Service could help him, so he was in a real rush to get back to Oslo.

The Rescue

The estate agent was standing in the middle of the living room in the apartment belonging to Torstein Heimdal and Anna Lisa Knoph.

It had grown very late and everything was perfectly fine. It was tidy in here. Quite attractive, in his opinion, now that all the cartons, boxes and piles were removed. He had employed interior decorators to furnish it, as selling empty apartments was a grind.

The young couple had not even got as far as moving in properly before they suddenly wanted to sell. By the time they bought the place, they knew they were to spend a period of time in the USA. Three weeks ago, however, Torstein Heimdal's old grandmother had died. He was the only grandchild and had been given the opportunity by his mother and uncle to take over her apartment in Frogner for a song. It was double the size of this one and the address was considerably better.

The first viewing would be held at the weekend. That was perfect now that everything had been accomplished. He had three more apartments as well as an old house in Mølla to get ready by Friday.

The Primehouse AS Company, where the estate agent was a senior partner, had an eye-catching logo. A bowl containing three mangoes. A year ago some bright spark had taken it into his head that a real bowl with real mangoes in it should always be placed in a central position in apartments during the viewing times. A kind of signature flourish — it was vital to show off a distinctive feature. The estate agent was therefore setting down an orange pottery bowl containing three ripe, colourful fruits.

From Tuesday to Friday, he thought, staring at the bowl.

Mangoes ripened quickly.

Too quickly, he realized. The fruit would smell rank by Thursday. Holding a viewing in an apartment filled with a sweet, rotting odour was out of the question.

Again he looked around.

This apartment would be sold at the earliest opportunity. Which was after twelve noon on Monday. The apartments here went like hot cakes. Just like the one he had sold yesterday.

And like the one he had helped Selma Falck to buy. That had been almost two years ago now and she had not recognized him. Cheerful and accommodating, pleasant and correct.

But she had not even recognized him.

He hated her.

Hate was a strong word. Maybe too strong. He was not entirely sure, but the rage that had surged from his gut and made his ears ring when she had introduced herself to him in January 2018, ready to purchase the only apartment with a balcony in the whole building, could not have come from anything other than hatred.

The worst thing was that she had not remembered him.

They had been in the same class at junior high school. When they were fourteen years old, Selma had been the death of him.

Not literally, of course, but the pain she had inflicted on him then had destroyed his life, as a life can so easily be crushed for someone who is only fourteen.

Estate agent Nils Kristoffersen had fallen in love with Selma when they were both twelve. She was not the prettiest girl in the class. Not even one of the very cleverest. What gave her the role of queen of the playground was something he had never really understood. Maybe it was just her gaze. There was something challenging in it. Something strong and purposeful that expressed itself in an intense energy in everything she did. Something frightening, to be honest, and he had fallen head over heels.

Sport was the basis of her power, he had later appreciated. She won the school championships in almost everything. She was in the local handball team before she was really old enough. The teachers adored her: she was cheerful and polite towards them. Little did they know what else she got up to. Selma Falck began as reigning monarch as early as the first class. As she grew older, she extended her territory. She held court with a group that steadily increased in size and consisted of both girls and boys.

Nils Kristoffersen was never one of them.

He merely followed Selma from a distance.

More and more in love, and more and more lonely. He noticed everything she did. What she liked. What she said. Once he had spent two whole weeks' pocket money on KIP, the little packs of chewing gum that had been Selma's favourite. For weeks he had looked for an opportunity to present her with this gift.

It never came. He had found the bag of cellophane-wrapped packets while clearing out the basement of his childhood home a few weeks ago.

As a young teenager, Nils had kept a diary. It was something only girls did, but since he was falling apart, torn asunder by emotions for which he had no outlet, he had committed them to paper. He had dreamed up stories that belonged only to him and in which Selma always featured. If by chance she ever as much as looked in his direction, he would write all night long.

In 1980, the year everyone in the class turned fourteen, a miracle happened. Nils's father, who worked for a large electronics chain, came home with an arcade machine in his cargo space. It had been damaged in transit from the USA, but only superficially. His dad had fixed it all up with plywood and *Casco* glue.

The cabinet contained the very latest of all games. Pacman.

For the first time, Nils experienced the taste of popularity.

The ability to play Pacman without having to pay for it became a honeypot, even for the kids who swarmed around Selma.

And for Selma herself.

The estate agent did not even want to think about it. He felt hot and wanted to go outside. The pile of prospectuses lay strewn on the kitchen worktop. He straightened them up and closed his eyes.

One time Selma came on her own to Nils's house to play.

Nils Kristoffersen had never really been able to think through what it was that had happened. Only in short, staccato glimpses of memory. It had to do with his diary, which Selma had found when Nils had gone the toilet to relieve himself. It had to do with what she had read on the sly. And how she had laughed, that terrible way of laughing she had, and about what she had told the others at school the next day.

It had to do with who he became afterwards.

Three months later, Nils's family had moved house.

He needed a change of surroundings, the psychologist had said.

Selma Falck was evil, Nils Kristoffersen knew that. For the rest of her life she had gone from success to success, from triumph to popularity and respect.

It was all undeserved.

He gathered up his things from the apartment, now ready for viewing. When he grabbed the bunch of keys to put them in his elegant little satchel, his eyes fell on the set that fitted Selma's old door locks. He had kept one after the transfer, just as he had made a note of the alarm code when *Verisure* had come to set it up according to Selma's wishes.

He was there, but she had hardly noticed him then either.

Again he felt an uncomfortable intense heat throughout his body. He took deep breaths and shut his eyes.

Now it was all over. He would have to give up when Torstein Heimdal and Anna Lisa Knoph's apartment was sold.

When Selma changed the locks, he had lost access to her apartment. No longer could he torment her with the small, select hints that she should not feel secure. Just as she had made the school playground a living hell for him, it felt in a sense like an entitlement he had. Tormenting her. Taking from her what he advertised every time he sold a new residence: the protective nest of the home.

He knew it had worked. She was flummoxed. He could sometimes hear her, from the window above her balcony when the door below was open. He knew all about where her daughter was. How the girl worked herself into a frenzy about her mother and might well be the only person in the whole world Selma Falck was afraid of.

He had also found her handball in the basement during his recent clear-out. When they were thirteen and Selma's mother had thrown it out at a time when Nils happened to be walking by, he had picked it up and taken it home with him. That had been when he was still infatuated and Selma had not yet spoiled everything.

He had dropped the ball from the window to her balcony. That had scared her.

And brought him pleasure.

Hoisting the satchel on to his back, he used both straps so that he could carry the heavy bowl more easily. He did not want to put the mangoes in his bag – they were too large. With a bit of effort he managed to lock the front door without putting down the bowl. He headed towards the elevator and summoned it.

Nothing happened.

'Shit,' he muttered, pressing the button again.

Still nothing happened.

The elevator had stopped. He would have to alert the management committee and get it going again, by Friday morning at the latest. Holding a viewing in an apartment on the fourth floor with no functioning elevator – well, you could just forget it.

He would have to use the stairs.

The stairwell was separated from the apartment entrances on each floor by a glass wall with a door in the middle. In stairwell A, where he was located, there were two apartments on the third floor. One of these was Selma Falck's.

He walked down carefully to avoid dropping the bowl.

With his eyes downcast: he was reluctant to think of her. He would no longer concern himself about Selma Falck. Just as he had almost passed the glass wall and was about to step on to the first stair leading down to the next landing, he raised his eyes.

A man was standing in front of Selma's front door.

There was something about him.

Nils Kristoffersen stopped. Concealing himself behind the brick wall of the stairwell, he peered into the little hallway shared by the two apartments.

He could see that the man was picking the lock.

Skilfully too. With a dexterity Nils thought he recognized from American films, he pushed the door handle down with such care that it could scarcely be heard. He looked around and Nils just managed to pull his head back in time. His heart was pounding and his throat felt constricted. He forced himself to take another look.

The man was on his way into the apartment.

Stealthily, he could see.

And with a gun tucked in at the back of his trouser waistband.

The mangoes fell to the concrete floor. One by one, with three thuds one after another. He only just succeeded in saving the bowl, which he was now clutching in one hand.

He wanted to run away.

Instead he opened the glass door as guardedly as he could.

He wanted to take to his heels.

Instead he walked up to the door that had been left open a crack.

He wanted to get out of the building and phone the police.

His hand reached out for the door instead and quietly pushed it wide open.

He heard voices. One voice. It was muted and Nils moved towards the open living room door. Inside there was a man, standing with a gun raised. It had a contraption to lengthen the barrel. A silencer, was what crossed Nils Kristoffersen's mind just before he stormed into the living room, lifting the heavy bowl that was the logo of the Primehouse Estate Agency and swinging it in a forceful arc in the direction of another living person.

After that it was difficult to say what exactly happened.

The man in the grey clothing had sensed his approach. He managed to turn halfway towards the estate agent, who had picked up speed in the course of the four metres he hurtled across the living room floor. One shot went off, but Nils Kristoffersen never heard it. The only sound he could later bring to mind was the hollow, sickening thump of heavy stoneware hitting a human skull.

And Selma Falck's first half-shrieked, half-sobbed question: 'Who are you?'

Even now she still did not recognize him.

THURSDAY 19 SEPTEMBER

At Home

'Do you think he was mad?'

Selma Falck was sitting on her own settee. In her own apartment. With yet another set of new locks, this time fitted by one of the locksmiths used by the police. They had offered for her to stay at a hotel for a while. Vanja and Kristina had tried to take her home with them to Pilestredet. Even Lars Winther had offered Selma alternative overnight accommodation for a time: she could borrow his parents' house in Disen. They had gone on a holiday postponed by little Leon's accident. Selma could pick and choose. She decided to go home.

This was precisely where she wanted to live.

It had taken exactly twenty-four hours for the police to complete their examination of the crime scene and all traces of the dead Birger Jarl Nilsen were now gone.

It would take time, but everything would be as before.

If that were possible.

It had to be.

'Mad ...' Fredrik Smedstuen tasted the word. 'That's actually the most difficult term in the world. Mad. Insane.'

He lifted his tumbler, half-filled with red wine from a bottle that had originally belonged to a star chef. He stared at it and let the liquid slosh around.

'According to my norms, he must have been. I mean, to carry out such a ... campaign. So ice-cold. So well planned down to the smallest detail. Insane in my book, but on the other hand his ability to follow through with it all suggests a rational state of mind. So if he'd been insane ...'

Tasting the wine, he let it linger in his mouth before swallowing.

'Medically? Maybe. Or ... I don't really know. Legally? We'll never find out. They decided ABB wasn't insane, after all, and what he did was even worse.'

'He whose name shall never be mentioned,' Selma said with a tired smile.

Fredrik smiled back.

'Why was Birger Jarl so afraid of me?' Selma asked, rubbing her eyes. 'From the very start, I mean? After he had broken in and stolen the document in which I practically proved he was the one behind it all, of course then I was a danger to him, but at the very beginning?'

'He'd probably been following you. Maybe seen you with Ewa Connert, for all I know. It was important to keep both you and the police away from her. Ewa Connert was Birger Jarl's Achilles heel. She knew Endre Cappelen's case in detail. It was for Endre's case he wanted to get revenge.'

Selma was scarcely able to string her thoughts together.

It had gone so quiet. The neighbours on the same floor had moved away during all the commotion. Johanna on the floor above had been admitted to the maternity ward that same day.

It was as if the building had fallen asleep from exhaustion.

The last forty-eight hours had become a blur. Selma had endured two lengthy interviews and would have to be prepared for several more. Hopefully, that would not happen anytime soon. Birger Jarl Nilsen's car had been found in a car park in Torhovsdalen. Selma's MacBook had been stowed under the passenger seat and the police had requested permission to retain it. Since Selma was aware they would seize it in evidence anyway, she agreed.

She knew the sound files from the Ministry for Children and Families were not on the laptop.

She had played them directly from the memory stick. That had disappeared completely. As had the one belonging to Lars. And his folder. The document in the yellow plastic cover, which Selma had written when she had clearly realized that Birger Jarl Nilsen was behind the murders of Linda Bruseth, Kajsa Breien and Børre Rosenhoff, was however intact.

To the great excitement of the police.

Despite being so exhausted, she had not said a word to anyone about the forgery of documents in the Ministry. First of all, she could no longer prove anything. Secondly, she owed Lars the opportunity to find new documentation. She had promised him that the evening they had gone to Selma's home together and discovered everything had been stolen. Although a lot had happened since she gave that promise, it did not prevent her from keeping it. Lars Winther was a good father who right now should be taking care of his boy, but above all else he was a journalist. A terrier of a journalist: there might still be a possibility that he would manage to track down fresh evidence at some point.

'Here's to you wrapping up this case – cheers!' Selma said, raising her cola glass.

'Wrapping it up?' Fredrik laughed loudly. 'It's now that it begins! It's going to take weeks and months to get to the bottom of it all. We still don't know exactly how Birger Jarl got hold of Judge Breien. And where she was actually killed. We have our theories, of course, good theories, just as we have about how Børre Rosenhoff ingested the ricin. But we're still not entirely sure.'

He cleared his throat and ran a hand over his scalp, which must have been shaved that same day.

'But thanks to you, this will be work of a completely different character. We know the perpetrator's name. It's then easier to find our way forward to what took place, of course. We've also already found ricin in Birger Jarl's home. One gram! Christ, what a substance! I'm glad we have a special crew to search for such things.'

He took another swig and gave a loud sigh.

'Amazing that he had such belief in his son. That letter we found at Birger Jarl's house, by the way we call it the Mandela letter now ...'

Selma laughed softly and yawned.

'... that really does give a totally distorted interpretation of reality. Lies and nonsense. But a beautiful little story, I must admit. If only it had been true. I can't think of any explanation other than that the boy must have deliberately lied.'

'You shouldn't be so sure of that. After years of drug addiction and otherwise terrible bad luck, anyone would start to think up alternative realities.'

'But to think Birger Jarl *believed* it! Enough to plan a fucking triple murder in revenge!'

Selma touched her arm. It was almost completely healed now. The scar would still be noticeable, though, and some arm movements made the stitch line ache.

'He *wanted* to believe. Maybe he simply had to. He had failed so hugely as a father. Throwing an impossible teenager out of his home three years after the very foundation of the family had gone ...'

She shook her head and said no more.

Endre's case was solid, she thought. And real. He had not been subjected to either falsification of documents or any other tricks. Endre Cappelen was his own worst enemy: it would not have been possible for him to look after a child for three quarters of an hour.

The silence was lovely. Selma closed her eyes.

'He denied his own son, damn it all,' Fredrik said indignantly. 'When I asked, that time a couple of years ago, and we—'

'I'm sure that didn't make the situation any better for him. Birger Jarl was a man who disintegrated through feelings of sorrow and guilt.'

Selma drained the rest of the cola in one gulp. 'I have to go to bed,' she said, yawning again.

'Your rescuer,' Fredrik said slowly without making any move to leave. 'The guy who killed Birger Jarl and saved your life ... he's not very keen on you, according to the people who've interviewed him.'

'Oh?' Selma said placidly. 'Did he explain why?'

'No. It's just an impression they've been left with. Was there anything that jarred when he sold you this apartment?'

'Not that I know of,' Selma said, rising from her seat. 'But now I really need some sleep.'

Fredrik stood up too, his movements stiff and laborious. 'See you, then,' he said as he made for the hallway.

'I'm sure you will,' Selma said, letting him leave by himself.

When she heard the door click shut out there, she headed for the bathroom. Stripped off her clothes and stood naked, studying herself in the mirror.

Nils Kristoffersen had saved her life.

Once upon a time, Selma had destroyed his.

That was what he claimed. While they waited for the police, he had told her who he was. She had been stunned by the whole situation – a man lay on her living room floor with his skull smashed and she had wet herself in fear when it had dawned on her that she was about to die. Nils Kristoffersen, however, could not be stopped. His voice was monotonous and insistent. He kept talking and the police never came. He talked about what Selma had done to him. About how his life had turned out. About how that autumn he had plagued her as horribly as he could, but that they could never, ever call it quits.

His story was awful. She didn't remember the details. Selma did not remember Nils. Not his name, not his face. Far back in her memory there was a recollection of a Pacman machine, but she only connected that with something bright and cheerful.

His story could not possibly be true.

Selma would never have behaved like that towards another human being.

All of a sudden she tore herself away from her own reflection and walked naked out to the hallway cupboard. Flicked on the harsh ceiling light. On a shelf high on the wall there was a folder of certificates, references and old school photographs. She eventually found the photo from year eight.

Selma sat in the centre of the first row. She was laughing, perhaps at something Vanja, sitting beside her, had said.

Her finger ran from person to person.

'Tina,' she whispered. 'Berit. Ann-Elisabeth. Terje. Guttorm.'

She remembered them all. Except for one, the boy on the far left. The teacher was standing on his right, closer to the other pupils, as if even the only adult in the picture did not think the boy belonged with the others.

Dark hair and a fringe that almost covered his eyes. A very solemn face. His hair had turned grey over the years, Selma realized now, but the chin was the same. Narrow, almost weak, with a mouth that looked too small under his big crooked nose.

It was Nils Kristoffersen standing there.

But Selma could still not remember him.

SUNDAY 22 SEPTEMBER

The Promise

'Why should we meet him here of all places?'

Lars Winther was standing in the Botanic Gardens, under a tree that appeared deep in sorrow for the events of the last few weeks. The branches bowed all the way down to the ground. The tree was bare: only here and there a yellow leaf still clung to the twigs, battling against the gentle north breeze.

'Don't know,' Selma said, shivering. 'He's from out of town. Maybe his knowledge of places in Oslo is limited.'

'Did he say what it was about?'

'Not really. Something to do with the forgery of documents. Not sure how he knows about it. I haven't said as much as a cheep to anyone other than you about it. I was a bit shocked when he phoned, so I agreed to meet him.'

Lars's face took on a grim expression and not because it was only six degrees out here in the open. Nor because the sky was threatening rain.

'I'll never forgive you for not telling me you got accessible sound files from Allan Strømme. And that you listened to them. And that you damn well went and lost them all.'

'Don't complain. I could have chosen not to tell you anything. Anyway, you've now discovered what the sound files were about.'

'I know it now, yes! But what is that knowledge worth when I can't write a single word about it! I have no proof, and no idea where to look for any.'

'It probably doesn't exist.'

'Why do you say that?'

'Just a feeling. At any rate, *Aftenavisen* has led the pack on this whole murder business. You're the only one who's been allowed to interview me, exclusively, because I refused to talk to anyone else on your editorial team. You should be grateful.'

For two days the story the media had chosen to call the *Triple Murder of Child Welfare Service* had been headline news on all channels. Fredrik Smedstuen was on his way to becoming a celebrity and the estate agent who had saved Selma by shattering the killer's skull with an orange mango bowl had been a guest on the Lindmo chat show. Selma turned down the chance to take part, despite the producer's energetic efforts to persuade her.

'It's actually not really about a triple murder, is it?' Selma said, slightly incredulous, out of the blue. 'They weren't committed at the same time. Surely we're talking about serial murder?'

'Whatever,' Lars replied tetchily.

A man came walking towards them on the path. Tall and upright, he was dressed all in grey. His impressive thick hair was the same colour as his clothing. He smiled when he caught sight of them and advanced more quickly.

'Karstein Braaten,' he said, shaking their hands in turn.

The park was almost empty. The man was getting on in years, Selma thought he must be around sixty, and he spoke with a deep, steady voice. His business was brief, he told them after a short introduction. He wanted to ask them most earnestly to keep quiet about what they thought they knew about the forgery of documents in the Ministry.

'Think we know?' Lars exclaimed angrily. 'We're not talking

about what we *think* but what we had proof of until only a few days ago!'

'And you no longer have that proof,' the man said calmly. 'I don't have the authority to force you to do anything. My task is simply to ...'

He shivered in the wind that had started to pick up. The last yellow leaves on the tree of sorrow came loose and whirled away.

'... set things right,' he ended. 'To make peace.'

'What the fuck,' Lars said. 'I know what's happened and I intend to find fresh evidence.'

'You can try, by all means. I can guarantee you will find none.'

'How can you be so sure of that?'

The man smiled but his eyes remained serious. 'It's part of my job to make sure of that. Just as it's part of my job to prevent all unnecessary fuss.'

'Where do you actually come from?' Selma asked sceptically. 'I didn't quite catch that on the phone.'

'From the Directorate of Public Security and Resilience,' he answered with equanimity. 'We're based down in Tønsberg.'

'What has that Directorate to do with ...' Selma had not quite gathered her thoughts.

'We don't need to go into that now,' the man said gently. 'I work on public security, you see. Falsification activity by the state threatens public security. That's how I come into this case. Expressed very simply. You can do as I ask, or you can leave it.'

He thrust his hands deep into the pockets of his woollen coat.

'I just want to spare you totally unnecessary work. Each and every claim that what happened really did happen will be countered in the most emphatic way. And of course it will become very unpleasant for whoever puts forward undocumented assertions.'

Now he was looking straight at Lars. Selma noticed the journalist was looking less assured.

'A great deal has already been taken care of,' Karstein Braaten continued. 'For example, Director General Horatio Bull-Pedersen, when all this ...'

He shrugged.

'... other business is over and the dust has settled, will accept early retirement. And Alvhilde Leonardsen in the same department has received strong ... incentives to step back prematurely. It will all be sorted out. The things it's not too late to sort out, of course. Mind you, some aspects are irreparable. But nor will things be repaired by creating even more fuss. Or by wasting time that could be spent on more sensible things.'

Once again his gaze shifted to Lars.

'So I'll thank you for taking the time to meet me,' the man said in a friendly tone. 'As I said, this is only a suggestion. My authority does not stretch any further than that.'

Selma could have sworn that he winked at her. Quick as a flash, and maybe she was seeing things, but his entire demeanour radiated a glimmer of something that took her back to last year's revelation of the illegal cells of manpower with licence to kill.

She took a step back when the man turned and began to walk away.

'Wait,' Lars said, and the man stopped.

Lars rummaged through his pockets. Taking out a note, he opened it flat.

'I'm still going to have one more shot at picking holes in this story,' he said, handing the note to Karstein Braaten. 'But all the same ...'

The man took the note, read it and looked up again.

'No matter whether or not I succeed, it seems that you can ... make things happen.'

'Aisha Mohammad,' the man read aloud. 'Tante Ulrikkes vei 4 in Oslo.'

'Yes. She's one of the people who were impacted by what I now can't prove. She works with us in *Aftenavisen* and had her child taken from her without ever being given a chance. To show that she could manage to be a mum, I mean. It's too late to give the child back to her. But could you …'

Lars seemed more indecisive than Selma had ever seen him. He kicked at the grass, looked down and clearly had difficulty finishing what he had to say.

'Could you make sure she at least gets to meet her daughter?' he finally asked. 'So that she can be reassured that all is well with her? And maybe see her a couple of times a year or something?'

Karstein Braaten folded the note again. Taking his wallet from the inside pocket of his coat, he opened it and, with calm movements, tucked the note inside.

'I can probably manage that,' he said, with a nod. 'That sort of thing does lie within the scope of what I can manage to arrange.'

He turned on his heel again and began to walk.

Selma's mobile peeped. She took it out and read the message.

Selma. Whew. What a week. Do you have time to see me for dinner this evening? You can choose where. Fredrik.

She considered this while she followed Lars. They walked in the opposite direction from the man from the DPSR, towards the Munch Museum where both Lars's bike and Selma's Volvo were parked. All at once she stopped and sent a reply.

Fredrik – thank you, but today I'm going to try to wheedle my way to a date with a very young man. What about tomorrow? Hugs from Selma.

She had not made up her mind until now.

She had not had the energy to try until now. Slipping her mobile into her pocket, she hurried to catch up with her long-legged friend sauntering ahead.

Skjalg

Selma was fed up waiting for the forgiveness that never came.

As she rounded the corner into the small cul-de-sac in Tåsen where her daughter Anine lived with five-month-old Skjalg, she made up her mind to stick to the truth this time.

It was best that way. Anine always saw through her, and in any case the media were so full of the revelations of the last twenty-four hours that it would be impossible to lie about it all. Even for Selma Falck.

The soles of her feet crunched as she opened the wrought-iron gate and stepped on to the gravel. She caught a glimpse of Anine at the window on the first floor, with Skjalg in her arms. Selma felt a stab of anticipation, a warm glow at the thought that everything was over with and her life was safe again. Nils Kristoffersen and his annoying story was something she had decided to forget and she had almost managed that already.

It was best that way.

At least for Selma herself.

Anine had spotted her and the door opened before she reached the top of the stone steps.

'Hi,' Selma said, stopping on the middle step.

'Hi,' Anine said without a smile.

Skjalg stared solemnly at his grandmother. Selma thought her heartbeats must be loud enough to hear. Clutching her chest, she said: 'It's over, Anine. I got mixed up in it through sheer accident. I just had to find a way out of it too. Some time or other, if you like, I can sit down and tell you everything. But right now ...'

Skjalg's face broke into a big smile and he met her eyes. He still had only the two top centre teeth and he was still the spitting image of his grandmother, even though he had grown bigger in the weeks since she had last seen him. More boyish, in a sense.

Even more beautiful.

'Right now I really desperately need to be with Skjalg.'

'Your need,' Anine said. 'Selma Falck's need. Well, we must be sure to meet that. As usual.'

Once again Selma touched her heart. 'Please,' she whispered.

Anine shook her head slightly. For a long time. Whether it was rejection of Selma's pleas or whether she was just in a mood, as usual, it was impossible to say. She moved Skjalg from one arm to the other. The baby leaned forward and his mother had to catch him round the stomach to avoid him falling as he reached out towards Selma.

'He recognizes me,' Selma said.

'It's three weeks since you saw him, Mum. Such small babies don't remember so far back. But ...'

A tiny backdraught from inside brought with it the scent of the boy. It was distinctive, so completely different from how Selma's own children had smelled. He was looking at her now, with a seriousness that convinced Selma at least that he understood how important she was. How close to him she would always be, no matter what barriers and sanctions Anine would find to use in the years ahead.

Tentatively, she stretched her hand out towards him. He grabbed it.

Again that smile: it was like looking at pictures of herself as a baby.

'OK, then,' Selma whispered at his touch. 'I'll just go.'

She glanced up. Anine was looking straight at her. Her face was impossible to read. Skjalg tugged at Selma's hand and made a contented, gurgling noise.

'OK,' Anine said at last, handing over the baby. 'You can come in, then. On the condition that you never, ever, ever, go out and get shot again. Or ever go anywhere near anyone with a gun.'

'I promise whatever it takes,' Selma murmured with her mouth on the silky-soft baby's head. 'Thank you very, very much.'

They went inside. Anine was first up the stairs, with Selma immediately behind, holding the baby close. An autumnal gust of wind shut the door behind them and really, all was well.

The Mandela Effect

Dear Dad,

She was mine the moment I saw her. And I was hers, even though it would still take hours before she saw me and realized that.

It was one of those nights in spring when everything is fine.

So fucking fine, Dad.

Victoria stood there, a bit shy, she'd had one drink too many and her friends had left her. I had spent the evening observing her from a distance. You remember how I was at that time, Dad. A disappointment. To you and me and almost certainly to Mum if she had still been alive. I had spent seven years making a mess of my life. For seven years I had missed Mum and run away from you and thought I would never be an adult. Everything turned around that night. If only you could have seen me. Seen us. If only Mum had still been around.

They were similar, Mum and Victoria. The same reddish-blonde hair, the pale eyes. Victoria wore high heels and was waiting for a taxi, feeling sorry for herself. I had seen that already, earlier that evening, when she picked lilacs in Frogner and tucked a flower behind her ear. They blossomed so early that year. The fragrance was everywhere throughout the city as we walked, her in front and me a block or so behind. I was following her. I had seen her when she met the others, the girls who let her down and the man who chose someone else instead of her.

Victoria was the breath of spring I had been looking for.

She had taken one drink too many. Only that. She sobbed a little that night and wanted to go home. When a rat came scampering out from the bushes at Spikersuppa and nearly frightened her to death, I had to show myself. She more or less fell upon me, Dad, in every sense. She grabbed my arm and pulled me towards her and was scared and a bit tipsy and so sweet in a way I had never known in a girl before. I was no longer that gay guy. I was Victoria's man. My heart was bursting. It exploded into starry sky pieces there and then, I was in love and knew it would last. She was too good for me, too much like Mum, and too much like everything I had run away from since the age of fourteen. But she was mine. I promise you, Dad, Victoria and I really belonged to each other.

We walked all the way to Manglerud.

She gave me her whole life as a gift. She sobered up as we strolled along and talked to each other about our lives. I'd smoked a joint on my own earlier that evening and as the effect wore off, my life and the air around me grew sharper. I loved her already. We walked through the city and along the streets, up the winding roads towards Ekebergåsen.

David came into being that night, Dad.

All our dreams were created one weekend in May.

Her apartment was big enough for us both. For all three of us when the time came. We stayed there for two days and nights. We didn't get out of bed except to get water and collect the food Victoria had delivered to the door. We had plans. We had a life. Most of all we had a dream about David.

The next day Victoria became ill.

At first she just threw up, and we laughed and said it was a delayed hangover. We hadn't touched alcohol since Friday night. We slept late into Sunday afternoon, the way we sometimes do without really meaning to lose track of time like that. When I woke, she was in the bathroom. Even there, naked and on her knees in front of the toilet bowl, she was gorgeous. My hands fitted perfectly into that slight curve over her backside when I crouched down to assist her. I held her hair back and stroked her shoulders: she retched until there was nothing left to get rid of. Victoria was pale and a bit dizzy, but she smiled when I carefully helped her to her feet and led her back to bed.

Close together, very close, we lay there, for as long as it was possible to move even closer.

She was really unwell. An ambulance came. Her mother came. An old bag. The apartment wasn't mine and I had to leave. Victoria was really poorly, something dangerous that had been left behind as we walked through the whole of Oslo and fell in love.

David was born nine months later.

I've told you this before, Dad. Now that I'm no longer with you, I want you never to forget. It has been so important to me that you should understand. That you should know that Victoria was the one, the only one, and that all the mistakes I've made, before and since, can't take away from me that I lived a real life. For just two days, that was all I got after Mum died, but it was enough for me. We created David, he belongs to Victoria and me, and when Victoria died, he became ours. Yours and mine, Dad. We were the ones who should have had him, and I have fought so hard to fulfil all the dreams and hopes that came into being that weekend with Victoria. They've told lies about me. They've blown up small mistakes and made up things I would never have done. Even my lawyer has been against me. The worst thing, though, is that they have taken my life from me. Our days together, Victoria's and mine. They have come up with a monstrous story about chance events and wickedness, as if David could have come into being in any other way than how he was made: from love.

Those lies have taken my life from me. No matter how much I fight, it's never any use. I couldn't manage to shoot myself. Nor to hang myself either. When you find me, I'll have chosen the most secure way, since no one can survive this poison in such a dose.

Thanks, Dad, for these three weeks. And for at least believing my story. You're the only one.

Your son, Endre.

AUTHOR'S POSTSCRIPT

This is a novel. The story I tell is therefore not true. I have, for example, no basis for claiming that our Civil Service falsifies documents. Or that the Directorate for Public Security and Resilience acts in the way I allow them to in this story. I've no idea whether the *Godt Brød* bakery and café in Grünerløkka has a back door, or for that matter whether it is legal to construct new buildings in Oslo with a single balcony on a huge and otherwise grey, smooth wall.

Overall I have taken a great many liberties, such as a novelist can and should do. Including pushing the disclosure of the NAV scandal (which is a catastrophe taken from real life) one month forward in time because it better suited the purposes of my narrative. I have also introduced a lot of twists and turns around the fact that Norway has received, and at the time of writing is still receiving, a real thrashing from the ECHR in a number of child welfare cases (which is also entirely true). This real-life legal fight raises more than a few difficult questions and I have written this book in political, legal and human incredulity.

A Memory for Murder was concluded during a state of emergency for us all. The pandemic came to Norway just as I was getting into top gear and the book was taking its final shape. Absurdly enough, one of the events that this book's Karstein Braaten was tasked with preparing for actually did happen. The depredations of the virus have scared and still scare me. If it had not been for the understanding shown and adjustments made by my editor, Espen Dahl, and his boss, Kari Marstein, this novel would never have been completed.

However, I am most of all grateful, as usual, to my sweetheart of more than twenty-two years. Along with many others, she too has had to put her shoulder to the wheel to salvage the activity, workplaces and culture of the publishing industry. All the same she has still had energy, time and love enough to be the rock of stoic peace and calm I cannot live without. And to give me a really good talking to when that has been called for.

Thank you, Tine, as always.

Larvik, 4 July 2020
Anne Holt

Read more of Anne Holt's bestselling series

'Step aside, Stieg Larsson, Holt is the queen of Scandinavian crime thrillers'

RED MAGAZINE